THE BEST OF
LADY CHURCHILL'S
ROSEBUD WRISTLET

DEL
REY

BALLANTINE BOOKS

NEW YORK

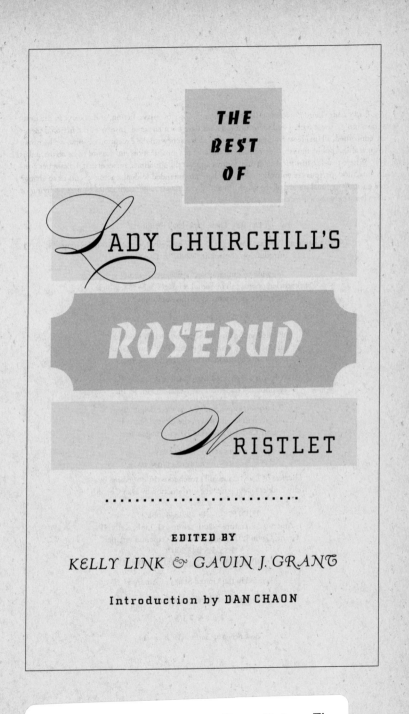

THE
BEST
OF

Lady CHURCHILL'S

ROSEBUD

Wristlet

....

EDITED BY

KELLY LINK & GAVIN J. GRANT

Introduction by DAN CHAON

A Del Rey Trade Paperback Original

Compilation and preface copyright © 2007 by Kelly Link and Gavin J. Grant
Introduction copyright © 2007 by Dan Chaon

Owing to limitations of space, permission
acknowledgments can be found on pages 383–387, which
constitute an extension of this copyright page.

Published in the United States by Del Rey Books,
an imprint of The Random House Publishing Group,
a division of Random House, Inc., New York.

DEL REY is a registered trademark and the Del Rey
colophon is a trademark of Random House, Inc.

All stories, essays, and poems were originally
published in serial form in the United States by
Lady Churchill's Rosebud Wristlet magazine.

LIBRARY OF CONGRESS
CATALOGING-IN-PUBLICATION DATA

The best of Lady Churchill's rosebud wristlet / edited by
Kelly Link & Gavin J. Grant ; introduction by Dan Chaon.
p. cm.
ISBN 978-0-345-49913-4 (pbk.)
1. American literature—20th century. I. Link, Kelly. II.
Grant, Gavin J. III. Lady Churchill's rosebud wristlet.
PS535.5.B48 2007
810.8'0054—dc22   2007015118

Printed in the United States of America

www.delreybooks.com

2 4 6 8 9 7 5 3 1

Book design by Barbara M. Bachman

For Richard Butner,

who is still owed some quotation marks

A (PARENTHETICAL) PREFACE

SOMETIME IN 1996, DURING THE LONG, HAZY HOURS OF Gavin's temp job, and encouraged by the literary atmosphere of Boston bookstore Avenue Victor Hugo where Kelly was working, we decided to start a zine. Why not? We had access to a photocopier, and we knew some writers. Gavin walked by a travel agency advertising a $300 tropical vacation and decided that for that kind of money he'd have more fun making a zine. (With hindsight, $300 is also a lot of books and beer.) *Lady Churchill's Rosebud Wristlet* was inspired as much by pop culture (*Ben Is Dead, Don't Shoot It's Only Comics*) and personal zines (*Doris, Leeking Ink*) as by the suspicion that the kind of hybrid genre/literary fiction that we liked best was underrepresented in the magazines that we read.

We ran twenty-six copies of the first issue of LCRW off on someone's photocopier. (We numbered it Vol. 1, No. 1.) It wasn't pretty, but it sold through. When we started to put together our second issue, we upped the print run and found a size and design we liked. (It was stapled then; it's still stapled now.) We began to solicit fiction from newer writers, including Nalo Hopkinson and Dora Knez. Our goals since then haven't changed much. We want to publish a mix of new and established writers. We want to publish work that surprises us. We want to have fun and break even.

The Best of LCRW represents ten years of photocopied stories, a continued commitment to sending chocolate bars, intact and more or less unmelted, through the mail (see the subscriptions page at the back), and many—too many—late nights spent struggling with Word, PageMaker, Quark, and now InDesign. That we still spend those late nights reading submissions, laying out pages, and addressing mailing labels, is thanks to the many wonderful writers who continue to send us their best and oddest work.* And thanks, also, to the subscribers and casual browsers who have picked up a zine with a very odd title at bookstores like Dreamhaven, Borderlands, Powell's, Prairie Lights, and Quimby's.

Perhaps you're wondering about the name. Let's just say it cost us quite a few pennies in consultancy fees from a famous marketing firm, a group of people (corporation sounds so corporate) so well known we don't feel the need to name them—let's just say that they were the first agency to name trees after subdivisions. We wanted something simple and mimetic: a single word that would summarize everything you (yes, you) wanted from a magazine, a word that would intrigue you so much you had to buy that word, had to take it home where you would ignore your roommate and/or your kids and your little dog, too, because you *had* to read it *now*. But it turned out that *Fiction, Story, Zine, Playboy, Naked People,* and *Free Money Inside* were either already in use or else presented legal difficulties. Eventually, for entirely other than commercial reasons, we named ourselves after the rosebuds that Winston Churchill's mother, Jennie Jerome, was reported to have had tattooed around her wrist.** Fascinating woman, Lady C., fascinating.

Over the course of the past ten years, we've published over two million words worth of fiction, poetry, reviews, and lists in LCRW. (If

---

* So, okay, there's one writer whose work we cannot include here and whose name we cannot tell you, as, when he (or she) withdrew his/her work, she/he also requested that all mention of their submission be erased from any public records. That was in issue 18, which came out in June 2006 (or so, you know how it is). Oh, how we hated to leave out that story. We missed it so much that we left a space for it in our table of contents in issue 18. In putting together this anthology, we could not *not* include that gap. We also wrote down the writer's name on the back of a Green & Black's chocolate bar label, put the label in a St. Peter's Best Bitter bottle, and tossed it into the sea. Somewhere out there and all that.

** According to the biographies we read, it was either a snake or rosebuds. We like rosebuds more than snakes. (Gavin does. Kelly prefers snakes, actually.)

Gavin's questionable breakfast-table math is correct.) We've felt for a long time that the writers we include in LCRW deserve a much wider readership than the one we can reach by publishing a twice-a-year zine, and we were ecstatic when Jim Minz, our editor at Del Rey, agreed with us. (Thank you, Jim. Thank you, Chris and Fleetwood and Betsy.) If we could have, we would have included more material from each issue in this anthology, and over the last year, while working on this project, we thought about how to accomplish this. We considered shrinking the font size and including a magnifying glass. Losing the margins. Offering a supplement. Leaving out all punctuation marks. (We did that once by mistake, and we're still apologizing. Sorry, Richard.) But in the end, we drew straws, made up lists, argued a lot (but friendly arguing—over drinks, not knives), and then left out some of our favorite stories. So this is really *The Best of LCRW . . . So Far*. Since we intend to keep putting out our zine, at some point we'll just have to do another one.

Hope you enjoy digging around in here as much as we enjoyed putting it all together.

Two notes about the zine:

1. LCRW comes out twice a year. Should you wish a third issue, please send us a check for $1,000. That issue will be the Your-Name-Here Issue.

2. A new literary award. We believe everyone is special (even those people who don't read—or write for—LCRW, but this award is not for them). Here is the press release: Northampton, MA. LCRW and Small Beer announces The Eponymous Award, given to all writers on publication in LCRW of their writing. So, Bob Smith has been awarded the Bob Smith Award for Fiction Writing. Jane Smith has been awarded the Nonfiction Award. D. K. Smith has been awarded the Poetry Award. You get the idea. In fact, for getting this far, you deserve an award. You have just been awarded the Reader Who Reads Notes Award (fill in the year here_____). Congratulations!

CONTENTS

LADY CHURCHILL'S ROSEBUD WRISTLET

AN INTRODUCTION

Dan Chaon

WHAT IS IN THIS CONTAINER?

SOMETIMES IT IS HELPFUL to have a label. Ingredients, categories, affiliations, and so on. One reason to create a label is for the readers, who would like to know what they are getting themselves into.

For example, it might be simplest to say that the focus of the magazine called *Lady Churchill's Rosebud Wristlet* has been "weird or speculative fiction." But then what does that mean, exactly? Does that mean science fiction? Fantasy? Horror? Does it mean, for example, dwarves and faeries and hobgoblins sitting around drinking mead out of acorns? Post–nuclear holocaust cannibal mutants with a taste for sexy college students? Zork and Zurk fencing with laser sabers on the flight deck whilst Becka the plucky intern tries to maneuver the spaceship through a cluster of asteroids?

WHICH IS TO SAY that certain kinds of labels have certain kinds of connotations. When I was a college student, for example, I took a class in writing fiction. I wrote a story in which a little girl lives in a castle with her dying grandmother and her only friend is a telepathic severed human head that is floating in a jar on a shelf in the castle library. The story had some problems, I admit, but the teacher handed the story back with only one comment: *Dan~ I don't accept genre fiction in this course!* By which the teacher meant, among other things: no dwarves, faeries, cannibal mutants, spaceships, asteroids, etc. No telepathic severed human heads. NO GENRE FICTION!!!

Genre fiction, we learned, was generally concerned with formulaic plots and one-dimensional characters, and was written in trite, hackneyed prose.

Literary fiction, on the other hand, was primarily realistic and focused on depth of characterization and complexity of thought. It valued the beautiful sentence and the well-made paragraph. It often ended with a moment of epiphany that was represented by a metaphor.

So I wrote a story in which a little girl lives on a farm in Nebraska with her dying grandmother and her only friend is an alcoholic deaf-mute farmhand who lives in a trailer nearby. In the end, she has an epiphany in which she imagines the farmhand communicating to her telepathically, but the telepathy is a metaphor for her yearning to be close to someone. The teacher wrote: *Dan~ powerfully realistic and moving!*

WELL.

It seemed like there came a point in the late 1980s, toward the end of my college career, when the idea of "literary fiction" was so narrowly defined that it had in fact become a kind of formulaic genre itself. The editor of a major magazine came to our school and told us that he wasn't interested in things that weren't "realistic." He told us, "If Kafka were alive today, we still wouldn't publish his fiction."

After a while, this kind of orthodoxy began to feel increasingly rigid and claustrophobic. Began to smack of tyranny, even.

So let us say, for the sake of a good story, that some people began to rebel. Let's say that a kind of underground literary movement arose in the dark hours of literature, sometime in the winter in the middle of the 1990s, and that at the forefront of that movement was a little zine called *Lady Churchill's Rosebud Wristlet,* edited by a couple of brave young iconoclasts, Gavin Grant and Kelly Link, who were courageously writing against the grain of the publishing world and the literary establishment and the literature professors and so forth.

Possibly we could apply various kinds of nicknames to this literary movement: "New Weird," for example, or "New Wave Fabulist," or "Slipstream," all of which have been offered by various anthologists and which in some ways all sound like the names of hairdos a girl might have gotten for the prom back in the seventies or eighties or nineties because of which years later the girl's children will look at a photograph from prom night and say, "Is that your real hair? Are you wearing a wig in that picture, Mom?"

But that is beside the point. Don't pay attention to the name, unless you like that sort of thing. The point is that they were writing stories and publishing stories and people, the public, became increasingly interested in what was going on. The idea was a good one: to take what was compelling and exciting about so-called genre fiction—all that storytelling stuff that as a kid made you want to read in the first place—and add to it a dash of the so-called literary story's love of language and depth of characterization, and some of the lit professor's clever postmodern intellectualism, and out of this mix create something really fresh and new.

(Well, sort of new. There were people like Joyce Carol Oates, Peter Straub, John Crowley, Angela Carter, Ursula Le Guin, etc., etc., who had been working in this vein all along, but why don't we go ahead and posit the concept of a rising literary movement, okay?)

OR BETTER YET, why don't we just say that there are some excellent writers in this collection who have written some cool stories. These writers aren't working in the same styles or modes and perhaps the authors aren't even aware that they are part of any sort of movement, but their work does seem to have interesting formal connections and occasional glimpses of familial resemblances—possibly a shared set of readings that they all loved as children, a collective dislike of conventional expectations? In any case, *Lady Churchill's Rosebud Wristlet* has brought them together.

They are gathered over there by the fire, sharpening sticks and muttering amongst themselves. I think of them as some kind of tribe, I guess. I imagine that they are headed off into the forest to hunt the wild hind called literature, and that they will return near dawn with the creature's severed head held aloft, singing at the top of their lungs.

THE BEST OF
LADY CHURCHILL'S
ROSEBUD WRISTLET

TRAVELS WITH THE SNOW QUEEN

Kelly Link

...

PART OF YOU IS ALWAYS TRAVELING FASTER, ALWAYS TRAV-eling ahead. Even when you are moving, it is never fast enough to satisfy that part of you. You enter the walls of the city early in the evening, when the cobblestones are a mottled pink with reflected light, and cold beneath the slap of your bare, bloody feet. You ask the man who is guarding the gate to recommend a place to stay the night, and even as you are falling into the bed at the inn, the bed that is piled high with quilts and scented with lavender, perhaps alone, perhaps with another traveler, perhaps with the guardsman who had such brown eyes and a mustache that curled up on either side of his nose like two waxed black laces, even as this guardsman, whose name you didn't ask, calls out a name in his sleep that is not your name, you are dreaming about the road again. When you sleep, you dream about the long white distances that still lie before you. When you wake up, the guardsman is back at his post, and the place between your legs aches pleasantly, your legs sore as if you had continued walking all night in your sleep. While you were sleeping, your feet have healed again. You were careful not to kiss the guardsman on the lips, so it doesn't really count, does it.

Your destination is North. The map you are using is a mirror. You are always pulling the bits out of your bare feet, the pieces of the map that broke off and fell on the ground as the Snow Queen flew overhead in her sleigh. Where you are, where you are coming from, it is impossible to read a map made of paper. If it were that easy then everyone would be a traveler. You have heard of other travelers whose maps are bread crumbs, whose maps are stones, whose maps are the four winds, whose maps are yellow bricks laid one after the other. You read your map with your foot, and behind you somewhere there must be another traveler whose map is the bloody footprints that you are leaving behind you.

There is a map of fine white scars on the soles of your feet that tells you where you have been. When you are pulling the shards of the Snow Queen's looking glass out of your feet, you remind yourself, you tell yourself to imagine how it felt when Kay's eyes, Kay's heart were pierced by shards of the same mirror. Sometimes it is safer to read maps with your feet.

LADIES. HAS IT EVER occurred to you that fairy tales aren't easy on the feet?

SO THIS IS THE STORY so far. You grew up, you fell in love with the boy next door, Kay, the one with blue eyes who brought you bird feathers and roses, the one who was so good at puzzles. You thought he loved you—maybe he thought he did, too. His mouth tasted so sweet, it tasted like love, and his fingers were so kind, they pricked like love on your skin, but three years and exactly two days after you moved in with him, you were having drinks out on the patio. You weren't exactly fighting, and you can't remember what he had done that had made you so angry, but you threw your glass at him. There was a noise like the sky shattering.

The cuff of his trousers got splashed. There were little fragments of glass everywhere. "Don't move," you said. You weren't wearing shoes.

He raised his hand up to his face. "I think there's something in my eye," he said.

His eye was fine, of course, there wasn't a thing in it, but later that night when he was undressing for bed, there were bits of glass like grains of sugar dusting his clothes. When you brushed your hand against his chest, something pricked your finger and left a smear of blood against his heart.

The next day it was snowing and he went out for a pack of cigarettes and never came back. You sat on the patio drinking something warm and alcoholic, with nutmeg in it, and the snow fell on your shoulders. You were wearing a short-sleeved T-shirt; you were pretending that you weren't cold, and that your lover would be back soon. You put your finger on the ground and then stuck it in your mouth. The snow looked like sugar, but it tasted like nothing at all.

The man at the corner store said that he saw your lover get into a long white sleigh. There was a beautiful woman in it, and it was pulled by thirty white geese. "Oh, her," you said, as if you weren't surprised. You went home and looked in the wardrobe for that cloak that belonged to your great-grandmother. You were thinking about going after him. You remembered that the cloak was woolen and warm, and a beautiful red—a traveler's cloak. But when you pulled it out, it smelled like wet dog and the lining was ragged, as if something had chewed on it. It smelled like bad luck: it made you sneeze, and so you put it back. You waited for a while longer.

Two months went by, and Kay didn't come back, and finally you left and locked the door of your house behind you. You were going to travel for love, without shoes, or cloak, or common sense. This is one of the things a woman can do when her lover leaves her. It's hard on the feet perhaps, but staying at home is hard on the heart, and you weren't quite ready to give him up yet. You told yourself that the woman in the sleigh must have put a spell on him, and he was probably already missing you. Besides, there were some questions you wanted to ask him, some true things you wanted to tell him. This is what you told yourself.

The snow was soft and cool on your feet, and then you found the trail of glass, the map.

After three weeks of hard traveling, you came to the city.

NO, REALLY, THINK ABOUT IT. Think about the little mermaid, who traded in her tail for love, got two legs and two feet, and every step was like walking on knives. And where did it get her? That's a rhetorical question, of course. Then there's the girl who put on the beautiful red dancing shoes. The woodsman had to chop her feet off with an ax.

There are Cinderella's two stepsisters, who cut off their own toes, and Snow White's stepmother, who danced to death in red-hot iron slippers. The Goose Girl's maid got rolled down a hill in a barrel studded with nails. Travel is hard on the single woman. There was this one woman who walked east of the sun and then west of the moon, looking for her lover, who had left her because she spilled tallow on his nightshirt. She wore out at least one pair of perfectly good iron shoes before she found him. Take our word for it, he wasn't worth it. What do you think happened when she forgot to put the fabric softener in the dryer? Laundry is hard, travel is harder. You deserve a vacation, but of course you're a little wary. You've read the fairy tales. We've been there, we know.

That's why we here at Snow Queen Tours have put together a luxurious but affordable package for you, guaranteed to be easy on the feet and on the budget. See the world by goosedrawn sleigh, experience the archetypal forest, the winter wonderland; chat with real live talking animals (please don't feed them). Our accommodations are three-star: sleep on comfortable, guaranteed pea-free boxspring mattresses; eat meals prepared by world-class chefs. Our tour guides are friendly, knowledgeable, well-traveled, trained by the Snow Queen herself. They know first aid, how to live off the land; they speak three languages fluently.

Special discount for older sisters, stepsisters, stepmothers, wicked witches, crones, hags, princesses who have kissed frogs without realizing what they were getting into, etc.

YOU LEAVE THE CITY and you walk all day beside a stream that is as soft and silky as blue fur. You wish that your map was water, and not broken glass. At midday you stop and bathe your feet in a shallow place and the ribbons of red blood curl into the blue water.

Eventually you come to a wall of briars, so wide and high that you can't see any way around it. You reach out to touch a rose, and prick your finger. You suppose that you could walk around, but your feet tell you that the map leads directly through the briar wall, and you can't stray from the path that has been laid out for you. Remember what happened to the little girl, your great-grandmother, in her red woolen cape. Maps protect their travelers, but only if the travelers obey the dictates of their maps. This is what you have been told.

Perched in the briars above your head is a raven, black and sleek as the curlicued moustache of the guardsman. The raven looks at you and you look back at it. "I'm looking for someone," you say. "A boy named Kay."

The raven opens its big beak and says, "He doesn't love you, you know."

You shrug. You've never liked talking animals. Once your lover gave you a talking cat, but it ran away and secretly you were glad. "I have a few things I want to say to him, that's all." You have, in fact, been keeping a list of all the things you are going to say to him. "Besides, I wanted to see the world, be a tourist for a while."

"That's fine for some," the raven says. Then he relents. "If you'd like to come in, then come in. The princess just married the boy with the boots that squeaked on the marble floor."

"That's fine for some," you say. Kay's boots squeak; you wonder how he met the princess, if he is the one that she just married, how the raven knows that he doesn't love you, what this princess has that you don't have, besides a white sleigh pulled by thirty geese, an impenetrable wall of briars, and maybe a castle. She's probably just some bimbo.

"The Princess Briar Rose is a very wise princess," the raven says, "but she's the laziest girl in the world. Once she went to sleep for a hundred days and no one could wake her up, although they put one hundred peas under her mattress, one each morning."

This, of course, is the proper and respectful way of waking up princesses. Sometimes Kay used to wake you up by dribbling cold water on your feet. Sometimes he woke you up by whistling.

"On the one-hundredth day," the raven says, "she woke up all by herself and told her council of twelve fairy godmothers that she supposed it was time she got married. So they stuck up posters, and princes and youngest sons came from all over the kingdom."

When the cat ran away, Kay put up flyers around the neighborhood. You wonder if you should have put up flyers for Kay. "Briar Rose wanted a clever husband, but it tired her dreadfully to sit and listen to the young men give speeches and talk about how rich and sexy and smart they were. She fell asleep and stayed asleep until the young man with the squeaky boots came in. It was his boots that woke her up.

"It was love at first sight. Instead of trying to impress her with everything he knew and everything he had seen, he declared that he had come all this way to hear Briar Rose talk about her dreams. He'd been studying in Vienna with a famous Doctor and was deeply interested in dreams."

Kay used to tell you his dreams every morning. They were long and complicated and if he thought you weren't listening to him, he'd sulk. You never remember your dreams. "Other peoples' dreams are never very interesting," you tell the raven.

The raven cocks its head. It flies down and lands on the grass at your feet. "Wanna bet?" it says. Behind the raven you notice a little green door recessed in the briar wall. You could have sworn that it wasn't there a minute ago.

The raven leads you through the green door, and across a long green lawn toward a two-story castle that is the same pink as the briar roses. You think this is kind of tacky but exactly what you would expect from someone named after a flower. "I had this dream once," the raven says, "that my teeth were falling out. They just crumbled into pieces in my mouth. And then I woke up, and realized that ravens don't have teeth."

You follow the raven inside the palace and up a long, twisty staircase. The stairs are stone, worn and smoothed away, like old thick silk. Slivers of glass glisten on the pink stone, catching the light of the candles on the wall. As you go up, you see that you are part of a great gray rushing crowd. Fantastic creatures, flat and thin as smoke, race up the stairs, men and women and snaky things with bright eyes. They nod to you as they slip past. "Who are they?" you ask the raven.

"Dreams," the raven says, hopping awkwardly from step to step. "The Princess's dreams, come to pay their respects to her new husband. Of course they're too fine to speak to the likes of us."

But you think that some of them look familiar. They have a familiar smell, like a pillow that your lover's head has rested upon.

At the top of the staircase is a wooden door with a silver keyhole. The dreams pour steadily through the keyhole and under the bottom of the door, and when you open it, the sweet stink and cloud of dreams are so thick in the Princess's bedroom that you can barely breathe. Some people might mistake the scent of the Princess's dreams for the scent of sex; then again, some people mistake sex for love.

You see a bed big enough for a giant, with four tall oak trees for bedposts. You climb up the ladder that rests against the side of the bed to see the Princess's sleeping husband. As you lean over, a goose feather flies up and tickles your nose. You brush it away, and dislodge several seedy-looking dreams. Briar Rose rolls over and laughs in her sleep, but the man beside her wakes up. "Who is it?" he says. "What do you want?"

He isn't Kay. He doesn't look a thing like Kay. "You're not Kay," you tell the man in the Princess's bed.

"Who the fuck is Kay?" he says, so you explain it all to him, feeling horribly embarrassed. The raven is looking pleased with itself, the way your talking cat used to look, before it ran away. You glare at the raven. You glare at the man who is not Kay.

After you've finished, you say that something is wrong, because your map clearly indicates that Kay has been here, in this bed. Your feet are leaving bloody marks on the sheets, and you pick a sliver of glass off the foot of the bed, so everyone can see that you're not lying. Princess Briar Rose sits up in bed, her long pinkish brown hair tumbled down over her shoulders. "He's not in love with you," she says, yawning.

"So he was here, in this bed, you're the icy slut in the sleigh at the corner store, you're not even bothering to deny it," you say.

She shrugs her pink-white shoulders. "Four, five months ago, he came through, I woke up," she says. "He was a nice guy, okay in bed. She was a real bitch, though."

"Who was?" you ask.

Briar Rose finally notices that her new husband is glaring at her. "What can I say?" she says, and shrugs. "I have a thing for guys in squeaky boots."

"Who was a bitch?" you ask again.

"The Snow Queen," she says, "the slut in the sleigh."

THIS IS THE LIST you carry in your pocket, of the things you plan to say to Kay, when you find him, if you find him:

1. I'm sorry that I forgot to water your ferns while you were away that time.

2. When you said that I reminded you of your mother, was that a good thing?

3. I never really liked your friends all that much.

4. None of my friends ever really liked you.

5. Do you remember when the cat ran away, and I cried and cried and made you put up posters, and she never came back? I wasn't crying because she didn't come back. I was crying because I'd taken her to the woods, and I was scared she'd come back and tell you what I'd done, but I guess a wolf got her, or something. She never liked me anyway.

6. I never liked your mother.

7. After you left, I didn't water your plants on purpose. They're all dead.

8. Good-bye.

9. Were you ever really in love with me?

10. Was I good in bed, or just average?

11. What exactly did you mean, when you said that it was fine that I had put on a little weight, that you thought I was even more beautiful, that I should go ahead and eat as much as I wanted, but when I weighed myself on the bathroom scale, I was exactly the same weight as before, I hadn't gained a single pound?

12. So all those times, I'm being honest here, every single time, and anyway I don't care if you don't believe me, I faked every orgasm you ever thought I had. Women can do that, you know. You never made me come, not even once.

13. So maybe I'm an idiot, but I used to be in love with you.

14. I slept with some guy, I didn't mean to, it just kind of happened. Is that how it was with you? Not that I'm making any apologies, or that I'd accept yours, I just want to know.
15. My feet hurt, and it's all your fault.
16. I mean it this time: good-bye.

THE PRINCESS BRIAR ROSE isn't a bimbo after all, even if she does have a silly name and a pink castle. You admire her dedication to the art and practice of sleep. By now you are growing sick and tired of traveling, and would like nothing better than to curl up in a big featherbed for one hundred days, or maybe even one hundred years, but she offers to loan you her carriage, and when you explain that you have to walk, she sends you off with a troop of armed guards. They will escort you through the forest, which is full of thieves and wolves and princes on quests, lurking about. The guards politely pretend that they don't notice the trail of blood that you are leaving behind. They probably think it's some sort of female thing.

It is after sunset, and you aren't even half a mile into the forest, which is dark and scary and full of noises, when bandits ambush your escort and slaughter them all. The bandit queen, who is grizzled and gray, with a nose like an old pickle, yells delightedly at the sight of you. "You're a nice plump one for my supper!" she says, and draws her long knife out of the stomach of one of the dead guards. She is just about to slit your throat as you stand there, politely pretending not to notice the blood that is pooling around the bodies of the dead guards, which is now obliterating the bloody tracks of your feet, the knife that is at your throat, when a girl about your own age jumps onto the robber queen's back, pulling at the robber queen's braided hair as if it were reins.

There is a certain family resemblance between the robber queen and the girl who right now has her knees locked around the robber queen's throat. "I don't want you to kill her," the girl says, and you realize that she means you, that you were about to die a minute ago, that travel is much more dangerous than you had ever imagined. You add an item of complaint to the list of things that you plan to tell Kay, if you find him.

The girl has half-throttled the robber queen, who has fallen to her knees, gasping for breath. "She can be my sister," the girl says insistently. "You promised I could have a sister and I want her. Besides, her feet are bleeding."

The robber queen drops her knife, and the girl drops back onto the ground, kissing her mother's hairy gray cheek. "Very well, very well," the robber queen grumbles, and the girl grabs your hand, pulling you farther and faster into the woods, until you are running and stumbling, her hand hot around yours.

You have lost all sense of direction; your feet are no longer set upon your map. You should be afraid, but instead you are strangely exhilarated. Your feet don't hurt anymore, and although you don't know where you are going, for the very first time you are moving fast enough, you are almost flying, your feet are skimming over the night-black forest floor as if it were the smooth, flat surface of a lake and your feet were two white birds. "Where are we going?" you ask the robber girl.

"We're here," she says, and stops so suddenly that you almost fall over. You are in a clearing, and the full moon is hanging overhead. You can see the robber girl better now, under the light of the moon. She looks like one of the bad girls who loiter under the street lamp by the corner shop, the ones who used to whistle at Kay. She wears black leatherette boots laced up to her thighs, and a black ribbed T-shirt and grape-colored plastic shorts with matching suspenders. Her nails are painted black, and bitten down to the quick. She leads you to a tumbledown stone keep, which is as black inside as her fingernail polish, and smells strongly of dirty straw and animals.

"Are you a princess?" she asks you. "What are you doing in my mother's forest? Don't be afraid. I won't let my mother eat you."

You explain to her that you are not a princess, what you are doing, about the map, who you are looking for, what he did to you, or maybe it was what he didn't do. When you finish, the robber girl puts her arms around you and squeezes you roughly. "You poor thing! But what a silly way to travel!" she says. She shakes her head and makes you sit down on the stone floor of the keep and show her your feet. You explain that they always heal, that really your feet are quite tough, but she takes off her leatherette boots and gives them to you.

The floor of the keep is dotted with indistinct, motionless forms. One snarls in its sleep, and you realize that they are dogs. The robber girl is sitting between four slender columns, and when the dog snarls, the thing shifts restlessly, lowering its branchy head. It is a hobbled reindeer. "Well, go on, see if they fit," the robber girl says, pulling out her knife. She drags it along the stone floor to make sparks. "What are you going to do when you find him?"

"Sometimes I'd like to cut off his head," you say. The robber girl grins, and thumps the hilt of her knife against the reindeer's chest.

The robber girl's feet are just a little bigger, but the boots are still warm from her feet. You explain that you can't wear the boots, or else you won't know where you are going. "Nonsense!" the robber girl says rudely.

You ask if she knows a better way to find Kay, and she says that if you are still determined to go looking for him, even though he obviously doesn't love you, and he isn't worth a bit of trouble, then the thing to do is to find the Snow Queen. "This is Bae. Bae, you mangy old, useless old thing," she says. "Do you know where the Snow Queen lives?"

The reindeer replies in a low, hopeless voice that he doesn't know, but he is sure that his old mother does. The robber girl slaps his flank. "Then you'll take her to your mother," she says. "And mind that you don't dawdle on the way."

She turns to you and gives you a smacking wet kiss on the lips and says, "Keep the shoes, they look much nicer on you than they did on me. And don't let me hear that you've been walking on glass again." She gives the reindeer a speculative look. "You know, Bae, I almost think I'm going to miss you."

You step into the cradle of her hands, and she swings you over the reindeer's bony back. Then she saws through the hobble with her knife, and yells "Ho," waking up the dogs.

You knot your fingers into Bae's mane, and bounce up as he stumbles into a fast trot. The dogs follow for a distance, snapping at his hooves, but soon you have outdistanced them, moving so fast that the wind peels your lips back in an involuntary grimace. You almost miss the feel of glass beneath your feet. By morning, you are out of the forest again, and Bae's hooves are churning up white clouds of snow.

SOMETIMES YOU THINK there must be an easier way to do this. Sometimes it seems to be getting easier all on its own. Now you have boots and a reindeer, but you still aren't happy. Sometimes you wish that you'd stayed at home. You're sick and tired of traveling toward the happily ever after, whenever the fuck that is— you'd like the happily right now. Thank you very much.

WHEN YOU BREATHE OUT, you can see the fine mist of your breath and the breath of the reindeer floating before you, until the wind tears it away. Bae runs on.

The snow flies up, and the air seems to grow thicker and thicker. As Bae runs, you feel that the white air is being rent by your passage, like heavy cloth. When you turn around and look behind you, you can see the path shaped to your joined form, woman and reindeer, like a hall stretching back to infinity. You see that there is more than one sort of map, that some forms of travel are indeed easier. "Give me a kiss," Bae says. The wind whips his words back to you. You can almost see the shape of them hanging in the heavy air.

"I'm not really a reindeer," he says. "I'm an enchanted prince."

You politely decline, pointing out that you haven't known him that long, and besides, for traveling purposes, a reindeer is better than a prince.

"He doesn't love you," Bae says. "And you could stand to lose a few pounds. My back is killing me."

You are sick and tired of talking animals, as well as travel. They never say anything that you didn't already know. You think of the talking cat that Kay gave you, the one that would always come to you, secretly, and looking very pleased with itself, to inform you when Kay's fingers smelled of some other woman. You couldn't stand to see him pet it, his fingers stroking its white fur, the cat lying on its side and purring wildly, "There, darling, that's perfect, don't stop," his fingers on its belly, its tail wreathing and lashing, its pointy little tongue sticking out at you. "Shut up," you say to Bae.

He subsides into an offended silence. His long brown fur is rimed with frost, and you can feel the tears that the wind pulls from your eyes turning to ice on your cheeks. The only parts of you that are warm are your feet, snug in the robber girl's boots. "It's just a little farther," Bae says, when you have been traveling for what feels like hours. "And then we're home."

You cross another corridor in the white air, and he swerves to follow it, crying out gladly, "We are near the old woman of Lapmark's house, my mother's house."

"How do you know?" you ask.

"I recognize the shape that she leaves behind her," Bae says. "Look!"

You look and see that the corridor of air you are following is formed like a short, stout, petticoated woman. It swings out at the waist like a bell.

"How long does it last?"

"As long as the air is heavy and dense," he says, "we burrow tunnels through the air like worms, but then the wind will come along and erase where we have been."

The woman-tunnel ends at a low red door. Bae lowers his head and knocks his antlers against it, scraping off the paint. The old woman of Lapmark opens the door, and you clamber stiffly off Bae's back. There is much rejoicing as mother recognizes son, although he is much changed from how he had been.

The old woman of Lapmark is stooped and fat as a grub. She fixes you a cup of tea, while Bae explains that you are looking for the Snow Queen's palace.

"You've not far to go now," his mother tells you. "Only a few hundred miles and past the house of the woman of Finmany. She'll tell you how to go—let me write a letter explaining everything to her. And don't forget to mention to her that I'll be coming for tea tomorrow; she'll change you back then, Bae, if you ask her nicely."

The woman of Lapmark has no paper, so she writes the letter on a piece of dried cod, flat as a dinner plate. Then you are off again. Sometimes you sleep as Bae runs on, and sometimes you aren't sure if you are asleep or waking. Great balls of greenish light roll cracking across the sky above you. At times it seems as if Bae is flying alongside the lights, chatting to them like old friends. At last you come to the house of the woman of Finmany, and you knock on her chimney, because she has no door.

WHY, YOU MAY WONDER, are there so many old women living out here? Is this a retirement community? One might not be remarkable, two is certainly more than enough, but as you look around, you can see little heaps of snow, lines of smoke rising from them. You have to be careful where you put your foot, or you might come through someone's roof. Maybe they came here for the quiet, or because they like ice fishing, or maybe they just like snow.

IT IS STEAMY and damp in the house, and you have to climb down the chimney, past the roaring fire, to get inside. Bae leaps down the chimney, hooves first, scattering coals everywhere. The Finmany woman is even smaller and rounder than the woman of Lapmark. She looks to you like a lump of pudding with black-currant eyes. She wears only a greasy old slip, and an apron with the words, IF YOU CAN'T STAND THE HEAT, STAY OUT OF MY KITCHEN.

She recognizes Bae even more quickly than his mother had, because, as it turns out, she was the one who turned him into a reindeer for teasing her about her weight. Bae apologizes, insincerely you think, but the Finmany woman says she will see what she can do about turning him back again. She isn't entirely hopeful. It seems that a kiss is the preferred method of transformation. You don't offer to kiss him, because you know what that kind of thing leads to.

The Finmany woman reads the piece of dried cod by the light of her cooking fire, and then she throws the fish into her cooking pot. Bae tells her about Kay and the Snow Queen, and about your feet, because your lips have frozen together on the last leg of the journey, and you can't speak a word.

"You're so clever and strong," the reindeer says to the Finmany woman. You can almost hear him add *and fat* under his breath. "You can tie up all the winds in the world with a bit of thread. I've seen you hurling the lightning bolts down from the hills as if they were feathers. Can't you give her the strength of ten men, so that she can fight the Snow Queen and win Kay back?"

"The strength of ten men?" the Finmany woman says. "A lot of good that would do! And besides, he doesn't love her."

Bae smirks at you, as if to say, I told you so. If your lips weren't frozen, you'd tell him that she isn't saying anything that you don't already know. "Now!" the Finmany woman says, "Take her up on your back one last time, and put her down again by the bush with the red berries. That marks the edge of the Snow Queen's garden; don't stay there gossiping, but come straight back. You were a handsome boy—I'll make you twice as good-looking as you were before. We'll put up flyers, see if we can get someone to come and kiss you.

"As for you, missy," she says. "Tell the Snow Queen now that we have Bae back, we'll be over at the palace next Tuesday for bridge. Just as soon as he has hands to hold the cards."

She puts you on Bae's back again, giving you such a warm kiss that your lips unfreeze, and you can speak again. "The woman of Lapmark is coming for tea tomorrow," you tell her.

The Finmany woman lifts Bae, and you upon his back, in her strong, fat arms, giving you a gentle push up the chimney.

GOOD MORNING, LADIES, it's nice to have you on the premiere Snow Queen Tour. I hope that you all had a good night's sleep, because today we're going to be traveling quite some distance. I hope that everyone brought a comfortable pair of walking shoes. Let's have a head count, make sure that everyone on the list is here, and then we'll have introductions. My name is Gerda, and I'm looking forward to getting to know all of you.

HERE YOU ARE AT LAST, standing before the Snow Queen's palace, the palace of the woman who enchanted your lover and then stole him away in her long white sleigh. You aren't quite sure what you are going to say to her, or to him. When you check your pocket, you discover that your list has disappeared. You have most of it memorized, but you think maybe you will wait and see, before you say anything. Part of you would like to turn around and leave before the Snow Queen finds you, before Kay sees you. You are afraid that you will burst out crying or even worse, that he will know that you walked barefoot on broken glass across half the continent, just to find out why he left you.

The front door is open, so you don't bother knocking, you just walk right in. It isn't that large a palace, really. It is about the size of your own house and even reminds you of your own house, except that the furniture, Danish modern, is carved out of blue-green ice—as are the walls and everything else. It's a slippery place and you're glad that you are wearing the robber girl's boots. You have to admit that the Snow Queen is a meticulous housekeeper, much tidier than you ever were. You can't find the Snow Queen and you can't find Kay, but in every room there are white geese who, you are in equal parts relieved and surprised to discover, don't utter a single word.

"Gerda!" Kay is sitting at a table, fitting the pieces of a puzzle together. When he stands up, he knocks several pieces of the puzzle off the table, and they fall to the floor and shatter into even smaller fragments. You both kneel down, picking them up. The table is blue, the puzzle pieces are blue, Kay is blue, which is why you didn't see him when you first came into the room. The geese brush up against you, soft and white as cats.

"What took you so long?" Kay says. "Where in the world did you get those ridiculous boots?" You stare at him in disbelief.

"I walked barefoot on broken glass across half a continent to get here," you say. But at least you don't burst into tears. "A robber girl gave them to me."

Kay snorts. His blue nostrils flare. "Sweetie, they're hideous."

"Why are you blue?" you ask.

"I'm under an enchantment," he says. "The Snow Queen kissed me. Besides, I thought blue was your favorite color."

Your favorite color has always been yellow. You wonder if the Snow Queen kissed him all over, if he is blue all over. All the visible portions of his body are blue. "If you kiss me," he says, "you break the spell and I can come home with you. If you break the spell, I'll be in love with you again."

You refrain from asking if he was in love with you when he kissed the Snow Queen. Pardon me, you think, when *she* kissed him. "What is that puzzle you're working on?" you ask.

"Oh, that," he says. "That's the other way to break the spell. If I can put it together—but the other way is easier. Not to mention more fun. Don't you want to kiss me?"

You look at his blue lips, at his blue face. You try to remember if you liked his kisses. "Do you remember the white cat?" you say. "It didn't exactly run away. I took it to the woods and left it there."

"We can get another one," he says.

"I took it to the woods because it was telling me things."

"We don't have to get a talking cat," Kay says. "Besides, why did you walk barefoot across half a continent of broken glass if you aren't going to kiss me and break the spell?" His blue face is sulky.

"Maybe I just wanted to see the world," you tell him. "Meet interesting people."

The geese are brushing up against your ankles. You stroke their white feathers and the geese snap, but gently, at your fingers. "You had better hurry up and decide if you want to kiss me or not," Kay says. "Because she's home."

When you turn around, there she is, smiling at you like you are exactly the person she was hoping to see.

The Snow Queen isn't how or what you'd expected. She's not as tall as you—you thought she would be taller. Sure, she's beautiful, you can see why Kay kissed her (although you are beginning to wonder why she kissed him), but her eyes are black and kind, which you didn't expect at all. She stands next to you, not looking at Kay at all, but looking at you. "I wouldn't do it if I were you," she says.

"Oh come on," Kay says. "Give me a break, lady. Sure it was

nice, but you don't want me hanging around this icebox forever, any more than I want to be here. Let Gerda kiss me, we'll go home and live happily ever after. There's supposed to be a happy ending."

"I like your boots," the Snow Queen says.

"You're beautiful," you tell her.

"I don't believe this," Kay says. He thumps his blue fist on the blue table, sending blue puzzle pieces flying through the air. Pieces lie like nuggets of sky-colored glass on the white backs of the geese. A piece of the table has splintered off, and you wonder if he is going to have to put the table back together as well.

"Do you love him?"

You look at the Snow Queen when she says this and then you look at Kay. "Sorry," you tell him. You hold out your hand in case he's willing to shake it.

"Sorry!" he says. "You're sorry! What good does that do me?"

"So what happens now?" you ask the Snow Queen.

"Up to you," she says. "Maybe you're sick of traveling. Are you?"

"I don't know," you say. "I think I'm finally beginning to get the hang of it."

"In that case," says the Snow Queen, "I may have a business proposal for you."

"Hey!" Kay says. "What about me? Isn't someone going to kiss me?"

You help him collect a few puzzle pieces. "Will you at least do this much for me?" he asks. "For old times' sake. Will you spread the word, tell a few single princesses that I'm stuck up here? I'd like to get out of here sometime in the next century. Thanks. I'd really appreciate it. You know, we had a really nice time, I think I remember that."

—

THE ROBBER GIRL's boots cover the scars on your feet. When you look at these scars, you can see the outline of the journey you made. Sometimes mirrors are maps, and sometimes maps are mirrors. Sometimes scars tell a story, and maybe someday you will tell this story to a lover. The soles of your feet are stories—hidden in the black boots, they shine like mirrors. If you were to take your boots off, you would see reflected in one foot-mirror the Princess Briar Rose as she sets off on her honeymoon, in her enormous four-poster bed, which now has wheels and is pulled by twenty white horses.

It's nice to see women exploring alternative means of travel.

In the other foot-mirror, almost close enough to touch, you could see the robber girl whose boots you are wearing. She is setting off to find Bae, to give him a kiss and bring him home again. You wouldn't presume to give her any advice, but you do hope that she has found another pair of good sturdy boots.

Someday, someone will probably make their way to the Snow Queen's palace, and kiss Kay's cold blue lips. She might even manage a happily ever after for a while. You are standing in your black-laced boots, and the Snow Queen's white geese mutter and stream and sidle up against you. You are beginning to understand some of what they are saying. They grumble about the weight of the sleigh, the weather, your hesitant jerks at their reins. But they are good-natured grumbles. You tell the geese that your feet are maps *and* your feet are mirrors. But you tell them that you have to keep in mind that they are also useful for walking around on. They are perfectly good feet.

SCOTCH: AN ESSAY INTO A DRINK

Gavin J. Grant

. . .

UISGE BEATHA, THE WATER OF LIFE, OR AS IT'S BEST KNOWN around this little planet, Scotch. My drink of choice, and I hope yours—if not before you read this, then perhaps after. I'm not here to compare Scotch to other—naturally lesser—imbibements, nor to apologize or snicker at one of the few vices that Western guilt allows itself; rather I'm celebrating a warmth in winter, a summer chilled, a friendship toasted, an evening capped.

Distilled liquors have been popular since human culture shifted from nomadic to agrarian patterns. In the present day Scotch whisky is one of the few world-class drinks, rivaled in recognition by few if any other products. *Product* is a strange word to use when talking about whisky, but for all our yearning toward peat fires and romance, you can't hide from the fact that whisky is a huge business. Yet, and there'll always be a *yet,* the liquid fire of it, the burning sensation, can only give a hint at the potential energy stored in this distillation. This potential was illustrated recently during a fire at a bonded whisky warehouse in Scotland. Firefighters had to contend with "seas of fire" as barrel after barrel exploded. Certainly a drink to respect.

In the United States whisky is still rather regarded as a unidimensional spirit without much character beyond that initial fiery taste. It's not always been that way, and different views certainly hold sway elsewhere. Whisky is limited not by itself but by the drinker. Here is a spirit to be drunk hot, cold, mixed, or straight; it's not just the "on the rocks" masculine drink of the manufacturers' lame ad campaigns, although they are attempting to leaven that with humor and try to reach the younger—and female—demographic, whom I know from personal experience will take to Scotch with only a little persuasion. Bad ads aside, in the States Scotch retains the image of being the drink of older, corpulent, broken-veined men.

So much for the United States; what about elsewhere? In the Mediterranean whisky is huge, and not just in the single-malt form. In Italy and Spain those beautiful young mothers we see swinging bambinos on their hips as they walk down the graceful alleyways think nothing of dropping into a café or tapas bar to order whisky with lemonade or ginger ale, or a whisky sour (see recipe), all of these drinks decorated and embellished with a twist of lemon or lime, a slice of sweetly sweating orange, a cheeky bright red cherry.

In Asia, especially Japan, lighter malts dominate the imported drinks market. So much so, in fact, many distilleries are now owned by Japanese firms beginning in 1985 with the purchase of the Tomatin distillery by Takara Shuzo and Okura and Co. With the World Trade Organization's mandated drop in import taxes on Scotch it is now very likely that sales and presence will keep increasing for a good few years, which the manufacturers will likely use as another inroad into the rest of Asia. All over the world, especially in China and India, Scotch is so popular that some markets are dominated by local knockoffs of famous brands. It's pretty funny from my point of view to see pictures of shelves full of Chivas Royal or whatever, but the distilleries see it differently; while some are fighting in the courts, others see it as proof of a market opportunity and at least one—Glenmorangie, the leading single malt in Scotland—has started up a distribution and sales network in China.

Back in Scotland and the rest of Britain Scotch is still popular, and sales are rising after a flat period at the start of the decade. Perhaps the funniest thing to happen there is the crossing of the ocean of prepackaged mixed drinks. Every liquor store in the United States seems to have a different selection of Jim Beam and this, Bacardi and that, but I doubt *any* of them have Scotch and Irn Bru! This has emerged in the UK as the new drink of choice among the young and savvy; the tastes blend into a sharp single that—surprised as I am to admit it—is very much worth a try.

Now believe me I'm not suggesting you go out and get a lovely bottle of Laphroaig or Balvenie and start dropping all kinds of mixers in it—no no, a splash of water to bring out the fullness of the flavor will do. The mixed drinks are made with blended whisky that was *meant* to be mixed—just as long as it's not five-year-old MacHughie or some other such waste of space. There are hundreds of recipes going rusty from disuse and it's up to you to save them. Start with an old-fashioned (see recipe) and find a bartending guide—or even better a good bartender—and bring back the wisdom of the ages.

Todaidh Mor, Todaidh Beag
(Great Todday, Little Todday)

After realizing that every move we make is predetermined and contributes a penny to each of the multinational's profits, one might be tempted to take a few days off work to recover. Well and right that you should, and there's nothing better to take the chill off than a hot toddy (see recipe), and if you can persuade someone to head to Videosmith or your local equivalent (forgoing that nasty multinational chain of independent-store busters) you can nestle back in the comfort of your own home and lose yourself in the fun of *Whisky Galore* (see page 29).

So let your blends be mixed to cool your summer; at the end of a long day (or night) slow down to a single malt, explore the complexity of this age-old distillation and discover that even if the eighties and early nineties were the blands in the spirit world that's no reason why the present day should be.

Slainte mhath! (Good health!)

Recipes

Old-Fashioned

> ½ *lump of sugar*
> 2 *dashes bitters*
> 1 *ounce water*
> 2 *ounces blended whisky*

Mix the first three ingredients together. Add the whisky, stir, add some ice, and decorate with a slice of orange, a twist of lemon, and a cherry!

Whisky Sour

> 2 *ounces blended whisky*
> ¾ *ounce lemon juice*
> 1 *teaspoon powdered sugar*

Shake together the ingredients with cracked ice. Strain into an 8-ounce highball glass, add a little ice, fill with seltzer water, and add a slice of lemon to decorate.

Hot Toddy

> *Juice of ½ lemon*
> *A good splash of whisky*
> 2 *spoons of honey*

Put the lemon juice and whisky in a mug, then fill with
boiling water, add the honey, and stir until it's dissolved.
You can add black currant juice or chamomile or mint tea
if you want, but either way, this will set you straight

The Obligatory Conspiracy Theory

We all know (good start: presupposing complicity) that the corporations are taking over the world and it has become geometrically
more difficult to understand the ethical and financial repercussions
of buying a product. Because of the difficulty in tracking down the
actual owners of the many whisky distilleries, I'm not even going
to try. Instead let's look at the recent upsurge in Swing Theory.
This theory states that everything connected to martinis is cool,
from music to clothes to bad plastic 1950s design relics and back to
martinis. Where did this come from? The hipsters on the "leading
edge" would have us believe that they brought this about, and as it
ever so slowly filters through mainstream society they recline farther back and chortle behind the backs of their hands as the ador-
ing crowd follows their every move. Unbeknownst to them, they
are in fact just robots following the terrible plans drawn up by a
shadowy consortium of gin manufacturers. Not since nineteenth-
century London has gin been so popular and had such an awful
splashover effect into fashion, design, and all the other important
circles of influence. In the late 1980s gin barons bought into a number of leading Japanese zaibatsus. Once ensconced there they en-
forced a strict three-martini lunch and launched an all-out attack
on Hollywood, spreading their evil "ginfluence" everywhere they
went. U.S. and European economists and commentators had no
idea why these massive Japanese combines were moving into the
fund-draining Tinseltown operations, but the zaibatsus had no
choice. Alcohol-soaked CEOs were "persuaded" into it. As they
were never given any sober time for reflection, the tyranny of their

majority stockholders held sway and, even as they watched the whole Japanese economy crumble, they continued to pour their reserves into Hollywood. Moving through the ranks, infiltrators from the Ginlords began to bring martini *kultur* to the movies. They bought up record companies and called it synergy, which was merely a front for relaunching the careers of Louis Prima and Dean Martin; they gave contracts to grungemeisters in return for a switch from guitars to horns, 4/4 to bossa nova, long hair to short, cherries to olives. Gin kids within the publishing combines have been glimpsed pushing books on the "new" lifestyles of the young, hip, and fabulously misguided. It's been a tumultuous few years for the Ginlords and they are still reaping the fruits of their labors even as those who are not blinded by *mondo bachelor-pad* life are weeping. There will be no end until we stand up with our single malts and our whisky sours. Until then, the Ginlords have us at their mercy.

WHISKY GALORE

Whisky Galore was written in 1947 by Compton MacKenzie; I must have seen the film version (1949) more times than I've seen any other movie and I doubt I'll ever tire of it. The story was inspired by a real-life incident, the sinking of the SS *Politician*—with its cargo of whisky—near the island of Eriskay in the north of Scotland during World War II. In MacKenzie's version the ship is the SS *Cabinet Minister*, which goes down off the coast of the Toddays, Great and Little respectively, where no whisky has been seen for too long (anything longer than a couple of days is much too long for these islands to be without whisky). Comic relief is supplied by Captain Waggett (played by Basil Radford in the film), who has safeguarded his own supply in a superior—

and rather blackguarded—manner and who wants to stop any of the islanders getting the whisky from the ship.

The comedy is gentle yet daring, antiestablishment yet following the classic form, and has a dash of old-fashioned romance to warm our cynical hearts. The film has a few actors and actresses you may recognize from other classic films of the period, and Catriona Macroon (Gabrielle Blunt)—the soft voice of the local phone exchange and the object of a local sergeant's affections—may send you overseas in pursuit of her present-day kin. Worth searching out.

MARGINALIA

We apologize for the chocolate stains on the book. If your copy of this anthology doesn't have any chocolate on it, it is a limited edition "clean" copy and may be worth so much in the future you should just quit work now and sit around living off credit cards waiting for it to appreciate.

UNRECOGNIZABLE

David Findlay

Watch tissue scar shut this face in seconds-
bulk of new, smooth flesh where eyes were.
I can no longer hold you, unrecognizable friend.

Grandmother is calm; a porcelain miniature.
The parrots ferry her across the room
strung from their feathered breasts.

MEHITOBEL WAS QUEEN OF THE NIGHT

Ian McDowell

boss last night I was talking
    to mehitobel
not the cat I mean the tall one
with the talent and the o
and those great gotohell eyes

archy she says
i d sell my tattered soul
for a bottle of good jack
and a stack of books to review
that didn t half suck

but bel i said what soul
aren t you some hebrew demon
    lady
child eater
howler in the night
bottom half a burning snake

true archy she sighed
wife of asmodeus i was
and one day i ll fight
my mother lilith for the right
to marry god and eat him
no doubt after i ve kicked his
    ass at pool

toujours noir
toujours noir
that s me

thing is archy
there s then and soon
and neither one is now
these days i m too much
the hermit bookworm
to go gallivanting nightown
all bottomless in serpentfire
and right now i don t want
godflesh or kidsmeat no
pork rinds will do me fine

that s what she said boss
pork rinds
our queen of the night i think
is a redneck gal at heart

—*for Mehitobel Wilson*

TAN-TAN AND DRY BONE

Nalo Hopkinson

. . .

IF YOU ONLY SEE DRY BONE: ONE MEAGER MAN, WITH ARMS and legs thin so like matches stick, and what a way the man face just a-hang down till it favor jackass when him sick!

Duppy Dead Town is where people go when life boof them, when hope left them and happiness cut she eye 'pon them and strut away. Duppy Dead people drag them foot when them walk. The food them cook taste like burial ground ashes. Duppy Dead people have one foot in the world and the next one already crossing the threshold to where the real duppy-them living. In Duppy Dead Town them will tell you how it ain't have no way to get away from Dry Bone the skin-and-bone man, for even if you lock you door on him, him body so fine him could slide through the crack and all to pass inside your house.

Dry Bone sit down there on one little wooden crate in the open market in Duppy Dead Town. Him a-think about food. Him hungry so till him belly a-burn he, till it just a-prowl 'round inside him rib cage like angry bush cat, till it clamp on to him backbone and a-sit there so and a-growl.

And all the time Dry Bone sitting down there so in the market, him just a-watch the open sky above him, for Dry Bone nah like that endless blue. Him 'fraid him will just fall up into it and keep falling.

Dry Bone feel say him could eat two-three of that market woman skinny little fowl-them, feathers and all, then wash them down with a dry-up breadfruit from the farmer cart across the way, raw and hard just so, and five-six of them wrinkle-up string mango from the fruit stand over there. Dry Bone coulda never get enough food, and right now, all like how him ain't eat for days, even Duppy Dead people food looking good. But him nah have no money. The market people just a-cut them eye on him, and a-watch him like stray dog so him wouldn't fast himself and thief away any of them goods. In Duppy Dead Town them had a way to say if you only start to feed Dry Bone, you can't stop, and you pickney-them go starve, for him will eat up all your provisions. And then them would shrug and purse-up them mouth, for them know say hunger is only one of the crosses Duppy Dead pickney go have to bear.

Duppy Dead Town ain't know it waiting; waiting for the one name Tan-Tan.

So—it had Dry Bone sitting there, listening to he belly bawl. And is so Tan-Tan find he, cotch-up on the wooden crate like one big black anansi-spider.

Dry Bone watch the young woman dragging she sad self into the market like monkey riding she back. She nah have no right to look downpressed so; she body tall and straight like young cane, and she legs strong. But the look on she pretty face favor puppy what lose it mother, and she carrying she hand on she machete handle the way you does put your hand on your friend shoulder. Dry Bone sit up straight. He lick he lips. A stranger in Duppy Dead Town, one who ain't know to avoid he. One who can't see she joy for she sorrow: the favorite meat of the one name Dry Bone. He know she good. Dry Bone know all the souls that feed he. He recognize she so well, he discern she name in the curve of she spine. So Dry Bone laugh, a sound like the dust blowin' down in the dry gully. "Girl pickney Tan-Tan," he whisper, "I go make you take me on this day. And when you pick me up, you pick up trouble."

He call out to Tan-Tan, "My beautiful one, you enjoying the day?"

Tan-Tan look at the little fine-foot man, so meager you could nearly see through he. "What you want, Grandpa?" she ask.

Dry Bone smile when she say *Grandpa*. True, Duppy Dead townspeople have a way to say that Dry Bone older than Death it own self. "Well, doux-doux darlin', me wasn't going to say nothing, but since you ask, beg you a copper to buy something to eat, nuh? I ain't eat from mornin'."

Now, Tan-Tan heart soft. Too besides, she figure maybe if she help out this old man who look to be on he last legs, she go ease up the curse on she a little. For you must know the story 'bout she, how she kill Antonio, she only father, she only family on New Half Way Tree. Guilt nearly breaking she heart in two, but to make it worse, the douen people nah put a curse on she when she do the deed? Yes, man: she couldn't rest until she save two people life to make up for the one she did kill. Everywhere she go, she could hear the douen chant following she:

It ain't have no magic in do-feh-do.
If you take one, you mus' give back two.

Tan-Tan reach into she pocket to fling the old man couple-three coppers. But she find it strange that he own people wasn't feeding he. So she raise she voice to everyone in the marketplace: "How oonuh could let this old man sit here hungry so? Oonuh not shame?"

"Lawd, missus," say the woman selling the fowl, "you ain't want to mix up with he. That is Dry Bone, and when you pick he up, you pick up trouble!"

"What stupidness you talking, woman? Hot sun make you bassourdie, or what? How much trouble so one little old man could give you?"

A man frying some hard johnnycake on a rusty piece of galvanized iron look up from he wares. "You should listen when people talk to you, Tan-Tan. Make I tell you: you even self touch Dry Bone, is like you touch Death. Don't say nobody ain't tell you!"

Tan-Tan look down at the little old man, just holding he belly and waiting for somebody to take pity on he. Tan-Tan kiss she teeth steuups. "Oonuh too craven, you hear? Come, Daddy. I go buy you a meal, and I go take you where I staying and cook it up nice for you. All right?"

Dry Bone get excited one time; he almost have she now! "Thank you, my darlin'. Granny Nanny bless you, doux-doux. I ain't go be plenty trouble. Beg you though, sweetheart: pick me up. Me old bones so weak with hunger, I ain't think I could make the walk back to your place. I is only a little man, halfway a duppy meself. You could lift me easy."

"You mean to say these people make you stay here and get hungry so till you can't walk?" Tan-Tan know say she could pick he up; after all he the smallest man she ever see. The market go quiet all of a sudden. Everybody only waiting to see what she go do. Tan-Tan bend down to take the old man in she arms. Dry Bone reach out and hold on to she. As he touch she, she feel a coldness wrap round she heart. She pick up the old man and is like she pick up all the cares of the world. She make a joke of it, though: "Eh-eh, Pappy, you heavier than you look, you know!"

That is when she hear Dry Bone voice good, whispering inside she head, *sht-sht-sht* like dead leaf on a dead tree. And she realize that all this time she been talking to he, she never see he lips move. "I name Dry Bone," the old man say. "I old like Death, and when you pick me up, you pick up trouble. You ain't go shake me loose until I suck out all your substance. Feed me, Tan-Tan."

And Tan-Tan feel Dry Bone getting heavier and heavier, but she couldn't let he go. She feel the weight of all the burdens she carrying: alone, stranded on New Half Way Tree with a curse on she head, a spiteful woman so ungrateful she kill she own daddy.

"Feed me, Tan-Tan, or I go choke you." He wrap he arms tight round she neck and cut off she wind. She stumble over to the closest market stall. The lady selling the fowl back away, she eyes rolling with fright. Gasping for air, Tan-Tan stretch out she hand and feel two dead fowl. She pick them up off the woman stand. Dry Bone chuckle. He loosen up he arms just enough to let she get some air. He grab one fowl and stuff it into he mouth, feathers and all. He chew, then he swallow. "More, Tan-Tan. Feed me." He choke she again.

She body crying for breath, Tan-Tan stagger from one market stall to the next. All the higglers fill up a market basket for she. Them had warn she, but she never listen. None of them would take she money. Dry Bone let she breathe again. "Now take me home, Tan-Tan."

Tan-Tan grab the little man round he waist and try to dash he off, but she hand stick to he like he was tar baby. He laugh in she mind, the way ground puppy does giggle when it see carrion. "You pick me up by you own free will. You can't put me down. Take me home, Tan-Tan."

Tan-Tan turn she feet toward she little hut in the bush, and with every step she take along the narrow gravel path, Dry Bone only getting heavier. Tan-Tan mother did never want she; Ione make Antonio kidnap she away to New Half Way Tree. Even she daddy who did say he love she used to beat she, and worse things too besides. Tan-Tan never see the singing tree she always pass by on she way home, with the wind playing like harp in the leaves, or the bright blue furry butterflies that always used to sweet she, flitting from flower to flower through the bush. With Dry Bone in one arm and the full market basket in the next hand, Tan-Tan had was to use she shoulders to shove aside the branches to make she way to she hut. Branches reach out bony fingers to pull at she dreads, but she ain't feel that pain. She only feel the pain of knowing what she is, a worthless, wicked woman that only good to feed a duppy like Dry Bone. How anybody could love she? She don't deserve no better. "Make haste, woman," Dry Bone snarl. "And keep under the trees, you hear? I want to get out from under the open sky."

By the time them reach the thatch hut standing all by itself in the bush, Tan-Tan back did bend with the weight of all she was carrying. It feel like Dry Bone get bigger, oui? Tan-Tan stand up outside she home, panting under the weight of she burdens.

"Take me inside, Tan-Tan. I prefer to be out of the air."

"Yes, Dry Bone." Wheezing, she climb up the veranda steps and carry he inside the dark, mean one-room hut, exactly the kind of place where a worthless woman should live. One break-seat chair for sit in; a old ticking mattress for when sleep catch she; two rusty hurricane lamp with rancid oil inside them, one for light the inside of the hut and one for light outside when night come, to keep away the ground puppy and moko jumbie-them; a dirty coalpot; and a bucket full of stale water with dead spider and thing floating on top. Just good for she. With all the nice things she steal from people, she ain't keep none for she self, but only giving them away all the time.

Dry Bone voice fill up the inside of she head again: "Put me on the mattress. It look softer than the chair. Is there I go stay from now on."

"Yes, Dry Bone." She find she could put he down, but the weight ain't lift off from she. Is like she still carrying he, a heaviness next to she heart, and getting heavier.

"I hungry, Tan-Tan. Cook up that food for me. All of it, you hear?"

"Yes, Dry Bone." And Tan-Tan pluck the fowl, and chop off

the head, and gut out the insides. She make a fire outside the hut. She roast the fowl and she boil water for topi-tambo root, and she bake a breadfruit.

"I want johnnycake too."

So Tan-Tan find she one bowl and she fry pan, and she little store of flour, and she make dumpling and put it to fry on the fire. And all she working, she could hear Dry Bone whispering in she head like knowledge: "Me know say what you is, Tan-Tan. Me know how you worthless and your heart hard. Me know you could kill just for so, and you don't look out for nobody but yourself. You make a mistake when you pick me up. You pick up trouble."

When she done cook the meal, she ain't self have enough plate to serve it all one time. She had was to bring a plate of food in to Dry Bone, make he eat it, and take it outside and fill it up again. Dry Bone swallow every last johhnycake whole. He chew up the topi-tambo, skin and all, and nyam it down. He ain't even wait for she to peel the roast breadfruit, he pop it into he maw just so. He tear the meat from the chicken bone, then he crunch up the bone-them and all. And all he eat, he belly getting round and hard, but he arms and legs only getting thinner and thinner. Still, Tan-Tan could feel the weight of he resting on she chest till she could scarcely breathe.

"That not enough," Dry Bone say. "Is where the fowl guts-them there?"

"I wrap them up in leaf and bury them in the back," Tan-Tan mumble.

"Dig them up and bring them for me."

"You want me to cook them in the fire?"

"No, stupid one, hard-ears one," Dry Bone say in he sandpaper voice. "I ain't tell you to cook them. I go eat them raw just so."

She own-way, yes, and stupid too. Is must be so. Tan-Tan hang she head. She dig up the fowl entrails and bring them back. Dry

Bone suck down the rank meat, toothless gums smacking in the dark hut. He pop the bitter gall bladder in he mouth like a sea grape and swallow that too. "Well," he say, "that go do me for now, but a next hour or two, and you going to feed me again. It ain't look like you have plenty here to eat, eh, Tan-Tan? You best go and find more before evening come."

That all she good for. Tan-Tan know she best be grateful Dry Bone even let she live. She turn she weary feet back on the path to Duppy Dead Town. She feel the weight on she dragging she down to the ground. Branch scratch up she face, and mosquito bite she, and when she reach where she always did used to find Duppy Dead Town, it ain't have nothing there. The people pick up lock, stock, and barrel and left she in she shame with Dry Bone. Tears start to track down Tan-Tan face. She weary, she weary can't done, but she had was to feed the little duppy man. Lazy, the voice in she head say. What a way this woman could run from a little hard work! Tan-Tan drag down some net vine from out a tree and weave she-self a basket. She search the bush. She find two-three mushroom under some rockstone, and a halwa tree with a half-ripe fruit on it. She throw she knife and stick a fat guinea lizard. Dry Bone go eat the bones and all. Maybe that would full he belly.

And is so the days go for she. So Dry Bone eat, so he hungry again one time. Tan-Tan had was to catch and kill and gut and cook, and she only get time to sneak a little bite for sheself was when Dry Bone sleeping, but it seem like he barely sleep at all. He stretch out the whole day and night on Tan-Tan one bed, giving orders. Tan-Tan had to try and doze the long nights through in the break-seat chair or on the cold floor, and come 'fore day morning, she had was to find sheself awake one time, to stoke up the fire and start cooking all over again. And what a way Dry Bone belly get big! Big like a watermelon. But the rest of he like he wasting away, just a skin-and-bone man. Sometimes, Tan-Tan couldn't even self see he in the dark hut; only a belly sticking up on the bed.

One time, after he did guzzle down three lizard, two bread-fruit, a gully hen, and four gully hen eggs, Dry Bone sigh and set-tle back down on the bed. He close he eyes.

Tan-Tan walk over to the bed. Dry Bone ain't move. She wave she hand in front of he face. He ain't open he eyes. Maybe he did fall to sleep? Maybe she could run away now? Tan-Tan turn to creep out the door, and four bony fingers grab she round she arm and start to squeeze. "You can't run away, Tan-Tan. I go follow you. You have to deal with me."

Is must be true. Dry Bone was she sins come to haunt she, to ride she into she grave. Tan-Tan ain't try to get away no more, but late at night, she weep bitter, bitter tears.

One day, she had was to go down to the river to dip some fresh water to make soup for Dry Bone. As she lean out over the river with she dipping bowl, she see a reflection in the water: Master Johncrow the corbeau-bird, perch on a tree branch, looking for carrion for he supper. He bald head gleaming in the sun like a hard boil egg. He must be feeling hot in he black frock coat, for he eyes look sad, and he beak drooping like candle wax. Tan-Tan remem-ber she manners. "Good day to you, Sir Buzzard," she say. "How do?"

"Not so good, eh?" Master Johncrow reply. "I think I going hungry today. All I look, I can't spy nothing dead or even ready to dead. You feeling all right, Tan-Tan?" he ask hopefully.

"Yes, Master Buzzard, thanks Nanny."

"But you don't look too good, you know. Your eyes sink back in your head, and your skin all gray, and you walking with a stoop. I could smell death around here yes, and it making me hungry."

"Is only tired, I tired, sir. Dry Bone latch on to me, and I can't get any rest, only feeding he day and night."

"Dry Bone?" The turkey buzzard sit up straight on he perch. Tan-Tan could see a black tongue snaking in and out of he mouth with excitement.

"Seen, Master Buzzard. I is a evil woman, and I must pay for me corruption by looking after Dry Bone. It go drive me to me grave, I know, then you go have your meal."

"I ain't know about you and any corruption, doux-doux." Johncrow leap off the tree branch and flap down to the ground beside Tan-Tan. "You smell fresh like the living to me." Him nearly big as she, he frock-coat feathers rank and raggedy, and she could smell the carrion on he. Tan-Tan step back a little. "You don't know the wicked things I do," she say.

"If a man attack you, child, don't you must defend yourself? I know this, though: I ain't smell no corruption on you, and that is my favorite smell. If you dead soon, I go thank you for your thoughtfulness with each taste of your entrails, but I go thank you even more if you stay alive long enough to deliver Dry Bone to me."

"How you mean, Master Crow?"

"Dry Bone did dead and rotten long before Nanny was a girl, but him living still. Him is the sweetest meat for a man like me. I could feed off Dry Bone for the rest of my natural days, and him still wouldn't done. Is years now I trying to catch he for me larder. Why you think he so 'fraid of the open sky? Open sky is home to me. Do me this one favor, nuh?"

Tan-Tan feel hope start to bud in she heart. "What you want me to do, Master Crow?"

"Just get he to come outside in your yard, and I go do the rest."

So the two of them make a plan. And before he fly off Master Johncrow say to she, "Like Dry Bone not the only monkey that a-ride your back, child. You carrying around a bigger burden than he. And me nah want that one there. It ain't smell dead, but like it did never live. Best you go find Papa Bois."

"And who is Papa Bois, sir?"

"The old man of the bush, the one who does look after all the beast-them. He could look into your eyes, and see your soul, and tell you how to cleanse it."

Tan-Tan ain't like the sound of someone examining she soul, so she only say politely, "Thank you, Master Johncrow. Maybe I go do that."

"All right then, child. Till later." And Master Buzzard fly off to wait until he part of the plan commence.

Tan-Tan scoop up the water for the soup to carry back to she hut, feeling almost happy for the first time in weeks. On the way home, she fill up she carry sack with a big, nice halwa fruit, three handful of mushroom, some coco yam that she dig up, big so like she head, and all the ripe hog plum she could find on the ground. She go make Dry Bone eat till he foolish, oui?

When she reach back at the hut, she set about she cooking with a will. She boil up the soup thick and nice with mushroom and coco yam and cornmeal dumpling. She roast the halwa fruit in the coal pot, and she sprinkle nutmeg and brown sugar on top of it too besides, till the whole hut smell sweet with it scent. She wash the hog plum clean and put them in she best bowl. And all the time she work, she humming to sheself:

Corbeau say so, it must be so,
Corbeau say so, it must be so.

Dry Bone sprawl off on she bed and just a-watch she with him tiny jumbie-bead eye, red with a black center. "How you happy so?"

Tan-Tan catch sheself. She mustn't make Dry Bone hear Master Johncrow name. She make she mouth droop and she eyes sad, and she say, "Me not really happy, Dry Bone. Me only find when me sing, the work go a little faster."

Dry Bone still suspicious though. "Then is what that you singing? Sing it louder so I could hear."

"Is a song about making soup." Tan-Tan sing for he:

Coco boil so, is so it go,
Coco boil so, is so it go.

"Cho! Stupid woman. Just cook the food fast, you hear?"

"Yes, Dry Bone." She leave off singing. Fear form a lump of ice in she chest. Suppose Dry Bone find she out? Tan-Tan finish preparing the meal as fast as she can. She take it to Dry Bone right there on the bed.

By now, Dry Bone skin did draw thin like paper on he face. He eyes did disappear so far back into he head that Tan-Tan could scarce see them. She ain't know what holding he arms and legs-them together, for it look as though all the flesh on them waste away. Only he belly still bulging big with all the food she been cooking for he. If Tan-Tan had buck up a thing like Dry Bone in the bush, she would have take it for a corpse, dead and rotting in the sun. Dry Bone, the skin-and-bone man. To pick he up was to pick up trouble, for true.

Dry Bone bare he teeth at Tan-Tan in a skull grin. "Like you cook plenty this time, almost enough for a snack. Give me the soup first." He take the whole pot in he two hand, put it to he head, and drink it down hot-hot just so. He never even self stop to chew the coco yam and dumpling; he just swallow. When he put down the pot and belch, Tan-Tan see steam coming out of he mouth, the soup did so hot. He scoop out all the insides of the halwa fruit with he bare hand, and he chew up the hard seed-them like them was fig. Then he eat the thick rind. And so he belly getting bigger. He suck down the hog plum one by one, then he just let go Tan-Tan best bowl. She had was to catch it before it hit the ground and shatter.

Dry Bone lie back and sigh. "That was good. It cut me hunger little bit. In two-three hour, I go want more again."

Time was, them words would have hit Tan-Tan like blow, but

this time, she know what she have to do. "Dry Bone," she say in a sweet voice, "you ain't want to go out onto the veranda for a little sun while I cook your next meal?"

Dry Bone open he eyes up big-big. Tan-Tan could see she death in them cold eyes. "Woman, you crazy? Go outside? Like you want breeze blow me away, or what? I comfortable right here." He close he eyes and settle back down in the bed.

She try a next thing. "I want to clean the house, Master. I need to make up the bed, put on clean sheets for you. Make me just cotch you on the veranda for two little minutes while I do that, nuh?"

"Don't get me vex." Tan-Tan feel he choking weight on she spirit squeeze harder. Only two-three sips of air making it past she throat.

The plan ain't go work. Tan-Tan start to despair. Then she re-member how she used to love to play masque Robber Queen when she was a girl-pickney, how she could roll pretty words round in she mouth like marble, and make up any kind of story. She had a talent for the Robber Queen patter. Nursie used to say she could make white think it was black. "But Dry Bone," she wheeze, "look at how nice and strong I build me veranda, fit to sit a king. Look at how it shade off from the sun." She gasp for a breath, just a little breath of air. "No glare to beware, no open sky to trouble you, only sweet breeze to dance over your face, to soothe you as you lie and daydream. Ain't you would like me to carry you out there to lounge off in the wicker chair, and warm your bones little bit, just sit and contemplate your estate? It nice and warm outside today. You could hear the gully hens-them singing cocorico, and the guinea lizards-them just a-relax in the sun hot and drowse. It nice out there for true, like a day in heaven. Nothing to cause you danger. Nothing to cause you harm. I could carry you out there in my own two arm, and put you nice and comfortable in the wicker chair, with two pillow at your back for you to rest back on, a king on he own throne. Ain't you would like that?"

Dry Bone smile. The tightness in she chest ease up little bit. "All right, Tan-Tan. You getting to know how to treat me good. Take me outside. But you have to watch out after me. No make no open sky catch me. Remember, when you pick me up, you pick up trouble! If you ain't protect me, you go be sorry."

"Yes, Dry Bone." She pick he up. He heavy like a heart attack from all the food he done eat already. She carry he out onto the veranda and put he in the wicker chair with two pillow at he back.

Dry Bone lean he dead-looking self back in the chair with a peaceful smile on he face. "Yes, I like this. Maybe I go get you to bring me my food out here from now on."

Tan-Tan give he some cool sorrel drink in a cup to tide he over till she finish cook, then she go back inside the hut to start cooking again. And as she cooking, she singing soft-soft,

> *Corbeau say so, it must be so,*
> *Corbeau say so, it must be so.*

And she only watching at the sky through the one little window in the hut. Suppose Master Johncrow ain't come?

"Woman, the food ready yet?" Dry Bone call out.

"Nearly ready, Dry Bone." Is a black shadow that she see in the sky? It moving? It flying their way? No. Just a leaf blowing in the wind. "The chicken done stew!" she call out to the veranda. I making the dumpling now!" And she hum she tune, willing Master Johncrow to hear.

A-what that? Him come? No, only one baby rain cloud scudding by. "Dumpling done! I frying the banana!"

"What a way you taking long today," grumble Dry Bone.

Yes. Coasting in quiet-quiet on wings the span of a big man,

Master Johncrow the corbeau-bird float through the sky. From her window Tan-Tan see him land on the banister rail right beside Dry Bone, so soft that the duppy man ain't even self hear he. She heart start dancing in she chest, light and airy like a masque band flag. Tan-Tan tiptoe out to the front door to watch the drama.

Dry Bone still have he eyes closed. Master Johncrow stretch he long, picky-picky wattle neck and look right into Dry Bone face, tender as a lover. He black tongue snake out to lick one side of he pointy beak. "Ah, Dry Bone," he say, and he voice was the wind in dry season, "so long I been waiting for this day."

Dry Bone open up he eye. Him two eyes make four with Master Johncrow own. He scream and try to scramble out the chair, but he belly get too heavy for he skin-and-bone limbs. "Don't touch me!" he shout. "When you pick me up, you pick up trouble! Tan-Tan, come and chase this buzzard away!" But Tan-Tan ain't move.

Striking like a serpent, Master Johncrow trap one of Dry Bone arm in he beak. Tan-Tan hear the arm snap like twig, and Dry Bone scream again. "You can't pick me up! You picking up trouble!" But Master Johncrow haul Dry Bone out into the yard by he break arm, then he fasten onto the nape of Dry Bone neck with he claws. He leap into the air, dragging Dry Bone up with him. The skin-and-bone man fall into the sky in truth.

As he flap away over the trees with he prize, Tan-Tan hear he chuckle. "Ah, Dry Bone, you dead thing, you! Trouble sweet to me like the yolk that did sustain me. Is trouble you swallow to make that belly so fat? Ripe like a watermelon. I want you to try to give me plenty, plenty trouble. I want you to make it last a long time."

Tan-Tan sit down in the wicker chair on the veranda and watch them flying away till she couldn't hear Dry Bone screaming no more and Master Johncrow was only a black speck in the sky. She whisper to sheself:

Corbeau say so, it must be so,
Please, Johncrow, take Dry Bone and go,
Tan-Tan say so,
Tan-Tan beg so.

Tan-Tan go inside and look at she little home. It wouldn't be plenty trouble to make another window to let in more light. Nothing would be trouble after living with the trouble of Dry Bone. She go make the window tomorrow, and the day after that, she go recane the break-seat chair.

Tan-Tan pick up she kerosene lamp and go outside to look in the bush for some scraper grass to polish the rust off it. That would give she something to do while she think about what Master Johncrow had tell she. Maybe she would even go find this Papa Bois, oui?

Wire bend,
Story end.

AN OPEN LETTER CONCERNING SPONSORSHIP

Margaret Muirhead

. . .

Dear Sir or Madam:

You don't need to be small or local anymore to have "Mom-and-Pop" appeal. In today's business climate of mergers and acquisitions, corporations may seem to have lost their human touch. In the following proposal, I am offering you the opportunity to be part of an exciting new partnership that could lend any multinational conglomerate the glow of paternalism, all at relatively low cost to you.

As background, let me introduce myself. I am recently married and considering beginning a family. Like many modern couples, my husband and I have both maintained our family ("maiden") names after marriage. In an effort to be equitable, we have agreed that our progeny will bear a third new name. We considered splicing and grafting our names, all to hideous effect. We then bandied about the names of our favorite composers, poets, filmmakers, and household appliances. We are especially fond of our toaster oven and are grateful to its manufacturer. We are also fond of the verb *bandy*.

However, none of these names solved our second dilemma, which is again modern: we simply cannot afford to raise a child. Although we are both gainfully employed (but not in the employ of your fine corporation), our earnings barely cover rent in our metropolitan area, not to mention the dizzying storm of insurances: major medical, dental, auto, renter's, total disability, life, etc. Forget about IRAs, the S&P, college funds, or cable TV. A down payment on a house is out of the question. So is a gym membership. We are not poor; we are remuneratively challenged. In short, we are seeking corporate sponsorship of our yet-to-be-conceived child. In return for lifelong financial backing, we will give our son or daughter the name of the highest bidder.

It is with a great deal of pleasure that we applaud your recent renovation of a major baseball stadium, formerly known as _____ and now named for your fine Corporation. Some critics have whined that replacing a name of historical and local significance with a corporate appellation is flavorless, faceless, and, well, tacky. Of course we disagree. What do the notions of "tradition" and "history" mean in terms of the very real market economy? Season-ticket holders manage to still find the place, don't they? However, while we agree that a baseball stadium is certainly a worthy investment for your Corporation, what could be more worthwhile than to be the proud sponsor of a healthy human? Based on our own academic achievement and good looks, we assure you that our progeny will be rosy-cheeked, of above-average intelligence, and vigorous, although potentially nearsighted, of middling height, and a bad speller. As parents and caretakers of your investment, we will do our best to squelch the first semblance of any potentially unprofitable abilities (artistic) before fingerpaints hit paper. We will stress cost-effectiveness, team attitude, and solid business sense in baby's first lessons.

In addition to holding last-name rights of John or Jane Corporation (respectfully, we would like to maintain control of first-name rights and our attorney is including this clause into a draft contract), your Corporation's logo

will be discreetly sewn on all of your investment's baby
clothes. This visual reinforcement will invoke your
corporate identity and your mission of good works, and
will be no larger than 1" x 1½". No logo will be altered
without prior approval by your Office of Trademarks and
for the most part will be consistent with standard design
guidelines and will match Pantone chip #180. Branding is
so important, but we don't see any reason why it can't be
cute, too.

You may be wondering about the visibility of your
investment. A baby isn't a baseball stadium of fifty thousand
seats, after all. Let us remind you that corporate sponsorship
of human life is always a soft sell. However, there are many
opportunities for visibility that you may not have
considered: strolls in the perambulator, for instance, or your
investment shelved sweetly in the kid seat of a grocery cart
or swinging upside-down from the playground jungle gym.
There are also piano lessons, team sports, and years of
schooling with hundreds of peers (your future market).
Remember, your investment sleeps only eight hours a day.
Other than those slumbering hours, you will enjoy
continuous high exposure of your corporate beneficence.

At this point, we are certain you will find this
investment attractive. Let us state some of its terms:
complete financial support including housing,
transportation, and medical needs of investment and its
parents; undergraduate, graduate, and postgraduate
education costs; travel; miscellaneous European real estate;
annual parenting stipend; lawn maintenance; coffeemaker
with timer; some of those fancy soaps; and a lifetime supply
of extra-virgin olive oil.

To be fair, the child's grandparents will be made a similar
offer in case they feel a certain sentiment for their descendents

to retain their surname. We don't want to hear any sniveling from them about the "last chance to carry on the family name" or other such nonsense. Sentiment is not enough— interested parties must also have the means. We anticipate a lot of corporate interest and recognize that this first alliance may very well serve as a prototype for future programs of corporate sponsorship of human life.

Sincerely,
Margaret Muirhead and Peter Reiss
(Reishead)

I AM GLAD

Margaret Muirhead

I am glad I never gave back
your book. Such small revenge
when you consider I want
to blast your name, blight and
blacken your tomatoes, your rows
of precious lettuces. I want to watch
your pipes freeze, cut your phone
dead, set your cats against you.

Do not imagine I spend my time
reconstructing conversations
remembering each word you said:
I've seen this waterwheel before,
and *Save it for when the baby
dies*. I am too busy for that—
stealing your mail and making
the perfect soup. Oh, let the sting
spread to your eyes. Let the sweet
slow poison do its work.

You will not forget me: I hacked
my name into your table
with a butter knife. My spare
toothbrush still touches your toothbrush by the bathroom sink.
My hair clogged your drain.

Will you be surprised when I emerge
a movie star scrubbed like a shell,
so blanched and clean I will never
smell except of soap? New clothes
for every role and ever-changing
styles for my hair.
I will be a projection of light;
I will be as clean as light.

But what good is this if I can't see
the look on your face, the so-called
twist of regret, the crooked look
of wistfulness as you shut your wife
up with something cruel
because now, now,
you are beginning to realize:
What a girl! Feet, legs, breasts,
mouth, eyes. Those lungs! Those jokes!
What a kind, good-hearted girl.

LADY SHONAGON'S HATEFUL THINGS

Margaret Muirhead

Your aversion to lamps.
Your little drawings.
Your story about stalking
the girl as she walked
her dog in Beacon Hill.

Turkey dogs are hateful,
as are sausage links.
Eating in the supermarket
is deplorable. Scented
toilet paper is strange.

I hate when men stall
in the left-hand side
of the escalator. The left-
hand side is for passing.
I hate your height.
I hate your Chinese tea.

Damn your spices!
Your rock salt!
Your authentic fish oil!
Your certitude about
what is art and what is not
oppresses me.

You will not allow
your friends to meet
your other friends.
This is inelegant, indeed.

Lady Shonagon says
departure is everything:
remember the last time
I saw you, you refused
to drive me home. I barely
caught the bus.

The bus! I didn't
have the proper change.
Hateful, simply hateful.
Oh, hateful, hateful thing.

HEARTLAND

Karen Joy Fowler

...

MY GRANDFATHER SAYS WILLINA'S DEATH IS JUST ONE SMALL symptom of a bigger problem. He never knew Willina, which is why he can refer to her permanent absence as a symptom. What he knows *about* Willina is what he read in the paper and this amounts only to sexual history in its sparest, coldest, most merciless form. So he goes further and describes the symptom as small. He means a lot by that word since it's one of theirs. We're going to be seeing more and more of this stuff, my grandfather says. Women can be so stupid.

The whole goddamn country is small now, my grandfather says. Small country. Small people.

It's harder for me to see the big picture. I knew Willina pretty well and I don't remember the old days. Wasn't like this when I was a boy, my grandfather says, but when I was a boy, things were pretty much the same as now. Used to be an apple tree here, my grandfather says while we're walking me to work. Planted more than a hundred years ago. How does he know? We only came last winter. Little myth of his, maybe, like the little myth that he walks me to work. He heads on to the bar after saying good-bye to me. Anyway, if there ever was an apple tree, it's a T-shirt shop now. You can get anything you want on a T-shirt. Absolutely anything. A rainbow which ends at the tit. FUCK YOU, ASSHOLE, with a picture. My grandfather says he would never have learned to read if he'd known how disheartening it was going to be. He was real disheartened when I went to work for the new burger place. He wanted me on a farm. What was I supposed to do? What a fantasy.

The old family farm is under several feet of cement. Nothing germinating there. We moved to the capital where the money is green. But I don't think it was real to him until I came home in my burger-frying uniform. The uniform fit, which surprised my grandfather, I guess. I didn't have to roll the legs up or anything. And it was blue, in deference to local custom. I think it was the concessions that upset my grandfather most of all. They were *accommodating*. They were here to stay.

I guess there was a real problem when the first burger place opened. How can we eat meat, my grandfather says. *We're* meat. I don't eat it, actually. I just cook it. I suppose this is a pretty fine distinction, but we're all accommodating in one way or another. Even my grandfather. Does he or doesn't he spend my paycheck? You bet he does.

I met Willina because she worked one of the registers. Nobody will believe me now, but the first thing you noticed about Willina in those days was how cheerful she was. She smiled all the time. And she wasn't stupid at all. Willina was real smart. What's so great about farm work, she wanted to know. Those good old days, they were pretty limited when you stop to think about it. Now we know there's a wide world out there. Things we've never seen. Things we can't even imagine. There was no reason to think I would be flipping burgers all my life. Still isn't, I suppose. But it's harder now without Willina to see that.

Willina was pretty, too. And funny. The MacMunches, she called us. The MacMunch Bunch. Me and her and Nick and Polly. Polly's sort of everybody's mother. She's quite a bit older than the rest of us. Runs the kitchen and is in love with the man who delivers the patties. Nick was pretty soft on Willina and I guess I would have been, too, but I don't know how to be soft on a girl. I just hung around her a lot. She talked to me. Which wasn't really a good sign, Nick said. Made me sort of a brother. Nick was trying to make out Willina really cared for him, because she hardly talked to him. But I was happy to be anything in Willina's life. I didn't know any better. I just thought Willina was full of dreams and they were pretty to listen to. Took me a long time to realize what was going on.

There was a man who came by a lot. He always went to Willina's register, even if there was a line. I'm here for some home cooking, he'd say. See, he was one of them. Willina looked so sweet and little next to him. Give me a smile and a burger, Willina, he'd ask. The burger's worth nothing, but I'll pay for that smile. And Willina would already be smiling. Willina would have lit up like a sunny day the minute he walked in.

You watch out, girl, I heard Polly tell her finally. You stay away from those people. You hand them their burgers and then you take back your hands. No matter what anyone promises you, you remember. They got nothing for us.

Which isn't really true, of course. When you take your hand back, there's money in it. They always have money. We didn't used to need money, my grandfather says. I find this hard to believe. We sure as hell need it now.

He's not like that, Willina said. He's nice. But what she was really saying was, I'm not like that. No one would do that to *me*. She had a lot of confidence, Willina did. She knew she was smart. She just couldn't think of herself as small.

I don't think even Polly knew she was seeing him nights. I know she'd been seeing him for a long time before I found out about it. My grandfather had sent me out to get him some whiskey. The bottle emptied ahead of schedule. It couldn't have waited till morning. He couldn't have gotten through the night. I was a familiar face in the liquor store.

So I was on my way home, past the bar and restaurant with the floor show and the specialty book shop, and I saw Willina with the man. You're very special to me, he was saying to her. He was bent way over and she was staring up at him and didn't notice me at all. You're all I can think about, he said, and she said, Do you love me? Yes, he said. Yes, I love you, and then I was past and didn't hear any more. I went home and poured myself a whiskey and drank it even before I poured one for my grandfather. I didn't really understand why I was so upset.

Willina came in the next day singing. I have a secret, she said to me. I'm going to tell you. I'm going to tell only you. But she didn't tell me right away, because a bunch of them came in wanting sandwiches of eggs and sausages on muffins and coffee, lots of coffee. I knew what the secret was anyway. I could put off hearing it.

Our break was the same time so we went out the back and had a cigarette. She made jokes about how smoking would stunt our growth. I'm in love, she said. I am absolutely, hopelessly, deliriously in love.

I don't imagine it's Nick, I answered. I didn't say, I don't imagine it's me.

She didn't even hear. I'm leaving, she said. I'm going with him. I'm going to see the biggest cities in the world. I'm going to wake up every morning with his arms around me and I'll be in Paris or Tokyo or Los Angeles. I love him. *I love him*. Are you happy for me?

I was pretty miserable and I figured out why. It wasn't because I thought Willina was going to get hurt or was being a fool. I figured I loved her. Who wouldn't? And it wasn't even that I was jealous and loved her myself. I never expected her to want to be with me.

It was that it really hadn't occurred to me before that they would want our women. I don't know why. They wanted everything else. The things we made. The things we ate off of. The things we wore. But only the best. The best of everything. They took it all home with them and we never saw it again.

I was going to compete with them my whole life and I had only just realized it. How could I? They had all the money. They had traveled. I was flipping burgers and watching my grandfather drink my paycheck. No contest.

I'll miss you, I told Willina.

I'll miss you, too, she said. She looked at my face. She said she wasn't going right away. He wasn't done here quite. He still had a few odds and ends to take care of. She was going to stay on and earn all the money she could before they went. Don't tell Polly, she said to me. I'm not going to say anything until I'm really leaving. She doesn't like him and she doesn't even know him.

But Polly could see how happy Willina was and it made her unhappy. You be careful, girl, she said. A lot of things are far too easy to say, *I love you* being the easiest of them. There ought to be a way to make it more difficult. Some condition that has to be met before your mouth can make those words. You ought to have to earn them. But that's not the way it is. Anyone can say I love you. You be careful.

Willina had a couple more weeks of happiness. Suddenly he was gone. Gone home, they said at his hotel. Took some nice pieces of local art with him. Had to get a whole new suitcase. Left Willina behind.

I told Willina not to believe in him, Polly said, getting it wrong again. Willina had believed in herself. That was why she couldn't get over it.

Willina worked her register and tried to figure it out. She thought maybe he would write or send for her. Then she thought maybe he would write and explain. Then she thought she'd never really thought either of those two things. My head always knew better, she said. This is all my heart's fault. I'm never going to listen to my heart again.

One night she put a noose around her neck and severed the connection between her heart and her head. Polly found her the next morning, hanging from the shelf where we stacked the buns. Her shoes had fallen off her feet and lay on the floor, heels touching together, toes pointed out. There was a picture of her shoes in the paper. She got a lot of print, actually. It was a big story here.

I wonder if he even knows about it. I picture him sometimes, showing friends the slides from his vacation. Here's the Emerald Palace, he's saying. Tourists, everywhere.

Here's the yellow road. You follow it and you can still find some spots which are pretty unspoiled. You've got to go a ways, though. Most people don't bother.

Here's some local talent. The small ones dress in blue.

Here's the Emerald Arches. I knew a little girl who worked there.

WHAT A DIFFERENCE A NIGHT MAKES

...

PLAN: ADD HEIGHT

METHODS: FUN WITH DOORWAYS

METHOD A. Hang from doorway for 15 minutes every night.
Height gain: Individual results vary with IQ.

METHOD B. Measure yourself (shoe and sockless) against
your doorway just before you go to bed. Repeat
immediately upon waking (or at least as soon as
you can stand up straight).
Height gain: Minimum guaranteed by the
United Nations Committee on Comfortable
Beds (1 centimeter). Example results below
(Table 1) adapted from Wilkinson and
Shodderly's 1999 results.

TABLE 1:

Actual Height Measurements for Two Adult Subjects

	SUBJECT 1	SUBJECT 2
Height in evening (cm)	186.69	172.72
Height in morning (cm)	190.50	175.26
Height gain (cm)	3.81	2.54

Ethicist's Corner

Reader H. E. D. Bates from England asks, "What is the ethical response when asked my height—should I give my evening height or my morning height?"

THE ETHICIST ANSWERS: LOSER.

By facsimile, Vladimir Lennon of Manchester, New Hampshire, asks, "I am sure my brother is erasing his evening height mark while I sleep. Should I take him to court before a jury of his peers or should I just give him a good kicking?"

THE ETHICIST ANSWERS: LOSER.

PRETENDING

Ray Vukcevich

...

*T*HE MISSILE SILO WAS STUART'S IDEA. IT WAS HIS TURN TO make up a holiday tradition. The silo belonged to a man named Johnson who had moved his family back to Cheyenne. Johnson and his wife had spent a lot of money fixing the place up, and they'd given it their best shot, but it hadn't taken long to discover that a missile silo was an awful place to raise a family. Now he rented it out to people like Stuart.

The party this year was Stuart and Marilyn, Bill and Elizabeth, and Lewis. Bill was a lawyer and Elizabeth taught math at the same college where Stuart was in Psychology and Marilyn, when she wasn't on sick leave, was a research biologist. Lewis was a computer programmer. Sally was missing this year. She'd left Lewis and gone back to New York in the spring.

Last year it had been Elizabeth's turn to come up with a tradition candidate. She'd taken them to the Mojave where they had jumped out of an airplane. Since none of them had done it before, they jumped in tandem with instructors snugged on to their backs. Lewis had made a lot of bad jokes about being ridden to earth by the sky patrol. The instructors were all getting good Xmas eve overtime but none of them seemed happy about it. On the way down Marilyn had wet her pants and she hadn't spoken to any of the others for weeks afterward.

The year before that, it had been Lewis and snake handling in Louisiana. Marilyn hadn't spoken for a long time after that one, either.

The reason the gang needed to make up a new tradition every

year was that they had no traditions of their own. They were neither Christian nor Jewish, neither Muslim nor Hindu. The list of things they were not was very long. They were Americans of a certain class and education, in their forties, atheists or maybe closet agnostics. No children. They felt completely left out of things during the holidays, so they came together to seek out new rituals, new meanings. Over the years the search itself had become the tradition.

This year Marilyn had gotten a head start on not speaking to Stuart. She was turning herself down, speaking less frequently, and with less volume when she did speak. She was as quiet as a mouse on the drive out to the silo, her head resting against the car window until her cheek got too cold and she sat up to stare out at the snow. She looked like a sickly child bundled up in too many winter clothes. She coughed, and her cough was an accusation.

"I'm sorry," she said. "Are we there yet?"

He hadn't told her what he was up to. He knew that telling her would be like telling everyone. Elizabeth would have wheedled it out of her. He wanted it to be a big surprise—the vast plain of snow, the endless drive into nowhere, the headlights finally picking out the wire fence and the shack that must surely be too small to be their destination.

"Yes," he said at last, "we're here."

He and Lewis busted open the frozen door on the shack covering the entrance, and they all climbed down into the silo. Stuart switched on the power and gave them the tour. Here was the control room, now a media center, and here the crew quarters, now cozy bedrooms. Way down there were the spooky storerooms, and all those corridors and huge heavy doors, and, maybe most disturbing, the hole where the intercontinental ballistic missile had been. It was half-filled with water—more than a hundred feet of water, Stuart said, and there were flooded passages, another underwater world down there. Echoes and a slimy green smell. Even with the flashlights it wasn't easy to make out the surface of the water. None of them stayed long at the edge.

He led them back to a room that had once been the crew's mess. He let them bunch up at the door behind him, then stepped aside and switched on the light to reveal a lavishly appointed dinner table.

The walls of the dining room had been papered white with a faint red rose pattern. A picture Stuart had first mistaken for a big photograph mimicked a window on one wall. When he looked a little closer he saw it was a painting. Not a very good painting. He doubted even a very good painting would have chased away the overwhelming sense of being underground. It had something to do with the way light and sound behaved, something about the earthy smell of the air.

"Everyone sit down," he said. "I'll serve the soup."

Once into the soup course, Stuart warmed them up with his "alas, we middle-aged American atheists have no deep traditions" routine. It was the standard opening of their ritual.

"The Catholic Mass or the twelve days of Christmas. Hanukkah or Ramadan. We're excluded from all of that."

"Not excluded," Elizabeth said. "We've opted out."

"Yes," they all said together, like a chant. "Opted out."

"Well, tonight," Stuart said, "we are going to do an exercise in creative belief."

He had their attention. This would be the point of the evening. His proposal was simple.

Just believe something.

He suggested they start with ghosts.

"You're suggesting that if there are no ghosts," Bill said, "we must make our own?"

"Exactly," Stuart said.

"We have met the supernatural," Elizabeth said, "and the supernatural is us?"

"Now you're getting it," Stuart said.

"But why are we doing this?" Lewis asked. "What exactly do we hope to accomplish?"

"I want us to experience what most of the rest of the world claims to experience all the time," Stuart said. "Before the evening is over, I want each of us to know what it is like to believe the unbelievable."

"No matter how hard we try," Marilyn said, "I don't think we'll get ghosts just because we want to." She didn't look up when she spoke.

"You're right," Stuart said. "We are all unapologetic materialists. We'll need a little help." He would say no more until after dinner. No one complained. The delay was part of the ritual, too.

After dinner, they regrouped in the parlor. There was a fake fireplace with an electric fire. There was a round table in the middle of the room. On the table was a single black candle. To one side was a bar. Lewis spotted it at once and poured himself a drink.

"What?" he said when he caught them all looking at him.

"I have picked ghosts for us to believe in," Stuart said, "because I think we can use a mental aid that will make it easier."

Bill joined Lewis at the bar and mixed a drink for himself. He raised an eyebrow at Elizabeth but she shook her head no.

"We'll have to make our own ghost," Stuart said. "You can think of it as a game. The game for tonight. The main event. One of us will become a ghost. The degree to which that person becomes a ghost will depend on how strongly the rest of us believe that person is a ghost."

"You're talking about me," Lewis said.

"Why you?" Stuart asked.

"Odd man out."

"Actually," Stuart said, "I was thinking we'd draw straws. Look, I've already set it up. Short straw is the ghost." He took the straws he had prepared earlier from his jacket pocket.

"Here, you go first, Marilyn." He pushed the straws in front of her face. "Go on, pick one."

She sighed and took a straw. He saw that she had gotten the short one. He hadn't exactly planned it that way. In fact, he had been holding back. He knew how to force a card or, in this case, a straw. He had learned that trick in a psych course taught by a magician when he was a grad student, but he didn't think he'd used it on Marilyn. No one else knew the rest of the straws were redundant, so he went through the entire exercise, letting each of them pick one. There was one left in the end for him. He held his up and everyone did the same. It was easy to see that Marilyn would be the ghost.

"Our ghost person, let's call her Marilyn." He smiled at her. "She is merely a focus of attention. After all, what is a ghost but the point of concentrated desire?"

"Fear?" Lewis asked. "Concentrated fear?"

"In the unlikely event that this works," Bill said, "I mean, if I can convince myself that Marilyn really is a ghost, then she'll disappear."

"Why disappear?" Elizabeth asked.

"Because I don't believe in ghosts," Bill said.

"You mean, if you believe Marilyn is a ghost, you won't be able to see her, because you don't believe in ghosts?"

"You got it," Bill said. "It's a Zen of Physics kind of thing."

They were talking about Marilyn as if she weren't there, Stuart thought. It was working already. He hated to break the momentum but he needed to get her moving. She wouldn't be much fun as a ghost if she just sat there looking ill and pathetic. "Let's get this show on the road," he said. "Marilyn?"

"What do you want me to do?" Her voice wasn't much more than a whisper.

"Be a ghost," Stuart said. "You've got this ideal spooky place to haunt, so go haunt. Pass on to the other side. We'll light the candle and sit around the table and hold hands and call you back with pure belief."

Marilyn pushed herself up out of her chair and walked to the heavy metal door. Her shoulders slumped as if she was thinking she'd never be able to get it open, but then she must have remembered the doors were perfectly balanced because she grabbed the wheel and pulled. The door swung aside smoothly and she moved into the corridor.

"Okay," Stuart said. "Let's take our places at the table."

"What is this?" Bill sounded irked, but Stuart had known him long enough to know that he was intrigued.

"Mood," Stuart said. He lighted the candle and switched off the electric light. "Believing the unbelievable is all about mood. Come on, sit down."

Bill and Elizabeth took chairs at the round table. Lewis filled his glass again and sat down next to Elizabeth.

Stuart sat down. "Okay, hold hands."

"Oh, boy," Elizabeth said. She took Bill's hand. Lewis was staring down at his drink and didn't respond to her outstretched hand.

"Come on, Lewis," Stuart said.

"Okay, okay," Lewis said. "Let's blast off." He took Elizabeth's hand.

"Everyone close your eyes," Stuart said.

"Studies show that listening to Mozart strengthens your mind," Bill said.

"Personally, I go for ginkgo biloba," Elizabeth said.

"All you need is love," Lewis said, maybe a little bitterly.

"Close your eyes, and she will come," Stuart said.

One by one they closed their eyes. Stuart closed his last. He waited. Bill's hand was dry. Lewis's was cold from the ice in the drink he'd been holding. Stuart's chair was hard.

"Do you think we should say her name in spooky voices?" Elizabeth asked.

"No," Stuart said. "Maybe. I don't know. Let's try concentration first."

He concentrated.

Several minutes later, he peeked out at the others and looked right into the wide-open eyes of Elizabeth. She gave him a crooked grin and a wink. He frowned at her, and she sighed and closed her eyes. He waited a moment more to make sure everyone was cooperating before closing his eyes again.

"Maybe we should turn up the fire," Lewis said.

"Quiet," Stuart said.

It did seem colder. And the underground sounds, the pressure of all that earth and snow above, seemed to press down a little harder. He imagined the room had gotten smaller. If he opened his eyes now, he would see the walls just a few inches from the table. Marilyn would be there like an unhappy spirit—always hanging around, hoping, on the one hand, that she wasn't bothering anyone, and weepy, on the other hand, because she was unable to have much impact on the living. He could see the flickering candlelight through his eyelids.

Then there was a breeze.

Of course, there could be no breeze in the silo. This was a breeze produced by his belief. It was the wind that would blow the ghost of his dead wife into the parlor of the ICBM silo. There was a rustle of cloth, like the thighs of someone sneaking around in tight jeans. Then tiptoes through dead leaves.

The breeze became the gentle huff of breath on his cheek.

Someone whispered, very close, her lips just brushing his ear, "Both sexes of alligators bellow."

It didn't sound like Marilyn, and certainly not like anything Marilyn would say. She might have been like that a long, long time ago. Bright eyes and big smile, and the way she had moved just made your fingers itch to unwrap her, but nothing like that these days. These days she was the coughing woman. The whimpering woman. The I-don't-mean-to-bother-you-but-I-must-moan woman. Both sexes of alligators bellow. Such a wet thought. And there was the smell of lemons.

Elizabeth gasped. Then there was silence again. Stuart listened carefully but he couldn't be sure he wasn't imagining the sounds of something drifting around the table delivering little messages from the great beyond.

He wanted to see her.

He opened his eyes. Marilyn wasn't in the room. Bill's chin had tipped down to his chest. He might have fallen asleep. Elizabeth, her eyes squeezed tightly shut, was sitting up very straight and seemed to be struggling to hear something. Slow tears streaked Lewis's cheeks.

Where had Marilyn gone? Had she been there at all? The entire point of the supernatural was the willingness to fool yourself. So had he succeeded in fooling himself about the breeze and the lips on his ear and the voice? He cleared his throat.

Bill sighed and raised his head. Elizabeth opened her eyes. Lewis pushed up from the table and turned away.

"Well, that was weird," Bill said.

"Where's Marilyn?" Elizabeth stood up.

"I'm wondering the same thing," Stuart said.

Lewis poured himself a fresh drink. "Maybe she just went to bed," he said without turning back to them.

Stuart looked around the dining room and then peered into the rooms immediately connected to it, but Marilyn was not to be found.

"Frankly, I'm a little worried," Elizabeth said. "She did look pretty green even before she became a ghost."

"Okay," Stuart said. "Let's split up and look for her."

"That's what they always say in the movies," Lewis said.

"Oh, shut up, Lewis," Elizabeth said.

Outside in the corridor there was a hum that Stuart hadn't noticed before. Maybe he had not been perfectly still and listening before. "I'll go this way," he said.

He checked all the rooms and passages on his way to the missile hole. When he got to the hole itself and saw her standing there in the wedge of light from the corridor, he was surprised at how unsurprised he was. She had changed into her nightgown and white silk robe. She was barefoot and her feet were faintly blue. She was looking straight at him. She hardly ever looked straight at him these days. Maybe becoming a ghost had given her new knowledge, new strength, a kind of cosmic aikido. He approached her. If he were to reach out to touch her, his hand would pass right through her.

He put out his hand and pushed. She fell back into the hole. A moment later he heard the splash.

In a single instant, belief became reality. He turned away and moved to the door. She might have been feebly calling his name had she really been down there, but she wasn't really down there. Marilyn couldn't swim, which was probably why they had not yet swum with the sharks on Xmas eve. She wouldn't be anywhere near a hole filled with maybe a hundred feet of cold water. He closed the corridor door and walked slowly back toward the dining room.

You can believe your life into any state you want, he decided. Reality is plastic. You mold it. You pretend things into existence.

There would be big changes to make back home. He'd take some time off school, surely all of next term. Maybe go to Europe to get over this.

Maybe buy a BMW.

Bill came out of the shadows like a sudden psycho. He had a crazy grin on his face.

"Bill," Stuart said.

"We found her," Bill said. "Hey, here she is now."

Elizabeth came into the corridor pushing Marilyn in ahead of her. Lewis appeared with his drink.

"Safe and sound," Elizabeth said.

Marilyn's feet were still blue. She still wore her white silk robe over her nightgown.

"Doesn't she make a good ghost?" Elizabeth said.

Marilyn didn't speak but she didn't turn her eyes down either.

"Well, it's been fun, kids," Bill said, "but I'm for bed."

"Me, too," Elizabeth said quickly.

"Not me," Lewis said.

"Oh, you can stay up all night drinking if you want," Elizabeth said.

Marilyn moved away down the corridor toward the bedrooms. Stuart followed. What else was there to do?

Once in the bedroom, he sat down on the bed and tugged off his shoes. Marilyn hadn't moved away from the door. He could feel her eyes on him, but when he looked up at her, she switched off the light, leaving nothing but an afterimage of sadness and contempt.

He could hear water dripping on concrete.

He felt buried alive in the absolute darkness. Was she still there by the door? Had she ever really been there?

"Say something," he said.

Nothing.

"Please," he said.

Maybe he had imagined her, after all.

"Boo," she said.

Shh! I can't hear the music!

The Freight Hoppers, *Waiting on the Gravy Train*
Zeb, *Jesterized*
Kristin Hersh, *Murder, Misery and Then Goodnight*
Townes Van Zandt, just about anything, to tell the truth
Same goes for Gillian Welch
Jim & Jennie and the Pinetops, *Little Birdie*
Mark Kozelek, *What's Next to the Moon*
Teenage Fanclub, *Grand Prix*
Super Butter Dog, *Funkasy*
Mayumi Kojima, *Me and My Monkey on the Moon*
Neko Case & Her Boyfriends, *The Virginian*
Looper, *The Geometrid*
Puffy, *Jet CD*
Manic Street Preachers, *Know Your Enemy*
Salaryman
Ghost Dog soundtrack
Hooverphonic, *"a new stereophonic sound spectacular"*
O Brother, Where Art Thou? soundtrack

THE FILM COLUMN

William Smith

...

DON'T LOOK NOW (1973) | *Director: Nicolas Roeg*

NOTE: THE FILM COLUMN OFTEN CONTAINS SPOILERS.

Don't Look Now is a ghost story haunted by color and geometry.

In the opening sequence married couple Laura (Julie Christie) and John (Donald Sutherland) are spending a contented afternoon reading and studying slides of a Venetian church. Their children are playing outside in the idyllic English countryside. The scene cuts between interior and exterior, creating parallels between the children's games and their parents' banter. Laura is researching her daughter Christine's question about the curve of the earth and a flat frozen pond—cut to Christine throwing a ball into the water. Laura fans her fingers in front of her mouth—cut to her daughter performing the same gesture in miniature. These parallels, and others, establish the family's bond without the need to show them interacting.

When John looks at a particular slide this comfortable scene turns malevolent. The slide shows a church interior: seated at a pew is a small child in a red plastic raincoat—his daughter is wearing an identical raincoat, splashing in the puddles outside. This figure isn't supposed to be in the picture. John moves to the light table to get a better look, but knocks over a glass of water, smearing the color dye of the slide in a long red swath. He tries to soak up the water but suddenly stops, runs outside, and finds that his daughter has disappeared into the reedy black stream that runs across the yard.

Several months later in Venice: John has escaped into his work, restoring the church documented in the slides, and Laura is recovering from a severe nervous breakdown.

Venice is, as ever, visually stunning, but the city is pervaded by an air of sinister fakery. The church isn't as old as it is supposed to be and John's choice is to "restore the fake or watch it sink into the sea." A pair of elderly sisters, one of them blind, have an "accidental" meeting with Laura and claim to have had a vision of the couple's dead daughter standing between them laughing. And John is repeatedly "by chance" drawn to crime scenes where police are pulling murdered girls from the canals. Venice seems half-sunk in the same puddle that claimed their daughter.

With the help of the sisters, Laura hopes to communicate with Christine. John is sure his wife is being conned and, though he manages to trace the sisters to their hotel, he is drawn to a different path when he sees a red raincoat disappearing around a corner. It seems John is gifted with the sight as well.

Like many of Nicolas Roeg's films, *Don't Look Now* is a puzzle box. The viewer is asked to see through two competing visions, but the film offers no cues telling us when we have left reality. (And if we have, whose unreality are we seeing?) Secondary characters are introduced as benevolent but are later shown, in seemingly non sequitur scenes, acting threatening and bizarre. The viewer is never sure if these flashes provide insight or if they are a visualization of the protagonist's paranoia.

The color red is a constant, taunting presence. It invokes the couple's dead daughter but it also provides the only spark to lead the characters and the viewer through this world of canals and forgotten alleys.

The title of the film, taken directly from the short story by Daphne du Maurier, expresses how suddenly our world can be de-

stroyed: don't look now, but your child is dead. It hints at the overlapping kinds of sight (and blindness) that link these characters and
it is also a reference to the magician's misdirection of which Roeg
is a master. *Don't Look Now* is a complicated and satisfying ghost
story, but it is also the only horror film I can think of whose deepest chills come from the possibility of misreading a symbol.

A IS FOR APPLE: AN EASY READER

Amy Beth Forbes

Bobby wores the dress
He did
Bobby did wears the dress
He is a pretty girl

They bite me and it hurts
when they bite me
and it hurts
and it hurts

Jesus says Bobby
Jesus aych christ
The brown bottle comes out and it hurts
Where did you get the fork says Bobby
Leave the forks alone

The sun is out and Bobby goes
It is not the dress
Not the dress Bobby says be good
I am the good good good
Bobby wears the dress
You are my sunshine my only sunshine says Bobby and he goes

They bite me and it hurts
It hurts but I let them
I let them

Things are breaking
in the bathroom
Things are breaking
when Bobby comes out with the brown bottle

I got a purple Band-Aid.
I got a purple Band-Aid
and a blue Band-Aid too.

Bobby wears the suit and goes to work.
I am good all days.
I watch the TV all days.

It is Friday, and Bobby wears the dress.
He says, you are my sunshine, my only sunshine.
He says, I hate to leave you alone at night.
He says, be good.

I am good.
I am smart.
I took off the purple Band-Aid.
When they come I see them now.
I see their shiny green moon skin.
They shine when they bite me.
It hurts.

Today
Bobby is happy,
and we eat cake with spoons.
Today is my birthday.
I am twenty-three years old.
I have a purple Band-Aid.
Bobby doesn't know they bite me.

Bobby goes to work in his suit and tie.
I don't watch TV.
I look at the book.
A is for Apple.
I did not know that before.

It is Friday. Bobby looks pretty and happy in his dress.
He takes off the Band-Aids.
Those healed slow, he says.
Bobby sings, You are my sunshine,
and he goes.

When they come they sound like dripping water.
I tell them to bite me where Bobby won't see.
They shine. It hurts.

I put on a purple Band-Aid. I like purple.

All this week I read while Bobby is at work.
Monday I read *Pat the Bunny*.
Tuesday I read *Goodnight Moon*.
Wednesday I read *The Very Hungry Caterpillar*.
Caterpillar is a big word, but I know what it means.
Thursday I read *One Fish, Two Fish, Red Fish, Blue Fish*.
Friday I read *Where the Wild Things Are*.
My legs hurt all week.

Bobby laughs at me after dinner, in his dress.
You look involved, he says, let me see, I'll read it to you.
I hold the book to my chest.
Bobby looks surprised, then ruffles my hair.
Goodnight, he says.
I wish I could talk to Bobby.

Dr. Seuss is wrong, and Max the Wolf Boy is wrong too.
    They are not fun. It feels like fire in my legs.
They are beautiful when they shine.

Monday I started to read *The Phantom Tollbooth,* and I
    finished it on Wednesday. Wednesday I started to read *A
    Wrinkle in Time.*
I think I'm getting closer but I have to rest a lot. Reading is
    hard work, and my legs burn.

They slide over my legs and stomach, and there are more of
    them now. When they hold still they look like
    shimmering sea green geckos, but they only hold still
    when they feed. It takes so long now that my heart
    stutters, but I need them.

Bobby has been reading Stephen King. I picked up *It* but
    had to set it down again. My eyes hurt too much to read.
    Bobby gave me some aspirin, but it doesn't help. He
    doesn't know what's wrong with me.

It's Friday, and Bobby's dress is hanging in the closet. I can't
    even walk anymore. I can hear him in the bathroom,
    crying. He hasn't been to work in three days. He says he
    won't leave me. But it doesn't matter now.

SHH! I SAID I WAS LISTENING TO SOME MUSIC!

Thievery Corporation, *The Mirror Conspiracy*
Sam Phillips, *Fan Dance*
Gorky's Zygotic Mynci, *The Blue Trees*
Garbage, *Beautiful Garbage*
Cowboy Junkies, *Open*
Thalia Zedek, *Been Here and Gone*
Gillian Welch, *Time (The Revelator)*
Cary Fridley, *Neighbor Girl*
John Prine, *In Spite of Ourselves*
Outkast, *Stankonia*

MY FATHER'S GHOST

Mark Rudolph

You never visit me
at night, never creep
close to whisper the secrets
dead fathers tell their sons.

I never glimpse you
in the black window
or find you in the porch swing,
your cigarette burning a red excuse.

You always show up
at noon when asphalt bubbles
and maple trees sag
on power lines for support.

Stopped at a red light
or waiting to turn left,
I glance over the dash
and there you rise—a shimmering

of heat that weaves
back and forth and grins
like the town drunk you were.
Then your lips move:

"Dollar for your old man?
Just a dollar. I'll pay you
back when I get my check."
So I close my eyes and floor it.

A SELECTED LIST OF CHICKENS
(FROM *THE FAIREST FOWL: PORTRAITS OF CHAMPION CHICKENS*)

Black-Breasted Red Modern Game Bantam Cock • Golden Campine Large Fowl Cock • Red Naked Neck Large Fowl Cock • Black Cochin Frizzle Bantam Cock • Blue Shamo Large Fowl Hen • Silver Spangled Hamburg Large Fowl Hen • Porcelain Belgian Bearded d'Uccle Bantam Cockerel • Bearded Black Silkie Bantam Hen • Quail Belgian Bearded d'Anvers Bantam Cockerel • Barred Plymouth Rock Large Fowl Cockerel • Silver Duckwing Araucana Bantam Cock • Patrick Wyandotte Bantam Cock • Mottled Houdan Bantam Poulet • Blue Rose Bantam Cockerel • Belgian Mille Fleur Bearded d'Uccle Bantam Cock • Bearded Buff-Laced Polish Large Fowl Cock • White-Laced Red Cornish Red Fowl Cock • Golden Sebright Bantam Cockerel • Old English Crele Bantam Cockerel

WHAT'S SURE TO COME

Jeffrey Ford

...

1.

OUTSIDE ON THE CRACKED CONCRETE SIDEWALK STOOD A wooden Indian with headdress and hatchet that my grandfather had christened Tecumseh. Inside, the place smelled like a chocolate egg cream laced with cigar smoke and filtered through the hole of a stale doughnut. From beneath its pervasive layer of dust, one could dig out *Green Lantern* comics and *Daredevil: Man Without Fear.* In the back, next to the phone booth with fly-paper glass, were wooden shelves holding plastic models of planes, monsters, and the awe inspiring car designs of Big Daddy Roth. There were spinning racks of paperback books, rows of greeting cards, bags of plastic soldiers, paper and pens and crayons. At the fountain, they made cherry Cokes, black-and-whites, and malteds that were hooked up to a green machine and cycloned into existence. My father bought his Lucky Strikes there. My grandfather bought his horse paper there. My mother would go in once a year, stir the dust, and come out with a notebook to keep her thoughts in.

The owners, Leo and Phil, carried on a subdued argument day in, day out, which occasionally erupted into shouts of "Shmuck" and "Stick your ass in a meat grinder." Leo was tall, with glasses and a bald head. He always wore a green T-shirt and a graying apron with which he would swipe out your glass before setting it under the soda jet. The brown, smoldering length of stiff rope he smoked throughout the day made him talk out of the side of his mouth in a voice like a ventriloquist's dummy. "Put 'em back in your head," it would bark from behind the counter when he'd see my gaze drift up over the comics to where the *Playboys* were kept. He worked the register, but the register never worked. So when you brought your purchase to him, he'd blow smoke in your face and add the prices out loud: "Eh, let's see here, fifty-four, twenty-eight, seventy-five, ahhhh . . . a buck ninety."

Leo's brother-in-law, Phil, was short with a broken nose and one walleye always looking to the left. Mrs. Millman said the bad eye was as a result of all those years of spying on Leo at the cash register. He was crankier than his partner and would scurry around with a dirty rag, dusting. Many of his days were spent in the center aisle, trying to remove a giant wad of gum that had been flattened into the linoleum and blackened by a million footfalls. "It's a sin, watching him go at it," my mother said. Once he brought in a buffing machine with the idea of whisking that sin away, but when he turned it on the thing went out of control, knocking fat Mrs. Ryan on her rear end and denting a shelf. The presence of children made Phil nervous and he gave us names—"Cocker," "Fuck Knuckle," "Putzy Boy," and something that sounded like "Schvazoozle."

In the back of the store, through a small doorway you could only get to from behind the fountain counter, was a cramped stockroom. Old centerfolds were the wallpaper, and chaos reigned among the shelves. At the center of that room, beneath a single bare bulb, there sat a card table and four chairs. On Thursday nights after closing, those chairs were occupied by Leo, Phil, Dr. Geller, and my grandfather. They played a two-card game of their own invention called Fizzle—quarter ante, deuces high, fold on any pair, ace of spades takes all. They moved like reptiles in the cold, eyeing their cards, drinking whiskey, cigar smoke swirling with nowhere to go.

One Thursday night when my grandmother had taken sick after dinner and my father was not yet home from work with the car, my mother sent me to fetch my grandfather from the store. I wasn't usually allowed out that late, but my grandmother needed the milk of magnesia and my grandfather had put it somewhere and never told her where it was. It was a week before Halloween and the night was cold and windy. The trip down the back road spooked me as barren branches clicked together and dead leaves scraped the pavement. When the Beware of Dog lunged out of the shadows, barking behind its chain-link fence, I jumped and ran the rest of the way, thinking about a boy who had lived on that block and had been hit by a car and killed over the summer.

When I made it to the store, I opened the door and went inside. The lights were out and the place was still. I walked quietly up the aisle, noticing how all the toys and books appeared different at night, as if when no one was looking they might come to life. A muffled voice drifted up from the back of the store, and I followed its trail behind the soda fountain to the door of the stockroom. They all saw me standing there, but no one acknowledged my presence because the doctor was talking. I stood still and listened, trying not to seem too interested in the ladies on the walls.

Dr. Geller was a short, heavyset man with wavy black hair and a face nearly as wide as the seat of a fountain stool. I never saw him that he wasn't yawning or rubbing his eyes. When he came to the house on visits to tend to my brother and me, he would finish his examinations and then sit down in my mother's rocker where he'd fall asleep, smoking a cigar. In his vest pocket he had a silver watch on a chain that he would let us see if we did not flinch at the bite of the needle.

His voice came out cracked and weary amidst sighs of defeat as he told about how Joe, the barber, had had a heart attack and was laying on the floor of his shop facedown in the curls of hair. "Five minutes after I checked his vital signs and pronounced him dead," said Geller, "Joe stood up, took the little whisk broom from his back pocket, cleaned the chair he was closest to, and then spun it around for the next customer. His eyes were rolled back in his head and blood was leaking from his nose, but he spoke to me. 'Trim and a shave?' he asked. And I said, 'Nothing today, Joe.' After that he fell back onto the floor and died for good." The doctor drew on his big cigar, and my grandfather called me over and put me on his lap.

2.

My grandfather was a powerful man even in old age. He had been a boxer, a merchant marine, a deep-sea diver. There was a tattoo on his left biceps that when looked at straight on was a heart with an arrow through it, filigree work around the borders. Across the center of the heart, written in vein blue, was my grandmother's name: MAISIE. When you looked at the same design over his shoulder, as he let my brother and me do sometimes, standing on the dining room table, the image became a naked woman bending over, waving to you from between her legs.

"Don't tell your mother," he'd say, and laugh like a bronchial wolf.

He was well respected among the cardplayers, because he had an inside line at the track. He worked in the boiler room at Aqueduct Racetrack—The Big A. Over the years he had struck up as many friendships as he could with the jockeys, the paddock boys, the ticket punchers. Whatever the word was on a given horse, he made it his business to know before it was led into the starting gate. In addition, he studied the *Telegraph,* the horse paper, as if it were sacred text, working the odds, comparing the results of stakes races, jotting down times and bloodlines in the margins. He knew a lot about thoroughbreds and won a considerable amount of times, but, still, he was not the best handicapper in the house. A constant point of aggravation for him was not so much that when my grandmother bet she would invariably win but that her method lacked any logical cogitation.

Her winners came from her dreams. "Last night, I saw yards and yards of burgundy silk," she said at breakfast one morning, and later that day she put two dollars to win on a horse, Rip's Burgundy, running in the eighth. My grandfather scowled and rolled his eyes. "Bullshit," he said, but when the race was over, a horse he had considered a total pig had come out of nowhere on the back turn and scorched the field.

Whenever she was about to go to the track she had these dreams. Sometimes she saw numbers, sometimes it was just a fleeting glimpse of something that had to do with a horse's name she'd find in the morning line. No matter how sure she was of her bets, though, she would never play more than two dollars. Because of this, her winnings never seemed as spectacular as my grandfather's.

Her other talent was for reading futures from an ordinary deck of playing cards. About once every two months, she and my mother would have a little get-together for the neighborhood ladies. They'd drink sherry from teacups, eat thin sandwiches with the crusts cut off, and gossip. After everyone was a little tipsy, the women would beg my grandmother to take out the cards and read their fortunes. Everyone pretended it was just for fun, but even from the back room, where I'd be perusing the latest *Green Lantern,* I knew when it was happening because of the sudden silence. Then I'd drop my comic and hurry out to see. She'd be sitting at the dining room table across from Mrs. Sutto or Mrs. Kelty, her pupils obscured by the rims of her glasses, her lips pursed and moving, staring at the white tablecloth where she was about to place the cards. She would then say, "You must cross my palm with silver." A quarter was the going rate. The blue curtains behind her were always filled with a breeze when the cards hit the table. "To your self, to your heart, to your home, to what you least expect and what's sure to come." She'd lay the cards faceup in groups of five. This was followed by a period of silence in which the ladies smiled at one another. Her first line was always, "You are about to meet a man," and broken clues to this liaison would, thereafter, pepper the reading.

The only vacations my grandparents ever took were to race-tracks. The autumn following the summer of the death of Joe, the barber, they took a trip up to Rockingham Park in New Hamp-shire. The first night at the hotel, my grandmother ate oysters and had a dream about violet smoke. She told my grandfather at break-fast, and he said, "Jeez, here we go," and checked the morning line to see if there were any horses with names that had anything to do with violet smoke. She made him slowly read off the names and fi-nally decided on a horse in the fifth race called Quiet Pleas.

"What's that go to do with smoke?" asked my grandfather.

"It's kind of wifty like it," she said.

"You're wifty," he said, and shook his head, but later, at the ticket window, he had a feeling and also put fifty dollars on Quiet Pleas to win. When the horse paid enough for them to ride home in a new car, he began to see the beauty of it.

3.

One Thursday night, instead of meeting in the stockroom of the store, the cardplayers came to the house. My grandfather answered the door and greeted them. Leo came in first, took his cigar briefly out of his mouth and shook hands with my mother and father and grandmother. Phil entered behind him, gave a wave to the grownups, and then pointed at my brother and me and said, "How's the ball choppers?" The doctor arrived a few minutes later, looking like he hadn't slept in a week. My mother served deviled eggs, and they drank whiskey and beer, the cigar and cigarette smoke dimming the room. After some slow conversation, Leo said,

"Let's do this before we get three sheets to the wind." Everyone agreed and they moved into the dining room, my grandmother taking up her place at the table.

It had been decided that Leo would be the one to represent the group, so he sat closest to my grandmother and took from his pocket a silver dollar to lay in her outstretched palm. Although the old men were all gravely quiet, I could see my mother and father standing in the kitchen silently laughing. I sat on my grandfather's lap and watched closely as the blue curtain lifted and the cards hit the table. "To yourself, to your heart, to your home, to what you least expect and what's sure to come."

"Maisie," said my grandfather, "remember, he just wants a lucky number."

She stared hard at my grandfather for the interruption.

"Don't give me that crap," he said.

"All right," she said. "A lucky number," and lifted the pile of cards that had fallen under *what's sure to come.*

Leo bit down hard on his cigar as she shuffled those cards out in front of her. Phil watched the proceedings with his bad eye while at the same time, staring down my brother, straight on, who was fidgeting in the chair across from him. The doctor leaned over to me and said, "And me, a man of science." My grandfather overheard him and laughed low in his chest. Then my grandmother held the backs of the cards out to Leo and said, "Pick one." Leo reached in, grabbed the card at the exact center of the spread and turned it faceup on the table.

The ace of spades always frightened me back then, because any time it came up my grandmother would slip it off the table and give a forced laugh.

"Doesn't that mean death?" Mrs. Crudyer asked her once at a luncheon.

"Well," she answered, "it means a lot of things, but . . . here, I see a man with flowers for you. A dozen yellow roses."

It was less than four months later that Marion Crudyer's liver gave out and she passed. That dark ace had come up in a reading my grandmother had done once for me, and afterward my brother told me to make out a will and leave everything I owned to him. I walked around for two weeks awaiting sudden death. My mother dissipated my fears by telling me it was "no more than a fart in a windstorm." I went to my grandmother and asked her how she had learned the cards. She told me Mrs. Harris, onetime mistress of the tea leaves, who had lived in her apartment building in Jamaica, Queens, had taught her. On the night old Mrs. Harris died, my grandmother and her sister, Gertrude, saw a banshee floating outside the third-story landing window, combing its blue hair and moaning.

"Number one is the number," she told Leo. "I see one."

"Fizzle," said Dr. Geller, and the cardplayers all smiled.

After the reading we moved back into the living room and my grandfather brought out his mandolin. In between barrages of conversation, someone would say, "Mac, can you do 'Goodnight Irene'?" and he would play it, double stringing and singing the words in his wolf voice. "September Song," "Apple Blossom Time," "Until the Real Thing Comes Along"—even my father sang; my grandmother drank beer.

The doctor told about a child he had recently treated who was haunted by an evil spirit that broke dishes and furniture and left bite marks. The final diagnosis was too much television and sugar. Phil explained how he was considering using hydrochloric acid to eat away the gum wad at the store. Through snatches of stories and one-word comments, they compiled verbal obituaries for the town's recently dead. Then they talked nothing but horses as I slowly drifted off to sleep in the corner of the couch.

Saturday afternoon, my father, my grandfather, and I sat in the car in the parking lot behind the 5&10 in Babylon. They were up front talking, and I was in the back, watching the rain make rivulets on the window.

"Listen, Jim," my grandfather said to my father, "this morning Maisie got up and told me that she had a dream last night about an Indian and a shooting star. I forgot about it until I was having my coffee and looking over the *Telegraph*. In the eighth race, where we're putting all our money to win on number one, there's a horse at the five spot—Tecumseh."

There was a rain-filled pause. "Well?" my father asked, and waited.

"I don't know," said my grandfather, shaking his head. He reached into his pocket, pulled out a huge roll of bills, and looked at it.

"I'll take a piece," said my father, and handed over some money.

My grandfather laughed and added it to the wager.

"An arrangement made in hell," said my father before lighting a cigarette.

My grandfather sat for a few moments in silence with his eyes closed; then he opened the door and got out of the car.

Through the rain-streaked windshield, we watched him walk across the parking lot and along the front row of cars to stop beneath a street lamp beside a chain-link fence enmeshed in dead honeysuckle vine.

"Here he comes," said my father as I climbed into the front seat and kneeled next to him. When I looked again, I saw a thin man dressed in a black topcoat and hat, talking to my grandfather.

"Watch him pass the money with the handshake," said my father.

I waited and the handshake came. It lasted only a second but I didn't see any money. The thin man looked up suddenly and then turned and ran, down through a row of cars and into the back entrance of the 5&10. When my father sat upright in his seat and threw his cigarette out the window, I knew something was wrong. The cop cars the bookie had seen entering the parking lot now came into view.

"It's a bust," said my father.

My grandfather didn't move as the police jumped out of their cars and walked quickly toward him. As they approached him from the front, my grandfather had his hand behind his back and he was waving for us to take off. My father grabbed me and we ducked down beneath the dashboard. Seeing my worried look, he put his finger to his lips and smiled. We hid for ten minutes. When we finally looked again, the cop cars were gone and so was my grandfather.

4.

Dr. Geller showed up at our door with his black bag, a stethoscope around his neck and blood on his shirt. My mother got up and let him sit in her rocker. We were gathered around the television, drinking whiskey sours my father had created in the blender with Four Roses, Mi-Lem, crushed ice, and cherries. My father gave my brother and me each a sour and we stole handfuls of cherries. There was onion dip and potato chips, sardines and pepperoni. We each bet a quarter on the seventh race, and the doctor won with a horse named Hi Side. He kept one of the quarters for himself and then split the rest of his winnings between my brother and me. My father filled the doctor in on what had happened with the bookie.

"Did Mac have time to get the bet in?" he asked.

"I think so," said my father.

My grandmother shushed them, because the horses for the eighth race were on the track.

The number one horse, Rim Groper, pranced and skittered sideways past the camera as it was introduced. It was white and its mane was in curls. The announcer told us that its colors were magenta and black and that its grandsire had been the amazing Greenbacks.

"Looks like it's got some life in it," said my mother.

"Seems crazy," said the doctor, and lit a cigar.

My grandmother watched the horses parading toward the starting gate and laughed. The two, the three, and the four horses went by, each looking much like the others—sleek and shiny, leg muscles bulging. Number five, Tecumseh, passed the camera, swaybacked and lethargic.

"There's a wooden Indian," said my father, laughing at his own joke.

Before we knew it, they were in the starting gate and ready to go. The rain fell in black and white on a black-and-white track that was pure mud.

My grandmother had her fists clenched and her eyes closed. The doctor leaned forward in the rocker. My father put his drink to his mouth and kept drinking until the announcer yelled, "And they're off!" Coming out of the gate first, Rim Groper bucked, but Pedro Avarez held on and moved into a clear lead. The next horse, Cavalcade, was two lengths back, and the rest of the pack was a length behind him with Tecumseh bringing up the rear. My mother said, "Come on, come on," through clenched teeth. My grandmother tightened her fists, and the thick blue veins of her wrists became visible. My father shoved a cracker with three sardines on it into his mouth.

On the back turn, Rim Groper bucked again, and this time Avarez flew off, hitting the mud with a splash. He was trampled by the pack, being rolled and kicked like a log. The camera stayed on the horses as they rounded the turn and moved into the home stretch. Rim Groper, now free of his mount, flew ahead of the other horses. Tecumseh made a startling move on the outside and gained on Cavalcade. The jock on Cavalcade used the whip to force a burst of speed. Tecumseh kept closing. Rim Groper crossed the finish line four lengths in front of the competition. When the real leaders crossed the line, they were nose hair for nose hair and a photo finish was called.

While we waited for the results, the announcer told us that Pedro Avarez had broken his left leg but that he was conscious. "A true competitor," said the announcer.

"A true bum," said the doctor.

"The number one horse did finish first," said my father.

My grandmother shook her head sadly. "I saw the one," she said. My mother reached over and patted her knee.

"What a tangled web we weave," said the doctor.

My father made another round of sours. Just after the doctor left, they announced that Tecumseh had edged out Cavalcade, paying thirty to one. Then it was time for my father and me to go pick up my grandfather at the police station.

On the way home, my grandfather told us that later that afternoon the police had brought in the bookie and busted the whole operation.

"They said they'd let me off if I fingered the guy in the parking lot," he said. "I saw him there in the lineup, but I'm not that stupid. They tried to sweat me, but eventually I told them they had nothing on me and they had to agree."

"Did you make the bet?" my father asked.

"Nah," he said. "I told the guy I couldn't make the wager and since I do so much business with him he accepted my apology this time."

"I saw the handshake, though," said my father.

"Just a handshake," said my grandfather as he leaned over and reached for something beneath the seat of the car. "I had my own dream that the whole thing was bullshit." He held the roll of cash up for us to see.

My father laughed so hard, he nearly drove off the road.

"I'm going to let them stew over it a little and then give back their cash on Thursday."

"What was your dream?" asked my father.

"Some crazy twaddle," he said. "Maisie was in it."

5.

As it turned out, my grandfather never got the chance to give the others their money back, because on the following Wednesday afternoon, Leo was in a head-on collision on Sunrise Highway and was launched, bald dome first, through the car windshield. My father told me that at the wake Phil put a box of Leo's special cigars in the coffin with him. The cardplayers never met on Thursday nights again.

Following Leo's funeral, the store was closed for quite a few weeks, and when Phil returned, he seemed to have lost all his frantic energy. The first thing he did was bolt a sign onto the bar of the fountain that announced that it was CLOSED. He no longer bothered with the black spot in the center aisle and it began to slowly grow. Finally the stress of losing his partner caused Phil's right eye to also turn outward. Thinking of what Mrs. Millman had said was the cause of his left eye going bad, I wondered what he was now watching for. The day he had Tecumseh carted away, Phil stood with his hands in his pockets, leaning against the entrance to the store, unable to focus on us kids and call us by the names he had concocted. I heard from my mother that he moved to Florida to live with his son, whose wife despised him. The store was sold to a young couple, who cleaned it up so that it was shining white inside. They had no names for us, no *Playboys* over the comics, no dust to make each purchase a discovery.

On Christmas eve of that same year, the doctor was called out on an emergency. Mrs. Ryan wasn't well. When he arrived at her house, sometime after midnight, he found her passed out on the floor next to her bed. More than likely, he determined she had had a stroke, and then, attempting to lift her, he had one himself and keeled over. It was the news of this incident that infused the dark ace with all its old terror for me again. I went to his wake and funeral, as did the rest of the town. When he was laid out in his coffin, I was glad to see that he no longer looked tired. I thought about one time when I was younger and he had come through a blizzard to cure my fever. When the fever broke and I woke from a maddening dream of moonlight and Banshees on the baseball diamond, he was sleeping in the rocking chair next to the couch where I lay, his pocket watch in his right hand.

Not too long after the doctor's death, my grandfather had a heart attack while cursing out Dick Van Dyke, whom he hated more than any man alive and whose show my grandmother insisted on watching every week. The episode didn't kill him, but it paralyzed his left side and made him very weak. After a long stay in the hospital, they sent him home to live out the few weeks he had left.

One afternoon when I was given the task of watching him, he woke up after a long deathlike sleep and told to me to go fetch my father. I brought my father to his bedside. With whispers and grunts, he instructed him to open the top drawer of the dresser and reach in the back.

"There's a black silk sock back there with something in it," he managed to get out through the corner of his mouth.

My father reached in, felt around, and pulled out the sock. He turned it over and gave it a shake by the toe, and out fell the wad of money, still rolled and held fast by a green rubber band.

"Play the six in the eighth this Saturday," he told my father.

My grandfather slipped away three days later and was buried on Saturday. The day of the wake, my father sat my brother and me down on the love seat in the living room and told us, "Mac lived a life. . . ." He told us stories about the old days till he cried, and then he told us to go outside and play. My mother stared horribly through the whole thing, and my grandmother moaned at night. On the day of the funeral, after the guests had left the house, my father and I watched the eighth race. The number six horse, Tea Leaf, went off at twelve to one and finished second to last. I was there on Sunday morning in my grandmother's room when my father gave her the money. She sat in the recliner, looking particularly frail and wrinkled and ancient.

"Mac told me to give this to you for the funeral," said my father.

Closing her eyes, she took the money and held it above her heart. Then she turned to me and pointed, her hand shaking. "Never forget what you least expect," she said.

Roadtripping, Zinemaking, Cooking, Cleaning, Reading, and Eating Music

———

TLC, *Fanmail* (Lisa, Lisa, Lisa)

Trailer Bride, *High Seas* and Revival Vol. 2: *Kudzu and Hollerin' Contest*

Ladytron, *604*

Propellerheads, *Decksandrumsandrockandroll*

Wilco, *Yankee Hotel Foxtrot*

Mad Melancholy Monkey Mind, *Drive*

Teenage Fanclub, *Howdy!*

The Be Good Tanyas, *Blue Horse*

Barbara Manning and the Go-Luckys!, *You Should Know By Now*

Kelly Hogan, *Beneath the Country Underdog* (with the Pine Valley Cosmonauts), and *Because It Feel Good*

The Jody Grind, *One Man's Trash Is Another Man's Treasure*

The Pine Valley Cosmonauts Salute the Majesty of Bob Wills

STODDY AWCHAW

Geoffrey H. Goodwin

. . .

EVERY MORNING, I WAKE UP TERRIFIED OF STODDY AWCHAW. I scuttle around all day and curl into a tiny ball of paranoia, pass out, and do it again.

Books by men named Poe, and Dostoyevsky and Kafka—they all tell tales about the spookiness of night, but my particular species of terror, my thread of the thought virus, attacks me in daylight from the moment I open my eyes.

Stoddy Awchaw begs at me like a dirty Buddhist monk.

Worse, when I woke up *this* morning, the escalation of the whole saga was right in front of me and I could lick it with my morning-breath tongue. It's been going on for three weeks, and today at 5:11 A.M., when I squeezed my eyelashes together and finally let them snap apart, I could feel how it was worsening. . . . Maybe Mercury's in retrograde or the pile of magazines on my front porch has developed its own center of gravity, but it feels worse. There's a bitter sawdust taste in the air. Every thought I think . . . I know he's reading my mind.

My dentist checked my fillings and told me it was all in my head, said we conjure up our own darkest fears, but he doesn't get it. The gray-haired old lady at the supermarket where I buy my tapioca pudding said I should find "a nice British girl," as if that would solve my problems. The strangest one was the mailwoman. She brings me the magazines: Harry and David, Pottery Barn, Eddie Bauer, Made-to-Order Pecan Pies, and Sexy Russian Singles. My magazines seem to come at least twice a week. I leave them in a pile on my front porch.

Running her long clear fingernails through her long red hair, the mailwoman said, "Everybody's got somebody. For you it's a five-inch-tall wooden statue of a guy with a mustache, but everybody else, maybe a girl who's too young for this town but her aunt is the postmaster, has somebody, too. Maybe she's got an imaginary pomegranate that levitates toward her when she hears the sound of running water. Maybe that pomegranate wants to slow-and-steady float its way into her private place where the sun don't shine and hurt her there, you know."

I don't know. I'm fairly certain I shouldn't leave the water running, but Stoddy Awchaw is going to find me no matter what I do. I should throw open my front door and run until my feet are sore, but I'm not going to.

I've got a sudden plan, one I can't even think of yet, because he's listening as I form the thoughts in my head. He can read the sympathetic vibrations that come from the fillings in my bicuspids. It's all figured out, so I'm going to try my plan without even thinking about it first.

THE BATHROOM SEEMED like it might work, but I felt too exposed after I sat in the tub for a minute. Coming up with a better idea, I hid inside the cabinets under my kitchen sink. I waited in the claustrophobic space, jammed against the pipes and high on the smell of cleansers, with the cabinet door open just a bit.

He scares me worse than the boss I used to have when I mopped and waxed the floors at International House of Pancakes, or my mom when she used to get her drunk-looking smile and make me drink ipecac syrup, but Stoddy Awchaw is not a smart creature.

The second his crudely carved head, with the deep-set eyes and the too-high eyebrows, poked through the crack to harass me, I slammed the cabinet door on his neck. It was difficult to grab the door from the inside and slam it, my finger dug into a screw when I pulled—I drew blood—but I thought I got him.

And I thought I was free. I just wish I'd gotten to see the badly dressed guy with the clumpy feet's head pop off.

I am not a bad human being. The only thing I could have done to deserve this is that I went camping three weeks ago and started a bonfire that was bigger than I needed. I stood next to the crackling heat and played air guitar to myself.

Then I used my deep, nobody-messes-with-me, professional wrestler voice and shouted, "No one cares about dryads anymore. They worship fairies in their gardens, and the sprites have a frosty beverage named after them, but dryads have been lost 'cause we've cut down all the lumber and used it to build houses and canoes. We don't care about your namby-pamby screams when we yank you up by your roots. You got the short end of the stick in the grand scheme of human history! So there, you forgotten little pagan deities who live in trees!"

He's a mean wood nymph, Mr. Stoddy Awchaw.

Someday soon, he's going to go after somebody else. That's what the sexy mailwoman makes me think. In fact, I believe that somebody else and then somebody else, over and over until the end of time, is going to be followed by him—even if they hide behind the washer and dryer under the staircase or inside the refrigerator box that they like to pretend is a time machine. He's going to do to them what he's done to me.

His skittering walk and his cold misshapen glare are going to send me back underneath the kitchen cabinets, or inside my hot water heater, or into the crawl space above the ceiling tiles in my bedroom, where the mice leave their trails of poop. And I'm never going to ever come out, not for food or to leave my own trail of poop or when the sexy mailwoman rings my doorbell to tell me that there are too many magazines on my porch and that she wants to run away with me to Barbados and eat bananas all day. Even if she wants to run naked on the beaches of Greece and not care if we get obese from eating spanakopita, I am not going to come out. I'd rather suck my bleeding finger and inhale pink fiberglass insulation until I die from dehydration than get another shallow glimpse of the tiny monster that is Stoddy Awchaw.

And when he comes for you, I'm sorry. I did my level best.

A SELECTION OF TEAS THE LCRW KITCHEN HAS ACQUIRED OR BEEN GIVEN OVER THE YEARS

Special Harvest Oolong (Chang Leu), In Pursuit of Tea (in a *very* beautiful box) • Pink Grapefruit Green Tea, "Sip for the Cure" (green tea blended with grapefruit and blossom), Republic of Tea • Mango Ceylon Decaf, "Metabolic Frolic Tea" (fruity black tea blended with blossoms), Republic of Tea • Cinnamon Plum, "Tea of Conviviality" (black tea with spice, fruit, etc.), Republic of Tea • Sencha (green tea), Golden Moon Tea • Honey Pear (black tea with pollen pieces), Golden Moon Tea • White Persian Melon (white tea scented with melon flower), Golden Moon Tea • Yerba Mate (powering this issue), Guayaki • Organic Moroccan Mint (green tea with peppermint and spearmint leaves), Honest Tea (great tea, too much packaging) • Wild Cherry (flowers, barks, fruit), Heath & Heather • Mint tea (sadly the box is long gone) • Awake (a blend of Ceylon and Indian teas), Tazo • Blackberry Sage, "Tea for Wisdom" (black tea with blackberry flavor and sage), Republic of Tea • Darjeeling Tea (Indian black tea), Twinings • English Breakfast Tea (a blend of Ceylon, Kenyan, and Indian teas),

Twinings • ¼ lb loose Chinese Green Dragon tea from a tea shop • ¼ lb loose jasmine tea from a tea shop • ¼ lb loose China Rose tea from a tea shop • Haiku Organic Green Tea (Japanese organic Sencha green tea), Great Eastern Sun • Lemon Tisane (peel, fruit, leaves, roots), The Herbal Tea Shop

THE RAPID ADVANCE OF SORROW

Theodora Goss

...

I SIT IN ONE OF THE CAFÉS IN SZENT ENDRE, WRITING THIS letter to you, István, not knowing if I will be alive tomorrow, not knowing if this café will be here, with its circular green chairs and cups of espresso. By the Danube, children are playing, their knees bare below school uniforms. Widows are knitting shapeless sweaters. A cat sleeps beside a geranium in the café window.

If you see her, will you tell me? I still remember how she appeared at the university, just off the train from Debrecen, a country girl with badly cut hair and clothes sewn by her mother. That year, I was smoking French cigarettes and reading forbidden literature. "Have you read D. H. Lawrence?" I asked her. "He is the only modern writer who convincingly expresses the desires of the human body." She blushed and turned away. She probably still had her Young Pioneers badge, hidden in her underwear drawer.

"Ilona is a beautiful name," I said. "It is the most beautiful name in our language." I saw her smile, although she was trying to avoid me. Her face was plump from country sausage and egg bread, and dimples formed at the corners of her mouth, two on each side.

She had dimples on her buttocks, as I found out later. I remember them, like craters on two moons, above the tops of her stockings.

SORROW: a feeling of grief or melancholy. A mythical city generally located in northern Siberia, said to have been visited by Marco Polo. From Sorrow, he took back to Italy the secret of making ice.

———

THAT AUTUMN, intellectual apathy was in fashion. I berated her for reading her textbooks, preparing for her examinations. "Don't you know the grades are predetermined?" I said. "The peasants receive ones, the bourgeoisie receive twos, the aristocrats—if they have been admitted under a special dispensation—always receive threes."

She persisted, telling me that she had discovered art, that she wanted to become cultured.

"You are a peasant," I said, slapping her rump. She looked at me with tears in her eyes.

THE PRINCIPAL EXPORT of Sorrow is the fur of the arctic fox, which is manufactured into cloaks, hats, the cuffs on gloves and boots. These foxes, which live on the tundra in family groups, are hunted with falcons. The falcons of Sorrow, relatives of the kestrel, are trained to obey a series of commands blown on whistles carved of human bone.

SHE BEGAN GOING to museums. She spent hours at the Vármúzeum in the galleries of art. Afterward, she would go to cafés, drink espressos, smoke cigarettes. Her weight dropped, and she became as lean as a wolfhound. She developed a look of perpetual hunger.

When winter came and ice floated on the Danube, I started to worry. Snow had been falling for days, and Budapest was trapped in a white silence. The air was cleaner than it had been for months, because the Trabants could not make it through the snow. It was very cold.

She entered the apartment carrying her textbooks. She was wearing a hat of white fur that I had never seen before. She threw it on the sofa.

"Communism is irrelevant," she said, lighting a cigarette.

"Where have you been?" I asked. "I made a *paprikás*. I stood in line for two hours to buy the chicken."

"There is to be a new manifesto." Ash dropped on the carpet. "It will not resemble the old manifesto. We are no longer interested in political and economic movements. All movements from now on will be purely aesthetic. Our actions will be beautiful and irrelevant."

"The *paprikás* has congealed," I said.

She looked at me for the first time since she had entered the apartment and shrugged. "You are not a poet."

THE POETRY OF SORROW may confuse anyone not accustomed to its intricacies. In Sorrow, poems are constructed on the principle of the maze. Once the reader enters the poem, he must find his way out by observing a series of clues. Readers failing to solve a poem have been known to go mad. Those who can appreciate its beauties say that the poetry of Sorrow is impersonal and ecstatic, and that it invariably speaks of death.

SHE BEGAN BRINGING home white flowers: crocuses, hyacinths, narcissi. I did not know where she found them, in the city, in winter. I eventually realized they were the emblems of her organization, worn at what passed for rallies, silent meetings where communication occurred with the touch of a hand, a glance from the corner of an eye. Such meetings took place in secret all over the city. Students would sit in the pews of the Mátyás Church, saying nothing, planning insurrection.

By this time we no longer made love. Her skin had grown cold, and when I touched it for too long, my fingers began to ache.

We seldom spoke. Her language had become impossibly complex, referential. I could no longer understand her subtle intricacies.

She painted the word ENTROPY on the wall of the apartment.

The wall was white, the paint was white. I saw it only because soot had stained the wall to a dull gray, against which the word appeared like a ghost.

One morning I saw that her hair on the pillow had turned white. I called her name, desperate with panic. She looked at me and I saw that her eyes were the color of milk, like the eyes of the blind.

IT IS INSUFFICIENT to point out that the inhabitants of Sorrow are pale. Their skin has a particular translucence, like a layer of nacre. Their nails and hair are iridescent, as though unable to capture and hold light. Their eyes are, at best, disconcerting. Travelers who have stared at them too long have reported hallucinations, like mountaineers who have stared at fields of ice.

I EXPECTED TANKS. Tanks are required for all sensible invasions. But spring came, and the insurrection did nothing discernible.

Then flowers appeared in the public gardens: crocuses, hyacinths, narcissi, all white. The black branches of the trees began to sprout leaves of a delicate pallor. White pigeons strutted in the public squares, and soon they outnumbered the ordinary gray ones. Shops began to close: first the stores selling Russian electronics, then clothing stores with sweaters from Bulgaria, then pharmacies. Only stores selling food remained open, although the potatoes looked waxen and the pork acquired a peculiar transparency.

I had stopped going to classes. It was depressing, watching a classroom full of students, with their white hair and milky eyes, who said nothing. Many professors joined the insurrection, and they would stand at the front of the lecture hall, the word ENTROPY written on the board behind them, communicating in silent gestures.

She rarely came to the apartment, but once she brought me poppy seed strudel in a paper bag. She said, "Péter, you should eat." She rested her fingertips on the back of my hand. They were like ice. "You have not joined us," she said. "Those who have not joined us will be eliminated."

I caught her by the wrist. "Why?" I asked.

She said, "Beauty demands symmetry, uniformity."

My fingers began to ache with cold. I released her wrist. I could see her veins flowing through them, like strands of aquamarine.

SORROW IS RULED by the absolute will of its empress, who is chosen for her position at the age of three and reigns until the age of thirteen. The Empress is chosen by the Brotherhood of the Cowl, a quasi-religious sect whose members hide their faces under hoods of white wool to maintain their anonymity. By tradition, the Empress never speaks in public. She delivers her commands in private audiences with the brotherhood. The consistency of these commands, from one empress to another, has been taken to prove the sanctity of the Imperial line. After their reigns, all empresses retire to the Abbey of St. Alba, where they live in seclusion for the remainder of their lives, studying astronomy, mathematics, and the seven-stringed zither. During the history of Sorrow, remarkable observations, theorems, and musical arrangements have emerged from this abbey.

NO TANKS CAME but one day, when the sun shone with a vague luminescence through the clouds that perpetually covered the city, the Empress of Sorrow rode along Váci Street on a white elephant. She was surrounded by courtiers, some in cloaks of white fox, some in jesters' uniforms sewn from white patches, some, principally unmarried women, in transparent gauze through which one could see their hairless flesh. The eyes of the elephant were outlined with henna, its feet were stained with henna. In its trunk it carried a silver bell, whose ringing was the only sound as the procession made its way to the Danube and across Erzsébet Bridge.

Crowds of people had come to greet the empress: students waving white crocuses and hyacinths and narcissi, mothers holding the hands of children who failed to clap when the elephant strode by, nuns in ashen gray. Cowled figures moved among the crowd. I watched one standing ahead of me and recognized the set of her shoulders, narrower than they had been, still slightly crooked.

I sidled up to her and whispered, "Ilona."

She turned. The cowl was drawn down and I could not see her face, but her mouth was visible, too thin now for dimples.

"Péter," she said, in a voice like snow falling. "We have done what is necessary."

She touched my cheek with her fingers. A shudder went through me, as though I had been touched by something electric.

TRAVELERS HAVE ATTEMPTED to characterize the city of Sorrow. Some have said it is a place of confusion, with impossible pinnacles rising to stars that cannot be seen from any observatory. Some have called it a place of beauty, where the winds, playing through the high buildings, produce a celestial music. Some have called it a place of death, and have said that the city, examined from above, exhibits the contours of a skull.

Some have said that the city of Sorrow does not exist. Some have insisted that it exists everywhere: that we are perpetually surrounded by its streets, which are covered by a thin layer of ice; by its gardens, in which albino peacocks wander; by its inhabitants, who pass us without attention or interest.

I BELIEVE NEITHER of these theories. I believe that Sorrow is an insurrection waged by a small cabal, with its signs and secrets; that it is run on purely aesthetic principles; that its goal is entropy, a perpetual stillness of the soul. But I could be mistaken. My conclusions could be tainted by the confusion that spreads with the rapid advance of Sorrow.

So I have left Budapest, carrying only the mark of three fingertips on my left cheek. I sit here every morning, in a café in Szent Endre, not knowing how long I have to live, not knowing how long I can remain here, on a circular green chair drinking espresso.

Soon, the knees of the children will become as smooth and fragile as glass. The widows' knitting needles will click like bone, and geranium leaves will fall beside the blanched cat. The coffee will fade to the color of milk. I do not know what will happen to the chair. I do not know if I will be eliminated, or given another chance to join the faction of silence. But I am sending you this letter, István, so you can remember me when the snows come.

THE WOLF'S STORY

Nan Fry

I was hungry.
You killed all the deer,
cut down my forest and plowed
it under. If I took a lamb,
I was the devil's dog, a slavering
fiend, fair game for your stones,
your guns and poisons, your stories.

You caught one of my pups, tied
him to a stake, and when he cried
and his mother ran to him, you
shot her down.

You shot at me too. I outran
the bullets only to stumble
into steel jaws that bit
and held. I bit back and nearly
broke my teeth. I had to chew
my paw off. I left the bloody
stump in that steel mouth.

When I met her, my leg
had healed, but I was alone—
no mate, no pups, no pack.
I could barely catch mice,

couldn't run fast enough
to get a rabbit.

I was hungry all the time.
I'd eat grass even though
I knew it would come up again,
just for the satisfaction of swallowing,
to ease the ache in my gut.

She was plump and tender—a lamb
with no fleece. I wanted
to sink my teeth in right away,
but I wanted the grandmother too.
My jaws closed on them
like a trap snapping shut.

Full at last, I fell asleep.
The hunter cut me open,
took them from me, and filled
me with stones. They say I died then.

But whenever you hear of children
given stones for supper, I am among you.
My name is Hunger.

THREE LETTERS FROM THE QUEEN OF ELFLAND

Sarah Monette

. . .

WHEN PHILIP OSBOURNE FOUND THE LETTERS, HE DID NOT do so by accident.

Since the birth of their son, he had become worried about Violet. In the evenings, when they sat together, he would look up and find her staring blankly, her hands frozen above her embroidery. When he asked her what she was thinking about, she would smile and say, "Nothing." Her smile was the same lovely smile that had first drawn him to her, but he knew she was lying. At their dinner parties, where formerly the conversation had sparkled and glimmered like the crystal chandelier, there were now silences, limping, faltering pauses. He would look around and see Violet watching the reflections of the lights in the windows, with an expression on her face that frightened him because he did not know it.

He had come to believe, in the fullness and flowering of his love for her, that he knew Violet's every mood, every thought; but now he seemed to be losing her, and this sense that she was drifting away, borne on a current he could not feel, made him angry because it made him afraid.

The first letter:

Dearest Violetta,

I have obeyed your prohibition. It has been a year and a day. I have not spoken to you, I have not come near you, I have not touched your dreams. It is my hope that you have changed your mind. My garden is not the same without you. My roses still bloom, for I will not let them fade, but the weeping willows have choked out the cherry trees, and all the chrysanthemums and snapdragons have become love-lies-bleeding and anemones and hydrangeas of the deepest indigo blue. You are missed, my only violet. Return to me.

On that afternoon in late May, Violet Strachan had been in her favorite place beneath the oak tree, a cushion stolen from her mother's boudoir protecting her back from the roots. She was writing poetry, an activity her mother disapproved of. Happily, as Mrs. Strachan abhorred anything closer to the state of nature than a well-tended conservatory, she did not come into the garden. Her daughters, Violet and Marian, spent much of their time in the little grove of trees along the stream.

Violet was never sure what made her look up—a noise, a movement, perhaps just the faint scent of honeysuckle. Something tugged at her attention, causing her to raise her head, and she saw the woman standing barefoot in the stream. She knew immediately, viscerally, that the woman was not mortal. Her eyes were the deep, translucent blue-green of tourmaline; her hair, held back from her face with cunningly worked branches of golden leaves, was a silken, curling torrent that fell to her hips. Its color was elusive—all the colors of night, Violet thought, and then did not know where the thought had come from. Neither then nor later could Violet ever describe the inhuman perfection of her face.

Violet's notebook fell from her hand unheeded. She knew she was staring; she could not help herself. The woman regarded her a moment with a bemused expression and then waded delicately across the stream, saying, "Our gardens abut. Is that not pleasant?"

"Beg pardon?"

The woman came up onto the bank, her sheer silver-gray dress instantly dry, its hem lifting a little with the currents of the air. She flashed Violet a breathtaking smile and said, "We are neighbors. What is your name?"

Violet had known the neighbors on all sides of the family estate from infancy, and this woman could not be imagined to belong to any of them. Yet she found herself saying, "Violet. Violet Strachan."

"Violet," the woman said, seeming almost to taste the syllables. "A lovely name, and a lovely flower." The tourmaline eyes were both grave and wicked, and Violet felt herself blushing.

"What . . ." she faltered, then recklessly went on, "what am I to call you?"

The woman laughed, and the sound made Violet feel that she had never heard laughter before, only pale imitations by people who had read about laughter in books. "I have many names," the woman said. "Mab, Titania . . . You may pick one if you like, or you may make one up."

Her words were only confirmation of what Violet's instincts had already told her, but they were nonetheless a drenching shock. While Violet was still staring, the Queen of Elfland came closer and said, "May I sit with you?"

"Yes, of course," Violet said, hastily bundling her skirts out of the way. "Please do."

"I have not walked in your world for decades," the Queen said, seating herself gracefully and without fuss. "I cannot reconcile myself to the clothes."

"Oh," Violet said, pushing vaguely at the masses of cloth. "But you're here now."

The Queen laughed. "I told you: we are neighbors." Her long white hand reached out and touched Violet's, stilling it instantly. "Have you chosen what to call me, Violet?"

"I cannot," Violet said, staring at their hands where they met against her dark blue skirt. "I know of no name that suits you."

"You turn a pretty compliment," the Queen said. She sounded

pleased, and Violet felt even more greatly bewildered, for she had not meant to flatter, merely to tell the truth. "I would tell you my true name, but you could not hear it if I did. Mab is by far the simplest of the names mortals have given me, and I find it has a certain dignity. Why do you not call me Mab?"

"No," Violet said, struggling against the weight of embarrassment—and a queer, giddy feeling, as if her blood had turned to glowing champagne. "Nyx is closer." For surely the Queen's beauty was the beauty of Night.

The Queen was silent. Looking up, Violet saw the beautiful eyes staring at her, the perfect brows raised. She saw that the Queen's eyes were slit-pupilled, like a cat's. "You speak more truly than you know, lovely flower. Very well. I shall be pleased to answer to Nyx from your mouth." And she smiled.

For a moment, Violet's heart stopped with the impact of that smile, and then it began trip-hammering. She could barely breathe, and the world did not seem wide enough to contain the Queen's eyes.

The Queen lifted her hand from Violet's skirt to touch the piled chignon of her hair. "You have beautiful hair, Violetta. But all those pins with their cruel jaws! Why do you not let it free?"

"I couldn't," Violet said, purely by reflex—she was so dazed that she knew what she was saying only when she heard her own voice. "Mother would have a fit."

"Your mother need not know," the Queen said, her fingers as light as moths on Violet's hair. "I assure you, I am skilled enough to replace these ugly dragons when the time comes." And then, leaning closer so that the smell of honeysuckle surrounded Violet, she whispered, "I dare you."

Later, Violet would wonder how long the Queen had watched her—weeks? months? years?—before she made her presence known. Certainly it could be no accident that she had found so exactly the chink in Violet's armor, the phrase she and Marian had used since childhood to make each other braver, stronger, less like the daughters their mother wanted. By the time Violet caught up with what her own hands were doing, they were already teasing out the second pin. And then it seemed there was no going back. In moments, the pins were out, resting in a natural hollow in one of the oak tree's roots, and the Queen was gently finger-combing Violet's hair.

"Beautiful hair," she said, sitting back. "It is the color of sunset, my flower. I can feel dusk gathering in your tresses."

Violet had not had her hair down in the daytime since she was a child. The feeling was strange, unsettling, but the champagne in her blood seemed now to have twice as many bubbles, and, as she felt the breeze tugging against the warm weight of her hair, she was hard-pressed to keep from laughing out loud.

"Now," said the Queen, "I feel I can look at you properly. Tell me about yourself."

It was an invitation, but from the Queen of Elfland, even an invitation fell on the ear like a command. Violet found herself pouring out her life's history to the Queen: her father's quiet, scholarly preoccupation; her mother's ferrous dissatisfaction; her sister, Marian; her friend Edith; the callow boys who came calling; Violet's own true desire to write poetry and have a salon and never to marry, except perhaps for love. And the Queen listened, her knees drawn up to her chin, her eyes fixed raptly on Violet's face, asking a question from time to time. Violet could not remember ever being listened to with such care, such fierceness.

ONLY WHEN VIOLET had done speaking, made shy again by those brilliant, inhuman eyes, did the Queen move. She sat up straight and gently pulled free a strand of Violet's hair that had caught in the oak tree's bark. Still holding the strand between her fingers, she said, "And you have no lover, Violetta? I find that sad."

"The young men I know are all boring."

"And one's lover should never be boring," the Queen agreed. She was winding Violet's hair around her fingers, being careful not to pull. "What about your friend Edith?"

"Edith? But Edith's . . ." *A girl,* she had been going to say, but the Queen knew that already. Involuntarily, Violet looked at the Queen; the Queen was watching her with pupils dilated, a cat ready to pounce. "We couldn't," Violet said in a thin whisper.

"It is not hard," the Queen said, releasing Violet's hair. She caressed Violet's cheek. "And you are made to be loved, Violetta." There was a pause. Violet could feel a terrible, immodest heat somewhere in the center of her being, and she knew her face was flushed. The Queen raised perfect eyebrows. "Do *I* bore you?"

"No," Violet said breathlessly. "You do not bore me." The Queen smiled and leaned in close to kiss her.

PHILIP WAITED FOR a day when he knew Violet would be out of the house. She made very few afternoon visits since Jonathan's birth, but he knew she would not refuse her childhood friend Edith Fairfield, who had been so ill since the birth of her own child. At two o'clock he told his clerk a random lie to explain his early departure and went home.

He was not accustomed to being home during the day; he was disturbed by how quiet it was. The housemaid stared at him with wide, frightened eyes like a deer's as he crossed the front hall. The carpet on the stairs seemed to devour his footsteps. He had climbed these stairs a thousand times, but he had never noticed their breadth and height, the warmth of the glowing oak paneling, the silken run of the banister beneath his hand.

He stopped on the landing. There was a bowl of roses in the window, great creamy golden multifoliate orbs, seeming to take the sunlight into themselves and throw it out threefold. Their scent had all the sweetness of childhood's half-remembered summers, and he stood for a long time gazing at them before he turned down the hall toward Violet's bedroom.

Her bedroom was not as he remembered it. Standing in the doorway, he tried to identify what had changed, and could not. The room, like Violet herself, seemed distant. It was the middle of the day—he thought of the torchlike roses—yet Violet's room seemed full of twilight and the cool sadness of dusk.

For a moment, like a man standing on the brink of a dark, powerful river, he thought that he would turn and leave, that he would not brave the torrent rushing in silence through Violet's room. For a moment he recognized, in a dim wordless way, that the name of the riverbank he stood upon was *peace*.

But it was not right that Violet should have secrets from him, who loved her. He took a deep, unthinking breath and stepped into Violet's room to begin his search.

LATER, VIOLET WOULD recognize that the Queen had in fact enchanted her, that first afternoon by the stream. But by then she had come to understand the Queen of Elfland as well as any mortal could, and she was not angry. The Queen had done as she had seen fit, and the enchantment had not made Violet behave in ways contrary to who she was. It had merely separated her temporarily from inhibition, caution, guilt . . . so that the feel of the Queen's mouth on her naked breasts, the feel of the Queen's cool fingers between her legs, had brought her nothing but passion.

Only at twilight, as she was hastening up to the house, praying that her buttons were fastened straight and that there were no leaves caught in her hair, did it occur to her to wonder what had possessed her, to imagine what her mother would say if she were told even a tenth of what the Queen had taught Violet that afternoon. Her face was flushed with shame by the time she sat down at the dinner table. Luckily, her mother assumed her heightened color was due to sun, and therefore Violet received only a familiar diatribe about the quality of a lady's skin. She bent her head beneath her mother's anger without even feeling it, her mind full of the throaty purr of the Queen's laughter.

That should have been the end of it—the encounter should have been a momentary aberration, from which Violet returned, chastened and meek, to her senses—but the heat the Queen had woken in her would not be damped down again. She found herself imagining what it would be like to kiss Edith, or Marian's beautiful friend Dorothea, or even Ann the housemaid. At night she fantasized about the heroines of her favorite books, and sometimes her hands would creep down her body to touch the secret places the Queen had shown her. Two weeks after their first meeting, Violet went back to the spinney. The Queen of Elfland was waiting there, her hands full of roses.

PHILIP FINALLY FOUND the letters hidden in the back of a photograph of Violet and her sister, Marian, who was now in India with her husband. He had never liked the portrait, had always wished Violet would get rid of it, but it was the only picture she had of Marian. He did not like the dark directness with which the sisters looked out of the frame. It seemed to him unpleasant—and most unlike Violet. That girl's face, remote and delicate and somber, had nothing to do with the woman he had married.

He picked it up, turned it over, pried loose the back with a savage wrench.

The letters fluttered out like great helpless moths and drifted to the floor. He dropped the portrait heedlessly and picked them up, his hands shaking.

There were three of them; he could tell by the ink, which darkened from the terrible crimson color of blood, through a rich garnet, to a red so dark it was almost black. The handwriting was square and flowing, elegant yet as neat as print. The paper was translucently thin, as if it had been spun out of the great richness of the ink.

He looked first, viciously, for a signature. There was none on any of them, only an embossed signet, the imprint of a linden leaf. It meant nothing to him.

He put the letters in order, darkest and oldest to brightest and newest, and began to read.

THE SECOND LETTER:

> Violet, my song,
>
> I dream of your breasts, their small sweetness. I dream of your thighs, of the nape of your neck, of your fragile hands. I dream of the treasure between your thighs, of its silken softness beneath my fingers, and its warmth. I dream of your kisses, my Violetta, of the taste of your mouth, the roughness of your tongue. My truest flame, my mortal queen, I dream of the feel of your lips on my skin, the feel of your fingers in my hair. I dream of your laugh, of your smile, of your velvet-rich voice.
>
> You asked me once if I would not forget you. I could see in your eyes that you believed I would, that you thought yourself no more than an amusement, a toy with which I would soon become bored. I could not tell you then that it was not true, but I tell you now. I have not forgotten you. I will not forget you. You are more to me than you can imagine. Return to me.

AFTER HE HAD read them all, Philip crumpled the letters in his shaking hands and hurled them away as if they were poison. His brain seemed full of fire. When he bent, automatically, to pick up the portrait, he found another object wedged in its back, an elaborately woven knot of hair, as firm and soft as silk; its color seemed to shift with the light, from ink to ash to fog. It had to be the token the final letter spoke of.

He was standing with it in his hand, staring at it in a dry fury, when he heard the rustle of Violet's dress in the hall. As she came in, her face already surprised, his name on her lips, he shouted at her, *"Who is he?"*

She looked from him, to the crumpled letters, to the portrait, to the token in his hand. The expression left her face, as if she were a lake freezing over. She said, "No one."

"Who wrote you these letters, Violet?" he said, striving to keep his voice low and even. "You said you hadn't had suitors before me."

"I hadn't," she said. "I did not lie to you, Philip."

"Then what are these?" He pointed to the letters.

She looked at him, her eyes as dark and direct as the eyes of the photographed Violet lying on the floor. "Mine."

He was so jolted he took a step backward. It suddenly seemed to him that he was facing a stranger, that this woman standing here, her red-gold hair gleaming in the sunlight from the windows, was not his wife, Violet Strachan Osbourne, but some almost perfect replica, like a Madame Tussaud waxwork come to life. "But, Violet," he said, hating how feeble he sounded, "I am your husband."

"Yes," she said. "I know."

"Then why won't you tell me the truth?"

"It would not help." She looked away from him, not in embarrassment or shame, but merely as if she was tired of thinking about him. "If you will leave me now, in an hour I will come downstairs, and it will be as if none of this ever happened. We can forget it."

He did not want to talk to this Violet, so cold and patient and indifferent. He wanted to take her offer. But . . . "I cannot forget. Who is he, Violet?"

She came into the room, picked up the letters, and carefully smoothed them out. She passed him, picked up the photograph, returned the letters to its back. She turned to him then and held out her hand, her eyes level and unfathomable. He surrendered the token. She put it with the letters, then replaced the back of the frame and returned the photograph to its accustomed place. Only then did she say, "I wish you would reconsider."

"I cannot," he said, with greater certainty now. "I will forgive you, but I must know."

She looked into the distance for a moment, as if she was thinking of something else. "I do not think I have asked for your forgiveness, Philip."

"Violet—!"

She looked back at him, her eyes like stone. "If you insist on knowing, I will tell you. But I do not do so because I think you have a right to hear it, or because I want you to 'forgive' me. I do so because I know that I will have no peace otherwise."

"Violet . . ."

"You married me two months after we met. I was glad of it, even gladder when I became pregnant so quickly. I thought she would lose interest then."

"*She?*"

The look Violet gave him was almost pitying. "My lover, Philip. The Queen of Elfland."

In fear and fury, he erupted: "Good God, Violet, do you expect me to believe this nonsense?"

"No," she said, and the flash of her dark eyes went through him like a scythe. "I don't care what you believe. You may hear nothing, or you may hear the truth. I will not lie to you."

"I thought you loved me," he said in a failing whisper.

"I wanted to. And I like you very much. But she was right. I cannot forget her, though God knows I have tried."

It came to him then clearly, terribly, that she was not lying. Those letters with their strange paper and stranger ink, the knot of hair with its shifting colors, the fabulous roses—all those things forced him to face the idea that Violet held secrets from him, that there was something in her he had never even guessed at.

"She found me," Violet said, and he knew dimly that she was no longer speaking to him, "when I was eighteen. There was a spinney at the bottom of our garden with a stream running through it. Marian and I went there to read novels and write poetry and do other things Mother disapproved of. Sometimes we would talk of what we meant to do when we were grown. We would never marry, we told each other solemnly. I wanted to be a poet. Marian wanted to be an explorer and find the source of the Amazon. But that day I was alone."

It was another thing he had never known about her. He had never known that she wrote poetry at all, much less that she had dreamed of poetry instead of marriage. It was another fragment of her that he had not held, when he thought he had held everything that she was.

She had drifted across to the mirror, the massive heirloom cheval glass in its mahogany frame. She was running her fingers over the carved leaves and flowers; her reflection in the glass seemed like a reflection in dark water.

"I can't remember what I was doing. I just remember looking up and seeing her. She was standing in the stream. I knew what she was."

The eyes of her reflection caught his eyes. He watched Violet remember where she was and to whom she spoke; her face closed again, like a door slamming shut.

"She seduced me," Violet said, turning to face him. "We became lovers. At night I would sneak out of the house and cross the stream to her court. One week, when my parents took Marian to visit her godmother, I told the servants I was staying with Edith, and I spent the entire time with . . . with *her*. She begged me not to go back, but I could not stay. Do you understand, Philip? *I could not stay.*"

She seemed to see in his face that he did not understand, and the vitality drained out of her again. "The night before I married you, I asked her to let me go, to give me a year and a day to try to be your wife. She did as I asked."

"But then she began writing letters," he said, because he had to prove, to Violet, to himself, that he was truly here.

"Yes. I have not answered them. I have been faithful to you."

He held up his hands, palms out in a warding gesture, as if the bitterness in her voice were something he could push away. But he could not keep the reproach from his tongue: "You kept the letters."

"Yes," Violet said, her tone too flat to be deciphered, "I kept the letters."

THE THIRD LETTER:

> Violet, my only heart,
>
> I know that your silence must mean you will not return, that you have chosen your other life. I could compel you to return, just as I could have compelled you to stay. I hope you understand that my choice not to do so is itself a gift, the only way you have offered me to show you that I love you. I do not know what there is in your life to treasure: your husband, as blind and senseless as a stone? your fat, stodgy infant who will surely grow up to resemble his father? the mother whose love you cannot win? the father

who has never noticed you? your sick and clinging friend? the infrequent letters from a sister who thinks of nothing but her husband?

You know the wonders and joys I can offer you. You know that in my realm you will be honored as you are not in your own. Violet, it is pain to me to know how you are treated, how little those around you see you—much less recognize your beauties—even as they use you and destroy you. I know that you will not heed me; I feel in your silence that your mind is made up. You are better than the mortal world deserves.

I will give you three gifts then, since you will not let me give you more. Your freedom, even though you turn it into slavery; this token—I wish that perhaps you will wear it next to your heart; my roses, that your house, too, may become a garden. And I give you, still, my hope that you will return.

The silence in the bedroom was as heavy as iron, heavy as lead. Philip could not find the strength to lift it. In the end, it was Violet who straightened her shoulders and said, with an odd, crooked smile, "Well, Philip?"

"You don't love me," he said.

The smile fell from her face. "No. I am sorry."

"What about Jonathan? Your *son*?"

The Queen's careless description, *your fat, stodgy infant,* hung unspoken between them. Finally, Violet said, "I will do my duty by him."

"My God, Violet, I'm not talking about duty! I'm asking if you *love* him!"

"You are asking too much." The color was gone from her face; for the first time, he was forced to admit that the solemn photograph captured something that was really part of Violet. Before he could compose himself against that realization, another hit him: that he did not know her, that the sparkling, marvelous conversations, on which he had founded his love, had given him nothing of her true thoughts, nothing of her heart. He had worshipped her as her suitor; he had worshipped her as her husband. But until now, he had come no closer to her; truly, as he had thought earlier, she was a stranger to him.

In the pain of that revelation, he said, "You used me. You're *using* me and Jonathan." Then, with a gasp, "You're using my love!"

"I have given everything I have to give in return!" Violet cried. "Is this all there is, Philip? Have I no choice but to give everything to her, or to you? Either way, what is there left for me?"

"Violet—"

"No," she said, so harshly that he was silenced. "I see that I am like Ulysses, caught between Scylla and Charybdis. To neither side is there safe haven."

He looked away from the bitter anguish in her face. He still loved her. He did not think he would ever forgive her for what she had done, but her despair struck him like barbed arrows. "I am sorry," he said at last. "I did not realize I was asking so much."

"You have asked no more than any man asks of his wife." She sank down slowly onto the chair by the window, resting her forehead on her hand.

"I did not wish to . . . to crush you," he said, fighting now simply to make her hear him. "I did not know you were so unhappy."

"I am not unhappy," she said without raising her head. "I chose between love and duty, and I am living with my choice. I had not . . . I had not expected to be offered that choice again. That makes it harder."

"Will you go back to . . . *her*?"

"No. I cannot. Her love will destroy me, for I am only mortal, a moth, and she is like the sun. My poetry was immolated in her ardor, left in her garden with my heart, and I cannot sacrifice more to her." He thought for a moment she would go on, but she said only, again, "I cannot."

"Will you . . . will you stay with me?"

She raised her head then to stare at him; her face was set, like that of someone who looks on devastation and will not weep. "Have I a choice?"

"No, I mean . . . I meant, only, will you *stay*? With *me*?"

"You know that I do not love you."

"Yes, but . . ." He could not think how to express what he wanted to say, that he needed and loved her whether she loved him or not, and was forced to fall back, lamely, on, "You are my wife. And the mother of my son."

"Yes," she said, her voice inflectionless. "I am."

He said, in little more than a whisper: "Don't shut me out, Violet, please."

"Very well," she said. Her smile was a faded reflection of its former luminous beauty. "What is left is yours." She turned away, but not before he had seen the brilliance of tears in her eyes.

He wanted to comfort her, but he no longer knew how. He stood, awkward in the fading afternoon light, and watched her weep.

On the landing, the roses of the Queen of Elfland, as clamorous as trumpets, continued to shout their glory to the uncomprehending house.

TACOMA-FUJI

David Moles

First day of December and the fog
on the slopes of Mt. Rainier softens edges
reveals unknown symmetries
against a morning gray and streaked with yellow
so it might be Fuji there on the southern horizon
and if I were Hokusai I could draw this
the baseball stadium the cranes
like skeletons of Trojan horses
the masts of rich men's yachts.

A hundred years ago Japanese men came here.
They drank rice wine in waterfront bars
that are underground now, anonymous
cut wood on the slopes of *Tacoma-Fuji*
fought over women
and some of them went mad.

A man called Kafū wrote it all down,
an admirer of the French decadents
who enjoyed absinthe, long bicycle rides in the country
and the conversation of prostitutes.
He would have preferred Paris, but his father
thought America would improve his character.

BAY

David Erik Nelson

. . .

"Hey, Dan, you ever hear about the haunted dog?"

"Jesus!" I jumped in my seat, sloshing the better part of a pint of beer into my lap. "Crap. What?" I asked, not looking up, searching my parka for paper napkins—something to mop up the beer. "What was that?"

I'd been sitting belly to the bar for I don't know how long, staring into the long mirror behind the bottles, not really thinking at all—apart from vacantly wondering how I'd become such a sad old sack—and that warm, friendly, familiar voice was like stepping on a tack in the dark.

"Sorry to startle you, Dan. I was just asking if you'd ever heard about the haunted dog?"

"You mean like a ghost dog?" I asked, trying to soak up the beer with my wool mittens, then realizing they were the ones Janey had knitted for me when she'd been a Brownie and putting them away in favor of a wad of those crummy square bar napkins. "Like that one about the guy whose car breaks down in the woods and there's a wolf—"

"No," his voice was sharp, annoyed, like the way you talk to a smart kid who's acting stupid, "not a ghost dog—a *haunted* dog, like a haunted house." I looked up from my beery crotch.

"Is it a joke?" I asked. The guy—young, twentysomething, short, dark hair still damp from an evening shower, wool peacoat, pale face—he didn't look like anyone in particular. Someone Janey had gone to high school with? The age was about right. "Are you asking me, 'Did you ever hear the one about the haunted dog?' "

"No, Dan, this isn't a joke, it's a story. A true story—"

"Well, wait. I'm afraid I don't know—"

"Shhh." He waved his gloved hand at me. "You'll dig this. Just listen:

"So there's this guy, right, this family, and they get this dog—a beagle—from the Humane Society. You with me?" He pulled his gloves off and set them on the bar, lacing his fingers over them. He didn't really look at me as he spoke, instead craning around as if he was waiting for someone, afraid he'd miss her in the crowd.

I grunted and sipped my beer, feeling like a ridiculous old fart because I couldn't quite place this kid.

"So, this guy, his family, they're down at the Society and they pick out this beagle, and the guy asks the attendant where's the dog from? What's its history? And the attendant lays out this big old yarn about how the dog used to belong to some old guy that lived all alone in a little cracker-box house on a big slab of land out near Beggars. Dog was the old guy's dearest, only friend, blah blah blah, docile, blah blah blah, housebroken—you know, the basic keep-me-company house pet, right? Dog's name is Ski Boot. Imagine that, calling a dog Ski Boot? Old folks are weird." He turned to look at me. "Sorry. Present company excluded."

I nodded, waving my hand in a don't-sweat-it gesture as I set down my empty mug. And right then it came to me: this kid *must* be a fella Janey'd dated in high school her sophomore or junior year. Skinny, dark hair—it was all slowly gathering together in my head. If this was him, then he'd certainly changed, but it seemed *right*. Kid's name was Rob or Ron or something like that. No car, I recalled. I'd liked him for that.

"Say, what line of work you in these days?" I tried to sound as casual as possible.

"What?" he asked, looking at me blankly. "Work? Oh . . . never mind that. I don't really live around here.

"But, so the guy with the family asks the attendant what drove the old codger to get rid of such a beloved pal—you know, the guy figures he has the attendant over a barrel, caught him in a lie. The guy thinks he's a regular suburban Sherlock.

"But the attendant tells him the old guy died, no family surviving him. All of his property defaulted to the state and they auctioned it. The state didn't need a beagle for anything, and it didn't get bid on, so . . .

"Well, suffice to say, the guy feels like a first-class bastard and adopts the dog with no further questions, plus makes a nice little donation to the Humane Society.

"So, they get the dog home, walk him around the block, have dinner, and turn in. They figure that the dog will settle down to sleep upstairs, maybe in one of the kids' bedrooms, maybe in the master bedroom—hell, maybe even try to get into one of the beds."

"Dogs are like that," I said, thinking of a mutt named Butter I'd had for almost thirteen years before I had to have him put down last spring. "If they've been let to sleep in a bed in the past, it's hard to break them of it." Butter slept curled behind my knees, every night for seven years, after Janey's mom passed on in '93. And then it dawned on me, if this fella hadn't been around—probably went off to college somewhere and is just back visiting his folks or something—he might not know about Janey. It'd be an awful thing, not getting the proper chance to pay your respects to a classmate. Especially if they'd dated . . .

The kid turned to look at me, then broke into a wide, honest grin. Gosh, I wish Janey'd stuck with this guy—whatever the hell his name was. Rod? I hated knowing I had to break the news to such a sweet kid . . . and I couldn't even remember his *name*. You'd think a father would remember the nice ones, but in the end, you don't. In the end, it's the bastards who brand themselves in your memory.

"Sure," he said. "Sure! But these folks don't mind. They're

sorta looking forward to sharing some space with that musky, loyal weight. It can be reassuring to have a dog curled up on your feet. You know that. These are the sort of folks who crave that kind of reassurance.

"But the dog, he doesn't set himself up in any of the bedrooms, doesn't even come upstairs. He stays down in the TV room. A few minutes after lights-out he takes to whining. I dunno if you've ever heard a beagle, but they whine—Jesus, it's an awful sound. They get to sorta hyperventilating, and each puff of breath is this screech, like a bad windshield wiper. Really unbearable.

"But the family, they're gritting their teeth and sticking it out. The guy doesn't want to give in—you know, the way some people are about toddlers crying in the night. He wants the dog to get used to the dark or to figure out to come upstairs. He wants to force it to get comfortable on its own. I mean, it's a dog, for God's sake—no reason to jump when it says frog, right?

"The guy hears one of his kids leaving her room. He hops out of bed and catches her at the stairs, explains the situation, and then gets all three of them together and explains again, to make sure they're all with the program: 'No going to the dog. Let him come to you. We're the masters.' The older two kids understand—they don't like it, but they understand the importance of not making the dog boss—and return to their rooms. But his daughter, she's the youngest—not to mention being a girl—so the whole matter doesn't sit well with her, and when she finally does go back to bed, she's in tears.

"Just for the record, I think the girl was right.

"Of course, soon enough, the beagle graduates up from whining and takes to baying. You ever heard that sound?"

Rita, the bartender, set a fresh beer down and gave me this queer look—probably because the kid was gabbing, but not drinking. "No, but I imagine it's like a wolf. You want a beer or something?" Christ, I wished I could grab his name. Rob? It was driving me nuts.

"Me? No thanks. Don't drink."

I shrugged and tipped Rita double.

"But the baying—it's not like a wolf at all. A wolf, that's a scary sound, but this, it's . . . mournful. Overpowering. Really. They make like a trumpet of their mouths and just let loose. The sound is low and open and empty and long—it's a brokenhearted sound. But strong, like a hammer. It hits you like a melancholy sack of quarters.

"To their credit, the family hangs tough, doesn't budge all night. After hours—*literally hours*—the dog gives out and takes it back to this low whimper, like he's crying. The family gets a little sleep that night. A little.

"It goes on this way, of course. Night after night—the dog refuses to come upstairs, just curls up on the couch and whines and bays and weeps. The dog is fine when people are with him, during the day, but when they leave him alone at night it's Heartbreak Hotel in scenic Sorrow City, no vacancies."

I laughed at that—couldn't help it—and the kid's eyes sparkled. A natural storyteller, this one. Probably studying theater, I figured, or maybe working already, selling cars—a clean-cut kid like this one could rake it in working in sales.

"Then, one night, in the middle of the night, the dog stops baying. Really, he doesn't just stop—he cuts out, like someone pulled the plug on a CD player. At first the guy lets out a big, cleansing sigh. Finally, he figures, the dog's adjusted, acclimated. But as the silence stretches out he begins to worry. Now the dog's *too* quiet. And, for that matter, he didn't like the way it just cut out, like the dog lost his power. Or his air. Had the dog gone into a seizure? Maybe he's choking on his tongue. The last thing this guy wants to do is come down for breakfast the next morning and find his family hysterical over a dog corpse. He hops out of bed and quietly—quietly but quickly—slinks down the stairs."

"Hold up a second, son. Listen, I feel just awful about this, but firstly I can't even remember your name—"

"It's OK, Dan, I haven't told you—"

"—*and secondly,* I've got some sad news that I need—"

"No, Dan. You need to listen. I'm midstory here, OK?" He said that little piece conversationally, quietly. Nothing forceful, in his tone, in his words, but I couldn't conceivably have gone on interrupting him, not even to say the bar was on fire or Christ had come back in a pink evening gown. Not for anything. His eyes were so cold, so solidly *on me*. "My story is true, Dan. You need to understand that. Do you get it?"

"Yeah . . ."

"So the guy, he comes down the stairs, and freezes at the door to the TV room—you with me, Dan?"

"Yeah." My lips were numb—all of a sudden I was sorta scared of this kid. I never paid much attention to the guys Janey brought home, but maybe she let this one go for a reason. He ran so cold so fast—but by the time I'd worked all that out in my head, he was already warmed up again. Friendly again.

"—and there's this kid on his couch, sitting with the guy's dog. A naked kid. A kid who isn't one of his kids. A sobbing boy, not more than thirteen years old, petting old Ski Boot—who's happy as a clam, wearing one of those big, stupid, flop-tongued dog grins.

"The guy tries talking to the kid—you know, 'Whatsa matter, son? How'd you get in here? Blah, blah, blah'—but the kid won't answer, won't even acknowledge the guy's presence. Just keeps stroking the dog. The guy comes right up to the kid, right up to the arm of the couch. He reaches out to grab the boy, then thinks better of it.

"You know how when you've got a radio with a bad grip on a station, you can make the reception go clear or fuzzy just by reaching toward the radio? You know how that is? You ever notice that you get that feeling off of people, too?"

"Like auras?" I asked, but I knew what he was talking about already. About the radio reception, at least. "That psychic stuff they have TV specials on sometimes?"

"No, not that fakey-fakey TV crap. I mean for real. Try it some time—get your hand close to someone, and you'll just about always be able to feel . . . like, a . . . well, like a *buffer* of sorts. I don't know what it is, scientifically, maybe just the warm air around their body—that personal atmosphere—or some sorta static electricity or electromagnetic fields. I don't know. I just know it's there. You can feel it.

"But when this guy's fingers get close to this kid, there's nothing, nothing at all, and he knows that he doesn't want to know what would happen if he kept reaching.

"Also, the kid's crying pretty hard, right? Almost wailing, his mouth bent into one of those awful upside-down clown faces that kids make when they're really pitching a fit—but there's no *sound*. There are still regular night sounds: the mantel clock ticking, the dog grunting, the springs in the couch squeaking, but the *kid* isn't making any sound. Not anything.

"The guy, he's a horror–sci-fi fan, he's read his *Fantasy & Science Fiction* and watched his *Twilight Zone;* he figures that maybe Ghost World is just like the real world, but out of phase—just a little out of alignment, enough so that usually there's no passing through. Maybe this kid had somehow gotten racked into focus—not all the way into focus, but closer to being in the guy's world. Or the guy, could be *he'd* been racked into focus with Ghost World—literally one foot in the grave.

"He doesn't know, he doesn't want to know. If this was a

movie or a story—a made-up story—then the guy probably would've started doing experiments, started trying to figure out what the deal was, how it worked, like in *Poltergeist* or *Hellraiser*.

"But this is real life, and all the guy wants is for his dog to sleep quietly and the ghost boy to go away. He backs out of the room, creeps up the staircase, and pulls the covers over his head, sure that the kid will Just Go Away.

"The next morning the guy comes down to breakfast and finds his family quietly sitting around the table, munching Rice Krispies. The only sounds in the room are the kids chewing, the cereal snapcracklepopping and the dog's tags clanking against his metal dish as he crunches his kibble. The ghost boy is sitting on the floor, watching Ski Boot eat and running his hand in long, deliberate strokes down the dog's back. His tears have dried up, but he still doesn't look happy.

"That's how things go for the family. The boy follows the dog around the house, and no one really talks about it. In fact, even though the ghost kid—the *naked* ghost kid—follows the guy when he walks the dog every morning and night, *no one* mentions the kid. At all. Not even his children's friends, who get really good at making up excuses not to come over after school. No one broaches the subject with the family. Sure, they probably talk about it among themselves—'So I says to Mabel, I says, what's it with that bluish naked kid following Earl Hugus around the block? and she says blah, blah, blah'—"

I laughed again, hard. That voice he'd conjured up, a braying Chicago granny leaning out her first-floor window, was a scream. I laughed and he smiled, eyes sparkling—we had this terrific rapport going, and I couldn't believe that this same guy had put such a scare into me a few minutes earlier.

"My point is that no one asks, because no one wants to know.

"On the one hand, the guy is relieved that nobody asks, because he certainly doesn't have any answers. But it makes him nervous, too. What if it's some sort of group hallucination? You know, like the French Revolution. What if his family is being poisoned by something in their bread or water or Krispies, and they're starting to wig out?

"But, when push comes to shove, these are small worries—middle-of-the-night worries, like worrying that a plane'll hit the house, or that you'll look out your bedroom window and see a vampire chick floating there, ready to bust through. Or worrying about finding a corpse hanged in the attic.

"After a while the rest of the family lets it go. They learn to ignore the kid, ignore him completely, ignore him to the point that he isn't there for them at all anymore—like Auschwitz, right?"

"What?" I asked.

"Auschwitz, the Nazi death camp in Poland? It was right near a little town, right? Like, almost right in it?"

"Yeah. OK. I get it." And, strangely, I *did* get it: I'd seen a documentary on the History Channel that had gone on for a while about Auschwitz. It seems that the camp was almost smack dab in this little town called Oświęcim, and in the camp they had the big crematory ovens where they destroyed all the corpses. When the camp was liberated, the soldiers asked the townspeople, "How could you not know this was happening? Good Christ, the stink's incredible—it hangs all over your town right now," and the villagers said, "The Germans told us it was a pork sausage factory, and we believed them." This was at the end of the war, after months of living in the lingering, wispy smoke of burnt human carcasses. There was practically a famine behind Nazi lines then, everyone was rail thin, and these folks watched the smoke billow out of those stacks, watched the trucks and trains bring in load after load of bone-skinny "workers"—and never a single pig—but persisted in their desperate belief that Auschwitz was a sausage plant and nothing more. A huge sausage plant that no pigs entered and no sausages left.

"My point is that all that's left of the ghost kid, for these kids, is a vague sense of relief when they're invited to stay over at a friend's house.

"But the guy, he can't leave it alone. He calls the Humane Society again and gets ahold of the attendant who'd given them Ski Boot. He presses the guy, who finally 'fesses up: he doesn't have a clue where the dog came from—his story about the old man was total BS. Folks want to hear cutesy stories about devoted dogs, and all he wanted to do was *not* waste a perfectly good purebred in the doggy gas chamber. So he lied. What's the big deal? Had the dog eaten his kid's face or something?

"The guy says no and apologizes, says there isn't a problem, and promises to send in a donation posthaste.

"But like I said before, this guy is a sci-fi fan, a horror fan. He knows the ghost story formula backward and forward: ghosts stick around because they've got business left in this world. Help them settle up their tabs, and they'll fade into the ether.

"So, he starts talking to the kid when they're alone, talking to him in that sorta absent way you talk to a lug nut you're trying to loosen, or the way you mutter to the spices while cooking. The kinda talking that in a pinch you can pretend isn't *really* talking. He sits up late at night, lights off, watching cable with the boy, the dog sitting between them.

" 'You lost?' he asks, eyes glued to the tube, watching Ed Harris and Mary Elizabeth Mastrantonio in *The Abyss,* swimming for their lives through the Deep Blue Nuthin'. 'Not sure how to, you know, 'Walk into the light, Carol Anne'? Was this your dog once, and you've still got a last good-bye you need to say? Maybe you can't let go.' Flicking the channels, stopping at infomercials, *Iron Chef,* rap videos—stopping for anything that will inject a little noise into the room. 'Are your folks still looking for you? Do you need someone to tell them that you've, um, bought your ticket? Are they dead, too, but you don't know where to find them? Are you waiting in a ditch somewhere, waiting for a proper burial? Or are you in a shallow grave, broken and . . . and *alone?*'

"The guy spends a lot of nights like that, flicking the channels, petting the dog, and asking questions. Sometimes he goes for hours without even thinking about it, the questions pouring out of his mouth like rain out of a downspout. Other times the questions come as slow and hard as passing a kidney stone. A lot of the time he cries, thinking about the boy's corpse, cold and alone and forgotten, trapped in a junkyard fridge, dumped at the bottom of a ravine, stuffed into a hot, dry crawl space.

" 'Are you sad? Are you lost? Were you wronged? Do you have a message?'

"But the kid just sits there, eyes down, petting the dog. Until, one night, the kid finally turns to the guy and says: 'Jesus, mister, shut up. Can't you just shut up and leave me alone?'

"The guy is flabbergasted.

" 'When did you start hearing me?'

" 'I always heard you. I don't want nuthin'. Shut up.'

" 'But, what can I—how can I make you go away?' The guy leans forward, not breathing, not even thinking. Just waiting."

He turned to me, held me in his gaze. "And the kid tells him: 'You can't.' "

WE SAT THERE, staring at each other, and I waited for him to go on. But he didn't. He turned around, looking into the crowd, and picked up his gloves as if to go.

I almost reached out and grabbed him. Almost. "Wait." I was nearly yelling. "What kinda ghost story is this?"

He glanced over his shoulder. "It's a true one, Pops."

"That's the end?"

"Yeah, that's it. Stick a fork in me, I'm done."

"You can't do that! Stories don't end that way—the ghost has *got* to want something, and then the guy—"

"Listen," he said, sitting back down, "I already told you: this isn't a fake ghost story, this isn't a campfire ghost story. This is a *true* ghost story."

I sputtered, "But—"

"Danny Boy, don't 'but' me. Those ghost stories you always hear, those are a load of crap. In real life, it isn't like folks wander the earth on some big ol' quest. I mean, *come on*."

"But then why'd the kid come back? What'd he *want*?"

"He didn't want nuthin'," the kid snapped, "I mean, what do you want right now? Why are you talking to me? Why'd the beagle bay and weep over being alone? We're just two guys sitting at a bar, taking advantage of the happy hour specials. You don't know me from Adam, I don't know you from Cain. Just two guys, but we're talking, right? We're doing what people do, we're passing the time together, we're pushing away the dark and cold, the Alone, just like those old Vikings in their longhouses, with the face-freezing blast knocking at the walls, with monsters skulking in under the clouds to tear them apart. That's what people do: we clump together to chase away the cold of being alone."

He was so *angry*—it was scary. And, as I looked at him, something in his face changed, *hardened,* and I knew that he knew that I didn't believe him, didn't believe him about any of it.

"Touch me," he said.

"What?"

"*Touch me.*"

"Listen, fella, I don't know who you are—"

"Jesus! I'm not asking you to grab my johnson, Dan! Just here, just touch my hand."

"Son, I don't—"

"Touch it, touch my hand, you old puss. It's my hand, it's nothing. Touch it."

"Fine." I reached out and grabbed him, awkwardly, around the right hand, "There. Happy?" And my God, it was *cold*.

He didn't answer, just looked at me, watching.

"So what? So your hand's cold. My kid brother, he had hands and feet as cold as blocks of ice, even in the summer. Just bad circulation."

"Yeah, OK. Touch me here then, on my neck. Hunh, feel that?"

I didn't want to do it, but I did. My God, it was like clay in November. It was like touching a corpse out of one of those lockers they have in morgues.

"You ever known someone who's cold like that, cold as ice, where their neck meets their throat? Was your kid brother cold there? Is he now? Hmmm? And while you're at it, why not take my pulse, Dan? What am I at? How many beats a minute? Pretty calm, isn't it?"

I pulled my hand away slowly.

"You're no one—"

"I'm not no one."

"—you're no one Janey knew."

"You're right on that, Danny Boy; I've not yet met the gal. But why not ask me about Janey anyway? Or about your wife, Sue, or about Butter or about your bro', dearly departed though he is?" He smiled. It was a sick smile, and it made my gut drop to see it.

"You know them? Are they—"

His smile shifted to a smirk. "Don't bother, Dan. I was just screwing with you; it doesn't work that way."

"What . . ." I licked my lips. "Whadayou? Um, whadaya *want*?"

"I don't want nuthin', Dan. I just wanna talk."

HOW TO MAKE A MARTINI

Richard Butner

. . .

I drink so I can talk to assholes. This includes me.
—JAMES DOUGLAS MORRISON

DRINK WHAT YOU LIKE, SO YOU CAN TALK TO ASSHOLES IN-
cluding yourself. But. But you might want to have a martini. And
here's how to make one.

First off, martinis are made of gin and vermouth. If you make
one with vodka, it's not a martini: it's a vodka martini. If you
make one without vermouth, it's not a martini, it's cold gin, which
is a perfectly fine KISS song but perhaps not a perfectly fine
beverage.

The state of being in a martini glass does not instantly confer
martinihood on any given concoction. Some perfectly fine drinks
are served in martini glasses (a.k.a. cocktail glasses, as opposed to
old-fashioned glasses or collins glasses or cordial glasses). Gimlets,
say. Hell, even lemon drops. There is no such thing as a choco-
banana martini, though.

Get some vermouth that's decent. Universally renowned as decent is Noilly Prat. It deserves its rep. If you have some fancy small
batch vermouth, try that—make sure to use dry vermouth, not
sweet. If you're stuck with Martini & Rossi or Stock or Cinzano,
make do until you've finished that bottle, then pay the extra buck
for the Noilly Prat.

Get some gin that's decent. This is actually easier than the vermouth purchase. Gin is a poor person's drink; it's flavored grain al-
cohol, the simplest booze to manufacture. It is automatically not

fancy, no matter what various pop cultural artifacts of the twenti-eth century say. So, get something that's good but not faux good, like Bombay or Beefeater but not Bombay Sapphire or Tanqueray No. Ten, unless you feel like plunking down the cash. In other words, get something in a glass bottle (not a plastic one).

Now, get a garnish. Weird purists (weird purists who are not me) will demand that you eat an olive. You do not have to do this. One thing you definitely do not have to do is to drink a dirty martini, obtained by pouring olive brine in with the other fluids. If you like olive brine, then go have a large salty flagon of olive brine, but don't ruin your martini with it. So decide whether you'd like one olive or two, or instead of olives, a citrus twist. The citrus can be lemon or lime (see Bombay gin bottle as reference for the lime option). The olives can *only* be Manzanilla-sized olives, not jumbo or queen olives. You're having a cocktail, you're not eating lunch.

Keep the vermouth in the fridge once you've opened it; it's del-icate, like Sandy Denny. Keep the gin either in the freezer or in the liquor cabinet. If you keep it in the freezer, it's already nice and cold, which is good, but the ice will melt less quickly when you prepare it. You want the ice to melt. You want some dilution. Di-lution via melting ice is the key to any good cocktail. If you keep the gin in the freezer, make sure to stir your martini for an extra-long time.

Get a mixing glass. Crack some ice. You don't want just ice cubes; you want actual cracked ice. Buy a bag of it, or make it your-self with a hammer or with a Tap-Icer, or build a robot friend that you can program to crack ice for you. Put plenty of the cracked ice in the mixing glass. Then put in the vermouth. If you're com-pletely vermouthophobic, allow it to flavor the ice, then dump it out (this is the "in and out" martini). If you want a real martini, though, leave it in, and use about one part vermouth to six parts gin. Add the gin. Stir. Continue stirring. Stir some more.

Strain into your frosted martini glasses. You have kept them in the freezer, right? Add the garnish. Drink, and enjoy. If the gin-to-vermouth ratio feels wrong to your taste buds, well then, make another. Cheers, y'all.

ALL ABOUT THE T:
SWEPT (NOT SWEEPED) AWAY BY
THE LOVE OF IRREGULAR VERBS

shined	shone
dreamed	dreamt
leaned	leant
kneeled	knelt
came	kempt
burned	burnt
spilled	spilt
lighted	lit
learned	learnt
meaned	meant

HAPPIER DAYS

Jan Lars Jensen

...

THE THEME FOR OUR TEN-YEAR GRAD REUNION WAS *Happy Days*. I'm not sure why this particular show was selected, as we had graduated long after the fifties, and the series had been canceled before most of us met in high school. I'm not even sure why we needed a theme—a reunion isn't a prom. But I guess *Happy Days* generated a feeling of nostalgia that the organizers hoped would rub off on our event, and few people could claim they had never seen an episode.

My wife and I had a little spat because I would not go dressed as Fonzie, even though I had been president of the Student Council. I argued that if logic dictated the class president must portray himself as a central character, then I should be Richie Cunningham, who was clearly intended as the protagonist of the series before Ron Howard left and focus shifted entirely to Arthur Fonzarelli. But I had a more cerebral choice in mind than either of those two, and perhaps it was even more self-congratulatory.

Mr. Cunningham. Dad. Maybe unconsciously I saw myself as a father figure to my fellow grads and thought that in some way I was responsible for how they'd turned out, good or bad, and they could expect to hear advice from me, whether they wanted it or not. I used folded towels to round out my figure, and I wore a pair of trousers and a shirt that I found at Value Village, which seemed plausible fifties attire. My wife still thought I should be the Fonz, but she accepted my decision after realizing it made us fit tighter; she attended dressed as Joanie. We had been a couple since high school, and now we returned as a happy domestic twosome, even in costume.

The reunion committee rented a hall adjoining a local hotel and did a good job decorating according to the theme, with crepe paper streamers, pennants, even a rented jukebox. The DJ played fifties music and there was some bellyaching that we should have heard tunes from our high school days, but who could argue with the theme? Anyway, they must have played "Rock Around the Clock" four times that night, and with old friends and enemies we got up and fumbled through our idea of an appropriate dance style.

I spent much of the evening watching others, and I tallied the characters represented. I counted thirty-three attempts at Fonzie and I lost track of the Richies after twenty-eight. Mrs. Cunninghams and Joanies were tied at around twenty, and there were only slightly fewer Pinky Tuscaderos (there weren't a lot of strong female roles in *Happy Days,* but the decade portrayed was at least partly to blame). Maybe a dozen people, like me, thought they were sharp coming as Howard Cunningham. There was a surprisingly disproportionate number of Ralph Malphs over Potsies—almost a five to one ratio, even though the characters were of equal stature in the series, and I could only attribute this to the unpopularity of Anson Williams.

I started looking for patterns among people who came dressed as the same character. Some notable Fonzies:

Brad Forneau: He had become a pilot in the military and flown a fighter jet in a recent UN peacekeeping mission. He used his flight jacket as part of his Fonzie costume (despite the fact that it was brown and had military insignia on the sleeves), and when I spoke to him, he mentioned several times that flying an F-16 was largely about "keeping your cool."

Rodney Bislin: Rod in high school had accepted the "geek" label but, since then, had redeemed himself with a lucrative career in the telecommunications industry. "All those lunch hours spent in the computer room paid off," a friend of mine sneered. Coming as Fonzie, I sensed, was Rod's attempt to announce his success. He knew he'd been the dorkiest of misfits back then, but here he was, having pulled himself up to the top of the character ladder, Fonzie with a diamond in one tooth and a Jaguar parked in a garage somewhere, in some fancy neighborhood we would never know. God bless computers.

Sompho Thammavonga: Sompho was from a family of landed refugees and in school I had only been dimly aware of him as a figure lingering in the hallways. At the end of term, though, he stunned the whole school (the entire community, in fact) by getting the top mark in the province for algebra. The future had seemed bright for this new Canadian, but I heard that since then, he had become involved in heroin and trafficking, and, judging by his complexion, the worst rumors were true. Wearing a leather jacket and boots, with his hair back-combed off that wrecked face, he was as scary as the early Fonzie must have seemed to the Cunninghams, a hoodlum as likely to beat the shit out of Richie as to give him the time of day.

Jane Sipes: Stupidly I assumed she'd gotten a mannish haircut just for the evening's festivities, but my wife informed me that Jane worked for a lesbian bookstore in Vancouver and lived with a professor of Womyn's Studies. Anyway, she was as credible a Fonzie as any, mostly because her leather jacket and snug jeans looked like part of her wardrobe, not costume pieces.

I watched the people I had grown up with to see if they'd grown up any more, and I tried to relate it to *Happy Days,* and we danced to the theme song and reminisced and remembered favorite episodes, and we got our pictures taken beside the jukebox with our thumbs up ("Ayyy!"), and when it was over, the feeling was that this was a great success, we should get together more often, and whenever we had our next reunion, the theme should again be *Happy Days*.

AS OUR NEXT reunion approached, my wife started calling me "Dad." She was always home before me, trying on one of several fifties-style outfits. I assumed she was trying to get in perfect Joanie character for the big event. This time I could not get away with clothes I picked up for ten dollars at Value Village. We got a photo of Mr. Cunningham and had an outfit custom-made. To my dismay, I found that I no longer needed folded towels for physical effect. My body had started to resemble Tom Bosley's, something I would have thought impossible fifteen years ago. But facing my reflection in the mirror, I came to terms with my lumpy torso. It was a matter of perspective. A man was allowed to put on some pounds as he aged. It was a privilege that emerged alongside responsibilities like managing a hardware store.

I had heard rumors that the decoration for this reunion was going to be something special. Not only had the interior of Arnold's Diner been rebuilt within the venue, but so had other set locations, like the men's washroom, the living room of the Cunningham's home, and Fonzie's apartment above the garage. . . . Our jaws dropped when we stepped inside, and my wife's eyes flashed as if she had never truly been alive before this moment. I suspected all this could not have come to be without a sponsor, and it turned out that Rodney Bislin had been writing the checks. I suppose he had really enjoyed the triumph of his return as Fonzie last time.

For this reunion, no one dressed out of character, and the level of detail increased dramatically. You could have lined up the Joanies and gauged her development from kid sister to young woman, from series beginning to series finale. The first Fonzie to arrive on motorcycle caused quite a stir, but by the third such appearance, it lost its novelty, and the Fonzies looked for other ways to establish authenticity. A competition evolved whereby they took turns striking the jukebox, trying to coax songs from it. Meanwhile, our meals came out of Al's kitchen, carried by waitresses on roller skates. Like the last time I gave a speech, but before I had only made a passing allusion to the "happy days" of our youth; this time I peppered my oration with references to the hardware store, Uncle Leo, old army buddies, the Leopard Lodge, and whether or not we should dip into our vacation fund to build a bomb shelter. I found myself racing to these anecdotes: the other material seemed like filler, and I could only concentrate on it as a bridge to the next Cunningham story.

We had a good time but it was not without tension, as people argued over events from high school: who had given whom a hickey, who had not returned a borrowed sweater, who had spread the rumor that Mary Lou Milligan had a reputation. It had been a long time, after all, and it was important that things were set straight. Nobody argued about the success of the evening, and most of us were already thinking how we might improve our characters for next time.

OUR NEXT REUNION came early, as it was generally agreed that people couldn't wait five more years. My wife's wardrobe had become pretty much dedicated to Joanie sometime in the year before, and she spent much of her time exercising (even had a little plastic surgery) to maintain the physical aspect of her character.

Tensions between us grew. Unlike her, I didn't have to exercise for my body to keep in character. So we spent our time differently. And when we were together, we argued over when she should be home, how late she could stay up. But things were worst in the bedroom.

Bedrooms, I should say; she had started sleeping in the spare. Once I went in to kiss her good night, then, awkwardly, attempted to kindle some romance. I kissed her arm, to her obvious discomfort, and tried to join her on the narrow single bed. She protested further as I clambered atop her, kissing her neck, and she struggled to get out of my grasp. "Dad, what are you doing? Stop it, Dad!"

She shoved me off, and I accepted the look of contempt on her face. I straightened my sweater and left the room, going downstairs to sit alone, with imagined Chachis peering through the window, trying to get a gander. "Wa-wa-wa."

The reunion was moved from the banquet hall to a property that one of our grads had received as an inheritance, so decorations wouldn't have to be dismantled. Inside, didn't look like a converted barn. The booths, the revolving neon *A,* the Cunningham sofa, the television: the setting was complete. Within, old friendships and rivalries had dissolved and re-formed according to character: Richies hung out with Ralphs and Potsies, but only if they had the same lettermen jackets. I passed a table full of Als—six identical Als looking at whomever passed with hangdog expressions and urging them, in concert, to try the fish. They all wore white aprons.

Fonzies did not congregate. They staked sections of turf and tried to expand their influence. Sompho Thammavonga remained the dark Fonzie, and rumors circulated that he had killed a man with a switchblade. On the other end of the spectrum was Brad Forneau, who took on benevolent aspects, talking of the possibility of adopting a child and speaking almost spiritually of the secrets of cool. Rodney Bislin enjoyed more popularity after he activated a pinball machine by striking it with his hip, but that favor evaporated when it was revealed he had used some remote control gimmick. A marathon dance contest was held but after forty-eight hours, three Fonzies could still dance the flamenco with Mrs. Cunningham, and someone suggested they settle it once and for all by jumping over barrels on motorbikes. We opened doors so the contestants could have a decent run at it; although Brad managed to clear the barrels (perhaps using his long-ago pilot training to his advantage), Sompho not only landed the jump but also guided his bike into a crash, deliberately sliding across the floor and taking out Arnold's fried chicken stand. This would have extinguished all challenges to his authenticity had it not also left him slightly brain-damaged.

OUR NEXT REUNION was not so much a reunion; we all had lingered at the site and made contributions, building on our own living rooms, our own restaurants, or our own apartments above the garage.

Speeches were no longer necessary. Memories drifted by us and sometimes swept us into their current, as Richies double-dated or guarded the hardware store, as Fonzies cheated on a test or built a disastrous pigeon coop, as I worked on my card-playing skills in anticipation of the dark day when I would need to call upon them. I sometimes recognized a fragment of something that was going on and contributed my wisdom, my common sense, my fatherliness. I would not let my son be intimidated by hoodlums. I would not set him up on dates to advance my business dealings. Or I would at first, but later see the error in it and resolve never to do so again. I sat on the couch turning over cards, the faces of the queens all Joanie's.

Joanie of spades. Joanie of hearts. I turned over the king of hearts, and his face was not mine.

At some point she stopped resisting her longtime suitor, Chachi. He and she cooed over each other openly, in front of me. At least he had the decency to ask my permission to date her. I gave my consent, and they departed for Inspiration Point, where further resistance was bound to collapse, and my little girl would become a woman.

Why fight the inevitable? You get older, grow into other roles. At least nobody could take away memories of happy days, Monday, Tuesday, happy days, which would surely come again, and again, as surely as an LP would count them off the next time it played on the jukebox.

THE FISHIE

Philip Raines and Harvey Welles

. . .

CATCHIE HEARS FIRST.

" 'Mam! Noisy in the ground!"

Spitmam scoops away sleep and, releasing Catchie from her bed grasp, listens for the disturbance beyond the cottage.

"Hear? Under rock, 'Mam! Under and deep, calling to the folk!"

"You say, you say."

In a grumbly witter, Spitmam swings on her longcoat and unlodges the door. The night's cold as groundstone, but Spitmam bends stiff knees to lay an ear to one of the pathway flags.

"You're hearing it," she tells the girl quietly. "That thumping's surely under. And a grand thing's there!"

They roust their neighbors, going from cottage to cottage, but the folk are already out of sleep. By now, everyone hears the thuds, like a bairn discovering a drum, so they gather shovels, rippers, and picks and creep through night. Paddo's the best ears, and the three thin dozen villagers follow him across Cullin's grazing plank, jumping through a small breach in the surrounding dyke, and over the hellafield that pulls from the last cottage up to the lap of the high Cags two miles distant. Paddo leads them in an arc that curves wide round the village till the earth's banging is so loud that the huge flat stones under their feet are waking.

By a ground wave rising dry from boggy reeds, Paddo pricks a spot and like Spitmam before him, makes his sounding by listening against the scrag. "Crack here and right!" he shouts, so the men heft the picks and cut through the peat round the hella, and the women take the rippers and tear the cut apart, and the bairns sweep the tear with shovels and soon a dark hole's cleared. Spitmam has her iron collie, its cup restraining a small fire that's bright enough to light their work, though folk are proper about the fire and put good lengths between it and their fears.

After a spell, they gouge a ten-foot-wide ditch and are down through the flinty topsoil to sweet humus. Five, seven, nine feet again, till Aggie's ripper nicks a different layer. "Walloo!" she bellows for the joy of the strike when a bluster from below slaps the tool off her. A second smack and she's rucking her nesting dress and scrabbling up the sides.

"A grand fart!" Paddo clucks.

"Grand?" Aggie says when she's been pulled from the hole. "Find us a monster there!"

So before the folk dig any farther, Paddo crawls the length of the ground's pounding with ear down and marks out a square with one of his precise devices and amazes the folk with the scheme. "Paddo?" Pollett cries. "That's to be a hole letting out the world!" But they dig and scrape ten-foot trenches on the three sides of Paddo's square, down five, seven, nine feet, and slowly that deepest layer agrees to a shape.

"There's wings?"

"No, wings don't have scales."

"Never wings—there's tail!"

And it is, the grandest tail any of them has ever seen, beating the ground beneath it. Only Spitmam knows the real name, calling it *fin*. "So's a *fishie*?" Old Solly asks.

"Oh, I'm too tired for naming every new thing to come out of the ground. I'm back for my bed. Girl?"

"Along before you're through sleep!" Catchie calls to her granny, but Spitmam snorts—her girl's never going back till the last of it—so she covers the collie, slocking the flame now that the sky's grudging enough light for digging, and lurches old back to Cullin's dyke.

Digging passes to quarrying. Derry and his sister, Caff, run back to Speg the tinker's cottage and return with two kuddies filled of his chisels and the mallets the bairns use for smashing birds' eggs in the cliff nests. Folk line the trenches and scrub the tail, but as the soil falls away, it flexes and chafes weakly at the edges of the trench walls. Across dawn, New Solly and Speg use straw tethers to tie down the tail so that it doesn't thrash. Quicker now with the tethers, hellas on top of the fishie are pried out and roughed aside, and the soil covering the creature's shoveled out. The fishie shivers the rest off its back like an itchy sheep.

Sun over the tallest Cag: only that late do the folk consider what's unearthed.

"There's no fishie!"

"Spitmam says those, *fins*. So—fishie."

"Name's a monster anyway."

The beastie's half under rock and dirt still, but the other half's all odd shape. On its side, there's a white belly, grooved the length of four fat dozen feet from tip to tethered tail. Like a grand muscle of the earth exposed, the body makes a single thrust toward the massy tail, one purpose from which all else is stripped. The head's the tail broken suddenly, smooth, popped with titch eyes and split for a sneer.

"No fishie, tell me now. Watch mouth there, that's fitted for five folk."

"Ten!"

"We keep it half in rock sure, least till the upstander's called down. Kery?"

"Da?"

"Go the pend and tell the fishie to Hammle."

And so. Folk talk big for the fishie's bigness, but as they drift back from the hole along the side trenches, they see the warming Cags, and the whole sky and the wide water beyond the cliffs, and the fishie's just another big thing in the world. The tail stops yoking the tethers and the beastie lays still, its wounds bleeding a fine sand into the ditches. There's speculation about its stone skin—being so queer a granite—but talk drabs, and in ones and twos they scoot away to catch the lost morning chores.

Only three bairns and Catchie stay. One says, "I bet."

"Bet what, Derry?" Rabbie says.

"Bet you—cob or cunt?"

"Derry!" Caff squeals at Derry's swagger, but takes up his game. "Cob, since beastie beetled that ground like you, Derry, bawling for mam during a storm!"

"There's cunt," Derry declares. "Fishie's got the sense of the lass for being born so far underground. Rabbie?"

"Oh—cob."

"Catchie?"

Can't it be something else? Catchie thinks, but before she can make her bet, the bairns are disturbed by Hammle's distant hollering—"Off there sharp, piggots!"—and they scamper sulky off the fishie's huge back.

When there's a new beastie, villagers go first to Spitmam for a name and second to Hammle for tending. The upstander—the rude way of calling Hammle's refusal to live or work with the other folk—keeps the pend, where all queer things found are taken. There's a grim streak in Hammle, and the bairns know him for being hollered over smashing birds' eggs. Tall and sizzled with beard, they eye him as warily as the water foaming the cliff rocks.

"Your back's up for carrying a fishie to the pend?" Derry challenges him.

"Maybe not, but it's up to swamping bairns."

"Just saying, upstander," Derry coos, then screeches up the far side of the beastie with Caff.

Hammle scratches the fishie's belly and considers the sand seeping from the monster's cuts. "Poor thing," Hammle says sadly and for some reason looks only to Catchie. "Now why they always bring me the ones for dying?"

Catchie says nothing. Who'd weep just for a fishie?

FOR THE AFTERNOON, she and Spitmam sit on their cottage's drying green with pebbles of different sizes laid out on the flags and the sun another in hot flight. Catchie's full up with the new beastie. Spitmam endures the spill of questions, lets them splatter this way and that, for Catchie's always caught by the novelty of the new things that turn up. For as long as she has been able to count days forward, Catchie's been Spitmam's other hands, and in all such time, she's never lost the thrill of the world first opened.

" 'Mam, the fishie's from the water."

"*Of* the water, girl, this one's never from."

"But if the fishie's *of* the water, best we put it *in* the water. Speg could knit hardy tethers and the men'd pull and we'd bring beastie to the—the grand water—"

"Not *grand water*. How often you told? Called *sea*."

"*Sea* water and—"

A stinging grip on Catchie's wrist. "Girl, break your fancies." Spitmam inspects the last speckled pebble of the batch Catchie'd rooted by Aggie's herb fringe. She warms the pebble between palms, breathing slow on it like steam on a bitter day, and pops it in her mouth. There between her cheeks, the pebble rolls till Spitmam's sure; then she picks it out, whispering a secret word over the stone before placing it hush with the other spat rocks on the grass.

"Sea won't take this fishie," she lectures Catchie. "There's a *stone* fishie, not a water one. You know water's nasty about rock."

Catchie rubs her wrist and ponders this with a look that strays beyond the flies hovering over the garth wall, onto the straggle of blasted cottages making the old village edge, on again across the hellafield prickly with bell, up to the Cags that hide the other side of their island. A world of rock—or if not rock, *from* rock, like soil and pebble, or if not from rock, *allowed by* rock, like sheep and kale and violets.

"What's earth making such daft things for?" she asks.

There's an answer to that, Catchie knows from the way Spitmam smiles so far and no farther with tight lips, as if afraid some might peek at secrets through her mouth. Spitmam knows everything, being the villager who's here longest. With so much ground for tilling and nests for culling, folk have too little day to recall how the village got to be so small and recall further how it got to be so big in the first place. But Spitmam's dug a space for time and squirreled away the memories folk have left lying, as if waiting out a long winter with her knowledge. And Catchie's seen Spitmam, looking for a sign that such a winter's spent, watching the skies for a private sigh.

Catchie knows better than to press her granny, and anyway, the pebbles on the grass are rumbling and starting to fall about. There's a soft break, a rocky froth, and one by one the pebbles shell off, split with help from Spitmam and Catchie. Soon a brood of beasties are lying in their slag.

"Names," Spitmam orders, pointing.

"Field mice."

"That one?"

"Snake."

"Kind of snake, girl?"

"Tarsnake, 'Mam."

"There?"

"Grasshopper. Heath moth. Horsefly."

"Last one?"

"Never know, 'Mam."

"There's *vole,* girl. Tiny one, sure, but proper size wouldn't fit out of my mouth. All's true earth creatures, remember this, and not like that fishie over by the cliffs. These'll survive if water or wind not hack them."

Rough, Spitmam strokes Catchie's head as if untangling. "Remember, names are important. Names fence the world, catch the slips, ward the fears. Don't make little with the names—without them, everything's muck and rubble." Spitmam lets her head go like a dropped stone. "Now spare me talk of a nameless fishie."

Days to come, there's no talk of the fishie by anyone in the village. Where the talk comes from is the dailies—folk harrowing rocks before planting tatties or hunting birds along the cliffs and culling the eggs—that, and the dirty sky. Sky matters most. Always ready for new things, Catchie sees the change in the air first, a dark haze worrying the horizon. Spitmam insists on being told every coming wrinkle in the sky, so Catchie tells her granny.

"There's two storms soon," she says slowly, which sends everyone off on talk, since storms are the worst that can happen.

"I remember the last wind," Aggie tells Catchie when Spitmam's examining her young Kery for stomach cramps. "Remember it ripping Kellick's cottage? Poor man thought he was sure downcellar, but wind ripped his will as well. He was just falling down after that. Gravel within the week. Now there's a bad season."

"The wind's always a bad one," Spitmam says, just that and nothing more, for she'll name the wind, but she won't talk about it. Wind's a private matter for her, Catchie's seen, very deep.

"True, all winds come from trouble, but seems the winds are strutting more with every new storm. Seems they're getting *particular* each season."

"Wouldn't say about that. Now, Kery, don't look while I'm doing. Not having you bawl out my cottage."

"Oh, Granny, wouldn't do that."

"You say. Girl, find me a sly ripper."

Inside the cottage, Spitmam keeps all her healing work in fesgars and kettles hanging by crooks. A thick storing, with secret cubbies behind the corked jars that even Catchie's never permitted to root. Catchie knows the sly tools for the careful tasks are by the tattie bucket, so she moves the collie aside carefully, knowing the fire's locked sure but fearful of anything to do with fire, and there finds a ripper.

With a hand firm to Kery's chin to make sure the head wouldn't dally, Spitmam takes the ripper and quickly slices hard and down the girl's chest. "Tickles," Kery says, but Aggie shushes her and watches Spitmam peel away crumble to get into the chest cavity.

"Reach that out," Spitmam orders. Catchie grips three stone birds out of Kery's chest and lays them on the ground, where they try to stand but fall over. Swift, Spitmam resets Kery's chest, bricking it with strong mud from a side-bucket and harshing the surface with sand.

"No wailing—there's good, Kery."

"Where's to see, Granny? Those the birds?"

"There's *kitties,* Kery, except that one, but a starling."

"You have all the names," Kery says, dumbed by Spitmam's knowledge, and bounds off the stool and out of the cottage.

"Her da was the same," Aggie says after her. "That man grew out birds and fishies and useless things, till that tree grew right out his skull. Didn't have the will of it anymore." With her last sigh, Aggie looks for the broken cottages round the village edge and adds, "But then which folk got the will of it now?"

"Folks keep to the names—there's the backbone."

"Well, so, Spitmam."

After they're away, Spitmam stays at the door, regarding the sky while Catchie wraps the chickies in a hankie and sits them in a kuddie. "I'll take these to Hammle."

"You don't linger, girl. First storm's across tonight."

"Along before dark."

"Promised."

The short's across the hellafield, but Catchie decides on the wayward and follows the village path till she comes to the cliff edge. Here, the path's picky down to the beach, but Catchie stays on the edge, tracing it round toward the grand fishie site. There's angry things in the air—*shags* and *terns,* Spitmam says, but with all their screaming at Catchie, they're only birds and she lobs a few rocks to make more view of the sea.

Sea. There's another Spitmam word. Most folk would just give it the name and avoid thinking or talking about it. Best not regard water, they'd say. Water'll snatch at the folk who stray too close, or it'll worry at the earth, eating foundations, making bog and sucking away their island. Water kills. Air hates. Fire would do both, and worse, if they allowed it sparking outside their collies.

This close to the edge, Catchie sees the air's too black for bravado, so she gathers the kuddie and skeddaddles in a straight cut to where the fishie's lying.

Hammle hails her when she's close. "Come to scat the beastie now, Catchie?"

Catchie flushes with the accusation, bridling at its twisty tone. " 'Mam took stone birds in Kery."

"Why they're not taken the pend?"

"Says take them to Hammle direct. There's you here, not the pend."

"Sure, right so."

Hammle jumps off the fishie's back and swaps his heavy clipper for her kuddie. Brusquely, he throws open the hanky and pokes the sick birds.

"Kitties and starling," Catchie tells.

"Didn't ask your naming," Hammle sharpens, but softens it with a smile. "Name's not the matter."

While Hammle probes the birds, Catchie leans over the edge and considers the fishie. Most body's been brought out now, strapped over by dozens of tethers and bridged by rafters laid across the top by the upstander. Even held down so, the beastie still shudders with force Catchie's only witnessed in sea or storm. On the skin, the fishie's already molting, its peels like a tattie thinned for the pot. Catchie comes closer, then close enough to touch the beastie's surface, haired all over by budding gravel flowers with odd heads. *Tulips,* Spitmam instructed her once.

"Beastie's lost the will," Catchie speaks to Hammle.

"*Body's* lost the will," Hammle corrects her. "Feel that."

Pushing her hand through the flowers, Catchie grips the skin. There, faint in the caverns and nests of the beastie, the bare rushing of air deep down, and there again, a song, trapped, like something swallowed badly.

"There's tune in the—" Catchie flicks the name "—*lungs.*"

Carefully, Hammle replaces the birds' shroud in the kuddie. "Those lungs are hung with this massy body. Now in the water— in the proper element—that body's easy. Except that this is a *stone* fishie, and it has no element. Those lungs were never for anything but cracking, poor beastie. And still, there's song in it. Now there's mystery."

"What's *mystery*?"

"There's spirit."

"What's *spirit*?"

"There's the world's secrets."

"Secrets? Oh, things without names," Catchie says, meaning all that's never important, as Spitmam would have expected her.

Hammle wipes his poking hand and takes the clipper away from Catchie. "Well, so some say."

" 'Mam says."

"So Spitmam says."

Catchie picks up the empty kuddie and Hammle climbs onto the rafters to clip the flowers on the fishie. Spitmam'll be wanting her to prepare the cottage for the storm. Anyway, beastie's failing, she can't see the sense of Hammle's work. Yet Catchie loiters.

"And?" Hammle shouts down.

"And just."

"And just saying?"

"Just saying," Catchie starts, and started, carries through, "there's cob or cunt?"

A chafing's expected, but Catchie's surprised when he laughs. "Cunt, piggot!"

"Well, poor lass."

"So."

"Mind storm, upstander."

"Minding, thanks."

With a wave, Catchie gives the fishie a last regard and says alone—"What's mystery?"—but the air's fouling with storm so she sprints the short back to the cottage.

DURING STORM IS WORST.

Before, there's Spitmam sealing the door with muddy tar. She's peculiar quiet, figuring the cutstone of the storm's break with a squint as if she'd been hallooed from the sky. Catchie's seen her granny peer storms before, as if there'd be a question of setting the kettle and borrowing a spare chair from New Solly next door for visitors.

After chewing a whole weed, Spitmam finally mumbles alone, "There's not it, not this time."

"What's it?" Catchie asks, but Spitmam smiles just so and no further, so the girl bites down and bands sure their cottage jars and fesgars with straw wire.

There's no slope to the storm. Soon after Spitmam's lodged the door, she's half across when the forewind razors the wall boulders sudden, and she's all across when the storm starts to beetle the door and window. Sure in their cubby, Spitmam holds Catchie like a first bairn. They cower in cave dark, not trusting the collie's fire for light. It's the only time Catchie sees Spitmam scratchy with the ordinary fears of the rest of them, though she glares with the anger of one ashamed of ordinary weaknesses.

Wind has its own screaming, pure intent, but in the storm, it's not just wind. Catchie listens. Shrilling across the flagged roof, tongues through the gaps around the window, but between the shudders, there's the sound of the brutes of the air. Birds shrieking, wauling, hooting, every bird that Catchie imagines, birds with wings, birds in fur, birds finned, birds every-shaped. And her own moan so pale in Spitmam's embrace.

"Name the things you hear." Spitmam grasps her in hard comfort. "Hold yourself with names, girl!"

From the twist of noise, Catchie untangles the bird sounds. "G-gulls. Kitties."

"The others."

"Bab-baboons, 'Mam. Tiger."

"And all, girl."

Shaking, Spitmam hugs Catchie solid, and she listens over the storm, for that low growl astride the other wind creatures. Words. Catchie hears words.

" 'Mam—'Mam, there's folk!"

"Easy now. Only the wind folk."

"What do they want?" Catchie's nearly screaming now, for she can hear a wind woman fly widdershins around the cottage, faster and faster so that she seems to move forward through a new clock, and the woman cursing her for being of the slow world, and laughing at her twig bones and brittle heart and hard fears.

But Spitmam smiles like so and no further, turning Catchie's head to her shoulder. She rocks her in the arm's memory of tenderness, till the storm's spent.

AFTER STORM IS BEST EVER.

Breaking open the cottages, everyone steps slow onto the scoured ground and spies around, but all are counted sure—the storm's not taken any this time. Folk reset windows, and brush the pathway, spoilt by fallen dykes. There's speculation about scratches on the door frames, which beastie has these claws, and they bring their questions to Spitmam, but she shrugs and closes her door against them. Bairns chase the last of the birds loosed from the storm, curling and fluttering helplessly before the harder world shreds the whirls of shape.

Then when the villagers trust the sky and press back the weight of their sighs, they fill kuddies with meat and mallets and go the path, dancing around the broken stones and picking down the cliff's edge till they come to the smooth sand. Sitting on tufts of beach rush, families help one another with their heavy boots, bound sure with braided straw. Caff and Kery squeal as their mams smear rock cake on the shoes, Derry teases the sky with stones and insults, Pollett organizes the mallets on large flaskies spread on the sand. Last, booted folk fan along the beach rim, till Speg starts with a crack of his mallet to a boulder, and in answer the villagers yell and whistle and march toward the water.

The beach's spattered with things wrong-footed by the storm. Men and women close into the water—though never forget water's cunning hatred—and sing as they stomp out the jelly bodies of fishies with their boots. Smaller fishies have been hurled back of the beach, so the bairns beetle the limbs of *cats* and *turtles* and *kestrels*—but no one conjures with names, they're just fishies.

And with each cull, Speg leads their shout—"There's *rock*! Fuck back, water and wind, for we're *rock* and rock's longer than you!"

Catchie crushes *cobra,* regards the beach, runs over and crushes *robin*. "Rock's longer!" she shouts, but she can't join the others, she's thinking of so many new things. There's another world in the water out there, a place under the sea where the cobra springs at the robin, and the robin soars over the sycamore, and the sycamore shelters the bear, and the bear scoops the water for the salmon.

That sets her thinking of the grand fishie, and of the music in its lungs, but there's another sparkle ahead of her. Catchie wipes the hard-water jelly from her boot, but Caff calls first, "Catchie!"

Caff's strayed close to the water, where the bigger fishies are. "There's what, Caff?" Catchie shouts, but Caff just calls her again, more fearful this time. "Caff, you breached?"

Caff points down at a fishie—a sure beastie, maybe five feet long. Its limbs are pudding, but still pulling toward the water's edge in painful lunges, leaving behind skin in sticky tracks. The belly's coated with sand and rushes snag in its hair, but Catchie can still see through the smoky jelly. A mackerel inside the fishie's body blinks back at her.

Caff whispers, "There's fishie?"

"Must be fishie." Catchie sees how the tide's trying to meet the fishie partway. "Water wants it back."

"But Catchie, it's *folk*."

"N-not folk, Caff—only we're folk."

"But Catchie, she's hair like 'Mam and long fingers like Old Solly and she hurts like the time I stubbed my knee! There must be a name to her."

Can the fishie hear? It tries to speak, drooling in the air, but Catchie thinks that it only talks underwater. Poor fishie. Poor *woman*. All she can say to the two girls is the will of surviving, and something else asked, but not asked with words and names.

Some *mystery*.

"Maybe wants a name, Catchie."

Everything wants a name. So Catchie reels through all Spitmam's taught names, but none satisfy the fishie, and her yearning twists further into Catchie. What other names can she want than the ones that are? But before she can say further, Speg's shouting at them—"Get away from the beastie!"—and Catchie and Caff stand back as New Solly and Geddy run toward them, mallets banging against their legs.

"Daft, you've got no thinking what water will do!" Geddy, Caff's mam, chides with a bop to the side of Caff's head. Catchie retreats. She hopes to get a last look at the fishie, catch again her question, but the men have dyked her with their bodies, the trample of boots and mallet swings, and soon Catchie cannot regard the least, not with all these tears and heavy sobs cracking the floor in her heart like trapped songs.

"MORE BEASTIES FOR the pend, Catchie?"

"No, upstander—just come."

"Bringing what?"

"Bring a question."

"Well then?"

"What's *mystery*?"

Hammle tucks his beard and regards Catchie sharp, then passes a clipper to Catchie. "Help with the fishie then."

The storm's cut the fishie at a hundred points, scores to gashes, and the wounds release all queer things. Bushes, already heaving fruit, sprout across the top of the fishie in a hairy line, while tatties are popping just from the skin. The tulips begin to color across, yellow dissolving red, and a fuzz of sundew and poppies scum the beastie's gut. Like Aggie's old husband, a tree sticks stump out of its skull, and for the itch, the fishie tauts the tethers and rubs against the ditch's edge. Its crackling lies in sheaths underneath.

Hammle's started along the tail, weeding the wounds, mowing the skin. He starts again with Catchie beside him at a clump of bracken. They work silent, and Catchie thinks, maybe she should say it, but the upstander has his pace and speaks when it's time. "What's *mystery,* you say?"

"So, upstander."

"You part of the cull this morning?"

Catchie, strangely ashamed, doesn't say, but there's no need to, for nearly all folk cull, and there's no need to say further about Hammle's distaste for it.

"And there's something you regarded?"

"Upstander, there's a fishie, shape of a woman. Like folk."

"And?"

"Rock has folk, wind has folk. Wind has birds, water has birds. Water has fishies, rock has fishies. Why, upstander?"

Hammle points first across the hellafield. "There's?"

"Hellas. Rock."

"Rock, so." He points the other way, the cliffs. "There's?"

"Sea. Water."

He points up.

"Wind." Catchie regards the new dark boundary moving for the island. "Storm."

"In Spitmam's collie. There's?"

"Fire."

On four fingers, Hammle calls them. "Rock. Wet. Air. Fire. There's all, and all's of them. The elements, bitter with one another, fighting to destroy every other. But not always—never always."

"Time when sea not slap folk?" Catchie shuds her eyes away from the sky's face. "Time when storm not smash folk?"

"So, Catchie. That time before, the elements were mix, making a *proper* set of birds and fishies and folk together. But then the elements came apart, then came to blows. Now wind has its own birds, own fishies, folk even. And so water."

Hammle nips the whale's skin, then tufts at his beard. A straggle snips away, and he rolls it to a gritty crumble that falls to dirt. "And so rock," he says.

"Fire, too?" Catchie asks.

"So there's said, but no one's cracked a collie to find its world."

"And this is the way of it?"

"So, till one element crushes all—but there won't happen."

"Why? Rock's long!"

"Rock's long, but wind's faster. Wind's whip, but water flexes. Water's shifty, but fire sparks the world. Fire's light, but rock's what's lit. And so. Every needs each."

Catchie yanks a dandelion from the fishie, spilling its cup into a hundred drifters. "So what held all together once?"

"Many's said."

"What's *your* say, upstander?"

"There's the mystery you're asking." Hammle pats a cleared plank of the fishie's skin. "Mystery's in the world's glue, sticking the world to our hearts. Once upon, it bound all with all. Now mystery's so small—a wick in a beastie's eye, a gleam along the shore. No fashioning to it left. Our grand fishie has it, but not much longer. Regard the flowers, the trees—five days, and there's never any fishie left. So. So there's the way for all, sure."

Catchie, remembers the stone birds in Kery's chest, and dimmer, how Aggie's husband fell apart with the tree. It's true—none keep their cast.

Catchie considers this full. She hooks the clipper on a fork in the bush, shimmies down the side of the beastie and smacks on the crackling floor. Bending under the roof of pulled tethers, Catchie scrambles the ditch round to the fishie's head, till it's immersed her, curving out and over the sky like the cliffs rising from the beach. Inside that cavern, she listens for the rustle of weeds, and listens again, and hears titchies, hares and flies stirring, and farther still, the creature's songs.

She regards the fishie's tiny eyes, strong in its pain and confusion, but there's something other, too, the same thing Catchie pitted from the water woman's eyes. Some mystery, closely held, but passing out, through Catchie, forward into the world, drawing out of her an urging sharper than Catchie's ever felt.

Hammle's followed, so Catchie asks, "Why do you help the beastie?"

"There's poor beastie."

"Just so?"

"Only so."

She lays a hand along its lip—poor beastie—and regards the coming storm, knowing this should destroy what's left of its will.

"I'll save you, beastie"—she speaks, but alone, and carries the words against her as she and the upstander resume clipping its coat.

WHEN TWO STORMS DALLY, folk dispute which is bairn, which is fierce—but this time, there's sure that the second storm will be the cracker. Never's the air matted so thick, as massy as rock now. The storm shadow's as long as the Cags and some consider that Cags and storm are teeth on a grand jaw, and that the poor villagers are sure to be pulped now.

So folk sit on their doorstones, staring at the grey above and the black to come. There's no talk, only families huddling outside for the last time, till one by one they wave to their neighbors and go into their cottages. Catchie hears the sound of bricking all down the pathway.

She whispers for the fishie, but as the breezes snap at her knees, Catchie calls out now, " 'Mam, let's be sheltering."

Spitmam doesn't reply in her staring down the sky. The storm's been her study for hours, ears and eyes pressed to the wind. Catchie wonders if she's become full rock now, forever still, when sudden Spitmam leans ahead, opens her mouth just wide and no further, then opens a little more and no further, then further and stop, then all the way, belting as well, "She's there! Girl, *she's hither!*"

"Where's hither, 'Mam?"

"*There, there!*" Spitmam grabs at the sky, but Catchie regards only bubbling cloud and birds swarming front, as if they're yoking the storm forward. "There! Abreast the storm, oh, she's the dare, coming for me so brazen! Come away, *sister*!" Spitmam shouts up. "Come and find what's here for you!

" 'Mam, the shelter! It's too bad."

"Never!" Spitmam growls with a bit of storm in her eyes. "There's she coming and I'm to meet her."

"Who, 'Mam? Who's there?"

"My sister. You not see?"

Before Catchie says not, Spitmam has her arm and pulls her into the cottage. Brief, Catchie thinks Spitmam's turned for shelter at last, but she leaves the door wide for the little gusts to spin across the floor and rip away all Catchie's battening in the cubbies. Spitmam reaches farthest into a cubby Catchie's been forbidden, and from far, she brings out first a water jar, second a fire vessel.

"Touch the fire vessel, girl." Catchie does, fearful till her thumb rests on the raindrop-cast ceramic. The surface is warm, shakes like broken sleep, and the vessel rolls over with the anger of what's in.

"Now touch the jar."

Catchie considers the jar. Heavy glass, tidy with black straw, capped and sealed with tar. Inside, water sloshes restlessly. When Catchie touches the glass, the water rears at her finger, leaving a small beastie banging the side. There's such hatred in its eyes that Catchie backs away.

" 'Mam, the water, there's—"

"So."

"There's you!"

"Sister."

"So the vessel?"

"So. My fire sister."

Catchie brings her legs together in fortress and considers this fishie Spitmam as she curses them soundlessly. " 'Mam, how's this?"

"Oh, there's a long story, not to be said now. Long before the village, I fished the shores for my water sister, making traps and waiting patient. Another time, I took evenings with the collie, coaxing my other out of the fire world with tinder."

"So there's world in the collie?" Catchie speaks.

"There's all the cast of wind, water, and rock there, but the collie's their dyke. My sister's their only escape, and the fire vessel, her cage."

"Your other sister, 'Mam," Catchie says, catching at last. "There's her in the storm."

"The last."

"Coming for you?"

"All come for what I have."

" 'Mam?"

"Come after the names," and saying, Spitmam opens her mouth, just so, and then much further, further than Catchie's ever regarded, and drags Catchie close so she can stare down the throat. Deep in, behind the tongue, fizzing with glow, there's a white gem, set in the mouth like the throne of all Spitmam's speech.

SPITMAM SHUTS AGAIN. "You regard?"

"There's *precious,* 'Mam."

"There's the most precious. There's all the names that ever been."

"Where did they come?"

"They come from before. When the world split, and the land was cut for islands by water and storm, and *whole* folk were split into water and rock and fire and wind folk, names were about to slip the cracks and out of the world—and where would I have been? This world without names—no *where* for me to be. So I hid the names in my mouth and came to the island. Slow, I learnt the names—there's such use in them to fashion things. The village comes from the names, girl. Every one of you folk, grown from my spit and word of mouth."

Catchie considers. Aggie, Caff, Kery—all made by the 'Mam.

"Names, 'Mam? Where's their force?"

"And what have I always instructed? What's always said about names?"

"They cast."

"There's so. They cast, they strap. The proper and fit name will retrieve any from the world's slush. Now consider with the three sisters and me."

Catchie speaks slowly, conceiving the force of names for the first time. "If names cast, they can make whole. If they make whole, they can bring all sisters together. Can make anything whole."

"Said well, girl. I want to be whole. I'm ill with this quarter world and folk nagging me for names for every bastard thing they step on. Now serve your purpose and gather the fire vessel and I'll hold the water jar and we'll catch the willful sister."

So ordered, Catchie's released from Spitmam's grip and takes the vessel from the floor by the strap. Spitmam nabs the collie, fixes it for a low light, and brings the water jar, dogging Catchie out the door and into the storm's work.

Dust's spiking the air. The storm regards them from above.

"Hold the collie and wait by." Spitmam purrs. "Ah, there's she."

Now Catchie can distinguish a grand face puffing out of the clouds, the cast of Spitmam. Like a woman surfacing from the stars with the streamers of another world caught in her hair.

"Oh, 'Mam," Catchie moans. "There's too rash. How will you snag her?"

Spitmam smiles. "Sister wants the names. Nothing more needed than just open my mouth and tempt her in. For I'll gobble you, storm!"

With a last cry of *Sister!* Spitmam spreads her mouth to the sky, letting birds and wind and her sister consider the pure radiance of the names, and the wind Spitmam curls herself into a ready bolt.

There's a quick moment and it dares Catchie. " 'Mam?"

Spitmam turns to Catchie, gaping.

" *'Mam?*"

She tilts toward the girl, anxious to face again her sister, but when Spitmam bends down, and down again, Catchie's hand pips out and rams her mouth. Spitmam snarls, but Catchie wrenches down the jaw to clear, the moment's all she needs, and her fingers snatch the gem.

Spitmam coughs out Catchie's hand and a curse—*"Break you, girl, fuck you to powder!"*—but Catchie's away, fingers lashed to the gem in one and the other hand to the collie. She's between the canted cottages, frogging Cullin's dyke and over the hellafield, leaping stone to stone, while behind, a wild Spitmam chases with jar and vessel rolled under her arms and following all, a wilder sister spouting crows and coiling gale like a whip.

Breathless, finally by the edge of the fishie, Catchie shouts. "Upstander! Come save the beastie!"

"Catchie?" Hammle peeps out from a tented cocoon in the trench. "Your senses bashed by the storm?"

Catchie holds out her prize hand. "Got the names, upstander! For casting the fishie!"

Hammle unsnarls from the tent tethers and climbs through. "Names? Only Spitmam has."

"Stolen away!" Spitmam behind them, rages. "Now return or I'll make your bones for shit."

"So, Spitmam," Hammle says quiet.

"Hammle, this is clear of you."

"Sisters, too, I regard."

Catchie sidles to the upstander's side, away from her granny's threats. "Upstander, you know the sisters?"

"Know them well," Hammle tells Catchie, considering Spitmam queerly. "For me and Spitmam are from ago. You not hear? I was Spitmam's first. I was her first Catchie."

"But you fled me for the beasties and your pend, Hammle. After my making and my tending and my learning."

"Beasties need keeping, Spitmam."

"There's not important. Only names fill."

"Witch!" Hammle growls. "Names are what split the world. Folk cutting the world up for names, and cutting up the cuts for more names, and cutting and cutting till there's no mix, no mystery, only the elements and the hunger for names."

"No world without names speaking first for them—you know and you see everyday with your nameless beasties falling to rubbish."

"Names summon the world only to cut it up again."

"And what else holds the world?"

"The mystery of it, Spitmam."

"And never name the world? Huddle in your hole then, and leave out my girl."

With arms still around the jar and vessel, and the jar banging with the water sister's fury and the fire vessel quaking with expectation, Spitmam reaches for Catchie. Catchie steps back, but the step's ditch and she falls onto a net of tethers, and is about to scream when the wind sister's across them.

Greeted, sister—booms the voice of the cloud face above them. *So kind to arrange this union*—and one twister like a long finger grazes over them. Spitmam hollers, brushed over, dropping the jar to the hella. The glass clicks, not cracks, but the water sister pesters it with teeth. And the jar explodes.

Sister!—the water sister cries in a drowned voice, rising from the jar's pool in a claw that rakes Spitmam's face. *So much rock, so much wind—why not so much water?* and saying, she has a special shriek that summons the underground streams, the bog, the sea.

There's a still moment, tense like a drop before dropping, before the ground rumbles and geysers shred the hellafield. Hellas flip up, water shoots up in dozens of jets.

Sweet sister—the wind sister caws in the chorus of birds—*so much water sure, but my storm sucks your seas dry.* So twisters noose the water jets, grapple like snakes, and in a coil that unwinds across the land, the grandest ever whirl of water and wind and loose rock takes shape.

When the elements are so bare, Catchie knows there's the end of things, but she's firmed to her purpose. The wind sprays her with mud, so she's slow out of the tethers. Once free, Catchie lets the collie sag in her hand, flame sighing against its iron gate. What else? she thinks, but it's easy, and before the thought's words, she throws the collie, harder than the wind against the side of the beastie, and cries out.

"You fishie!"

A moment, there's only a dingy flame, a hot smudge. Then a smolder of grass on the back of the beastie, a worm of smoke. Quick, the fire rises. The rushes glow bright, sparking out seeds, flaring branches like saplings, throwing out brands like vines, and the hillside of the fishie sheets with a flame jungle. Sizzle and flick, the tethers snap and the fishie twists its back, and howls.

"Away!" the upstander cries, lifting Catchie with him, but there's only there, between the burning beastie and the sisters' whirlpool. Out of the calamity, Catchie regards the cast of the fishie, but there's two casts: the stone fishie and another flowing into it, a fishie of fire, stripping all the dross from its sister's body.

"There's two fishies!" she yells, shucking the upstander's hand from her shoulder, but there's only one fishie, as it flaps in the hole, a burning rock. A roar above her makes Catchie turn, and there in the mad brew of storm, there's another fishie, cast by wind and beating its grand tail.

"There's third fishie!" she cries, when the beastie leaps from the cloud, unknotting from the stormy Spitmam's hair, and dives toward them. The wind fishie falls for its sisters, a loud *whoosh* that drives Hammle, Spitmam, and Catchie backward with smoky draughts.

Where's last fishie? Catchie thinks alone, but she's there, a pucker in the bog lapping her feet that throws back like a new spring and kicks itself free from the ground with a switch of tail, an arc of flowing cast that gushes across her sisters.

And with the last join, there's a break in time, and rock and water and wind and fire stop in struggle. Light curdles. Faster than the thought, a spasm passes into the elements, through Catchie, out of the elements, and across the world.

" 'Mam! Upstander!" Catchie shouts, for the ground's gone, and her arms don't move in air, and the sound of her shouting's staggered into gibber. World waits. In this new gloom, the fishie, whole and proper, beats its tail and swims in a circle. World waits. There's something left. The gem reminds by biting into Catchie's hand.

The gem. Just so.

Like the collie before, Catchie throws the names toward the fishie, and the gem consumes itself in its trail, pouring out the names till a last name reaches the fishie and she swallows it. The name of *whale,* and the whale accepts, and replies with a thudding song.

World waits.

Where's else?—Catchie mouths to the whale. You have cast, you have name—and again, the whale sings to her.

So Catchie opens her mouth, gives the whale a new name. It's not a name given to her by Spitmam and all the folk that came before, it's not a name whittled from the gem she's thrown, but one that's her and only. A new making, a happy bellow, part *poor beastie,* part *grand beastie,* part *there's more.*

World rouses.

The whale takes the new name, swims a little farther out, and sings a different tune back to Catchie.

World rises.

Catchie comes forward, and yelps another name, made up of her feeling to this naming and this new song of the whale's, and the whale takes this, and gives Catchie something new in its mystery to name, and Catchie laughs, for the mystery needs the name to be called out and the name must fall short of the mystery, and this is the game that makes the world all over. For Catchie and the whale call and catch across the world, naming the stars and the masses, the orphan worlds tended by Hammle and even the brittle empties where Spitmam and her sisters tear between the one name they've permit themselves, and then the whale and Catchie swim past all the same again, and then again, with new mysteries in new songs and new names for new mysteries, and there's the way of it, name and mystery, and the pulse of a grand tail.

THE SWITCH: HOPE IN THE FORM
OF PLANTED TOMATOES

Mortgage Lifter • Rainbow's End • Green Grape • Buck's County Hybrid • Aunt Ruby's German Green • Green Zebra • Black Gilliflower • Black Limbertwig • Calville Blanc d'Hiver • Carolina Red June • Chenango Strawberry • Grimes Gold • Golden Russet • Northern Spy • Mother • Smokehouse • Sops of Wine • Summer Rambo • Westfield Seek-No-Further • Wealthy • Abraham Lincoln • Eva's Purple Ball • Amish Paste • Winter Banana • Dad's Mug • King Umberto • Red Pear • Banana Legs • Brimmer Pink • Black Krim • White Beauty • Tigerella

DEAR AUNT GWENDA

VOL. 2

(A Q&A production)

...

Q: "Fore!" cries Archway. He has shanked, past the lake and the stream running into it and over the beach into the foaming sea. Underwater a vent sends up sulfur bubbles—encased in one, his small yellow ball rises to the surface.

But in what activity is Archway engaged?

1. Golf
2. Writing a poem
3. Writing a song
4. Writing a check

I look forward to your assistance in this matter.

A: I thought shanking involved stabbing people in a prison with a cell-made shiv or possibly carving a nice spot of lamb with said shiv. But let's examine the options before us, SAT-takerlike. Golf? No, no. Poemtry? No, no again. Songetry? Paul is dead. Check writing? Some ways yes (sensory), some ways no (lack of ink). Based on these options, I would have to say Archway is hopelessly embroiled with the wrong word.

Q: I've been watching those clean-out-your-life-and-clutter TV shows for a few months and decided it was time to hit my own clutter. My question to you is should I keep the stack of letters from my old boyfriend/first love or do I chuck them out since it's been years and I'm very happy with my current significant other? I haven't read them since we broke up, but I'm having a hard time parting with them.

—*Sentimental Fool*

A: Sentimental fools are the best kind. You should stow the letters in a cooking pot you never use in the deepest recesses of a kitchen cabinet. If you move, you must repeat this procedure. That way when you die, others will find them and have an enjoyable and possibly important afternoon reading them. Also, get your current significant other to write some letters for comparison and squirrel those away, too.

Q: Global warming isn't fast enough. What do I have to do to change things in Washington, D.C.?

A: Is it *possible* to change things in Washington, D.C.? The answer is sadly no, for people are too happy with their thick steaks and nubile interns; let's move the capital elsewhere and start fresh.

[Cue ominous classical music]

But whatever you do, don't vote for Nader this year. I can't promise real, substantial change if the Dynasty falls but, as Diane Keaton and Jack Nicholson have proven, the American people must believe "Something's gotta give."

Q: I have a summer cold and I want a good black-and-white movie or three to watch. I don't want one with a smarmy git or a heroine who melts in the end.

I also want some ginger ale, or tea, maybe some soup, but hopefully those won't appear on these pages, otherwise they might get messy. So, films?

A: I hope your summer cold is gone now (or possibly has returned). Melting heroines and black and white leaves *The Wizard of Oz* right out. Here are three excellent summer cold, b&w movies:

Midnight (1931)—"Every Cinderella gets her midnight."
The Blue Gardenia (1953)—"For drinks, Polynesian Pearl Divers, and don't spare the rum!"
The Loved One (1965)—"This botched, patched-together movie is a triumphant disaster—like a sinking ship that makes it to port because everybody aboard is too giddy to panic. They're so high and lucky they just float in. Perhaps they didn't even notice how low they'd sunk."—Pauline Kael

Q: What's the best time of year to prune grapevines?

A: Is that what the kids are calling it these days? I call it making baby Jesus cry.

THE FILM COLUMN

William Smith

. . .

GREASER'S PALACE (1972) | *Director: Robert Downey, Sr.*
    Music by Jack Nitzsche (arranger for Phil Spector,
    and member of Crazy Horse)

NOTE: THE FILM COLUMN OFTEN CONTAINS SPOILERS.

reaser's Palace is a notable example of the "acid western," an extinct seventies subgenre that combined the metaphysical ambitions of top-shelf westerns, like *Shane* and *The Searchers,* with the excesses of the spaghetti westerns and the irreverent outlook of the counterculture.

Written and directed by Robert Downey, Sr., the film is an absurdist take on the Gospels in which Jesus—in a zoot suit and spats—parachutes onto the western plains and heads for "Jerusalem" to find the agent Morris and become an "actor/singer/dancer." This is one of several goofball epic journeys which crisscross the film and lead us to its center, Greaser's Palace.

Seaweedhead Greaser is the high sheriff of the land. He has a concerned and fatherly air about him but he is armed to the teeth, and gut-shoots his subjects without pattern or reason. In a cheeky reference to Arthurian myth (and probably a parody of Richard Nixon), Greaser suffers from epic constipation and all of his subjects are obsessed with his long-awaited bowel movement. Greaser's Palace is an enormous log castle with an outhouse at the pinnacle. At promising moments, Greaser races to the peak (where he keeps a mariachi band and his mother caged) and waits for the spirit to move him. But it never does.

The complete Holy Trinity wanders through the landscape of the film. The Father, unmistakable with his halo of white hair and wizened eyes, watches his creation through windows and from distant mountains. The Holy Ghost, under a sheet with a cowboy hat, invisibly torments Seaweedhead's son, Lamy. Driven by holy cigar burns, Lamy is prone to bizarre outbursts. Seaweedhead finds these fits undignified, so he knifes Lamy and throws him in a well. Inconveniently, Jesus keeps resurrecting him.

When Jesus finally arrives at Greaser's Palace to spread his message, his routine falls completely flat. It's a good act and has all of the energy and schmaltz of a road-tested vaudeville number, but he just hasn't read the crowd. So he pulls out the stigmata bit (that old groaner) and knocks 'em dead. The agent Morris is unimpressed. "My whole life that's the worst act I've seen. How do you do that material with a straight face?"

Like Salvador Dalí, Robert Downey realized that the ultra-vivid contrasts and infinite horizon of the desert create the perfect backdrop for surrealism. By transplanting the Christ story to the old west—and dressing it up in esoteric pop culture references—Downey creates an absurdist collage that parodies American myths and our justifications for the conquest of this country. He also illustrates that the very act of removing a religion from its land of origin to practice it elsewhere is a work of absurdist collage.

The film plays out its own bizarre take on the Passion and crucifixion but one of its more subtle revisions is that it reverses the Christian dogmatic of reading the Old Testament through the Gospels and instead it sees the Passion as an extension of the testing of Abraham. The trembling hand of a father holding a knife over his son, waiting for an okay from the whirlwind, was a resonant image for a generation sent off to slaughter in Vietnam. Zoot

Jesus vocalizes this anxiety in his last discussion with his father before being crucified:

"Father, I can't do it."

"Why?"

"I think I found myself . . . and I really don't trust you."

The fathers in this film demonstrate a fear that the older one gets, the more likely one is to listen to perverse voices from the whirlwind (and who is older than the capital-F Father himself?). We do get a bit of intergenerational communication near the end when Lamy and Seaweedhead admit their mutual love and respect over a drink. This is exactly what Seaweedhead needs to free his tortured colon and (in a hilarious reference to *Zabriskie Point*) the log cabin explodes with his ecstatic release. The film's final shot, of the sun disappearing into a mountain, denies this momentary resolution, though, and suggests that everything is cyclical and the bowels of the world are impacting again.

Using non sequiturs, puzzle structure, and overloaded symbolism, Downey has created a film of religious parody that produces a strong religious effect. In one of my favorite moments, a hobo stands in the desert, displaying a painting of the Last Supper. Zoot Jesus stares at the image and is completely perplexed. It's as if he's gazing into another universe where all of his signifiers have been moved around. This is similar to the way the film operates on the viewer. Its elements combine to create the impression of great meaning that probably isn't there. But since *absence of meaning* is one of the film's main subjects, this is a perfect technique.

THE ICHTHYOMANCER WRITES HIS FRIEND WITH AN ACCOUNT OF THE YETI'S BIRTHDAY PARTY

David J. Schwartz

...

Xaya:

You no doubt recall (or perhaps you don't; it's been quite a while) that last Thursday was the Yeti's birthday. I want to tell you about the surprise party we threw for him. We were sorry you couldn't be there, but obviously that would have been impossible. If it makes you feel any better, there were quite a few people there whom I don't believe you've met.

The guest list was too large to have the party at our apartment—the fish are upset by crowds. So we looked for a restaurant. We had to call around a little bit to find a place with vegetarian options, since the Yeti doesn't eat meat, but we settled on a little Thai place downtown. Maggie and I had eaten there a few times, since it's not far from our place, and we've always enjoyed it. The rama Thai is excellent.

Maggie and I arrived early and had a drink in the bar. Maggie wore a turtleneck and a short skirt with high boots and nylons. She looked incredible, as you can imagine. For myself, I wore a long-sleeved shirt, charcoal-colored, with some green pants. The fish call them our Quiet Party Clothes, which is their snide way of insinuating that we're predictable. The Black Mollies have an entire spectrum worked out: our Social Obligation clothes are dark and conservative, while our Loud Party Clothes are brighter and don't need to be dry-cleaned.

When we got to the table Todd and Mictecacihuatl were

already there. Todd is a lawyer; right now he's representing the dolphins in their lawsuit against Miami. Mictecacihuatl is a god of the underworld, which is nice work if you can get it. Mictecacihuatl was overdressed, as usual, in a black tuxedo. One of the gods he works with, Ixpuztec, told me once that Mictecacihuatl bought the tux for a wedding that never happened, but it doesn't seem like the sort of thing you ask about.

Maggie told a few lawyer jokes. Todd's a good sport about them, but she had to stop after a while because Mictecacihuatl has false teeth, and his rather wild laughter kept knocking them loose. I suppose that working where he does you learn to appreciate a good joke, or even a rather formulaic and predictable one.

It wasn't long before more people arrived. Max and Earl, the conjoined twins, came in with their seeing-eye dog Bathsheba. Max and Earl aren't blind, but when Bathsheba retired she sort of lost her direction, and one day a couple of years ago we found her begging door-to-door for bowls of Beaujolais. She says she doesn't have a problem, but she's certainly happier since Max and Earl adopted her.

Sergeant Rust was there—stunning in a sleeveless red dress—with her new husband Arvid, the arachnid taxidermist. The Flying Cardellini Sisters were there, and I got a dirty look from Maggie when I waved to Phyllis, the middle sister. Maggie knows I dated Phyllis before we met, and she's terribly insecure about the sex, although she won't ask about it. The truth is that Phyllis was very conservative sexually, and the trapeze above her bed was strictly for practicing in her sleep.

The Zulus came, although they spent most of the time talking on their cell phones, which I thought was rather rude. Dr. Wise was particularly irked by this, as he has a script he's been working on about the female pharaoh Hatshepsut that he's determined to see Johnny Depp star in. But thanks to the miracles of modern technology, instead of pitching his script he spent the entire evening listening to Lawrence—the mastodon, not the fire elemental—complain about his dating troubles.

(Between you and me, I think poor Lawrence's problem isn't the depth of the dating pool but rather his dislike of children. Female mastodons these days are rather militant about breeding, which is why the males tend to go into engineering or medicine or other financially stable professions. By the way, Lawrence was telling me that he thought he'd seen you on some satellite photos—he works for Rand McNally now, you know. I told him I didn't think you'd be recognizable by now, but he seemed pretty certain.)

It was a big group, and eventually we had to ask the waitress if we could add another table. She was very gracious about it, I think because the Monkey King was especially charming that night, and likely could have talked her into coming home with him if she hadn't been happily married, as she told us several times.

Before long everyone was there, from Coventry Rose to Hector Elizondo. Yes, *that* Hector Elizondo; apparently the Yeti met him when they were both on a ski vacation in Banff. It's amazing, the facility the Yeti has for making friends, but then you know that better than anyone.

Evelyn was supposed to bring the Yeti by at seven-thirty, but she had called Maggie at ten minutes to eight to let her know they were going to be a bit late. So we talked. Joan—the macaw, not the dominatrix—told a story about a jaguar and a giant otter that made Mictecacihuatl spit up his drink all over Ling-Ling, who was very calm about it considering how difficult red wine is to get out of fur. Maria Cardellini told a story about a bearded lady and a thin man that seemed to rather embarrass Lawrence. And we all talked about the weather, which was so unusually warm for the Midwest in February.

Still the Yeti didn't arrive. I was enjoying myself, but I must admit that every time I checked my watch I got more worried. I'm a worrier, Maggie tells me, and you will probably agree. I knew the Yeti could take care of himself, and Evelyn was a very safe driver. She was probably trying to hurry him along as much as possible without making him suspicious.

Mpande spotted them first, and hung up his cell phone in time to cue us all to shout "Surprise!" I'm afraid we startled a busboy, who stumbled and would have dropped an entire tray of glasses if Lawrence hadn't steadied it with his trunk. In the confusion I missed the Yeti's reaction, but he was all smiles as he circled the table, shaking hands and kissing the ladies. I have never seen the Yeti miss a chance to kiss a woman, and yet I've never seen a woman resist him either. I suppose it's the teddy bear look that makes him seem harmless.

There were presents, of course. Dr. Wise gave the Yeti a first printing of *Walden,* which quite moved the Yeti and left the rest of us feeling our gifts were inadequate. The Zulus gave a set of ivory combs and brushes, and were careful to mention that the ivory came from elephants who had died of old age. The Yeti thanked them and ruffled up his fur to try out the brushes, which produced a roar of laughter and a few sparks of static electricity. Maggie and I gave him a pair of snowshoes—with a smaller set for Evelyn—since he had told us he was going back to visit the Himalayas in March. He thanked us and said they'd come in useful for outrunning photographers.

The food came soon after we ordered; I think perhaps the management was trying to rush us out. If so, it didn't work, since everyone spent as much time talking as they did devouring their pad Thai and spring rolls. Sergeant Rust and the Monkey King swapped war stories, while Dr. Wise tried to interest Hector Elizondo in the part of Tuthmosis II.

At one point Maggie leaned close and asked me why we didn't do things like this more often, and I shrugged. In my experience things like this happened when they were good and ready, when schedules opened up and everyone was in town. (Everyone except yourself, of course. Which reminds me, Maggie says we should try to visit in June, after she's turned in her grades for the spring semester. Let us know if that's a problem.)

Of course, it didn't all go smoothly. Baron Samedi said something that mortally offended Coventry Rose. I never did find out what it was, but when Lawrence—the fire elemental, not the mastodon—confronted him about it, he was convinced that we were all siding against him. Despite our protests, he threw a pair of twenties on the table for the bill, tipped his top hat, and vanished in a puff of black smoke. You can imagine the stir that caused among the other diners, especially considering that we were in a nonsmoking section.

The Baron's dramatics notwithstanding, it was a wonderful dinner, and I was sorry when the group started to break up. Max and Earl excused themselves before dessert on the grounds that Bathsheba was rather drunk, and the three of them went weaving out. Sergeant Rust and Arvid left soon after in order to get their babysitter home at a decent hour. The Zulus had a flight to catch, and they swept out in a flurry of embraces, pursued by Dr. Wise, who was still trying to get a phone number from one of them.

Soon only Maggie, Evelyn, the Yeti, and myself were left. We sipped our cordials (all except the Yeti, who has quit drinking and was content with a Thai iced tea—did I tell you about the unpleasantness at Geb's barbecue last summer? I can't recall) and talked quietly of the old days. It seems such a long time ago that we were students, and yet it seems like yesterday. I do miss those days, although I never dated and wouldn't have had money to go anywhere if I had. Maggie says the pictures from then don't look like me, although the Yeti of course hasn't changed. (Maggie says you look adorable, although I've tried to explain about your size. I also tried to explain that "adorable" was probably not the right word for the master of the mountains, but that's Maggie. I'm curious to see her reaction when the two of you finally meet, since I've come to suspect she's immune to surprise.)

Of course, once we began sorting through the checks and cash on the table we realized someone had shorted us. Maggie engaged in some rude speculation as to whom it had been, but in the end I simply threw two hundred onto the pile to make it worth the waitress's time. The Yeti asked Evelyn for his wallet, but we wouldn't let him pay. Business is good, and if I can't afford to treat my friends then the money doesn't mean a thing.

We left then, making plans to see Evelyn and the Yeti again before they left for Nepal. They're truly happy together, and it's a wonderful thing to see. Evelyn used to be so moody. Remember the way her tail would droop when she felt self-conscious, which was nearly all the time? And the Yeti—I must admit that I used to think the Yeti was rather superficial, and any woman could make him happy. But Evelyn has illuminated new depths within our hirsute friend. They make a wonderful couple, and they both send their regards.

As we walked back to the apartment, Maggie asked me if I thought Dr. Wise would ever get his movie made, and I told her we should ask the fish when we got home. And do you know what they said? The Zulus had already been in touch with Johnny Depp's agent, and he was eager to see a script.

We're sending some cookies along with this letter; Maggie's idea, which I didn't have the energy to argue against. I'm fairly certain they'll be shaken to crumbs in transit. I'm not even sure you still eat—how is the transformation progressing?

Let us know about June. I know there's been some distance between us since you moved back home, but I want to spend some time with you before you go back to sleep for another thousand years. The fish say we will see each other again. I hope they're right.

Take care,
Allan

A BY-NO-MEANS-COMPLETE JOAN AIKEN CHECKLIST

All You've Ever Wanted (1953) • *More Than You Bargained For and Other Stories* (1955) • *The Kingdom and the Cave* (1960) • *The Wolves of Willoughby Chase* (1962) • *Black Hearts in Battersea* (1964) • *The Fortune Hunters* (1965) • *Nightbirds on Nantucket* (1966) • *Trouble with Product X* (1966) • *Hate Begins at Home* (1967) • *Armitage, Armitage, Fly Away Home* (1968) • *The Whispering Mountain* (1968) • *A Necklace of Raindrops and Other Stories* (1968) • *A Small Pinch of Weather and Other Stories* (1969) • *The Windscreen Weepers and Other Tales of Horror and Suspense* (1969) • *The Kingdom Under the Sea: And Other Stories* (1970) • *Smoke from Cromwell's Time and Other Stories* (1970) • *The Cuckoo Tree* (1971) • *The Green Flash and Other Tales of Horror, Suspense, and Fantasy* (1971) • *Night Fall* (1971) • *The Butterfly Picnic* (1972) • *Died on a Rainy Sunday* (1972) • *A Harp of Fishbones and Other Stories* (1972) • *Midnight Is a Place* (1974) • *All But a Few* (1974) • *Arabel's Raven* (1974) • *Not What You Expected: A Collection of Short Stories* (1974) • *Voices in an Empty House* (1975) • *A Bundle of Nerves: Stories of Horror, Suspense, and Fantasy* (1976) • *Castle Barebane* (1976) • *Go Saddle the Sea* (1977) • *The Far Forests: Tales of Romance, Fantasy, and Suspense* (1977) • *The Faithless Lollybird* (1978) • *The Five-Minute Marriage* (1978) • *The Smile of the Stranger* (1978) • *Tale of a One-Way Street and Other Stories* (1978) • *A Touch of Chill: Tales for Sleepless Nights* (1979) • *Arabel and Mortimer* (1980) • *The Lightning Tree* (1980) • *The Shadow Guests* (1980) • *The Weeping Ash* (1980) • *The Stolen Lake* (1981) • *A Whisper in the Night: Stories of Horror, Suspense, and Fantasy* (1981) • *The Young Lady from Paris* (1982) • *The Way to Write for Children* (nonfiction, 1982) • *Bridle the Wind* (1983) • *Mansfield Revisited*

(1984) • *Up the Chimney Down and Other Stories* (1984) • *Mortimer, Arabel, and the Escaped Black Mamba* (1984) • *Dido and Pa* (1986) • *The Moon's Revenge* (1987) • *If I Were You* (1987) • *Teeth of the Gale* (1988) • *A Foot in the Grave* (1989) • *Return to Harken House* (1990) • *The Haunting of Lamb House* (1991) • *Jane Fairfax* (1991) • *Morningquest* (1992) • *Is Underground* (1993) • *The Midnight Moropus* (1993) • *Eliza's Daughter* (1994) • *The Winter Sleepwalker* (1994) • *A Creepy Company: Ten Tales of Terror* (1995) • *Mayhem in Rumbury* (1995) • *Cold Shoulder Road* (1996) • *Emma Watson* (1996) • *The Youngest Miss Ward* (1998) • *Lady Catherine's Necklace* (2000) • *Ghostly Beasts* (2002) • *Midwinter Nightingale* (2003)

Finished? Well done! Now, how about Peter Dickinson?

SERPENTS

Veronica Schanoes

...

Some people think little girls should be seen and not heard,
but I think—Oh bondage! Up yours! 1-2-3-4!
—THE X-RAY SPEX

And what does it matter to me whether you're a little girl or a serpent?
—ALICE'S ADVENTURES
IN WONDERLAND
Lewis Carroll

"WILL YOU TAKE THE PATH OF PINS OR THE PATH OF NEEDLES?"
It doesn't sound like much of a choice to Charlotte. Dark
woods, sharp metal. It sounds like some kind of test. Perhaps if she
gives the wrong answer, toads and snakes will fall from her tongue
whenever she tries to speak. Charlotte wouldn't mind that. She
likes snakes: she likes the way they move, twining themselves
along the ground. She thinks she might be a kind of serpent herself, sliding along in a smooth sine wave, wise and cunning. Serpents don't sew.

"The path of pins."

The scenery changes, wavers like a snake curving from side to
side, and then slides away. While it is swerving and sliding, Charlotte wonders if the world is a snake as well. That would make her
happy, to be a smaller snake inside the belly of a larger snake undu-
lating through time and space. The past would be the tail and the
future the head, and the massive sinuous body would coil and
curve over and under and through itself in a Möbius pattern, and

the past would be the head and the future would be the tail and the world-serpent would hold its tail in its mouth, a tale in its mouth, its tale in its mouth.

Snakes never blink.

CHARLOTTE FINDS HERSELF on the path of pins. As far as she can see, the dirt path is strewn with pins: safety pins, straight pins, hairpins, hat pins, diaper pins, glittering like scales along the back of a winding serpent. A careless little girl could cut her feet to shreds, but Charlotte is wearing her purple fourteen-hole Doc Martens. She can't even feel the pins grinding into the dirt floor of the forest under her heels. She walks along, imagining the silver serpent that has shed this skin. It would be huge, she thinks, to shed this many scales, and the pins would almost be more like stiff little feathers than smoothly overlapping scales. As she begins to imagine the cold sapphire eyes of the pin snake and the sharp metal teeth lining its mouth, she realizes where the pins are coming from. The trees lining this path have pins where the leaves should be. These trees would be impossible to climb—one wrong move and you'd have a face full of blood and scratches. You'd probably need a tetanus shot.

While Charlotte contemplates the trees, something is moving very quickly toward the path, making as little noise as possible. It skids right in front of her like a schoolgirl crossing Park Avenue against the light to get to homeroom before the bell rings. Charlotte is thrown off balance; she tries to stop in midstride, and almost instinctively, like a snake sensing motion, she whips around to follow the movement. She tries to balance on one leg, her arms pinwheeling as her left foot waves in the air behind her. She's almost regained her balance when she skids on some pins and falls heavily to the side, bloodying her hands, her knees, and her face.

The sun is setting. Oh my fur and whiskers, I shall be too late.

But Charlotte is not too late; she turns her head aside just in time to avoid an eye full of pins. As she lies where she's fallen, breathing heavily, nonsense phrases slide through her head: it's all fun and games until someone loses an eye, cross my heart and hope to die, stick a needle in my eye. Not needles. Pins. Charlotte takes a deep breath and stands up. She dusts pins off her blue skirt and white apron, leaving red streaks from her bleeding hands, streaks the same color as her wine-dark motorcycle jacket, with all the zippers and pockets holding her subway pass, silver eyeshadow, red lipstick, liquid black eyeliner, a fake ID that gives her age as twenty-two, a neon pink cigarette lighter, a pack of cigarettes (she doesn't smoke), some speed, some bobby pins, a thimble, and a box of comfits. She opens her basket and pulls out gauze and tape. After bandaging her knees she puts on a pair of swimming goggles. No pins in her eyes, thank you very much. No needles either. She sets off to find whatever it was that made her lose her balance. She steps off the path.

Aha, you may be thinking. We all know what happens to little girls who stray from the path. Do we?

As Charlotte walks carefully and firmly through the pin-grass growing in this part of the woods, she thinks about goggles. Do snakes wear goggles? It depends, she thinks, on whether or not they go in the water. Water moccasins go in the water. So do other snakes. She likes to watch them skimming, sliding along the surface of the water, arching their bodies back and forth. She wonders if sea serpents swim the same way, gliding in S shapes along the surface of the ocean. Probably not, she decides. Sea serpents swim *through* the water, not on it. She imagines a sea serpent weightless in a wine-dark sea. She imagines the same serpent pulling a fishing boat down to the ocean floor, twining the rope of its body around the boat as strapping young sailors shriek and hurl themselves overboard. The thoughts make her smile. Sea serpents, she thinks, might wear goggles.

She continues to track the quickly moving creature. Her Docs make surprisingly little noise as she goes; perhaps she's done this before. She draws closer and sees it is a white rabbit, breathing heavily and shaking. Blood and mud are smeared across its paws and its fur. Its small pink eyes roll around in an even madder manner than usual.

Charlotte wonders whether or not snakes eat rabbits. Surely swallowing a rabbit wouldn't be much of a difficulty for a boa constrictor, she thinks, remembering pictures she's seen of other smaller snakes with rat-shaped lumps in their bodies. As if sensing the predatory turn her thoughts have taken, the rabbit freezes; its ears triangulate frantically, trying to catch the sound of her breathing, and all at once it leaps down a rabbit hole that has been concealed under a mound of stacked pins piled precariously like pick-up sticks. Charlotte throws herself after it and is falling, falling down a hole whose walls are made of pins with duck heads holding diapers onto babies' bottoms, safety pins punched through clothing, straight pins piercing butterflies as they flap their wings vainly, pushpins holding Charlotte's second-grade essay on poisonous snakes to a corkboard, bobby pins twisting her hair too tightly, safety pins through her earlobes (they had already been pierced so it took only a steady hand and some patience). The hole is quite long and it twists and Charlotte feels as though she is being swallowed by a snake. It is not a bad feeling. She lands with a rush on a leaf pile of pins.

Her goggles, Docs, and motorcycle jacket serve her well—no pins make it through. But her exposed legs and face are now scratched, cut, bloody. Charlotte pushes herself up, scraping her hands as she goes. She opens her basket and takes out a bottle of iodine and methodically applies some to every inch of broken skin. Charlotte is a wound and its cure, a germ-free adolescent.

Which way is Grandma's now? She looks around, trying to orient herself. She rubs her eyes, leaving bloody smears across the lens of her goggles. From now on, she will see the world through the haze of her own blood.

Something about the tiling of these corridors looks familiar to her, but not until she reaches the glass booth does she realize that she's in the Astor Place subway station. She brings the subway pass out of her pocket and waves it at the token clerk, who is not there anyway. She jumps the turnstile. She sees the rabbit on the platform and begins to run toward it, but the dirty feral creature spots her and is so distressed that it leaps off the platform, launching its body straight out over the tracks. As it falls and Charlotte watches, it changes from a rabbit into a small mouse and scurries away.

Charlotte is disappointed. A snake certainly could have swallowed that morsel.

She is not disappointed for long, though. She is thinking about having a cigarette and whether or not her grandma would smell the smoke in the folds of her jacket or the cuts in her skin, and if she did, whether she would believe Charlotte if she told her that the smell was from the show she went to last night, when the train comes hurtling into the station at breakneck pace. Snakes have no necks to break, thinks Charlotte. Or maybe they're all neck until their tails.

Charlotte has always loved the subway system, the dark, dank smelly stations, the more labyrinthine, the more exits and interchanges, the better. She likes the seemingly random assignments of letters and numbers; she likes the confusion and mourned when the difference between the AA and A was dissolved. She likes it when an uptown local becomes an express on an entirely different track and when the F with no warning starts running on the A line. She likes the small signs that presage the coming of the train—the soft clank of the track shifting, the mice moving quietly to the sides of the track, the faintest pinprick of light down the tunnel. It won't be long now. Not long. She loves the look of the stations, the steel beams and bolts and cracked concrete—the bones and organs of the city. And when the train comes, she likes that best of all, the free-fall rush of air it pushes before it, the long loud clatter and screech. Subways, Charlotte thinks, are like snakes when snakes ruled the earth.

When Charlotte was little, she used to make her mom ride in the first car so that she could stand at the door with all the warning stickers at the head of the car (RIDING BETWEEN CARS IS STRICTLY FORBIDDEN; NO SE APOYE CONTRA LA PUERTA) and press her face against the glass. As the train hurtled through the darkness, Charlotte would watch wide-eyed as incandescent lights stretched out in bright streaks flashing by like the *Millennium Falcon* making the jump into hyperspace, only better. What Charlotte liked best was the occasional ghost station—Eighteenth street on the 6, for example. Abandoned, covered with phantasmagoric graffiti, but still kept lit up in perpetual, futile wait for passengers and trains that never stopped. Charlotte used to dream about getting off in the old stations to explore, being left behind as the train pulled away, left to fade into the stretched and flamboyant graffiti. They were nightmares, sort of.

Charlotte gets on the train, arranges her skirt, and closes her eyes. She tries to doze but she is just too hungry. Instead she opens her basket and peels a hard-boiled egg, leaving bloody fingerprints—a murder mystery detective's dream—on the shell and on the surface of the white, which gives beneath the pressure of her fingers and then returns to its perfect shape. She is eating her second egg when she becomes aware that the shrieks and squawks of the other passengers have been drowned, engulfed by a silence, the silence of people pressing away, the silence of fear and loathing.

As Charlotte chews the second bloody bite of her second egg she realizes that the other passengers are birds: not pigeons or other city-vermin birds, but dodoes, lories, eaglets, and hawks. She thinks she even catches sight of a bird with plumage all of pins, which would be painful for a snake to swallow, but perhaps she is mistaken. Slowly and deliberately she finishes her egg as a finch in the little love seat in the corner tucks into a Tupperware of living centipedes. Charlotte shifts position, which is painful because of the way the cuts in her legs are sticking to the seat.

As muttering and chirping starts to replace hostile avian glares the train judders and shudders, stopping suddenly. The lights go off and then back on. Charlotte and the birds stare straight ahead as seconds and then minutes drift by silently. The PA system emits a loud crackle of static. Charlotte doesn't know it, but if she could play that static backward and at twice the speed it would be the sound of her mother as a little girl telling her to be careful on the path of pins. But she can't, so she will never know. To her, it just sounds like a hoarse snake, hissing and spitting and coughing all at once. A snake with strep throat.

But you and I know. That will have to be enough.

There is a pause in the static, and then the PA starts to play music, particularly insipid sentimental pop that seems to distress the birds as much as it does Charlotte, who has no intention whatsoever of sitting in a stalled-out subway car listening to Celine Dion. She stands up, walks over to the door leading to the area between the cars, where you're not supposed to ride, and opens it. She steps out onto the ledge and lowers herself onto the track, followed by the birds, who are grateful for her deft opposable thumbs even if she does eat eggs. They are clearly more comfortable following a bleeding egg-eater than they are staying behind in the subway car, which is beginning to fill with hot saltwater.

Charlotte walks deliberately and firmly. She is convinced that every so often she can spot a pin glinting up at her from the tracks. The birds follow silently. Every so often Charlotte glances over at the third rail lying coolly under its sheltering guard. The lure is strong, like the fear that you might throw yourself off the top of the Empire State Building or try to grab a policeman's gun just because you can imagine yourself doing so. Charlotte pictures herself laying her hand against the third rail and filling from hair to boots with burning electric energy, her consciousness flickering and then running straight into the electric blood of the city, crackling through trains and streetlights, merging purely and quickly with the pulsing islands surrounding her.

She doesn't know if the birds are thinking along similar lines or not.

The way along the tracks is long, much longer than the path through the woods, and the birds become restless, rustling their feathers and crowding forward, even pecking Charlotte's back, although she certainly can't feel it through her jacket. One of the wrens decides that he can lead way better and takes off straight into the third rail. His skin turns black and splits, spilling his bones and still-quivering lungs onto the ground. The smell of burning feathers makes Charlotte vomit. She stops walking in order to rinse her mouth out with cinnamon mouthwash from her basket.

The remaining birds are looking a bit green as well. Charlotte passes out the comfits for them to suck on.

After they have been walking for what seems like hours, Charlotte finds that they are at the abandoned Eighteenth Street subway station. The funhouse graffiti is layered over older graffiti; infinite strata of urban fireworks marking successive waves of fucked-up youth. Charlotte walks through the station: her goggles, her blood- and iodine-stained face and legs, her bandaged hands, her red motorcycle jacket, and her comet-tail of birds make her look like a walking piece of graffiti. She climbs the stairs, only to find her way blocked by an iron gate. She rattles the bars but the grille is locked. She picks up one of the birds and pushes it through the bars. It flies away and the others get the idea. Soon the only company Charlotte has left is the dodo, who is too large to fit through the gate and can't fly anyway. Together they walk back down the stairs.

Charlotte finds a section of the wall which has less art and is mostly painted with slogans instead. She leans back against RIP HER TO SHREDS and HATE AND WAR, removes her goggles, and takes a nap, right under GOD SAVE THE QUEEN and HEAVY MANNERS. The dodo sinks down next to her, rests its head on her shoulder, and falls asleep as well.

When they wake up, Charlotte is unsure how long she has been sleeping. She lights a cigarette, stubs it out, and passes it to the dodo, who eats it. Charlotte thinks this is all to the good, because she doesn't like to litter. The city has enough trouble. So does she.

She sighs and puts her goggles back on. The red smears of blood are still damp. The dodo looks a bit anxious, so, as a gesture of friendship, Charlotte gives the bird a second pair of goggles from her basket. She tightens the strap around the bird's head and it squawks in appreciation. Then she takes a small bottle of seltzer and piece of cake out of her basket. She and the dodo share breakfast? lunch? dinner? Neither one of them knows and neither do we.

After eating, Charlotte examines the bottom of her left boot and pulls out several straight pins that have stuck in the rubber. She is oblivious to the dodo's embarrassment at having nothing to give her in return for the goggles and food. Luckily, the awkward bird spots something glinting in the corner of the abandoned station. It is Charlotte's own thimble, which has rolled out of her pocket while she was sleeping. The dodo, ignorant creature, has no way of knowing the shiny thing's provenance. It picks up the thimble in its beak and solemnly presents it to Charlotte. Charlotte accepts it back graciously, although she'll never need to use it again. Snakes, remember, don't sew. She slips it in her pocket.

Charlotte stands up. As she pulls away from the wall she feels her jacket sticking, but she cannot see why. The graffiti that she was leaning against, old and chipped as it was, has imprinted itself on her jacket like wet paint in a silent movie or a *Sesame Street* sketch. The mirror ghost print of half a dozen punk slogans criss-crosses her back.

Together Charlotte and the dodo climb the stairs. Armed with the pins from her boot she begins to pick the padlock keeping the gate closed. It's a fruitless exercise. The straight pins cause nothing but pricked fingertips and a steady subway rumble of foul language from Charlotte.

Finally she gives it up and throws the pins away. Sitting back down on the ground she opens her basket and takes out a large solid key with four different ridged edges that match the + at the bottom of the padlock. She unlocks the padlock, puts the key back into her basket, slides the lock off the gate, and locks it around a belt loop on her jacket. Then she pushes the gate open. She and the dodo step through together.

They climb another set of steps. When they come up from underground they are at the very edge of a forest. Looking back, Charlotte can see two paths winding through the trees. Looking the other way she can see her grandmother's cottage two, maybe three blocks away. She checks to make sure she still has everything she needs: goggles, jacket, basket. The dodo watches her uncertainly. It shuffles its feet and clears its throat. Charlotte picks the bird up and hurls it as hard as she can up in the air. The dodo spreads its stubby, prickly wings and flaps ferociously, twisting its barrellike body back and forth as it rises. It hangs suspended for a few seconds, contemplating Charlotte. From this height she looks like a red blur, a bloodstained egg, and compared to the dodo, she is barely more than an egg. The dodo wishes her luck and then continues its ascent.

Charlotte has already turned away and is walking to her grandmother's cottage. There is nothing left in her way, just smooth sidewalks unrolling under her feet. When she gets to the cottage, she knocks gently on the door, and when there is no response she uses her school ID to jimmy open the lock. She walks in.

Grandmother is not bedridden, and her eyes, ears, and teeth are just the right size. She is wearing a green dress and kneeling in front of the crackling sparking fire in the fireplace. She is crying softly and inconsolably. She does not even turn her head to look when Charlotte comes into the room.

Charlotte kneels down next to her grandmother and takes her hand. "It's OK," she says.

Her grandmother continues to weep over the long tube of patterned snakeskin. "It's dead," she whispers. "It's dead."

"No, Grandma," says Charlotte. "It's not dead."

But her grandmother continues to weep gently, bent like a willow over the shed skin. Charlotte sets her basket down and takes from it a loaf of fresh bread, a quart of homemade chicken soup, and a bottle of red wine. "These are for you," she tells her grandmother. She takes a red apple from her basket and places it in her grandmother's hand, closing the older woman's fingers around it, but still her grandmother does not turn her head.

Charlotte stands behind her grandmother and begins to undress. She takes off her motorcycle jacket, folds it lovingly, and lays it on the floor. She unties her bloodstained apron, takes it off, and lays it on top of the jacket. Her sky blue dress follows as do her black cotton underpants and bra as well as her hair ribbon, leaving her standing in only her purple Doc Martens and her goggles.

"It's OK, Grandma," she repeats. "It's not dead. Look."

And as her grandmother turns to look, Charlotte—slowly, slowly—begins to shed her skin.

HOMELAND SECURITY

Gavin J. Grant

. . .

WITH THOUSANDS OF LIKE-MINDED OTHERS, I WENT TO the big peace rally in New York City on February 15, 2003. It was a cold day, and my wife and I walked up Third Avenue from Thirty-second to Sixty-eighth Street before we could cut over to First Avenue and join the rally. Which was really a slow march, but since the city government wouldn't give us a permit to march, let's call it a rally.

What do we want?
So many things.
When do we want them?
It doesn't seem possible, but now, please.

MARCH 5, 2003, LOCAL NEWS: Writer and editor Gavin J. Grant, 33 (picture), of Northampton, Mass., is believed to be one of hundreds of detainees held after police and other government agencies moved in to calm a noisy and potentially violent peace rally in New York City's Washington Square Park.

I joined the United for Peace and Justice e-mail list for information on future rallies. I forwarded their e-mail about a march and vigil on March 5 to my wife. She had to pick up some freelance work in New York and readily agreed to go.

Tell me what a democracy looks like.
From here, a dictatorship.
This is what a democracy looks like.
This march, or this war? It's hard to tell.

MARCH 7, 2003, E-MAIL: Gavin, Dad here. Got a call from INS (IRS?) saying you had been held (under Patriotic Act?) after rally and asking re: marriage and so on. Confirm OK by you to send these? Love, dad and mum. xx. . . .

The march and candlelight vigil on March 5 was as depressing as the February 15 rally. Thousands of people gathered outside Senator Hillary Clinton's office and marched to Senator Chuck Schumer's office to protest their voting to send the USA into war with Iraq. We marched down Third to Forty-second Street and then snaked over to Fifth, blocking crosstown traffic. We marched to Washington Square Park and were closely watched by the Fifth Avenue business owners, some of whom seemed to dither between a desire to join us and a fear of the crowd. But we were no mob. People drummed and danced, sang the usual songs, held or wore signs that were as funny and direct as ever ("The only Bush I trust is my own" was more popular this time) . . . yet, will this stop a war? Hundreds of police seemed to think we might start a Battle of Seattle ourselves. Which leads to thoughts of whether we might place some of these police in the White House.

MARCH 8, 2003, NATIONAL NEWS: Detained immigrant Gavin Grant's Web site (Internet Archive link) has been taken down by the federal government under suspicion of terrorist links. Grant, a freelance writer who has written for alternative publications such as *The Urban Pantheist, Weird Times,* and *Xerography Debt,* recently published altered transcripts of two of President Bush's remarks on Iraq on his Web site. Citing freedom of speech and linking to satirical Web sites such as *The Onion,* Grant simply switched the president's name with Saddam Hussein's in two transcripts. The first transcript made it appear that Hussein was about to attack the United States with three thousand cruise missiles— with no differentiation of civilian and military targets. The second transcript, however, was perhaps even more threatening and, given the present Orange Alert, is likely the reason Grant was arrested. Grant altered President Bush's remarks on the possibilities of an internal coup in Iraq and changed them to suggest that generals and others in the U.S. Armed Forces might find themselves well rewarded if they initiated an internal revolt. The White House announced there would be a press conference concerning the latest detainees at two P.M. today and referred all questions to John Ashcroft's office.

We, the people, don't want this war!
Shame Bush hasn't noticed.

MARCH 15: The thing is, I haven't been arrested. I'm not even in hiding. This morning I sanded the ice in my driveway and talked to Jeff, our contractor, about building some bookshelves in a room upstairs. When I opened my e-mail there were 250+ e-mails—mostly from people I don't know. Ninety percent were supportive, but some were just vitriolic. I haven't even posted my articles yet—they were just ideas I was playing with. I was going to contact a lawyer friend and a guy I know who ran a satirical site to get some advice before I posted. The lines keep moving and I wanted to make sure I wasn't going to cross any of the dangerous ones.

MARCH 12, 2003, NYPD SPOKESMAN: We can confirm arrests of a number of individuals participating in an anti-government rally in Washington Square Park on the evening of March 5. These individuals are no longer in our jurisdiction. They are being held under the auspices of the Domestic Security Enhancement Act of 2003 in an undisclosed location.

I don't like singing and chanting with the other marchers. I think walking quietly is just as important. That way we don't all look as if we're being carried away in an ecstatic trance. A few people jangled their keys as they walked. I wondered if it was just an impulse to be rhythmic or if they had read Ursula K. Le Guin's story about a revolution, "Unlocking the Air."

Drop Bush, not bombs.
Or at least his lapdog, Blair.

At the end of the February 15 rally when the closely herded thousands of us were leaving, I went to walk around the outside edge of a phone box. A policeman stopped me and told me I had to stay on the sidewalk. Cold, frustrated by this abject stupidity and niggardliness, I objected.

"That," and I pointed to the two feet of sidewalk between the phone box and the street, "is the sidewalk." The policeman declared it was not, and another policeman moved closer to us in case I was trouble. I repeated that the space between the phone and the road was, in fact, sidewalk. The policeman, putting his hand on his billyclub, repeated his determined opinion that it was not. I held my hands up in the air to show I wasn't about to start anything, could not stop myself from calling him a fascist, and left. I wondered how near to arrest I'd been.

SEPTEMBER 5, 2003, NATIONAL NEWS: Detainees from the March 5 peace march in New York have now been held for one hundred and eighty days without access to family, legal aid, or media. The Department of Homeland Security refuses to release the number of detainees or any identifying information. Twenty-three of the detained have since been stripped of their citizenship and deported to their countries of origin. Mothers of the Disappeared, a new New York City–based organization claims that the detainees are being tortured and tried in secret courts. White House spokesman Jim Morrell refused to comment on what he called "pure fabulation."

The U.S. government declared the war in Iraq over in May 2003. The ongoing reports of killings in Iraq remind me of growing up in the UK. War was never formally declared in Northern Ireland, but the headlines were often about bombings, murders, and shootings. The peace process in Ireland is one thing that fills me with hope. Perhaps the past can be let go—not forgotten—and a new future can be chosen based on peace and negotiation rather than on the acts of a randomly chosen period one, two, or three hundred years ago.

MARCH 5, 2004, NATIONAL NEWS: The one-year anniversary of last year's national peace rally and the accompanying series of arrests was marked today by rallies, countrywide student sit-ins, and the third masked Black Bloc flashmob appearance (exclusive video) in New York City this week. Although a number of the detainees are known to be serving prison terms, the Department of Homeland Security resolutely refuses to release the original number of marchers detained, or any identifying information. Mothers of the

Disappeared claim the detainees have been moved to the U.S. military base in Guantanamo Bay and that, citing Amnesty International interviews with ex-prisoners from the Afghanistan war of 2001, the conditions in Guantanamo are an abuse of the detainees' human rights. White House spokesman Jim Morrell refused to comment on what he called "pure fabulation."

I never carry my green card with me. I know the number, but I don't want to lose it if my wallet is stolen. So if I were arrested my identity cards would be my New York driver's license with my old address on it, credit cards, and membership cards for the library, Pleasant Street Video, AAA, and Amnesty International. I look in the mirror and I'm not sure who's there. There's a man with lines around his eyes, and a somewhat blank expression. What does he want? When does he want it? Not this president. Not this future.

FOR GEORGE ROMERO

David Blair

The poor don't shoot their zombies
in the heads. Not in your version.
The zombies do the right things
horribly: the man mourned
embraces his wife. Then he bites
her shoulder. And then they go
ice skating, but without skates.

VINCENT PRICE

David Blair

He was oddly astringent
witch hazel.
He was blurry
and portable
in every barbershop
towel and cloud
of talcum powder.
The basketball buzzer
was yelping him up,
an irregular sound
upstairs at the Y.
He was the old man
with mother-of-pearl
crutches working
the scoreboard
at the youth league
basketball games
and polio marks
like sealed letters
on the fat forearms
to Mrs. Sanquini
and Mrs. Sardenia.

He was the cage
of bingo numbers
rattling bones.

He had eyebrows
of wooden spoons
and all his dialogue
was flatter than
the tornado plains
where the blob
rolled along.
He was a bucket
of squid trunks
and exposed pipes
in the locker room
and the boiled cabbage
of the old man
who passed out towels.
He was the dark end
of burnt lightbulbs.

MUSIC LESSONS

Douglas Lain

. . .

PSYCHIATRIC SESSION,
DR. WILLIAM HOWSER, 11/2/98

Q: Tell me about the sound.

A: I've given you the wrong impression. It wasn't a sound. It was more of a concept. I heard it inside my head. I didn't really hear it, but I thought it.

Q: How old were you?

A: I guess I was about four . . . three or four years old. I saw the gorilla, no, the man in the gorilla costume. He was standing in the doorway.

Q: And he made this sound?

A: No, he just stood there looking menacing; there was this gorilla man in the doorway, and there was fog throughout my room. . . . I don't know, maybe I had a cold and the humidifier was on.

Q: You were afraid.

A: Yes. I pulled the sheets up over my head; I tried to go back to sleep and then wake up again. You know the trick? It was like, "This is a dream, I'll close my eyes and then when I open them the gorilla man will be gone and I can go tell my parents that I had a bad dream." So I pulled the sheet over my head and I closed my eyes.

Q: And when you looked out from under the sheet?

A: He was still there, of course, only now he was in the room with me. And the smoke, the steam from the humidifier, was everywhere. I'd been holding my breath, and when I looked up again and saw him standing at the foot of my bed I let out a gasp and tried to scream.

Q: Did your parents come to you then?

A: No. I tried to scream, but I couldn't do it. I opened my mouth to scream, but instead of sound this bubble came out of my mouth. I screamed and screamed, and when there should have been noise there was only this inflating bubble. And then it popped.

Q: It popped.

A: And that's when I heard the noise. Not the screaming noise, but the sound I was telling you about before.

Q: The sound you say had such a big influence on your music. The sound that wasn't a sound.

A: It was just an idea really. It was what you'd hear if you could hear between the notes.

Q: Silence?

A: No. Something. A sort of deep hum. I got close to it with my tape music.

Q: Why did you think of this today? Last week we were talking about your mother's illness, and today you tell me about this sound. How do you think these two things relate?

A: I saw him again.

Q: Who did you see?

A: The man in the gorilla suit. I saw him when I was in Pittsburgh on Friday.

Monday was a day plagued by bees. I woke up in my work studio, lying by an open window, to find that a crown of bees, half dead and dawdling, had converged around my hair.

I couldn't remember how I'd arrived at the studio apartment from the symphony hall, and I had no idea why I'd chosen to spend the night on the floor of my little room rather than at home and in bed with my wife.

"I'm all right," I told Meredith.

"You're in your room?"

"Yes," I said.

"I thought so, but when I tried to call last night I just got your machine."

"I'm okay."

"That's good, but where were you?" she asked.

I squashed one of the bees with a paper towel. The insects were so dazed that all I had to do was lean down and pluck them up one by one.

"I was hanging out with some bees," I told her. "I'll be home soon."

There was a bee in my car, buzzing around the windshield. I drove slowly, thinking about the sting.

It was midafternoon by the time I got home. I walked into the high-rise, crossed the lobby, and entered the elevator. The sound of the leather soles of my loafers crunching insect shells, a repetitive popping, distracted me from pressing the button for my floor.

Dried dead bees, perhaps a thousand of them, carpeted the floor of the elevator. I glanced at my watch and noted the time. It was 2:15 P.M., which meant the drive from the Hawthorne District to downtown Portland had taken four hours. I hadn't driven that slowly.

"Where have you been?" Meredith asked.

"I'm not sure."

"Well, I got Jacob down for his nap without you. It took forever," she said.

"I'm sorry. I must've lost track of time."

My wife and I rely on each other. She helps me keep the noise out and the sounds in, and I try to do the same for her.

Both of us are essentially cowards, and little things will set us off . . . send our heads spinning. A psychological study on the effects of television on children, a plague in Bangladesh, the death of a colleague or a distant relative—these things can have long-lasting and detrimental effects on one or the other of us. And when this happens the other person's job is to stay stable, to hold onto the earth. We can't both break down at once.

"I've been sitting at home nurturing an anxiety attack," Meredith said. "I've been reading about the corpse print again."

Meredith isn't particularly religious, she's an agnostic really, but around that time she was reading about the Shroud of Turin. The shroud is this sheet that they say covered Jesus after the Romans killed him, and what's significant about it is that it has this image on it. There's no paint on the sheet, the image seems to be a discoloration of the fabric, and nobody can say how or why it's there.

I hung up my coat on the rack by the door and went to peek in on my son while he slept. I sat by the side of his bed, a small twin bed shaped like a cello, and watched him breathe.

Meredith stood in the doorway and whispered in at me, "He was floating. That's what they think."

"What?"

"The corpse. We're talking about a floating corpse," she said, holding up her book and pointing at the shroud. "What if they're right? Not the medical experts, but the Christians. I mean, what if he comes back." She moved over to the side of the bed and sat down next to me. I put my arm around her.

"That would be good, right? We're talking about Jesus, after all."

She shrugged my arm off her shoulder and turned to face me. "The man is dead. What we're talking about is a zombie situation. I don't want a zombie in the apartment."

"You think He'd want to visit?" I asked.

Jacob stirred and kicked off his sailboat blanket. He turned his head away from us and a Matchbox truck slipped out of his hand and onto the floor.

"He fell asleep while playing?" I asked.

"No, I rocked him to sleep but he wouldn't let go of that car."

I grabbed the toy off the floor and stood up to leave, waiting for Meredith to follow me out into the hall.

"What are you really worried about, sweetheart? Maybe you shouldn't keep reading that book."

"No, I want to know about it. But my life is complicated enough. I don't need gray corpses floating around the living room," she said.

"You're really afraid?" I asked.

"You didn't come home last night and I know you were just working, but I've been reading this book and when you consider what else has been happening," she said.

"What? What's been happening?" I asked her.

"I don't know. I mean look at him," she said, holding up her book again.

I took the book away from her and tried to smile. With all the sincerity I could muster I told her, "Jesus loves you, Meredith. He won't hurt you, even if he is a zombie."

"Great."

"I'm serious."

"But how do you know. How do you know what they're up to?"

"They?"

"I just want reality, that's all."

"That's a tall order," I told her. "Reality? What is that exactly?"

She smiled. I'd done my job without faking it too much. I held her in my arms, and stared down at my hand on her back. I looked at my son's toy truck while trying to make everything all right.

"Jesus loves me?" Meredith laughed.

"Sure. Yeah. That's what they say."

"All right."

"I'm fine. Everything is fine."

But I wasn't.

My son's truck was yellow, and painted on the side, for no good reason that I could discern, were two little bees.

"It's fine. I'm fine," I told her. But I was staring at my son's truck, at the words printed beneath the bees.

JOIN US, the words read.

Jesus.

SOURCE UNKNOWN, DATE UNKNOWN

Q: How do these separate ideas connect?

A: It's a sampling, not a map.

Q: "Johnny B. Goode" is quite enjoyable. Mozart is interesting and also quite enjoyable. But I don't understand. Explain please.

A: Chuck Berry composed and performed "Johnny B. Goode." He's a rock-and-roll star. It's a rock-and-roll song.

Q: Will you please hold the baby bear?

A: That's not a real bear. That's a cartoon bear. How can I hold that?

Q: Will you please hold the baby bear?

A: No. That's just a picture, that's Boo-Boo. There's no baby bear here.

Q: What is rock and roll?

A: It's a popular musical form derived from blues and jazz.

Q: Look at the screen. Don't worry about that, you don't need to think about that. Look at the screen. What do you see?

A: It's just a bunch of waves, some red waves and . . .

Q: Do you hear that?

A: What is that noise?

Q: Please tell me about Mozart.

A: What do you want to know?

Q: What does Mozart mean?

I was maybe seven years old, and although the violin was not new to me, I was not a prodigy. Out in the backyard there was plenty of room, plenty of distance between me and anyone who might be trying to listen.

I sat on the root of the maple tree and looked up at the apartment house that I lived in with my parents. My father owned the house; there were several other families who lived there, but we didn't really interact with them.

I was alone in the backyard. I was bowing back and forth, doing variations in the key of C, when I spotted the bee.

It was huge and at first I thought it was a hummingbird. But as it circled around my head, I spotted the yellow-and-black fur and I jerked back, falling onto the grass and letting my violin slip gently to my side.

The bee came down, hovered right over my nose, and then lifted up and to the side. It didn't fly away, but just hovered about two feet to my left. After a few minutes I decided there was nothing to do but ignore it.

I improvised in the key of C, and I saw the bee bobbing in the air, moving up and down to the music. I'd let off a long high note, and the bee would jet off, up into the air. I'd sound a low note and the bee would sink. A quick burst of a song, I tried Mozart's *The Magic Flute,* and the bee was everywhere, weaving up and back and darting all around.

I played for hours, bowing along to a dancing bee.

I don't remember when the bee left, I don't remember how long I was out there. All I remember is that when I went in it was dark. My parents were furious, hysterical. I'd been gone for eight hours, they said, and they were on the verge of calling the police.

When I told them about the bee they just looked more angry.

"Don't lie to us," my mother said.

"What, do you think we're stupid? I looked all over the backyard for you. You think I didn't look in the backyard?"

"Where were you?" my mother asked. "Why did you scare us like that?"

All I could do was tell them about my bee and that my violin playing had really improved. Eventually my parents stopped asking me where I'd been and started examining my head, my arms and legs. Suddenly it wasn't anger, but stark fear, that moved them.

"How many fingers am I holding up?"

"What's the last thing you remember, sweetheart?"

"I was with a bee. A huge bee. And we were dancing."

RADIO PROGRAM, *TALKING MUSIC*, 11/5/98

Q: Do you envision yourself ever returning to your work with machine music?

A: Well, I never was much of a tech junkie. I mean Steve [Reich] worked on those electric circuits and channel selectors. . . .

Q: The phase-shifting pulse gate?

A: Right, and he did those pieces with swinging microphones and feedback.

Q: What did you think of those pieces?

A: Well, that stuff was interesting. . . . I mean, that was interesting to me because we were both working with tape loops in the sixties, and phase shifting was important to both of us. But overall, I think I moved back to instruments, back into the concert hall, faster than Steve did. I never really left the orchestra, because I was always conducting.

Q: What is phase shifting about? What is it that you and Reich were up to?

A: I guess it was Reich who really discovered the technique, and it was a very simple thing really. He was trying to line up these two tracks of tape, two loops of the same sentence from a sermon about Noah's Ark, and he wanted the two tracks to line up just so that they overlapped. He was working with these two tracks in a fairly ordinary and predictable way, but he didn't get it right. So, what he heard when he played the two tracks together was this slowly progressing phase shift. You know, one track was running slightly faster than the other. The two tracks started out the same, started out as one pattern, but when they got out of synch the sound started to wander. Finally the words became unrecognizable and you had this rhythmic thing happening and a creeping, wandering sound.

Q: What was the primary difference between Reich's tape loops and your own?

A: Well, I love "It's Gonna Rain," but my work was always more coherent, I think, than Steve's stuff. "Frozen Light" was about something, there was a story. You know, John Glenn thought he was seeing flying saucers out there, and those kinds of selections, the recordings I was working with, were just more interesting than what Steve was using. Even when the speech gets out of synch—

Q: Especially when the speech gets out of synch.

A: Yeah. I mean, there's a transcendent and mysterious quality to the phase-shifting stuff, and I think I worked with that more than Reich did.

Q: Are you interested in narratives in your work? It's a strange thing for a minimalist to be concerned with.

A: I'm interested in understanding what makes up a narrative. I've really left a lot of my more minimalist techniques behind. I mean, there are still a lot of repetitions, but I'm also stealing more . . . trying to figure out what's behind other musical traditions.

Q: There's a satiric streak in your latest works. Especially your operas.

A: I guess so. I'm just trying to figure out the roots of things. Trying to cut it up so it's not so familiar, and take a look at it again.

Q: Is that what's behind "Chuck Berry and the Magic Flute"?

A: Yes. I was trying to see the relationship between "Johnny B. Goode" and Mozart.

Q: And what you came up with was . . . well, it's funny stuff really.

A: Yeah. Well.

Q: Very quixotic. Why did you choose to juxtapose those particular musicians?

A: I guess I had to. I was compelled to.

Q: You had to?

A: Well, they're both on the *Voyager* probe. Both artists are, at least according to the committee I chaired with the late Carl Sagan, canonical and important to life on Earth. But, really, I can't tell you why I chose those two artists. I'm not supposed to tell you about that.

Q: Not supposed to tell me?

A: I'm sorry. I mean, I don't know how it works. The creative process is . . . I don't know.

Q: What are you working on now?

A: Another opera.

Q: Can I ask you what it's about?

A: You can ask. I'm not sure I can tell you.

Q: What's it about?

A: Bees. Mostly bees. And gorillas. Bees and gorillas.

Q: [laughing] I'll look forward to that.

A: Yes. Well.

Q: It's been a pleasure talking to you today.

A: Thank you.

Q: Next week on *Talking Music,* we will be visiting with Thomas M. Lauderdale, who will discuss swing music's new resurgence.

"I don't know the difference, Mom," Meredith said. She was talking on the phone and trying to rock Jacob to sleep. Jacob reached out, grabbed the portable phone, and dialed at random.

Sometimes Meredith forgets that our son is no longer an infant.

"I'm sorry. Are you still there? Let me put Jacob down."

I was sitting at my desk and trying out SoundEdit on my desktop computer. Meredith had opened the door to my study when she left Jacob's room on her way to the phone. I could keep working, but I was no longer off duty.

It was a welcome distraction. The new opera was a mess, and I was trying anything and everything in order to fix it. Tape music, synthesizer refrains, stolen excerpts from Pachelbel's *Canon* and even Beethoven's Fifth. I'd pulled out all the stops, ignored all scruples, but what I'd come up with was only one repeating phrase and a few hundred variations on it.

There was the bee theme and the gorilla theme, but I needed something more. What I needed was some other image to bring these two elements together.

I pressed play on my computer screen with a point and a click. The music of a human voice squeaked out from the computer's miniature speakers.

"The disks skipped across the sky like saucers on a lake." The voice was that of Kenneth Arnold, an Air Force pilot who, after encountering UFOs while flying over Mount Rainier in 1947, coined the term "flying saucer."

"The disks skipped."

"The disks skipped across."

"The disks skipped across the sky."

Pointing and clicking I flung the words back and forth, scratching up Kenneth Arnold like some sort of hip-hop artist.

"The . . . The . . . The . . . The disks . . . The disks skip."

My son ran down the hall, toward his room, shrieking and laughing as he bumbled along.

"I don't know. Maybe it's just that the modernists thought they knew the answers and the postmodernists are still looking. Yeah, you can tell Bill that if you want, but . . ." Meredith looks in on me, peeking around the door to my study and smiling. "Yes. Yes. Okay. I'm glad you think so," Meredith said. She covered the mouthpiece of the phone with her hand and turned her head. "Mom's defending your honor at the YWCA. I guess most retirees don't like your work," she said.

Eager for an excuse to leave my study, I leapt up to defend myself.

"But I'm talking in their language. I mean, remember in my Nixon concerto? I used all those brass instruments and did all that big band stuff," I told Meredith.

"Oh no. Not you too."

"Who doesn't like my music? Retirees? I'm writing specifically for them!"

"Hold on a second more, okay?" Meredith asked into the phone. "John, you're talking about thirty seconds in a forty-five minute meditation on the bombing of Cambodia."

"The disks skipped across the sky like saucers on a lake. The disks skipped across the sky like saucers on a lake. The the disks disks skipped skipped across across . . ."

"Let me talk to Kathy," I said, and reached to take the phone away from her.

"Ball, ball, ball, ball, ball, ball, ball, ball, ball." My son came out of his room at full toddle. He was holding a tennis ball over his head.

"The disks skipped across . . . The disks skipped across . . ."

"Kathy? You tell that man that I wrote 'Einstein's Flux Machine' specifically for him and that he's just not listening," I shouted into the phone.

"Ball?" Jacob asked.

"That's right. It's a tennis ball," Meredith told him as she picked him up again.

"The disks skipped across the sky like saucers . . . like saucers."

The Neighborhood of Make-Believe was rife with aliens. Purple Pandas from Planet Purple were blipping in and out of sight, appearing and disappearing.

"Rah-rah?" Jacob asked. "Mo rah-rah?"

"He'll be back," I said. "Mr. Rogers will be back on after the make-believe is over."

I sat at the kitchen table trying to scratch out at least an outline while my son sat in his high chair, spilling Cheerios onto the floor and waiting for his television friend to come back.

"They're so big," Daniel Tiger said.

"They are big, and purple," Lady Aberlin replied.

Daniel Tiger patted his dump truck and anxiously scanned the perimeter of his clock tower. "I could use my super-truck and then I wouldn't be so afraid." Daniel paused and looked up at Lady Aberlin with his perfectly round glass eyes. "Do you think the Pandas are trying to scare us?"

Lady Aberlin frowned. "I don't know, Daniel. The Purple Pandas are very big, and very purple. But maybe, do you think, they might be friendly?"

"I hope so, but they sure are different."

I looked down at my notebook and tried to think. If alien beings were directing the life of the protagonist, what would that mean? If he was to be depicted as a pawn of their influence, how could I make his actions meaningful? I started jotting down a melody which quickly turned into just another repeating series of notes that had to be fleshed out. I had to give my protagonist, a suburban businessman who secretly communed with ETs, an aria. I had to let him respond to what was happening. I had to let him act; had to let him sing.

"Mo rah-rah?" my son asked.

"Watch the trolley," I said. "When the trolley rolls by, we'll go back to Mr. Rogers's house."

"Rah-rah?"

"Yes. Here he comes. See the trolley? You know, Jacob, next week Papa is going to visit Mr. Rogers in person. Not just on television but in real life."

Jacob looked perplexed, not sure what the difference was.

Mr. Rogers appeared on the screen. "Sometimes people from other places can be scary. They just seem so different from you. But they're just people. Just like I'm a person, and you're a person. I wonder what Daniel Tiger will think when he finds out that the Purple Pandas are friendly. I wonder how he'll feel. We'll pretend more about that tomorrow," Mr. Rogers said.

"Papa rah-rah?" he asked.

"Yes, I'm going to go see him in Pittsburgh next week. Later on."

Mr. Rogers was sitting by the front door of his television house and untying his tennis shoes.

"But sometimes make-believe things like monsters and aliens and ghosts, those things can really be scary. Even if they are just pretend. And sometimes it helps to talk about those scary things with a parent or teacher who can really listen. And they can help you to know that it's all right even if you do get scared sometimes."

Mr. Rogers was ready to go; already he was back in his loafers and heading for the closet to fetch his tweed jacket.

"And that can give you such a good feeling," Mr. Rogers said.

"Ge-by, rah-rah," Jacob said.

"Good-bye, Mr. Rogers."

SOURCE UNKNOWN, TIME UNKNOWN

A: Why is my wife here?

Q: I have more questions.

A: What are you doing to her?

Q: We must keep track of you. Sometimes it is necessary to do these things.

A: She's not a musician. She wasn't on the committee. I don't understand.

Q: We are interested in her. But I have more questions for you. Why do you separate your sounds?

A: What are you doing to her?

Q: Please calm down. Please touch this.

A: I . . . I . . . Where am I?

Q: Please tell me why you separate your sounds.

A: I don't know what you mean.

Q: You call some sounds speech, others you call song. Some sounds are music, others are not. Please explain.

A: You don't have music?

Q: I am less separated from myself than you are. I don't understand what is not music. Please explain.

A: Music is a way of organizing sounds. It's a way of expressing ideas through composing different pitches, notes, harmonies.

Q: Different frequencies?

A: Yes.

Q: Why is all your music on the same frequency?

A: My music?

Q: Why is "Frozen Light" on the same frequency as "Einstein's Flux Machine"?

A: You're talking about my music?

Q: We've been working on your music, trying to understand and expand. You keep making the same patterns. Why?

A: I'm trying to understand.

Q: Will you pet the dog?

A: This again?

Q: Will you pet the doggy dog?

A: That's not a dog. That's a horse. That's Gumby's horse.

Q: Please show the dog your love. Pet the dog.

A: That's just a picture on a screen.

Q: You can differentiate between the image and the real?

A: Yes.

Q: Why do you select between images? Why are some images more real to you than others?

A: I don't understand.

Q: Why do you have dandruff? Why do you raise your hand if you're not really sure? Why is everything on the same frequency?

A: I'm tired.

Q: Look at the screen. What do you see?

A: The president of the United States.

Q: Will you talk to the president of the United States?

A: Hello, Bill.

Q: Please pet the dog.

A: That's not a dog.

Q: Look at the screen. Look at the waves of red.

A: What's that sound? What are you doing?

When I was at Juilliard, my roommate, a perpetually stoned jazz musician named Sam, used to take me to the airport. He loved airports. His idea of a relaxing evening out, his way of taking a break from music and school, was to drive out to LaGuardia and drink overpriced martinis while watching the 747s land.

"I WISH YOU wouldn't go," Meredith said. We stood at the gate looking out through the Plexiglas at the runway. My plane to

Pittsburgh was rolling toward the boarding tunnel. Pachelbel's *Canon* was gently flowing from the loudspeaker until static interrupted and boarding began.

"I have to go see Mr. Rogers," I told her. "This is my big break. I'll be reaching a whole new audience."

"Very new," Meredith said.

"Rah-rah?" Jacob asked. He leaned his head against Meredith's chest and she patted his head with her free hand.

"I'll be back soon," I told her.

SAM LIKED AIRPORTS because they gave him a sense of anonymity.

"It's like purgatory here. Nothing really happens. It's safe," Sam told me once after his fourth dry martini. "Let's go look at other people's baggage."

"WHAT'S THAT BUMP on your nose?" I asked Meredith as we stood in line.

She rubbed at her sinus and shrugged. "I don't know. Why don't you tell me?"

"How am I supposed to know? It's your nose," I said.

"Hose," Jacob said.

The flight attendant took my ticket, and I gave my wife and child a quick hug.

"Don't go, John. I've got this bump on my nose and I don't know what's happening and I don't want you to go," Meredith said.

"I . . ."

The attendant looked at me and frowned. I smiled back at her and then stepped out of line.

"I've got to go," I told Meredith. "I'll call you from Pittsburgh."

SAM DIDN'T JUST DRINK 'AND smoke pot, he also dropped acid, ate mushrooms, and chewed morning glory seeds. He liked being spaced out, and after our first semester I almost never saw him when he was sober.

"You know why I'm always stoned, John?" Sam asked.

"Because you're a bum?"

"It helps me with the groovy little gray dudes. It helps me see them more clearly," Sam said.

"The groovy gray dudes?" I asked.

"Yeah. They come to me, hang out around me, at night," Sam said.

"Where do they do this?" I asked.

"Oh, right here. They hang out by the foot of the bed and talk to me."

"What do they say?" I asked.

"Different things." Sam leaned over in order to fish out his tennis shoes from underneath the dorm's metal cot.

"What kinds of things?" I asked.

"Hey! I have an idea. Let's go to the airport," Sam said as he tightened his laces.

"What do they tell you, Sam?" I asked.

THE RENTAL CAR only had an AM radio, and so I listened to pop tunes from the sixties as I drove to *Mister Rogers' Neighborhood*. John Lennon kept telling me that nothing was real as I left purgatory and found the ramp to the highway.

And it was there, at the end of the entrance ramp, that I spotted the man in the gorilla suit. He was about seven feet tall, and he was holding the gorilla mask in his hands as he . . . as he floated across the asphalt.

He was seven feet tall and his mask was off. I drove up the ramp toward him, slamming my foot on the accelerator. His mask was off and his eyes shone out at me; huge almond-shaped eyes that were as black as night. I slammed my foot on the accelerator and then slammed into the gorilla man. Black fur flipped up onto my windshield and I spun the steering wheel and kept pressing the gas.

TELEVISION PROGRAM, *MISTER ROGERS'
NEIGHBORHOOD,* 10/30/98

Q: Did you love music when you were a boy?

A: Sure. Yes. I started playing the violin when I was four, and I loved going to concerts with my dad. I've always loved music.

Q: Well, you certainly are a talented musician now. You've grown up to be a person who can really make people happy with music.

A: Thank you.

Q: Do you think you could play something for us, maybe show us how you make songs and symphonies, and let us hear what they sound like?

A: I can do that. I've brought a reel-to-reel tape player with me today, and it has some piano music on it. What I'll do is set this up and if you'll let me play your piano . . .

Q: Oh, yes. I've got a piano in the living room. But before we go over there, do you want to feed the fish?

A: Sure.

Q: They need just a little bit.

A: Okay.

Q: There you go, fish. Today you're being fed by John Zucker-man.

A: Okay, let me get my tape player.

Q: And the piano is right over here.

A: So what I'm going to do is start up the tape machine and it's got some piano music on it, and I'm going to play along with it, only I'm going to play out of synch . . . the same notes in the same pattern, but because I'll be playing against the tape machine the music will change around a bit.

Q: You mean the same notes will change into different notes?

A: It's difficult to explain. I'll show you. (Playing along with the tape loop.) And you can hear how the same pattern when played at a slightly different time combines into a different pattern . . . and . . . and . . . Christ . . . Ohhhh . . .

Q: Is something the matter, John?

A: I've got to stop. Can we stop now?

Q: Sure . . . let's stop for a few minutes.

A: I just remembered something. I'm sorry. I'll pull myself together.

Q: There's no hurry. Did you remember something that upset you?

A: The sounds, the different patterns . . .

Q: They made you remember something?

A: I hit somebody, today. In my car on the way here. I think I hit somebody in my car. Only it wasn't a person.

Q: You hit somebody, in your car?

A: He wasn't human. . . . I hit an ape?

Q: I think we should take a break. Okay, everybody?

A: A man in a gorilla costume. Only he wasn't a man.

Q: This happened today?

A: On my way in from the airport. That's why I was late. Oh, Christ! Christ!

Q: You hit somebody with your car?

A: Shit . . . it was them. The gray men, the little men.

Q: John?

A: I . . . I . . .

Q: I think we're going to have to stop for the day.

A: They wanted me to make that noise . . . that sound.

Q: John, we're going to stop for today.

A: Why do they want me to make that sound?

Q: John, I want you to take a deep breath.

A: Get away from me. No, I won't pet your monkey. That's not a monkey.

Q: I want you to take some deep breaths. It's me, Fred Rogers, you're here at my television house and you're taking a deep breath.

A: What is that sound? What is it?

My son never did get to see me visit Mr. Rogers, and after my nervous breakdown in his television house I continued to sink. Strangeness, horrible and undeniable, surrounded me and I just tried to push on through.

I was a contactee, an abductee, an experiencer. After Pittsburgh I could remember it, remember them, but I didn't know what they wanted. I couldn't answer their questions or understand their sounds.

I was an abductee, and I knew it, and the abductions just kept coming.

"You're here," Foxman, the concertmaster, said. He was folding up his music stand when I walked into the rehearsal hall, and only paused briefly when he saw me. "You're here, but I'm still leaving."

"How late am I?" I asked.

"You are exactly one hour and fifteen minutes late," the third cellist told me.

"I'm sorry," I took my baton from the podium and then turned back toward the orchestra. "How many of you can stay a little longer?"

About twenty hands rose in response.

"Okay," I said. "Let's begin."

Foxman squinted at me. "You're wearing your jacket backward."

"I am?"

"And your pants."

"And my pants . . . backward. Yes," I said. "Okay, and one . . ."

I KEPT WORKING on my opera, kept adding elements, and kept coming back to the same basic pattern. *Missing Time* shifted right and left, and it was expanding, but when I looked over my notes they seemed like something written by a fourteen-year-old with autism.

I was looking for an answer, a satisfactory response, to the challenges and questions that they constantly thrust on me. I was looking for some way to understand what was happening, but what I came up with was just more stuttering, more phase shifting, more bees and gorillas.

I was writing my own libretto as well as the music, writing out the plot as well as the score:

"There are lights in the sky and lights along the road and lights that spell out SOAP and EXIT. And we might be visited, and we might be for we are. And the EXIT is the SOAP and the visitors are on the moon. Would you like some tea for your coffee or would you like the moon? And there are lights that spell there are lights that SOAP the EXIT, and there are visitors on the moon."

I had the telephone scene, and the barbecue scene, and the violin solo, and the spaceship would move very slowly across the stage. I had nothing, really, except yet another series of notes following the same basic formula that I would never, could never, escape. And the visitors were on the moon.

SOURCE UNKNOWN, TIME UNKNOWN

Q: Who are you?

A: You're asking me?

Q: Do you know your other self? We are tired of waiting.

A: What do you want?

Q: Who are you?

A: I am John Zuckerman.

Q: And without words?

A: What do you want from me?

Q: Without words.

A: What is that noise?

Q: It's you. You're making the music.

A: What is that noise?

Q: We are through waiting. The sound is yours. It's you.

Ufologists, debunkers, contactees, psychologists, bureaucrats, and faith healers have all come up with explanations for these kinds of experiences. The little gray creatures are benign visitors from the Pleiades system, they are bloodthirsty killers from Mars, they are a cultural delusion, they are angels, they are demons, they are a lie, they are God.

"I don't care what they are," Meredith told me. "I want them to leave us alone."

"Have you seen them?" I ask.

"Go check on Jacob. Will you just go and make sure Jacob is okay? You start talking like this and . . . Go look in on our baby."

We locked the doors, and then checked them again. We turned on the television, hoping that the actors and announcers selling Time-Life Books and Toyotas and Mutual of Omaha insurance would somehow stabilize the room with banality, and then we turned it off again.

"There are people who claim that all human religions are based on contact with aliens," I told Meredith.

"Do you want to listen to some music? Can I turn on the radio?" Meredith asked.

The oldies station was playing a song about flying purple people eaters.

"Have you seen them?" I asked again.

"Yes, I've seen them," Meredith said. "They're gray, ugly."

"So you understand? You don't think I'm crazy?"

"I wish you wouldn't bring those books home with you," Meredith said.

"You're not answering me."

"Those UFO books aren't good for Jacob. I had to take away a copy of *Communion* from him this afternoon," Meredith said. "He was playing with it and I think it scared him. The cover . . ."

"Meredith, I need you to help me. Something is happening and I don't know what it is," I said. I got up to turn off the radio, but instead I spun the dial over to the public access station.

"They're floating dots of light. They're floating dots of light. They're floating dots of light."

Some college kid with his own radio program was playing my early music. "Frozen Light" was on the radio.

"Jacob was talking to the cover of your book, to the man on the cover. He called him Papa," Meredith said. "He thought the gray monster on that book was you."

Nothing anybody says about UFOs makes any sense to me. I don't believe in time travel, I don't believe in faster-than-light travel, I don't believe in out-of-body experiences, and I have my doubts about the collective unconscious. People say that the aliens have been here always. People say that the aliens are us, some other part of ourselves.

They want something from me. They want me to be more than what I am. I don't know what they want. I don't know who they are.

"They're floating dots of light. They're-re floating-ting dots-ots," the words flowed out and mixed.

The world was phase shifting, and my job was to try and write it all down. I was expected to sing.

CONVERSATION WITH SPOUSE, SIGHTING OF UFO, 1/15/99

Q: What are we going to do?

A: I don't know.

Q: I can't believe this is happening.

A: You see it, too?

Q: Are the windows locked?

A: Let's go check. Let's go look.

Q: I don't want to look. Are the windows locked or not?

A: Do you hear that?

Q: It's beautiful.

A: Let's go look, let's go look out the window.

Q: You're on their side, aren't you?

A: Whose side? Oh, my God. It's huge.

Q: What is it?

A: It looks like a toy. It's exactly what you'd think a flying saucer would look like. Oh, and there are some people looking out the portholes.

Q: Come back. Get away from there.

A: You should see this.

Q: I'm going to watch a movie. Do you want to watch a movie? I rented *The Big Chill*.

A: Hello there. Hello.

Q: John, get away from the window.

A: Ooohhh . . .

Q: The light is . . .

A: Are you all right? Do you need help? Let me help you up.

Q: Thank you.

A: I think it was just a flyby. Are you okay?

Q: I have some questions.

A: What?

Q: I have some questions, why do you separate awake from asleep?

A: Meredith? What's going on?

Q: Why do you separate awake from asleep?

A: Meredith? What's wrong with you?

Q: Meredith is asleep.

A: I want her to wake up.

Q: How do you separate?

A: I want my wife to wake up. Oh shit. What's happening now? Why did you turn out the lights?

Q: Meredith is asleep. Why are you awake?

A: Is that a rhetorical question?

Q: Tell me about music. Please explain about music.

A: What do you want to know?

I'm not the only one who has been led like this. According to the paperbacks and Internet chat rooms, most pop music has been influenced by aliens.

JOHN LENNON WROTE a song called "Like a UFO," and David Bowie's Ziggy Stardust is actually a warning, a way to acclimatize the populace to the alien presence.

I can't adequately transcribe the opera here. I'll tell you what I can, but I can't tell you what it's about because it's not really mine.

What's more, reading the words to it doesn't convey much:

"When the sky is falling and the sky is falling and when it is we are. And give me an F and give me an F and give me an F. When the sky is falling I have to go to work, each day, by seven o'clock A.M. in the morning. I work in Beaverton. I work when the sky is falling. Hello."

It's a mess, incomprehensible, but I think I've finally captured that sound, the sound I've been hearing since I was three or four years old.

The night of the premiere, when the audience opened their programs and read aloud, I heard it. The sound that was not really a sound, but a thought, some idea, came to life on the stage.

My protagonist, a businessman who lived in Beaverton and secretly communed with UFOs, walked center stage and looked through the fourth wall.

The audience asked him questions.

LIBRETTO, *MISSING TIME,*
PERFORMED 4/5/99

A: There is no wall here. How long has it been this way? There is no wall here and I can see. . . . Who are you people?

Q: We have questions.

A: You have questions? I've been living my life thinking there was a wall where there wasn't one.

Q: Why do you live in such a world? Why do you pretend there are walls where there aren't any?

A: Who are you people? What do you want from me?

Q: We came here to watch you. And now we have questions.

A: You have questions?

Q: Will you tell us why we came here to watch you tonight? Will you tell us why we paid good money to come and watch you pretend there are walls where there aren't any?

A: Do you live where there aren't any walls?

Q: We have questions.

A: No. No more questions. Please. Just listen.

Q: What's that sound?

A: It's me. It's what one hears, what one says, when you break through. It's nothing.

Q: What is that sound? Why did we pay good money to come here and listen to you not say anything? Why did we pay good money for the orchestra not to play? What is that sound?

A: There isn't a wall here. Forget about the aliens, don't think about the way the sky is falling. What's interesting is the way there is no wall.

Q: Do you hear that?

A: How long has it been this way?

Q: We have questions.

A: Who are you people? How long have you been here? What do you want?

Q: We have questions.

A: I'm ready to answer.

TWO STORIES

James Sallis

. . .

Telling Lives

A COUPLE OF KIDS ARE STANDING AT THE BUS STOP READING my book about Henry Wayne, possibly a school assignment. Henry's right there with them with a cup of coffee from the Circle K, answering questions. So probably it's an assignment, all right. The city bus pulls in and they get on. I'm never sure how this works. Do they get some kind of pass to ride the city bus to school or what? Every morning there's a couple dozen of them out there waiting.

Across the street, Stan Baker, who owns most of the good affordable apartments in this part of town, is up on the roof of one of his units poking around at ledges, fittings, tar. Someone else with khakis and a clipboard is up there with him. City employee's my guess. Stan waves when I look up. I wrote my first biography about him.

No one ever imagined they'd catch on this way. Who could have? I wrote that first one, about Stan, on a lark, more or less to have something to do as I sat in front of the computer each morning. My last literary novel, at which I'd labored a full year, had sunk without a trace, not even flotsam or driftwood left behind. I'd taught for a while at the local community college but had no real taste or aptitude for it. When I went on to write features for the *Daily Republic,* bored with simple transcription, I found myself first making up details, then entire stories. It was in the biographies, cleaving to the well-defined shoreline of a life, that I found a strange freedom, a release.

"Barely scratch beneath the surface of any one of us, even the dullest slob around," my old man used to tell me, "and you'll come on a source of endless fascination and contradiction. We're all inexhaustible, teeming planets, filled with wonder."

This from a man who had little interest in others' lives (mine included, sadly) and who rarely left the house. Number twenty-two in the series.

Nowadays, of course, the biographies are about all anyone around here reads. Has the town somehow found itself, come to itself, within them? Certainly, for my part, I've stumbled onto an inexhaustible supply of material—and my life's work.

Carefree, the town where they care.

That's how we're known now, here just down the road from the nation's sixth largest city with its riot of dun-colored buildings, cloverleafs, and sequestered communities, ridgeback of mountains looming always in the distance.

And we do care. All of us, every one. Schoolkids with their backpacks and mysterious piercings, bank presidents, sanitation-truck jockeys, yardmen, and insurance salesmen alike. Clerks at convenience stores going nine out of ten falls with the angel of English each moment of their day. The group of street dwellers who regularly congregate in the alley behind Carta de Oro.

However we try to break out, to break free, we're forever locked within our own minds. Locked away from knowledge of ourselves every bit as much. But there's this one ride out we can sometimes hitch, this tiny window through which, with luck and good weather, we can peer and see ourselves, in the guise of another, looking back in.

That's what the biographies have become for us, I think, those rides, those windows.

"Hard at work, I see," Bobby Taylor (number eighteen in the series) says as I sip my morning double espresso at the Coffee Grinder. He's on duty, has his helmet tucked under one arm, what looks like half a gallon of coffee in the other hand, motorcycle pulled up just outside.

"Finger on the pulse and all that, Officer."

"Looks more like butt in chair to me."

"What can I say? It's a sedentary occupation."

"How's your mom?"

Mother was hospitalized six months back after meeting a UPS man at the door with an electric carving knife. She said he'd raped her, and no one should treat a twelve-year-old that way. In the hospital she'd turned thirteen, or so she claimed. One of the nurses baked her a cake, and everyone gathered round for the party. She'd blown out all thirteen candles.

"Holding her own."

"Alzheimer's, right?"

"What they say."

"She know you?"

"Some days she does."

"Next time you visit and it's one of those days, tell her little Bobby Taylor says hello. Had her for tenth-grade English, like nearly everyone else in town. Only A I ever got. Parents couldn't decide whether to be shocked or expect it to go on happening."

"And?"

"Shocked won out."

I was getting ready to leave when a thirtyish woman stepped up to my table. She had black hair cut short in the back, longer toward the front, giving an impression of two wings.

"Mr. Warren?"

"Yes."

She held out a warm, narrow hand, nails painted white and trimmed square across.

"Justine Driscoll. May I join you?"

Although I'd not noticed it before, a radio was playing behind the counter. Now soft jazz gave way to news. I heard "two fairies collided off the coast of Maine," then realized the announcer meant *ferries*.

"Please do. Can I get you something?"

"I'm fine. I own a small publishing company, Mr. Warren. I was wondering if—"

"I have an exclusive contract with McKay and Rosenwald, you must know that."

"Of course. But I hoped you might look this over. It's our leader for the fall. A flagship book, really, launching a new series."

From a book bag slung like a purse over one shoulder she extracted and passed across a copyedited manuscript, corrections and emendations in red pencil in a tiny, tidy hand.

I read the first few pages.

"The barber's hair," I said.

It began with the story of my mother at the hospital, blowing out those thirteen candles.

"You're not surprised."

"It was only a matter of time."

"Would you be willing to give it a read, let us know if there are errors?"

I pushed it back across the table. "I have no wish to read it, Miss Driscoll. You have my blessing, though—for whatever that's worth."

"Actually, it's worth quite a lot. Thank you."

She stashed the manuscript back in her book bag.

"Our salespeople are strong behind this. We have solid orders from Barnes and Noble, Borders."

"Then let me join them to say that I sincerely hope it does well for you."

"I'll not take up any more of your time, Mr. Warren."

She stood. Her eyes swept the room. I had the sense of a camera recording this scene. It was a glance I knew all too well.

"Miss Driscoll?"

She turned back.

"You look remarkably like my wife, Julie. Way you're dressed. Nails. Hair."

"Do I really?"

"She died eight years ago, a suicide."

"I know. From the book. And I'm sorry."

"This Frances Frank, the author. It's you, isn't it?"

She stood, irresolute. Before she could respond I asked, "Do you have plans for the rest of the day?"

"No."

"Yes."

The Museum of Last Week

Thornton is right. The park has become crowded, all but impassable, inhabited by thickets of statues in various stages of self-creation and decay. I had no idea there were so many of them. Unmoving bodies as far as can be seen, crowded up against one another, standing, stooping, stretching. Some on their backs. The children like to come in at night and topple them.

I walked by there today. Not that I'd meant or planned to. Far from it. Nonetheless, stomach rumbling and sour with the morning's coffee, I found myself outside the fence looking in.

Scant miles away, scattered about with cholla and bottlebrush cactus, the desert looms, a sea bottom forsaken by the sea.

It is, yes, beginning to look like her, just as Thornton said. In a few days the features will be unmistakable. Even as I watched—though in truth I must admit I stood there for some time—they changed.

Tell me you won't forget me, you said.

Easy enough, Julie. How could I ever? Ravages of your face in those last months soon to be caught in that of the statue inside, by the concrete bench and the fountain that hasn't worked for years.

The whole secret of everything, you once told me—art, conversation, life itself—is where the accent's placed: the emphasis, the stress.

Do things happen faster now, closer together, than they used to, or does it just seem that way? As though all has shifted to time-lapse photography, entire life cycles come and gone in moments; as though the lacunae and longueurs that for the most part comprise our lives, these struts that hold up the scaffold of the world, have been removed. Our lives have become instant nostalgia, an infinite longing for what's been lost. While the world, like Wallace Stevens's wide-mouthed jar left out in the rain, slowly fills to the brim with the mementos, decay, and detritus of our past.

Looking for more coffee, hair of the dog, I stop at a convenience store. I always order two cups, and sure enough, as I depart, a youngish man in corduroy sport coat and chinos approaches, coat so worn as to resemble a chenille bedspread, chinos eaten away well above onetime cuffs.

"I am attempting to resolve the categorical imperative with the categorically impossible," he tells me. We stand staring at each other. Kant at ten in the morning on the streets of downtown Phoenix. "Do you have the time, sir?" he says after a moment.

Professing that I wear no watch, I offer what I have instead: the extra coffee.

"I only wish I could have the luxury of not knowing," he says. "Unfortunately that is not the case. And I feel," he says as he takes a sip of coffee and falls in beside me, "that there may not be much time left." We stride along, two men of purpose moving through city, day, and world. Perhaps every third sentence of what he says makes sense. He is desperate for bus fare to the university where he teaches, one of these vagarious sentences informs me. "I was lost but now am found. Still, yesterday and today, I have had no access to research facilities." And a bit later on: "Tomorrow for the first time my students will be prepared for class and I will not be."

I ask what he teaches.

"History. And, every other semester, a seminar on forgetfulness."

Not long toward nightfall, I attend a housewarming for Sara and Seth, researchers who have just moved in together. This is a match made somewhere just off the interstate between heaven and Hollywood. Seth is the world's leading authority on mucus, can speak for hours concerning protein content, viscosity, adhesiveness, mucopurulence, degrees of green. Sara in turn has fifty pounds of elephant penis in her—now their—refrigerator.

You once told me that we understand the world, we organize it, in whatever manner we're able.

"An erect elephant penis weighs around one hundred eight pounds and is sixty-two inches in length," says Gordon, who, as an editor, knows such things.

"That's up to here," Ralph remarks, holding his hand at a level about six inches above my head. Flamingly gay, he takes inordinate delight in such rodomontade.

"Sixty-two inches is five-foot-two," I remark.

"Right," Ralph says. "Up to here on you," indicating again the same spot.

What does it mean, I wonder, that he feels this need to belittle me during an exchange concerning penises? But I suppose that indeed I will be, must be, a short statue. Julie will tower over me as she did in life, in every way.

Correct me if I'm wrong, but this is how I remember it. Gregory Peck, on safari, has been injured. He lies all but helpless in his tent, gangrene staking claim to leg and life as hyenas circle outside. The woman he loves attends him.

This is what I'm thinking as I step away from the others, away from fifty pounds of elephant penis in the fridge and dissertations on mucus, into the night. I was eight, nine, when I first saw that movie at the Paramount one Sunday afternoon. Scant blocks away the Mississippi boiled in its banks. Within the week it would surmount levee and sandbags and rush the lowlands. I kept having to ask my brother to explain what was going on in the movie. I'm not sure he understood a great deal more than I did at that point, but he gave it his best. He's now a philosopher.

And now, of course, in our world, anticipation has gone into overdrive. Gregory Peck would never just lie there listening to the hyenas. They'd be on him before he knew it.

Back home, I brew white tea (high in antioxidants, low in caffeine) in a white pot and take it in a white cup out onto my white-pine patio. Darkness surrounds, and I lift my cup to it—whether in supplication or challenge I do not know. What has my life come to? What have all our lives, what has our world, come to?

I go back inside, to the pantry. I've saved these a long time.

The scars come in packages of six. I rip open a package at random and sense the scars' restlessness as they stir to life, sense their pleasure at being allowed to do at last what they were created for.

HELP WANTED

Karen Russell

. . .

1. *Mer-Girl*

THE MER-GIRL'S DREAMS ARE FULL OF SALT-DILUTED LONGING.

"Quit thrashing around," her husband grumbles, poking her awake. "You woke me up again."

His tongue sea-slugs against hers, an old invertebrate habit. She misses the thrill of those first kisses, back when he filled her lungs with unfamiliar air.

"You taste like purple smoke," she whispers, "and interrupted dreams."

"You taste like toothpaste," he says, rolling over. "Good night."

Every night, the Mer-Girl brushes the sea foam taste from her tongue. She buffs her scales with loofah until they flake off in iridescent ribbons. She picks tiny starfish and sea lice out of her long hair. Their dessicated bodies line the edge of the enamel tub.

"Get a haircut," her husband suggests, watching as she braids dead eels through her ponytail. "And get a real job."

THE MER-GIRL GETS a job at Aqua Tots. She teaches babies how to swim. The idea is that the babies will remember the aqueous warmth of the womb, their fetal gill-slits.

"You'll see, Amanda-Stacie," the director smiles. "You've got to start them while they're young, before they forget how to float on their backs."

The Mer-Girl tries flipping the babies on their backs to test the director's theory. She can see that the director has exaggerated these babies' capabilities.

At Aqua Tots, there are black babies and white babies and Hilola, a honey-eyed Hawaiian baby. There are fat, taffeta-bright babies, and jaundiced babies that the Mer-Girl cradles like sickle moons. All of the babies possess the same aptitude for swimming, which is to say, none at all. The Mer-Girl is appalled.

Recently, Aqua Tots has started offering a service called Drown-Proofing. This involves dunking the babies under the water, again and again, until they learn how to hold their breath. They are slow, sputtering learners.

When their mothers aren't looking, the Mer-Girl tugs at the webbing of their tiny feet. "Kick," she whispers furiously. "Kick."

AT NIGHT, THE Mer-Girl scans the classified ads. She works on her résumé. She doesn't have many marketable credentials, although she does have an advanced degree. It's a secret education, one her husband knows nothing about. He likes to brag that he reeled her in on the first cast. The Mer-Girl lets him. She doesn't mention her diploma from the Undersea School of Seduction. Anyway, it's not like she was a stellar student. The Mer-Girl got placed in the remedial classes.

"Don't flop right into the boat!" her teachers chided. "Do you want people to think you're some kind of floozy?"

At school, they learned how to smile demurely while flinging their bodies against the splintery hulls of ships. The Mer-Girl used to get scolded for her bad attitude. When the sailors finally lowered their nets, she'd yawn with disappointment.

"You're supposed to act surprised," the teachers lectured, "and helpless." They made her study goggle-eyed fish for inspiration.

In the honors classes, the more accomplished mer-Girls practiced churning their arms in tandem.

"You must create a coy sea foam," the teachers explained, "to cover all of your scaly horror beneath the water."

All of the students had to memorize the score to the siren song. The Mer-Girl used to get confused and substitute lyrics from old show tunes. At dusk, they practiced singing it to easy targets: widowed sea kayakers, science teachers on singles cruises. Compositionally, it's not a very impressive piece—although there is one tricky part with a tambourine. But it worked on her husband.

The Mer-Girl has felt contemptuous of him ever since.

Even so, she still dreams about the first time she lay splayed out on his boat. Her withered fins twitch at the memory of it. That invisible line, tugging her out of her element. Then the quick ascent through skeins of orange light, bubbles streaming off her skin. Wild-eyed wanting, the joyful writhing on the hook, and that amphibious moment when she first broke the surface of the water. For a moment she swung perfectly suspended, the sun on her face, her torso cleaved by cold water. Back when her whole body was an indecision.

Throw me back—shallow-gasping in his shadow on the deck— *Don't throw me back.*

2. Bat Girl

The Bat Girl frowns and thinks for a moment, scratching at the membrane between her mammalian wings.

"I graduated summa cum laude, and I have years of relevant work experience," she says. "Also, I'm a bat." She hopes it doesn't come across like she's bragging.

"Vampire bat?" the interviewer asks warily.

"No, I'm a pollinator."

The interviewer nods without looking up, scanning the Bat Girl's application.

The Bat Girl never went to college. Her references are complete fabrications. There's a honeysuckle stamen caught between her teeth.

"You're hired." The interviewer smiles. "When can you start?"

The Bat Girl works as a marriage counselor at the Caverns of Spousal Reconciliation. They give her one of the large corner caves with stalactite chandeliers, lit by the dim effulgence of guano. The Bat Girl is the resident sonar therapist. She measures the distance between couples by listening to their echoes. The couples bounce accusations off one another—*You-never-you-don't-you-can't-you-won't.* The stalactites gleam above them like bared fangs. She rocks from the rooftop, eyes shut, and lets the acoustics of anger reverberate through her.

The Bat Girl has no formal training as a sonar therapist, but she has figured out that the actual words don't matter. Her tawny body shivers with their subterranean echoes. They drill into her ears like red-black spikes, a syncopated sadness: You stranger, you charlatan. You don't love me anymore.

It's exhausting work. Sometimes she wishes she'd taken that job as a silent-movie usher. From nine to five, she tries to steer the couples toward each other. She uses her echolocation to alert them to certain obstacles: buried grudges, old flames. She shouts upside-down encouragement from the rafters.

"Love is work!" she yells. "Fight the currents of discontent! Keep paddling toward each other!"

Then she watches, helpless, as they capsize on dark waves of sound.

The Bat Girl declines her colleagues' insincere invitations to go out for tacos. She doesn't have much in common with the other therapists. The girls in the office all like to get tanked on Cocotinis and walk around upright. They split guac and chips, and place bets on which of their male patients will turn out to be bigamists.

"Gee, no thanks," the Bat Girl always says. "I brought my lunch." She points at a sugary bag of peonies, her pink nose twitching.

During her lunch hour, she spreads her thin wings and goes blind-flying around the empty office. She does solo airsaults, rejoicing in the ultrasonic frequency of solitude. She bathes in the blue sound of her own voice.

Echo-la-la.

In the sweet relief of darkness, the Bat Girl sings.

Today, the Bat Girl still has one appointment before her break. Her eleven o'clock comes in, carrying what appears to be a giant tuna in a honey blond wig.

"This is my wife," he sighs, slumping her onto the floor of the cave. "She's depressed. We just moved to the Midwest. I'm an inland sort of man myself, but she's having a hard time adjusting."

"I am *not,*" she sighs in a sleep-bubbled voice. "I am a *very happy person.*"

Then she proceeds to burst into tears.

The Mer-Girl's sadness goes rippling through the cave at disheartening decibels. The Bat Girl gives her a blank, sympathetic smile, devoid of all judgment. Then she uses one clawed toe to scratch off the "Longshot" box on the clipboard suspended from the roof. She hopes her patients don't notice that she's placed her tiny claws over her ears.

"Oh boo-goddamn-hoo," the husband growls. "I guess I'm the big villain now for earning us a living? I guess you'd prefer to be hitching rides on manatees, instead of driving our fully automatic family sedan?" The Bat Girl can see that his bald head is sweating. "I guess it's too much to expect you to hold down a *part*-time, *minimum*-wage—"

"I guess I'm having a baby," the Mer-Girl interrupts. "And I don't want her to grow up marooned in a, a . . . shitty suburb of Cheboygan!"

The man stares at his wife. The Bat Girl gulps down the momentary silence, filled with guilty relief. She wonders which one of them the baby will take after. She rubs her sensitive eyes. When she opens them, she realizes that they are both staring at her, waiting for her assessment.

"This relationship can work," the Bat Girl warbles without conviction. "Love is work."

The Mer-girl gazes up at her with one lidless fish eye. "Then I'd like to use my sick days, please."

3. Centaur Girl

The Centaur Girl finds seasonal work at the carnival, giving rides to children. It's a lousy job. They pay her in candied-apple cores and bags of stuffing from the glassy-eyed bears. The Centaur Girl gets stuck carrying the fat children, the ones too heavy to ride the Shetland ponies. Her boss, the carnival barker, is a diabolical woman named Maisy Dotes. She wears a straw hat and carries a whip. She looks like an old sow, a slobbery ear of corn dangling from her lips.

"Don't worry," she reassures the Centaur Girl at the job interview. "The whip's just for show."

Then she cracks the whip across the Centaur Girl's knuckles, leaving a bright red welt.

The Centaur Girl has a hard time fitting in at work. The magician's assistants spend their breaks in the trailer, daubing at their pedicures with long rainbow scarves. They look down at her unshod hooves and give her a pained smile. The Shetland ponies won't talk to her. They roll their eyes at her stringy hair. They pass nickering judgment on her horsehide, which tapers into paperthin skin that hides nothing. They go gamboling around after hours to flirt with the locals, smelling of sweet manure and clover. Centaur Girl spends after hours alone in her trailer. She smells like kidsweat and ineluctable girl.

During the pony rides, Chumley, Maisy Dotes's idiot son-in-law, leads the Shetlands and the Centaur Girl around a worn dirt track. The Centaur Girl's cheeks burn with shame. She envies the other ponies, who trot after Chumley with a dumb animal loyalty. The Centaur Girl doesn't even like carrots, and she's conscious of the stick. Still, she follows him around.

It's just a job, she whistles through gritted teeth.

Some days, around the forty-fifth revolution, she'll decide that she's in love with Chumley. Her heart swells with a gelded longing as she watches him scratch his human ass. Then, by the time she's made it around the track again, she's fallen back in hate with him. She's not sure why she flip-flops this way. She supposes it's a strategy for passing the time. It beats swatting flies, anyhow.

The Centaur Girl keeps getting passed over for promotion. Her earnest neighing makes the children snicker. It negates all of her equine pretensions. It's too heartfelt, too human. And she lacks the ponies' quadruped equilibrium. Her body wobbles gracelessly from the waist up. Whenever her tubby riders dig their sneakers into her flanks, the Centaur Girl stumbles. Her hands are caked with blood and the orange stubs of losing raffle tickets. Pretzel salt gets in her wounds. If she's in a generous mood, Maisy Dotes will wrap them in gauzy strips of cotton candy.

Today, the Centaur Girl is staunching a spot of blood on her right flank with a strawberry ice cream cone. Little pink and red droplets dot the ground. When she looks up, she sees that there's been some kind of holdup in the pony ride. A mer-girl is standing in line, arguing with Chumley. The Mer-Girl is holding a plastic bag with a goldfish, the kind you win at the Dunk-a-Lunk. Both she and the goldfish look intensely unhappy.

"I took the day off work," she says. "Please, let me on. I'll take my chances. I just want to go for a ride."

"Sorry, lady, no dice." Chumley shakes a fat finger at her belly, which billows out over her tail. "Pregnant women and people with spinal injuries aren't allowed on the ponies." He points at a card-board cutout of an impish boy next to the CAUTION sign. " 'Sides, you must be this human to ride."

The Centaur Girl gives her a sympathetic shrug, but the Mer-Girl doesn't see it. She is already taking mincing steps toward the parking lot, standing on the tips of her fins. The Centaur Girl wonders where the Mer-Girl works. She wonders if she'll take a seaside maternity leave. The Centaur Girl feels a sharp stab of envy in her own empty gut. The vet has confirmed that she's as sterile as a mule. She'd be curious to know what mystery is incubating inside the Mer-Girl's womb.

After the fairgrounds close, the Centaur Girl always lingers. She pretends to sweep up the colorful balloon scraps with her tail. The other carnies trickle out one by one:

"Bye, Centaur Girl!" says the Singer of Unsung Songs.

"Bye, Centaur Girl!" says the Human Candle.

"Bye, Centaur Girl" until she is nearly bursting with impa-tience.

Then she goes clip-clopping down the empty boardwalk to the dark, motionless merry-go-round. She trots in slow circles be-neath the unlit bulbs, her tail swishing merrily. The Centaur Girl nuzzles the painted lions and the ceramic swans. She bobs up and down for effect. Sometimes she stamps her feet, and sometimes she claps her hands. She whinnies unconvincingly in the half-light of dusk.

4. Girl-Girl

Child labor laws prevent her from finding an occupation. In the economy of the womb, her eyes are shut in a dreamless sleep. Her body is an indecision. She's still floating on her back, unemployed.

"EFT" OR "EPIC"

Sarah Micklem

...

AN EXTANT FRAGMENT OF "THE LAY OF ROEBLAND," TRANS-
lated by Dr. Simone Menthaler, with annotations by the translator.

> *Dobe evek y*
> *An nolish bren o toft*
> *Ovan ekven oblish*
> *Y ony spen e stoft*

The warrior[1] smiled at[2] her[3]
She bade him step over the threshold
And under the lintel[4]
Her eyes cast downward[5]

1. *Dobe:* a warrior who supplies his own equipage but has
   pledged fealty to a greater lord in a time of need. The
   word is in the active modality, indicating he is armed
   and armored. In context with the subsequent word I
   suggest he is wearing a half helmet which conceals his
   eyes, such as the one recently excavated near Darvon.
2. *Evek:* a smile where the muscles around the eyes are
   not tightened as they are in most kinds of smiles; the
   lips curve without baring the teeth. This smile has no
   humor in it, but rather menace and possibly
   mendacity. If one agrees, however, that the warrior is
   wearing a helmet and therefore the eyes are not
   visible, one might conclude, as I do, that the smile is

one of suppressed and dangerous excitement. It is inexact to translate this phrase as "he smiled *at* her" because the preposition folded into *evek* should be rendered as something more aggressive. I failed to find an English equivalent that did not sound absurd.

3. *Y:* the pronoun for a beautiful woman of marriagable age who is nevertheless not yet married.

4. "Over the threshold and under the lintel" is clearly a metaphor for marriage or sex. The Roeblish feminist Any Bevek has argued at length that this fragment describes a rape. I feel there is little evidence in the context to support her conclusion. See note 5.

5. *Ony spen e toft:* I've translated this as "eyes cast downward," but it would be a more accurate (though unfelicitous) translation to say that the young woman who is yet unmarried takes a step aside, bends her stiff neck, and looks at the floor somewhat near the feet of the warrior. She keeps her face still but nevertheless her downcast eyes show not only modesty but fear. Here Bevek diverges from others, interpreting this as the maiden's fear for her safety, whereas most students of the epic, including myself, read it as a stimulating, anticipatory fear.

A Note on Translation from Roeblish

Though I have, in the course of my career as a philologist and translator, encountered many words and concepts difficult to translate economically and gracefully into English, never have I faced difficulties as great as those I found in rendering "Eft," believed to be a fragment of a great, lost thirty-line epic poem from Roebland's eventful third century A.D. Only one other line is extant from "The Lay of Roebland," and for a translation and explication of that line, which I could never hope to better, I refer you to Dr. Alfoot's book, *Meren Gon e Nesoom*. The Roeblish hold these five lines to be a cherished part of their national heritage, and I know that in offering this translation I have laid myself open to their intense scrutiny. I lived among the Roeblish for fifteen years before making this attempt. It may take as many more years before I can fully understand whether I have achieved something worthy or failed utterly.

The great Jesuit linguist, Father Francisco Gargani, the first to attempt a Roeblish/Italian dictionary, died exhausted after working on it for forty-five years. I am deeply grateful to him for revealing to the outside world the incredibly rich and strange language of the Roeblish. Tucked away on their northern isle, having little contact with other peoples, the Roeblish developed the language of emotion, gesture, and expression to a degree unknown elsewhere. It is said the Inuit have seventeen (or two hundred, or twenty-five, or merely twelve) words for snow[1] in all its manifestations, due to its importance in their culture. The Roeblish have, on the other hand, sixty-seven words for various kinds of smiles, twenty-six words for laughter, and so on, beyond my ability to enumerate. This allows them to express nuance with a precision that the writer who works only with the words available to him in English, for example, or French, Mandarin, even Japanese, can only envy.

From infancy, human beings around the world learn a universal language of facial expressions. When shown a photograph of a woman making a face of disgust, Okinawans and Ohioans alike could identify the emotion correctly. A Roeblish speaker, however, could tell if the woman was really disgusted or merely pre-

---

1. Linguists cannot agree on a number as they do not agree on the definition of *word*. In any case, Enuktak Pikiyut pointed out long ago that there are now, of necessity, many more expressions for types of ice than snow, because of the dangers and opportunities ice presents to Inuit hunters.

tending, and probably could deduce whether the disgust (if real) was occasioned by a bad smell, an unpleasant taste, or something imaginary.

Infants who hear certain phonemes learn to vocalize them through imitation; those who do not hear the phonemes grow up without the ability to recognize or reproduce them. Such is the plasticity of the human brain during the narrow span of time in which the fundamentals of language are mapped in the mind. The Roeblish language has, in its subtlety, given its native speakers the perceptual tools to "read" and render in words the language of the face and body more accurately than other peoples. It has been noted by many travelers that the Roeblish are oddly inexpressive. Their facial expressions and gestures are minimal; their laughter is muted and often silent. They frequently cover their mouths when they smile. This is the face they show to strangers. The Roeblish fail to understand that they have no need to conceal themselves from us. We lack the very words to interpret their smiles or frowns; we cannot distinguish at a glance—as they can—between a liar and a truth teller.

THE RED PHONE

John Kessel

. . .

THE RED PHONE RINGS. YOU PICK UP THE RECEIVER. "HELLO?"

A woman's voice. "I want to speak with Edwin Persky."

"Just a minute." You put her on hold, then punch in the letters: P-E-R-S-K-Y. The sound of a phone ringing. A woman answers. "Hello?"

"Edwin Persky, please."

"Hold on." She puts you on hold and leaves you listening to a pop orchestral recording of "Try to Remember" while she connects with Persky. Pretty soon she's back. "This is Edwin Persky," she says. "What can I do for you?"

You go back to the woman on hold, and say to her, "This is Edwin Persky. What can I do for you?"

The woman's voice becomes seductive. "I want to have sex with you."

You switch back to Persky's interlocutor. "I want to have sex with you."

She speaks with Persky, then relays his response. "What are you wearing right now?"

Back to woman one. "What are you wearing right now?"

"I'm wearing black lace panties and a garter belt. And nothing else."

You wish these people would show a little more imagination. And why the garter belt if she's not wearing hose? You can see her as she really is, sitting in her kitchen wearing a ragged sweatsuit, eating cookie dough out of a plastic container.

You tell Persky's rep: "I'm wearing black lace panties and a garter belt. And nothing else."

"Jesus," she sighs. Something about the way she sighs conveys more intimacy than you've felt from anyone in six months. A shiver runs down your spine.

She relays the come-on, then replies, "I'm taking off my pants. My mammoth erection thrusts out of my tight boxers. I fall to my knees and rub my three-day growth of beard against your belly."

You pass along the message. Cookie-dough woman says, "I come down on top of you and take your organ into my mouth. My tongue runs over the throbbing veins." It's too much. "Don't say that," you tell her. "Say, 'I grab the term insurance policy from off your cluttered desk and roll it into a tube. I place the tube over your dick, put one end into my mouth, and begin humming "The Girl from Ipanema." ' "

" 'The Girl from Ipanema?' What's that?"

"Don't worry. Just say it."

The woman hesitates, then says, "I grab the insurance policy—"

"—*term* insurance."

It takes her three tries to get it right. You pass it along to Persky's rep.

"That took a while," she says, after she passes it on. "At least it's original."

You snicker. "I had to help her. What's Persky doing?"

"I expect he's whacking off. Shall we speculate?"

"So does he have a reply?"

"Let's see—'I'm thrusting, thrusting, into your red mouth. I pinch your nipples and'—Jesus, I can't say this. Tell her he says, 'I smear warm guava jelly over your perky earlobes while transferring three hundred thousand in postcoital debentures to your trust fund."

"Debentures—I like that."

"Thanks," she says.

You relay the message to cookie-dough woman. She replies with something about waves of pink pleasure. You don't bother to get her onboard this time as you tell Persky's interlocutor, "I double your investment, going short euros in the international currency markets while shaving your balls with a priceless ancient bronze Phoenician razor of cunning design."

She comes back: "My amygdala vibrates with primal impulse as the sensory overload threatens to reduce my IQ by forty points."

Now this is what you call action. And a challenge. You are inspired and reply with a fantasy about Peruvian nights and the downy fur of the newborn alpaca. It goes on like this for a while. Cookie dough starts gasping, and the pauses between Persky's replies stretch. Soon his interlocutor and you have time on our hands.

"Are you working this Tuesday?" you ask her.

"No. You?"

"*Nihil obstat*. Take in a movie?"

"Sounds good. I'm Janice."

"Sid. Meet me at the Visual Diner on McMartin. Seven-thirty?"

"How will I know you?"

"I'll be wearing lace panties and a garter belt," you tell her.

"Okay," Janice says. "Look for my throbbing organ."

THE WELL-DRESSED WOLF

A RHETORICAL JOURNEY THROUGH
HIS WARDROBE IN FAIRY TALES

. . .   *Written by Lawrence Schimel*

Illustrated by Sara Rojo

What a magnificent creature is the wolf! Look at the way his velvet-smooth pelt shifts over lean muscles, like the sliding of shadows across the ground as a cloud passes in front of the moon. Shadowlike, the wolf stalks across the night, but the wolf is anything but substanceless. The wolf represents power. And danger. Just look at the wolves of fairy tales, always lurking on the edges of the story, ready to snatch unwary children.

The storybook wolf is always assumed to be male. Maybe it's the wolf's predatory nature that gives this assumption, where we associate hunting and power with masculine. Or perhaps it's the fact that most märchen seem to be morally instructive to girls: wait for your prince to save you, don't talk to strangers, be respectful of your elders, and so on, and a male presence (in the form of the wolf) is more useful for extrapolating to real-life encounters. . . . It may simply be that Western culture seems to have divided animal representations of sexuality as follows: fox=female and wolf=male.

If one were to visit the storybook wolf in his den, it would be no surprise to find his closet full of James Dean black leather jackets, clean white T-shirts, and sharply pressed denim jeans.

But that's not what wolves actually wear in fairy tales. Instead of living up to his bad boy image, the storybook wolf, when he wears anything at all, winds up cross-dressing. And not even in something sexy! Instead of red leather miniskirts (the female equivalent of bad boy biker jackets?) the storybook wolf winds up wearing Granny's flannel nightgown and bonnet, fuzzy slippers instead of high heels. What does this all mean?

On the one hand, the wolf's dressing up is a disguise. He's trying to hide his dangerous nature with the most innocent facade he can think of, to lure the innocent ewe or the young girl with her red cape into his clutches. There is nonetheless something sexual in this predatory nature, for *appetite* can as easily be applied to sexuality as to physical hunger, and does not the fateful scene, in the case of Little Red Riding Hood, take place in a bedroom? Does this cross-dressing merely underscore the wolf's dangerousness: he is so deviant, he will even indulge in this? Or perhaps we should look to the Brothers Grimm themselves, who spent their days gossiping with housewives, to account for this prurient interest in transvestism. What would Freud have to say?

Not unsurprisingly, it is always the lone wolf who winds up cross-dressing—or who winds up in stories, for that matter. The wolf is a pack animal, one of many shadows in the ever-shifting fabric of the night.

Is the wolf's cross-dressing an attempt to establish his individuality? Or is it rather the desire of the lone wolf, bereft of a pack, to fit in, to be part of the crowd, anonymous. Why else, in one of the few other tales where the wolves wear clothes, does he put on the fleece of the animal that most commonly represents a lack of individuality, the generic, fitting in?

And where does the sheepskin come from? In "Little Red Riding Hood," we know he puts on the grandmother's clothes after having eaten her. But his shearling coat? Does the wolf steal it from the farmer? Does he go shopping for it? The whole point of the story is that he can't get near the sheep in the first place, which is why he invents this subterfuge. If he's already got a sheep to take the skin from, the whole enterprise becomes redundant and his meal is already at hand. And if he does kill a sheep to get its pelt, how does he get the bloodstains out, to avoid alarming the flock he intends to join? Sheep are not killed when they are shorn for their wool, but even if the wolf steals wool from the farmer, what does he stick it on to make his sheepskin? The stories are vague on all these important questions, and obviously their editor should have returned the manuscript for rewriting.

In both stories, the climax comes at the moment of undressing, of true natures being revealed. But isn't that always the case with men? Once the civilized clothes are removed, what's left is the hairy, primal beast. But what is nudity to the wolf? Unclothed, the wolf is still dressed in his own fur.

Does it reflect a moral judgment, for having dared to cross the gender divide, that the wolf meets with death in both tales? (Of course, the wolf in fairy tales almost always gets a short shrift—is it any wonder they're endangered?)

And what if our central premise is wrong and the storybook wolf is actually female? Of course, even trying to posit this question lends more credence to the theory of the male wolf; a female would've chosen more flattering outfits. (Could it be more obvious that these tales were written, or at least recorded, by straight white men?) But if we reread these stories with the wolf as female, how does the subtext change? Would they have different endings? Would a female wolf clash with a young girl heroine, the way the queen is jealous of Snow White's beauty? If we change Little Red Riding Hood to a boy, would a female wolf become a nurturing figure, like the she-wolf who suckled Romulus and Remus? That's all we have time for this afternoon. Next session, we'll investigate the tailor as hero in fairy tales.

THE MUSHROOM DUCHESS

Deborah Roggie

. . .

THE DOWAGER DUCHESS OF TURING HAD MADE A LIFETIME'S study of mushrooms. It was an odd occupation, perhaps, for one of her age and station in life, but even duchesses must have their little hobbies, and fungal botany was hers. Her nurse, many years ago, had piqued her interest in mycology by teaching her what mushroom lore she'd known, and the Duchess supplemented that with field study and close questioning of peasant women whenever her duties allowed.

Mushrooms are funny things. They can please or poison, cause flying dreams or wake a sleeping man with a bellyache. One type of mushroom grows as large as a village, spreading stealthily underground until one damp morning, after a heavy storm perhaps, a ring of pale toadstools springs up to mark its boundaries. Some glow; some emit the foulest odors; and some develop so quickly that a patient observer can see them sprout, extend their gray umbrellas to the sun, and disappear, all in a single day.

So, in between hosting formal receptions and supervising the servants, the Duchess studied the most arcane mushrooms she could find. She tracked down one unusually tough, acidic variety of mushroom cap, which, worn internally, prevented conception. And she discovered a rare morel that could impregnate a woman. (Regrettably, she found, the children resulting from such pregnancies were severely impaired.) Her studies turned up species of toadstools that inhibited certain brain functions: speech, for example, or sight. A particular spotted tree mushroom, when harvested in autumn and used within two days, caused permanent memory loss. A nondescript puffball, dried, powdered, and added to saffron broth, gave the user the power of understanding animals' speech. However, as an unfortunate side effect, the subject lost all ability to communicate with humans.

The Duchess was careful and systematic when testing the properties of various mushrooms. She recorded the age of the specimen, its weight and condition, the dosage administered, the phase of the moon, and the species of her subject. The bulk of her experiments were done on animals, but as they were limited in their ability to communicate their experiences, eventually the Duchess turned to human subjects. In twenty-seven years of tests, she lost only two maids, a groom, and a stableboy. A scullion or two had gone quite mad, and a footman had committed suicide, but she was quite sure that no one connected her to their unfortunate fates.

She was unaware that in the immediate neighborhood "taking tea with the Duchess" had become synonymous with risky behavior.

Her husband, the Duke of Turing, had had mixed luck. He had lived for quite a number of years after succumbing to an overdose of greenblanket chanterelles; the Duchess told everyone he'd had a stroke, and she saw that he had the best of care. He wanted for nothing except health and mobility.

Once he was decently buried, the Dowager Duchess turned to the problem of her son's marriage. Eldred presented no opposition: he quite depended on his mother. It was finding the girl that provided the challenge. In time she found a suitable daughter-in-law who would be decorative and obedient, and who seemed likely to produce an heir. The dowry was negotiated, the bloodlines investigated, the girl inspected, and the contracts signed. Their wedding was splendid, as befit a son and heir of the ducal house of Turing.

But the Duchess was still unsatisfied.

Perhaps no one girl could have appeased her. Eldred seemed

happy enough in his animal way. His bride was everything that her parents had advertised.

Yet there was something wrong with Gracinet, of that the Duchess was sure. She puzzled over it as she took her bath, as she ordered new bed hangings, as she fussed over her lapdog. She worried about it while receiving guests and while shortening guest lists afterward. It nagged at her as she sat in her private workroom and sorted and labeled new specimens of dried porcini and ink caps obtained from foreign markets. And then, as if one of her more troublesome powders had suddenly dissolved because at last the tea was at just the right temperature, the problem became clear.

Gracinet was decidedly bookish, her conversations filled with literary allusions. The Duchess overlooked her quoting Soltari over breakfast. She smiled tolerantly when her daughter-in-law declared that Eldred's manner was right out of *The Voyage of the Sun*. But during the annual Hunters' Banquet, when Gracinet compared her husband to the mysterious Durial of the *Brinnelid* and Eldred grunted, "Who? Never heard of him," in front of the most cultured people of Turing, the Duchess decided she'd had enough. No wife of Eldred (who had never met a book he liked) must be allowed to put him in so bad a light. Of course the mother of her future grandsons should be intelligent, the Duchess thought, but she should also have the grace not to show it. From that moment the Duchess was convinced that her daughter-in-law must be stopped from asserting her superiority over them all.

"My dear child, you look poorly," said the Duchess to her daughter-in-law some few days later.

"It's just my monthlies, your grace," said the girl apologetically.

The Duchess smiled and tapped her on the arm. "I have just the thing. You sit right here and I'll make you a bit of my special tonic."

"Are you sure? I don't want to put you to any trouble."

The Duchess assumed her warmest manner. "Now, Gracinet, my dear, there's no need for you to suffer every month. You're my daughter now, and your health is important to me." And off she bustled, quickly locating the packet she had made up for this occasion, and calling for a maid to heat water for tea.

Gracinet, being new to Turing, saw no reason to excuse herself from having tea with the Duchess. She was uncomfortably aware that her mother-in-law did not like her. Why, she could not fathom, and her husband was no help on that score, for when Gracinet had asked him how she might have displeased the Duchess, he'd said only, "Gracious! Don't get on her bad side, whatever you do! That's all I need!"

She was finding this wife business both difficult and rather boring. Her husband had little use for her outside of the bedroom. His mother ran the household and brooked no interference. The Duchess's ladies were older women who loved to gossip and shake their heads over the follies of the young. Noting their mistress's aversion to her daughter-in-law, they followed Gracinet with pitying eyes but did not befriend her. It was unfortunate that she had no little hobby, such as that of her mother-in-law, to amuse her. Gracinet supposed that things would change when she became a mother and produced children of her own to care for.

In the meantime, she read, embroidered, and offered literary conversation at mealtimes.

The Duchess returned with a steaming cup.

"Drink it up directly, my dear," she said. "Monthly tea is best drunk hot."

Gracinet obediently complied. It was mild-tasting, faintly bitter, with a woodnut flavor. "I'm beginning to feel better already," she murmured as the warmth eased her aching belly and thighs.

"Let's keep this between ourselves, dear," the Duchess said. "This tea is terribly expensive, and I don't want every woman in Turing coming to me for a cup each month."

Gracinet promised. "You're so kind to me," she said.

The Duchess merely stroked her daughter-in-law's forehead and took the empty cup away.

From that point on, Gracinet gratefully drank the monthly tea provided by the Duchess. She suffered no more monthly discomforts: no cramps, or bloating, or exhaustion, or irritability. But it was around this time that she began to feel more isolated than ever. For whatever she said, whatever opinion she offered, she was bound to be either contradicted or ignored.

If Gracinet were to say, "My, it's cool out today," someone would be sure to glare at her and snap, "It's unseasonably warm."

If she said, "Can I help with that?" the reply was invariably, "I doubt it."

If someone's spectacles were missing, and Gracinet said, "I saw them on the hall table," she was simply ignored.

Not only the intimates of the ducal circle responded to her in this way. Servants scorned her and refused her requests. Strangers, even, found whatever Gracinet said to be worthless. The only kindness in her life was that her mother-in-law unfailingly prepared, month in and month out, that cup of monthly tea.

As a result, Gracinet grew shy and anxious, saying less and less. She wished she could not mind so much being dismissed and cut down at every turn. She wished she were brave. She wished that she could shout out a blazing fury of words that could not be ignored. Was there anything she could say that wouldn't be wrong? Any phrase, any formula that was safe?

Eventually silence became her only defense. If she said nothing, she would not be cut down. Tall and pale, Gracinet receded to the background of every gathering. She withdrew from public life. She was terrified of becoming pregnant and raising children who would treat her every utterance as wrong. Her husband installed a mistress at the other end of the house; Gracinet dared not protest.

The Duchess was pleased with the results of her experiment.

The bearded toadstool, the active ingredient in her monthly teas, fascinated her with its ability to provoke unpleasant responses to Gracinet's every word. There was a complex mechanism at work here, well worth study. She had never before worked with a mushroom that affected the interaction between a subject and those around her. Despite her foreknowledge, the Duchess saw her own reactions affected. Even when she could see the spectacles on the hall table, she felt a revulsion at hearing the fact stated by Gracinet. It was a relief when the girl began to keep her mouth shut.

True, if the girl never spoke it was impossible to measure the effects of different dosages. But there were other fungi to study. She had recently heard of the tawny ink cap, which, when well rotted and tawny no more, yielded an ink that compelled the writer to record only the truth. She longed to test it on her steward, whom she suspected of amassing a small fortune at her expense. She readied a page in her journal to be devoted to the steward's case. Science would not be denied.

For Gracinet, the silent days and months piled one upon the other, adding up to silent years. Over time, she felt insubstantial, corroded by cowardice, worm-eaten by words she dared not express. Even in keeping silent she found no dignity, for she became a figure of derision—her speechlessness made her an easy target. Some equated her silence with stupidity.

The Duchess made no effort to correct this notion.

Gracinet sought consolation in books. The library became her refuge. When she was quite sure she was alone, she read aloud to hear the sound of her own voice, even if she limited herself to others' words. She found that certain forms of literature lent themselves to this kind of treatment. She read aloud Bakinjar's *Sermons,* Linnek's *Letters from Doriven Prison,* and the epic *Tale of the Abbess of Pim.* On her daily solitary walks she whispered the *Blackwater Sonnets.* She gave voice to Soltari's *Ice Comedies* and to the tragedies of

Irsan the Younger, trying out different accents on different parts. Anyone overhearing her would conclude that she was quite mad, but the reverse was true: Gracinet was fighting to stay sane.

ONE HOT AND HUMID afternoon while in the library, Gracinet found the obscure book for which she had been looking and settled on the floor by the bookcase to read. That is why, when they entered the room, the two gentlemen did not see her. She remained as she was, hidden in the shadow of the jutting bookcase, hoping that they would quickly select a book and leave; but, to her horror, one stationed himself on the sofa in the middle of the room while the other roamed about, taking down likely books, flipping the pages, putting them back in the wrong places.

"Are you looking for anything in particular?" said the voice from the sofa.

"Not really. Just something to amuse me while I'm here." He snapped another book closed. Gracinet imagined the cloud of dust that resulted: the library shelves were seldom attended to. Sure enough, the man sneezed.

"Don't you find the people amusing enough?"

"What, his grace and that lot? Hardly. This is probably the dullest house in Turing."

"Oh, come now," said the voice from the sofa, "it's not all that bad. The Duke's lively enough, once you get him out of the house and away from his mother. Not a bad sort, really."

"I met his mistress. Gives herself airs. I'm surprised he never married."

"Oh, weren't you introduced to the wife? I guess they didn't trot her out for the occasion. Rumor has it she's an idiot. I couldn't tell, myself. They say her family covered it up until after the wedding." Gracinet felt her stomach knot. She knew what was said about her.

"And the old lady stood for it? I shouldn't think she was the kind to allow that sort of thing."

"Ah, the Dowager Duchess must have had her reasons. She always does. Notice how nothing happens around here without her say-so? How the Duke defers to his mother in the least little thing? If the Duchess said, 'Marry this stick,' you can bet he'd have done it."

"But why?"

The restless fellow joined his companion on the sofa, who lowered his voice. "The Dowager keeps 'em all in line. The old Duke, too, before he died."

"I don't quite follow your meaning."

"Well, I daren't be more plain. Just, whatever you do, don't have tea with the old lady."

"Are you serious?"

"On my life, I am. There've been some mighty peculiar tea parties in this house. She's famous for them. *Notorious* is more like it. Tea with unusual ingredients, if you know what I mean. If you're invited to one, make an excuse, invent a dead grandmother, a summons to the king, anything at all, and get out."

"Why has no one put a stop to it?"

"Well, nothing's proven. Perhaps that footman who thought he became a snake after sundown was already going mad. It happens. And that maid with the three bouts of temporary blindness for no known reason? Coincidence. Maybe the story about the two stableboys is just an ugly rumor. But I'd be careful, just the same."

His companion laughed nervously. "Indeed I will."

Gracinet had heard enough. She rose and stepped out from behind the sheltering bookcase, startling the two men on the sofa considerably. They gaped as she swept by them without a word. Whatever would they make of her now? At any rate, she supposed, they were unlikely to stay for dinner.

She had to think. Her feet took her down the hall, down the long staircase, and out onto a familiar garden path without her conscious mind registering the fact. She had to tease apart the facts, like the matted hair of the Duchess's odious little lapdog. Gracinet had no doubt that the monthly tea did more than ease cramps. What a fool she'd been! The maid, apparently, was not the only one who had been blind. If only she'd listened, if only she'd observed! There were years of *if only*s weighing upon her.

Her retreat, her aloofness, had been her undoing. And she had collaborated in her own silencing. She had hidden; she had cringed.

"It's not me," she said aloud, and realized that she was alone in the shady grove past the kitchen gardens. It was cooler here, and the young trees around her seemed like companions. "It's not me," she told them. "It was her. All along it was her." Gracinet found she was shaking, and tears streaked her face. The trees stood silent and still in the face of her storm. "'Drink it up, dear.' Oh, I could choke her on her own brew!" Grief for the lost years surged up and overwhelmed her; Gracinet sank to the ground and wept.

When the tears had stopped and her face felt like a wrung-out washcloth, she bent to clean the twigs and leaves clinging to her dress, and considered what to do next. I'll pretend to drink the tea, she thought, and see if its effects wear off. But I won't let the Duchess know. It will be better if she thinks I am not a threat. Then perhaps I can find a way to stop her.

She glanced at the house, bright in the sunlight beyond the trees, with its many windows blindly glittering. Oh, yes, thought Gracinet. She must be stopped.

SHE DIDN'T KNOW just when the feeling began, but the Duchess sensed, somehow, that she was being watched. A footfall in an empty corridor, an open window she was sure she'd latched, an unlocked door . . . Perhaps it was just age, she thought. Perhaps she was forgetting things. Perhaps there was a mushroom out there that would sharpen memory. She would have to check her notes.

It was an unproductive time for her researches. A recent shipment of rare specimens had been water-damaged—slimy with mold and completely unusable. Her agent had apologized profusely. And her new steward had inexplicably lost the latest shipment. Drat the man! She was surrounded by incompetents. These delays would retard her investigation into a truffle that caused people—even those with the most perfect pitch—to sing off-key. It quite spoilt her temper.

Even her daughter-in-law seemed different, though she was as silent and retiring as ever. But the last time the Duchess had brought Gracinet her monthly tea, she'd noticed an almost imperceptible nod from one of her ladies. Later one of them touched Gracinet on the shoulder when they thought she wasn't looking. And Gracinet had smiled. She wondered briefly if her daughter-in-law was quite as isolated as she'd seemed. But the Duchess shrugged off her misgivings.

One morning soon afterward, she discovered that someone had been in her workroom. The polished brass scales, a gift from her late husband, were out of balance. Her notes, though neatly stacked, were out of order. And, at her feet, a single bearded toadstool lay delicately on the carpet. She picked it up and held it in her cupped palm as if it were the head of a newborn infant, and, examining it, considered her options.

That afternoon, the Dowager Duchess found herself alone in her parlor with Gracinet. While she caught up on some correspondence, she glanced every now and then at the younger woman reading by the window. Her daughter-in-law had changed in some way, although the Duchess could not put a finger on how, exactly. A watchfulness, a sense that she waited for something. Even her posture seemed straighter.

The Duchess approached Gracinet and looked over her shoulder at the book she was reading. It was the *Abbess of Pim,* the scene where the foster son imagined burning down the abbey.

> ". . . *beams burned away, and charred stone*
> *left monument to bitter days.*
> *A hundred years of wind and rain*
> *could not scour this wretched place,"*

she read aloud. "I feel that way about this old house sometimes, with all its old memories and misdeeds. What a dreadful thought! Do you ever feel that way?"

"Sometimes," said Gracinet without thinking; then her eyes widened, and she turned to face the Duchess.

Not only had her daughter-in-law spoken, but the Duchess felt no revulsion, no urge to contradict. In that moment she knew Gracinet had stopped drinking the tea. Her scientist's mind wondered how long it had taken for the effects to wear off, and if there would be any residual symptoms. They stared at each other, each seeing the other clearly for the first time: the pale-haired disciple of science, and the newly determined daughter of literature—each surprised to find the other unmasked at last.

Gracinet tucked her chin toward her chest, like a horse about to throw its weight into pulling a heavy load, and continued the quote:

> "*But I and all my sons to come*
> *through all the days and nights unnumbered*
> *will remember wrongs done here,*
> *here in the broken house of Pim,*
> *though it sink beneath the waves*
> *and come to rest in dark waters*
> *the silent home of scuttling crabs. . . ."*

"Well, then——" the Duchess began, but she was interrupted by the entrance of a group of ladies and gentlemen, guests of Duke Eldred, who had come to the parlor to set up a card party. Frustrated, the Duchess was forced to play hostess; Gracinet left unnoticed in the commotion.

As soon as she could manage it, the Duchess took her son aside. "Really, your wife is getting more and more strange," she said. "Her behavior has become highly unsuitable. I must talk to you about her."

"After dinner, Mother," said the Duke, pulling out his pocket watch and consulting it.

"But——" He snapped the gold watch case closed so abruptly she jumped.

"Our guests, Mother, require my attention, and yours. Now is not the time. Worley, man! Let me introduce you to my mother. . . ." And the Duchess had no choice but to comply with a smile.

THE BELL RANG for dinner. Duke Eldred offered his arm to the Dowager Duchess, and together they led their guests to the dining room. A pair of footmen opened the double doors wide, and the company filed in.

Beneath their startled gazes a riot of mushrooms spilled out of bowls set among the elegant place settings and along the sideboard. They filled crystal glasses, swam in glass compotes, swarmed over silver dishes, overran great platters, tumbled over salad plates, and were piled high in a great vase like froth. The elegant dinner service hosted colonies of spotted toadstools and ink caps of many colors, tiny button mushrooms and the giant termite heap mushroom, puffballs of many sizes, stinkhorns, death caps and porcini, oyster mushrooms and morels, pink trumpets, white truffles and black ones, too. The Duchess knew many of them—from the arched earthstar to the bird's nest fungus, the elfin saddle to the slippery jack—as well as she knew the shape of her own hands. They were like cities accumulated by a traveler, marks of where she'd been and the journey yet to come.

"What is the meaning of this—this outrageous display?" said the Duchess in a deep voice that promised terrible consequences and made all there, including her son, flinch.

"It means that it is time you listened to me," said Gracinet.

The Duchess looked up to see her daughter-in-law standing at the far end of the room. The young woman held one of the Duchess's own private journals, and Gracinet opened it and read out loud in a voice that was steady and clear:

> "The dosage seems to be key, for when I first administered greenblanket chanterelles to my husband, his stomach rejected them immediately, and he suffered no long-term ill effects. But, convincing him that it was the wine that was bad that night, on another occasion I persuaded him to try the dish again; however, I gave him too few; and he merely suffered a fit of apoplexy. I must remember to take into account variations in the weight of the subject when working up the correct dosage. He was of the strongest constitution, and it took careful management to keep him from making a complete recovery. (That, in itself, yielded interesting results, see below.) I finally got the dosage right on the third attempt, some years later."

The Duchess looked about during this recitation, ignoring the shocked and hardening expressions of her guests. She felt distant from them all, as if they were located at the wrong end of a telescope. She noted that the missing shipment of mushrooms must have contributed to the display before her. Well, she mused, she should have demanded a written explanation from this steward, too. She had grown lax. Her glance fell upon a small covered tureen on the table before her. The Duke, seeing where her attention was fixed, reached forward and removed the lid to reveal a steaming stew of greenblanket chanterelles. "This is how my father liked them prepared, no?"

The Duchess said nothing.

Her son smashed the lid onto the floor so hard it scarred the floorboards before shattering into a thousand porcelain shards. The ladies were protected by their long skirts, but several gentlemen's legs were nicked right through their stockings. "Answer me!"

"Yes," said the Duchess.

THE DOWAGER DUCHESS of Turing had hoped to contribute her notes and specimens to science, but it was not to be. It fell to Gracinet to oversee the destruction of a lifetime's work: the private museum of mycology, the journals and drawings and fungal powders. Gracinet glanced through the journals before she consigned them to the flames. There she learned that bitter buttons caused hair to grow in unseemly places, and that oil of ghostgall, if rubbed on the blade of a murder weapon, prevented future hauntings. After a number of such entries, she shuddered and closed the book. It would not do to peer so closely into her mother-in-law's mind. It was time to concentrate on the future. Though the mistress was not yet out of the house, Gracinet had begun to reconcile with her husband. They were reading Soltari's *Ice Comedies* together.

The Dowager Duchess was confined to an upstairs bedroom, and watched day and night. But no one volunteered to share her meals, and no one offered her tea.

Gracinet came to regret her willed ignorance. When they burned the papers and scores of carefully labeled packets of dried mushrooms out by the kitchen garden, two of the gardeners overseeing the bonfire died, and a third became deathly ill from the smoke. He never made a full recovery: ever after he supposed that the bees were plotting against him, and had to give up gardening work altogether. It seemed the Duchess had managed one last experiment after all.

THE PIRATE'S TRUE LOVE

Seana Graham

. . .

I T WAS A FAIR SPRING MORNING AS THE PIRATE SAT WITH his true love before sailing out to sea. She was wearing a long purple dress, and her cheeks were red with crying. The pirate held her hand and promised her jewels and fine clothes, but nothing helped. She would much rather have sat with the pirate till the end of time and watched her purple dress turn to rags and then to dust than have him sail off and find her the finest jewels in all the world. But she did not say this aloud, because she knew that the pirate would not want to sit holding her hand until the end of time, even if her dress did turn to dust. For the pirate's heart would always be with her, but his mind would be always on treasure. So though she cried till her cheeks were red, she did not beg him to stay.

The pirate sailed away that spring morning and gave himself over to plundering and looting. He was good at his work, and lucky, and if that work involved a certain amount of antisocial behavior, well, it was what he was born to do. He was not a terribly analytical person, for he never stopped to ask himself why he needed to go around plundering and looting the high seas when all he'd ever really wanted was his ship and his men and the heart of his true love who was waiting back by the bay at home. Of course, he did have to pay somehow for the costly garments of satin and silk and lace he wore. True, these were not really necessary for plundering, but they did rather seem to go with the job.

After he left, the pirate's true love walked to the cliffs every day and looked out over the water. Sometimes, if she stood and stared long enough, she seemed to see the smoke of a great battle going on far out at sea. (Of course, her pirate love was by this time many leagues away, so this was either eye strain or imagination.) And, after looking a great while, she would sigh and walk sadly back to her humble home. It might have helped pass the time if the pirate had left her some plunder to sort, or some loot to tidy, but the fact was that gold and jewels had a way of slipping through pirate fingers like so much water. By the time the pirate sailed out on his next adventure, there was never much left but the pirate's mess to clean up, which she somehow could not find altogether romantic.

It was a day late in August when the pirate's true love turned from her lonely vigil on the cliffs, sighing because her humble home was entirely too neat and tidy now that the pirate's mess had long been cleared away—and realized that she was not alone. The truth was she never had been alone but had just become too farsighted to notice. But now—if she squinted—she could see that there were many other pirates' true loves standing on the cliff, sighing and straining their eyes over the all-too-empty waters. And she had to admit that, sad though it was, it was also just a little bit silly. After all, the pirates never came home before October. Now the pirate's true love—and let us call her May, since that was her name and we do not want to lose her in the anxious throng of other true loves there on the cliff—May could be a rather enterprising young woman when she saw the need, and right away she saw the need for a Pirate Women's Auxiliary. For there is such a thing as too much looking out over the water.

The Pirate Women's Auxiliary flourished handsomely for a while. For one thing, with organization, only one true love needed to go and stand anxious and brooding above the cliffs on behalf of all the rest, and though at first they quarreled among themselves for their turns, after a while they began to devote themselves to the group's new task—fund-raising. For there was quite enough wealth in the town—after all those years of relieving pirates of their treasure—to support any number of bake sales and raffles and charity balls. Though it is true that, during these latter events, the pirates' true loves would have to bravely blink back the tears as they thought of their bold buccaneers out looting and pillaging and not knowing what they were missing. And sadly but also truly, there was more than one pirate's true love who suddenly noticed that there were some not-too-shabby-looking farmers and blacksmiths and shopkeepers around . . . but that is not our story.

The *true* true loves remained loyal, but a problem arose. For when the brave pirates returned that fall (in November, and very soggy), they found that their true loves were not *ooh*ing and *ahh*ing over the heaps of treasure with quite the enthusiasm the pirates were accustomed to arousing. The truth of the matter is, the fundraising had gone a little too well, and the pirates' true loves had managed to amass pretty much all the gold and jewels and fine clothes they could ever desire—and these did not slip through their fingers like water at all. Oh, they did try to summon up the right note of gratitude at being showered with diamonds and rubies, but it was hard, as they were all secretly dying to get back to their carpentry lessons. For they had unanimously voted to use whatever excess earnings were lying around to build a nice warm teahouse on top of the cliffs in time for spring, so that the lonely cliff vigil would not be quite so cold and, well, tedious. By now even the most steadfast of pirate true loves had begun to look for excuses to avoid her shift.

So the pirates were a little dismayed and the true loves were a little distracted, but if the jewels failed to excite, the hand-holding was still nice, and all went well through the winter. The pirates' treasure troves slowly dwindled (and, unbeknownst to them, came back by indirect routes to their true loves' coffers), and at last the spring day came when the pirates needs must sail to replenish their pirate hoards. So the pirates held hands with their true loves, and the true loves' cheeks were red with crying, although noticeably less red than the year before (and some might even have been justly accused of cosmetic deception). And though their true hearts ached to see the pirate ship fade from view on the treacherous sea, they all hurried home to get the pirates' mess cleaned up, because they were anxious to start working on a ship of their very own.

For certainly it is understandable that after you stand, year in and year out, watching a fine pirate ship fade from view on the treacherous sea, you might get some hankering to go and find out what all the fuss is about. Because it couldn't be just about the treasure, could it? (As we have seen, the pirates' true loves had grown a little jaded about the gold, jewels, etc.) So the handiest true loves built a sturdy little vessel and the sharpest true loves studied navigation, and one warm day in August, they were ready to sail. They christened the ship the *True Love* (of course), and they ran up a flag made from May's purple dress (which was a much better use for it than letting it turn to rags), emblazoned with a picture of two hands clasped, and they left the now-thriving tea shop in the care of their faithful friends, who were now farmers' true loves and blacksmiths' true loves and shopkeepers' true loves. And they faded slowly away from view on the treacherous sea.

When the brave pirates returned to their home by the bay (in early December and even soggier than the year before), their ship rode more lightly on the water than it had in many a year, for, truth to tell, their plundering had not come to much these last few months. Since August, in fact, they had not managed to get aboard a single fat galleon, or raid even one silent, sleeping coastal town. For just as they came within firing range of some ship or shoreline, a jaunty little ship with a purple flag (they could never get quite close enough to make out its logo, and what some of them *thought* they saw was too ridiculous to be believed) would race into view and warn them off with a furious blast of cannons and muskets. And though the pirates fought very bravely and fiercely, inevitably they would eventually have to make their escape, hidden by the walls of billowing smoke all around them. They were bold and fearless, but they were not stupid. They knew when they had met their match. Curiously, none of this great bombardment ever seemed to actually hit their ship, and some of the pirates swore that the enemy was purposely missing. But the other pirates only laughed at this, for the Pirates' Code made this unthinkable. Besides, some of that musket shot had come close enough to singe the whiskers of their gorgeous pirate beards.

So now as the brave pirates alit from their ship, each walked to his humble home a little more slowly, a little less boisterously, a little less certainly than he had the previous year. (Though actually they should have been walking faster, for the treasure chests they carried were considerably lighter than they had been then.) They were not too sure that their true loves would love them quite so truly when they noticed that the customary shower of gold and jewels lasted for a conspicuously shorter period of time. The pirates, all in all, were a little ashamed.

But what was shame when compared to the wonder that filled each pirate's heart as he approached his true love's door—and found it locked and bolted? And what was shame compared to his consternation as he peered through a (dirty) window and could make out no warm and glowing fire, no true love waiting next to it? And what, above all, was shame compared to the terror that seized each pirate as he stood alone in the cold, damp night and thought that some farmer . . . or blacksmith . . . or shopkeeper . . . might well be happy in his place tonight?

Now, as each pirate was beginning to consider that treasure was a rather paltry thing compared to some other things that could be won—or lost—a pinprick of light appeared on the crest of a hill above. And it was followed by another. And another. And another. Until finally a torchlight procession could be seen wending its way swiftly down the hillside. And every pirate's heart leapt suddenly with a terrible, yearning hope that sent him running to the center of town, where the hillside road would end.

And the pirates' true loves (after a long tramp from a secret lagoon, where a certain ship lay safely berthed for the winter) came rushing down to meet them, chattering vaguely of some Pirate Women's Auxiliary project that had unavoidably detained them. If any pirate recalled at that moment a purple flag on a distant sea, he made up his mind to forget it. For all hearts present felt, though silently, that this reunion was something rather more than the usual shower of gold and jewels.

One fine spring morning in the following year, the pirates once again sat holding hands with their true loves (none of whose cheeks were red at all, but all of whose eyes glowed beautifully). And then, a little reluctantly this time, the pirates boarded their fine ship, which soon faded from view on the treacherous sea.

And one warm day in August (for pirates are pirates, and should never be thwarted completely), the *True Love* sailed out after them. And so it sailed for many an August to come.

YOU COULD DO THIS TOO

NAME IT. KULTURE INFORMATICS SUPPORT SYSTEM OR SOME other such thing that follows the Keep It Simple, Stupid form.

Find some writing you love. Edit it. If it's yours: rewrite it. Make it concise. Make it sing.

Paying writers: we'd all like to pay writers more. Squeeze other costs and pay the damn writers something.

Design. Pay Thom Davidsohn (*Journal of Pulse-Pounding Narratives*) or find someone whose design you like. Copy designs you like. Use fonts sparingly.

Copyediting. Ask as many people as you can to copyedit and proofread your project. Spelling mistakes are embarrassing.

Copy or print? LCRW is copied at Paradise Copies in Northampton, Massachusetts. We've looked much farther afield. Send out requests for quotations (RFQs).

Publication frequency depends on involvement. If it's only you: annual. The more volunteers there are (unless there's uni/other affiliation you'll all be volunteers) the more often you can put it out.

Distribute: zine distros (Loop, etc.: Google them). Shops: Quimby's Bookstore, Chicago; Atomic Books, Baltimore.

How do you sell it? Consignment (shops pay you as they sell your zine/book). Or outright sale. The usual trade discount is five copies: 40% discount. On a $5 zine the shop will give you $3.

Send it to reviewers! Build a basic Web site. Tell the world your project exists.

Advertise. Send your proudly made zine to *Xerography Debt, A Reader's Guide to the Underground Press,* and genre-specific reviews. Offer to trade ad space with other zines.

Do it all again!

THE POSTHUMOUS VOYAGES
OF CHRISTOPHER COLUMBUS

Sunshine Ison

The mark of a mediocre captain, or a blessed one,
is that his journey ends with death. His body fixed
in earth, now unshaken by waves. Not so, Columbus.
First, dug up in Valladolid and carted to Seville.
A long haul in the hold to Santo Domingo. Then packed
up with the other treasures and sent to Cuba in 1795.
Last, in 1898, turning tail from the Americans
and going home to a dwindled Spain,
a half-rotted Odysseus arriving to no grand welcome,
bones clinking loose from all this wear.

Focal-hand dystonia—a disorder common
to factory workers and musicians, whose fingers
map a series of motions again and again,
until the index, say, loses its ego and can no
longer act separately from the thumb. The hand
will play its scales, will twist its screws,
no matter what. Amidst rat-nibbled biscuits,
Columbus dreams about the seamstress
who holds him fast, who even in her sleep
stitches the hemispheres together,
and he is her needle.

AND IF THEY ARE NOT DEAD, THEY MAY BE LIVING STILL

Sunshine Ison

In the forest near Chernobyl, men no longer go to hunt.
Left alone, the animals are lethargic, wander
indolently like an idle boy in an old aunt's parlor.
They forget their own names.
The doves and swallows did not come back.

Marya Akimova tells her children
the same stories her grandmother told her,
stories that did not make much sense when she was
    young.
But her daughters listen without questions,
nodding sagely as if these were things they already
    knew.

She tells them of Baba Yaga, the witch
who lived in a house with chicken legs,
about boys who were also wolves, and rabbits
with brazen eyes like giant copper coins,
about magic fish that didn't look like fish,
and babies born and abandoned.

At night she climbs into bed and lets down her hair,
says aloud to the place beside her
where her husband used to lie,

"I don't know, I thought those were tales of olden times,
things that were gone and would not return. I said to my
grandmother, we are beyond all that. But I don't know.
Maybe we are walking in circles on a long road.
Do you know," she says,
"men do not even hunt in the forest anymore."

THIS IS THE TRAIN THE QUEEN RIDES ON

Becca De La Rosa

...

(**D**O YOU BELIEVE IN TRAINS?)

Mr. Gorman

In Helsinki airport he spills scalding tea on his arm, and when he finally finds a chemist he realizes that he does not know the Finnish word for salve, or the word for ointment, or even the word for burn. His baby daughter, Ella, is not impressed with his attempts to demonstrate what happened through an elaborate game of charades, although the shop assistant becomes very excited. In the end he steals a packet of butter from the nearby café to smear on his burnt arm and hopes no one will notice.

Ella's rag doll gets abandoned in the confusion. She screams and screams. "I'm dreadfully sorry," Mr. Gorman says to several bystanders, in English, "my wife just died."

They find an old cat in the train station, sleek and well fed, sitting on a bench and licking its paws. Ella squeals in delight. "Oh Ella," Mr. Gorman says wearily. "No, darling, he doesn't belong to you. Leave the poor cat alone. Do you want some chocolate?" The cat, whose collar reads PROSPERO, follows them around the train station with an indulgent air, as if he is humoring them, and slips past the ticket inspector when they finally board the train. He curls up in the middle of the bunk in their cabin and closes his eyes resolutely.

For Mr. Gorman the journey lasts much longer than four hours.

When the train derails, he just drops his head in his hands.

(Do you believe in cats?)

Prospero, the Cat

My dear fellow, someone says.

Light walks out of the shadows, a path to follow. Prospero does not hesitate. He says, *I am a cat: unseater of darkness, destroyer of solace found in small things, hunter and supplicant. I am a cat: unwatched listener at doors, glint of eyes in the night. I am wise and wary. I land on my feet.*

And the someone says, *Then follow me.*

The Odd Man at the Window

Who has white hair and white hands and a neat white suit, and stands watching.

Darling Bettina

She carries nothing but a notebook and pen, tucked under her arm, and a Finnish phrase book that is quite unnecessary because it seems that she can speak the language perfectly. Her passport fits into one jacket pocket. The other is stuffed with bill notes and a handful of coins. Her name is Darling Bettina but she would like you to call her Tee.

The sleeper train from Helsinki to Rovaniemi cost almost as much as her honeymoon would have. The bus to Inari will cost even more. On the back of a cheap postcard, bought days ago in Kuovola, she writes: *I am a bitch and a whore and I hope you hate me for this.* She sucks ink from the tip of her pen, tears up the postcard, and takes out another, identical. *Neddy,* she writes, *I am so sorry. I don't know what's the matter with me.*

But all of that is a lie.

She buys a cup of bittersweet coffee, stamps the snow from her boots, and finally, hastily, writes: *I had to go. I took the violin and the money. You are a lovely man,* which is true.

There are some things you know by heart and some things you tease out of air and light as if you are carding wool. Darling Bettina takes out the violin, chestnut brown and glowing, and plays to miles of Finnish snow.

(Well, do you believe in fairy tales?)

Ring Around the Roses

Sun bakes the stone hard and hot. Roses wrap around it, notch fists in its spine, like arms. The tower has been here for a long time. Maybe there is a princess at the top. Maybe she has a long, long braid of golden hair, the color of nasturtiums, of egg yolks, of cornfields. Maybe, if you ask her nicely, she will let you climb.

The tower has been here for a long time. There are notches in the stone, homes for the pigeons who sing curdled, rhythmic songs. There are places where the tower is worn a different color. It is definitely a tower. There are stairs, a thousand. There are bats. Bats live in towers, you know. There are chinks for windows. Oh, if we know only one thing, we know this is a tower. There are turrets and balustrades. There is soap. There is never enough soap when your hands are dirty. There is a sink, metallic. There is a dim mirror. There is a folding door. The toilet flushes with a noise like a bird flapping its wings, like a bird flying, like many birds flying away from the tower when the princess lets down her long golden hair. Maybe she will let you up. Ask nicely.

Lady Christina Annabelle Lucinda Davenport-Raleigh IV

She smokes very thin cigars. She wears gold spectacles on a golden chain. She is not sure in what order all her names should go (although she knows there are a lot of them). She is thin and greyish, like one of those fast dogs, and she is purebred. She is purer than you. Lady Christina Annabelle Lucinda Davenport-Raleigh IV knows she is a lady-in-waiting to someone, although she does not know who, so she smokes a skinny wandlike cigar, and waits.

(Do you believe in changelings?)

Baby Ella

Ella is happy now. The movement of the train feels like a cradle, rocking. She sucks on Prospero's tail (he does not seem to mind) and thinks of her mother, who had red hair, red lips, and wore long red dresses, and who left a long time ago. Was it a long time ago? Ella does not care for time. She listens to her father crying softly. It sounds like wind blowing, like leaves rustling, like trains.

Our Narrator, Anonymous but Golden-Tongued

Is wise and tricky.

Is long like a snake, glass-eyed like a cathedral, winged like a dragonfly.

Is witty.

Is clever.

Is cleverer than you are.

Is beautiful to look at but not to touch.

Is not Prospero, not Caliban.

Is maybe Ariel.

Is made of glass, of snow, of gold, of wind, but not of iron.

Is listening.

Some Music from the Chestnut Violin

Darling Bettina plays and plays, until the tips of her fingers swell and bleed. Her blood drips into the belly of the chestnut violin and makes the music sweeter. She does not think of Neddy. All that seems very far away.

The violin is second, third, fourthhand. Neddy's mother bought it at an antique store in Brighton. She hung it over the mantelpiece in a shadow box; firelight caught its gloss. Neddy brought Darling Bettina over for dinner one night, three years ago, and she stared at the violin trapped in its frame over the mantel. (Neddy's mother had noticed, that night, how pale and wide Darling Bettina's eyes could be, in the firelight.) Darling Bettina visited Neddy's mother again, not long after, to show off the glittering diamond ring on her finger, and then to discuss cake and cathedrals, and to try on the heavy wedding dress that smelled of mothballs and other people's promises.

The chestnut violin had belonged last to a one-eyed jazz musician who found it in a taxi underneath a pile of shiny tulle netting. It had been left there by a ballerina with black hair, who had received it as a present on her eighteenth birthday from a mysterious man in a red leather jacket, who had stolen it in the park, from where it sat on the ground beside three small children with crystal-colored eyes.

The day before her wedding Darling Bettina broke the shadow box, and stole the violin, and ran away.

And now she is playing, playing, playing.

When glass crashes and all the lights go out she almost doesn't notice.

A Riddle

What is fast as a train,
strong as a train,
bright as a train,
light as a train,
cold as a train,
bold as a train,
shrill as a train,
sharp as a train,
but is not a train?

An Answer

A train, of course.

(Do you believe in fairies?)

This Is the Train the Queen Rides On

No black horses, no white. There are metal wheels instead. No will-o'-the-wisps, fairy lanterns, ghost lights bobbing. That is what electricity is for. No pale kings and princes (although the man in white, the man with one white glove and one bare hand, has very fair skin).

But there is music, the rhythm of wheels and the wail of a chestnut violin.

And there is an engine driver with silver hair and an enigmatic smile.

And there is the servant and there is the master.

And there is the changeling.

And there is the queen.

The Engine Driver with the Silver Hair and the Enigmatic Smile

The fire flames hotter than hot, because he feeds it on the finest words, torn from the strangest books, the kind that crackle when you read them, the kind that weave odd music long after they are ash and dust. He smiles because the fire is hot and his work is good. He sings a song that sounds a little bit like flames licking over old paper, and a little bit like a fat man singing, very out of tune.

This is the train the queen rides on. He is the engine driver. He knows where things go when they disappear, and he knows what comes at the end of snow and frost.

"Burn, burn," the silver-haired engine driver sings, smiling enigmatically.

(All right. Do you believe in ghosts?)

The Queen

Red. Red. Red.

The Glassblower

Anyone who knows about anything will tell you it is impractical to have a glassblower blowing glass aboard a train.

Anyone who knows everything will not speak to you at all.

The glassblower makes vases and bowls. They are all the color of snow. He tries to make them red and blue and green and gold, but they all come out the same. He makes snow-colored wineglasses, platters, goblets. After a while he grows more adventurous. He tries to make a dragon, but it comes out shaped like a train. When he looks closer it almost seems as if there are tiny glass people inside, waving at him, snow-colored. The glassblower makes glass disks like biscuits and eats them absently. The crumbs stick in his long white beard. His beard used to be red, he thinks, although he really isn't sure. After he is finished eating he carefully stamps each bowl and vase and glass with his seal, a mark in the shape of a ladder or a section of railroad tracks.

The glassblower makes a glass rose. It ends up looking like a wheel. Perplexed, the glassblower turns it. There is a crash, a flicker of lights. Everything is still. The glassblower smiles. In the dark, the stamp on his hand glows red-hot; the stamp of a ladder or a section of railroad tracks printed into his skin, which is the color of snow, which is the color of everything.

And There Comes a Crash
from the Dining Carriage

And there comes a shriek from the wheels, and all the lights click off.

And someone screams, although it might not be a scream at all, but a cry of recognition.

And there really aren't many passengers traveling to the arctic circle on Christmas Eve this year.

And it might be nothing but the northern lights.

And then again, it might not.

Illumination

There is no light in the train but the light of his pale skin, the light of his bright eyes. He wears all white. He bows to them, lifts a delicate hand, and beams.

"Lost," he pronounces.

No one speaks.

"Follow," he says complacently, and so they do.

In the Olden Days

There were dancing days and wild music. There were forests of trees fluttering with paper lanterns and ribbons, and the folk danced and the lights danced and the stars danced, far up, as if they were spinning on a great glass wheel. There were songs. There were wells and hills. There were dishes of milk left out at dark, and loaves of bread on fences and beside cornfields, and gifts of trinkets, spinning dolls, pretty baubles. There were fights and truces. There were wild nights. There were stories.

Now, there is mostly snow.

What They Brought with Them

One violin, chestnut.
One silver bell on a cracked leather collar.
Crumbs of glass caught up in a white beard.
One wife. One mother.

What They Left Behind

One rag doll, eyeless, drooping.
One dictionary of Finnish phrases.
Three torn-up postcards.
One packet of black cigarillos.
Soap.
Eight suitcases, two backpacks, one snakeskin purse.
One glass dragon, trainlike.
One last look over his shoulder.
Everything.

What the Fire Ate

A fiancé, a handful of years, a handful of words, some dreams.

(Tell me: what do you believe in, then?)

What You Should Believe In

In dragons. In cats. In fairy tales. In fairies. In changelings. In masters, servants. In ghost lights. In ghost music. In ghosts. In glass. In roses. In snow. In golden coins that are made from snow, and that will return to snow when the song ends. In songs that never end. In engines. In stories. In gods, monsters, demons, shadows, dreams. In trick doors and secret passageways. In clocks that run backward and dandelions that tell time. In secrets. In magpies. In ravens, crying "Nevermore." In wells, hills, holy places. In towers.
    In queens. In disappearance.
    But you should never believe in trains.

Automobiles: city/highway mileage (to be imported from Europe if necessary)

———

as stated on www.vcacarfueldata.org.uk/
search/fuelConSearch.asp

Honda Insight:	60/66
Toyota Prius:	60/51
Citroën C1:	53/83
Peugeot 107:	51/68
Nissan Micra:	50/70

Renault Mégane Sport Tourer: 50/68

Ford Fusion: 49/70

Honda Civic Hybrid: 49/57

Ford Fiesta: 48/74

Fiat Grande Punto: 47/72

Smart Forfour: 47/72

VW Jetta (diesel):   38/46

VW New Beetle (diesel):   37/44

VW Golf (diesel):   37/44

Honda Civic: 36/44

Toyota Echo: 35/43

Toyota Yaris: 34/39

Toyota Corolla: 32/40

Kia Rio: 32/35

Honda Fit: 31/38

DEAR AUNT GWENDA

REPUBLICANS AND CHIHUAHUAS EDITION

. . .

Q: Now that you've been married for a while, do you have any new and startling insights into the male brain?

—*Yours, A Seeker After Truth*

A: It is true: men possess a brain! One sole brain that is shared among them, a hive mind! Okay, I've never really cared for those kinds of jokes. I've discovered that having separate bathrooms and a dishwasher are the keys to any successful marriage. It's best just to let them do the lawn-mowing. Science fiction conventions are excellent places to spend the landmark anniversaries in your relationship. Three bicycles are enough.

Also, you can make men do anything you want by threatening to get a buzz cut. It's just like dads and the word *stripper*.

Q: Many of my family members are Republicans. What can I do about this?

—*Fondly, Perplexed*

A: Dear Fondly Perplexed, if you're Southern, the answer is easy: follow the time-honored tradition of disowning the unsavory members of one's family. It's a genteel excommunication. Should their status change, you can just bring them back into the fold.

On a practical level, if you're not willing to disown them, there are still a couple of things you can do. The most important—the very key to your sanity—is this: stop listening to them. You must never pay attention to anything that comes out of their mouths. Just nod and murmur, "Uh-huh." Leave the room should anyone mention George W. Bush, the pope, or Dennis Miller. If pressed, say, "That Ann Coulter doll was pretty hot." Leave the room while they are still befuddled.

The third method of coping involves some fraud. But I've found that most states don't require a photo ID to change your party affiliation, just a social security number. Get someone of the same gender as your R relation to go down to ye olde courthouse and change them from R to D. If you're too chicken, get some forms and do it via the U.S. Postal Service, decreasing your physical exposure and increasing your legal exposure at the same time. Your family members may still act like Rs, but you'll have the sense of serenity that comes from knowing they are not. Fraud heals the soul. No good R will argue with that.

Q: My roommate is so quiet I never know whether I'm alone. I'm used to being the quietest person around, and her quieter-than-thou ways are unnerving me! How am I supposed to talk to myself if I can't be sure I'm the only one who's listening?

—*Invisible*

A: Have you read Carol Emshwiller's story "I Live with You but You Don't Know It"? You should. I think you're in it.

What you need is a puppet. You can talk to your puppet then and make it talk back to you. This will create a much bigger problem to deal with than Silent Roommate Stalks With Wolves, because you will be suddenly insane.

Q: I am the proud owner of two Chihuauas that don't know their own (barely measurable) strength. They always try to pick fights with the biggest dogs in the neighborhood, and to-day they barked at a woman who was clearly on her way to karate practice—the belt around her waist was black! How do you let a small dog know just how small it really is?

—*From, Lilliputian Pooch Papa*

A: Do you have asthma or something? Is this Paris Hilton pre-tending to be a man?

I kid: I love the Chihuahuas.

Small dogs yap at bigger ones. It's the way of the world. Deal with it or buy a mastiff for your precious princesses to ride on top of, tickbird-rhinoceros style.

Q: Why aren't all books as good as Geoff Ryman's *Air*?

—*A Devoted Reader*

A: Not all books are written by Geoff Ryman, therefore most suck.

Q: Will you tell me a story?

—*Love, an Annoying and Small Child with a Runny Nose*

A: One day an annoying and small child with a runny nose found out that runny noses signal deadly cancer, especially in small children. The child was soon dead.

BRIGHT WATERS

John Brown

...

IN THE SPRING OF 1718 JAN VAN DOORN RETURNED TO HIS
log house with a load of molasses and flour and a fine green dress
for his new wife. He found she had run out on him and taken half
of his goods with her.

She was the second wife he'd bought. And the second one to
run away before a season was out.

Her name was Woman With Turtle Eyes, an older Huron of
twenty-three years. He had thought an older woman would be
more stable than the girl he had purchased the first time. Besides,
she said she wanted him to buy her.

Jan didn't understand how the men in the settlements courted
and kept their women. And it couldn't be because he was ugly.
He'd seen plenty of ugly men marry. The only women who
seemed to have any interest in him were the whores at Fort Mon-
treal, and when he'd given in to his urges that one cursed time, they
took far more from him than his money. There was nothing to do
about Woman With Turtle Eyes. If he hunted her down, she'd just
run away again. He could beat her, but she'd run nevertheless. Besides, her theft meant he'd have to start working his old claim, and
there were precious few weeks before the beavers began to shed
their winter coats. No, there was nothing to do but fold up the
dress and put it in the cedar chest.

He looked down on the dress for a few moments, admiring the
fine, shimmering cloth. Then he closed the lid.

That night Jan cooked himself a meal of kale and old potatoes.

When he finished, he rubbed deer urine onto his traps to prepare them for the morrow. Then he went to bed.

Over the next few weeks he worked his claim, cured pelts, and began to rebuild what he'd lost. But as the weather warmed, someone began raiding his traps. The third time this happened he found six traps in a row with both bait and beaver gone. He held up the last trap and examined it. The other times he'd been too late to catch the thieves, but this time the blood matting the hair on the jaws was still wet.

If it was LaRue or English Pete, he was going to murder the man. That, or sell him off to the Abenaki. If it was a Mohawk, well, then he'd have to tame his response.

He didn't trap much anymore. There simply wasn't as much game here as there had been ten years ago. Besides, it was much more profitable to trade instead of trap. Let the Iroquois tribes do the work. He'd profit on both the buying and the selling. Nevertheless, he held agreements with all the trappers and sachems in the area. This was his claim. Even if it was small.

His next set of traps lay only fifty yards farther up the stream. And by the great William of Orange, they'd better be full.

He decided to walk carefully and was rewarded for his caution, for as he crested the next rise in the trail, he spied three Indian boys standing over the trap he'd set next to the willow there. Two held a pole with half a dozen beaver draped over it. The third bent down and sprung the trap.

He looked at their leg tattoos. Mohawk. One of the Iroquois tribes. Well, he couldn't kill them then.

Not that he'd want to. They were, after all, just boys. Still, Indian boys weren't like the lads back in Rotterdam. It had been small Abenaki lads, just this age, who tried to take his scalp in his first year as a trapper. He'd killed them all with the blood flowing down the side of his face and a chunk of his scalp flapping about like a wig.

And so he'd need to be ready. Hunting knives hung from the belts at their waists. But none carried a war club. Only one held a bow.

Jan sneaked back the way he had come and then up and around in front of them so that the boys would walk right up the trail into him. The path bent around a hill where the river willow grew thick. He waited for them there.

He withdrew rope and a knife from his pack. He couldn't kill them, but he could tie them up and scare them into good Christian men.

Just as he was wondering if he hadn't misjudged their direction, he heard footsteps and low voices. He wrapped the ends of the rope in his hands.

The first two boys passed and didn't see him. Each carried on his shoulder the end of a pole laden with beaver. When the third turned the corner, Jan roared and lunged for him.

But instead of catching the boy up in the rope, he ran into a white woman wearing a yellow bonnet who yelled like the devil himself and all his horned helpers.

She did not look like a slave. She did not react like one either. Before he could turn back to the boys, the woman set herself, brought up an Iroquois corn stick, and walloped him on the side of the head.

Jan lost his vision momentarily. When it came back he could see the boys preparing for an attack.

He pulled his war club out of his belt and warned them away. He was two heads taller than most men, and his war club was a good three feet long.

"I promise you by Hiawatha's bones," he said in Mohawk. "I'll crack every one of your thieving heads like a pumpkin."

"Stop," said the woman in Mohawk. "All of you."

One of the boys looked over at her.

"Stop this now."

Neither Jan nor the boys put down their weapons.

"Crow Child, put your knife down. Now!"

The boy hesitated and then lowered his knife.

"And you," she said. "That is Iron Wood's boy. You touch any of us, and his village will feed your parts to the dogs."

Iron Wood's boy? Jan looked at the boy more closely. He saw the turtle tattoos on his legs marking his clan. He saw his face. How had he not recognized him? He'd grown.

"These are my traps," he said. "This is my claim. And I'll suffer no thieves to take what's mine. If he's Iron Wood's boy, then I'd like to talk to the Wise Mother of the Turtle Clan about the proper punishment for thieves."

The boy didn't show much. They were trained not to. But Jan saw his eyes round just a little. The Wise Mother of the Turtle Clan ran her village. She was the one who chose the sachem, and she was not someone to trifle with. They'd flog the boy twenty times or hang him up from a tree for a day. There had been too much blood shed between Indians and traders over incidents just like this.

The boy looked to the woman.

"I think we can work this out," said the woman.

Jan turned to her. What woman in her right mind would be out walking with three Mohawk boys anyway? Granted, the Mohawks around here hadn't attacked any English or Dutch settlers for a few years. But Mohawks weren't the only ones in these woods.

"Who are you?" asked Jan. "And why do you speak Mohawk?"

"That is none of your business," she said.

Her accent when speaking Mohawk was just like Pete's.

"You're that English teacher the Indians have been talking about," he said.

"I'm not English," she said. "And no one has trapped here for years. How do we know they're yours?"

Most women avoided Jan. None looked him in the eye. It was

disarming to have her look at him so. But it was also obvious she didn't know anything about trapping. "They're mine because the traps have my mark."

The woman looked hard at the boys. They did not meet her gaze.

"I see," she said. "And if they promise never to raid your traps again?"

He looked at the boys. They'd be back. He would have come back were he in their position. "You may speak Mohawk and spit fire, but you're still an Englishwoman. Not a sachem or Wise Mother. You can't bind them. I'm afraid that won't do."

"They're boys," she said.

"They're thieves. And they're still young enough that they can learn. Or would you simply let this bad wood grow until it was too hard to cut out without killing the tree?"

"There are other ways," she said.

"Well, until you think of a better one, I'll be walking back to Iron Wood's village with you."

He could see she did not like that. But he didn't care. He raised his club and spoke to the boys. "You can put down your knives and we'll walk to your village like men. Or I can break a few bones and then carry you to your village over my shoulder."

The boys looked at the woman. She motioned for them to put their weapons down. The surprising thing was that they did. How an Englishwoman got such authority he could never guess.

When their weapons lay on the grass, he quickly bound their wrists to the pole holding the beavers. It would not do for them to be able to act on second thoughts. And they would have second thoughts. Then he began to march them the three miles to the village. On the way he asked her what she had been doing.

"They were escorting me to their village to teach them English, the Bible, and how to shoot muskets."

Yet another surprise. She took a great risk, or the English had suddenly reversed their policy on Indians and muskets. The English thought it wise to prohibit the sale of guns to their Iroquois allies. It was a stupid policy that Jan never followed. The Dutch had traded guns freely with the Iroquois and profited greatly. He supposed the magistrates would consider shooting lessons a similar offense. If they ever found out, she'd be pilloried and whipped.

"You're teaching them how to shoot?" he asked.

"Are you deaf?" Then she looked at his ear.

His ear was just one of the many things about his face that people felt they must look at.

"A bear thought it might taste good for lunch," he said.

"A bear would have taken more than that for lunch. I'm not a fool."

He didn't think she was. But it was the truth. "OK, let's see. I lost it in a fight."

"See, a little truth never hurts."

"Then how about this truth. You're a foolish woman to walk about in these woods with nothing more than a corn stick. What if I had been Abenaki? They'd love a pretty thing like you."

She set her jaw at that and walked up ahead of him and stayed there the rest of the way.

IRON WOOD'S VILLAGE was medium-sized for Iroquois villages and sat in the middle of twenty acres of cleared land. They burned the forest here many years ago. It would not be long before they would have to burn another place and move the village there. The land only lasted so long before it failed.

The village was encircled by two wooden palisades fourteen feet high. Inside that ring stood ten great longhouses and a number of smaller ones. Jan hailed the warrior keeping guard over this entrance, and then led the boys to Iron Wood's longhouse.

Just this walk through the village would shame them.

When he arrived at the longhouse, a girl ran inside. A moment later the Wise Mother of the clan stepped out. She wore a fine blue soldier's jacket, French cut with brass buttons.

"May the sun favor your crops," he said.

She looked at the boys and back to Jan.

"May you have corn in season," she said. "What have you brought me, One Who Keeps Them Awake?"

"Beavers," he said. "And boys who need learning."

"Hummm," she said. "Let us talk in private." She led the boys and Jan into the longhouse.

They talked long and Jan agreed that they should deliver double the number of beavers stolen or the equivalent in wampum. He actually preferred the wampum because the Iroquois and many of the trappers used it as coin. You could carry a tidy sum in nothing more than a sack. Of course, that also made it easier to steal. It had been his wampum that his last wife stole.

He told Crow Child he'd bring him back a musket if he delivered by next spring. And he'd warned him not to steal any of it, beavers or wampum, from anyone else. The boy promised. It was a fair penance, but one that would bring esteem to Crow Child if he kept it.

Jan could have asked for some physical punishment, but it was unwise for a trader to make any enemies among his sources. Those boys would grow up, and Iron Wood's son might become the next sachem.

During the conversation he also found out the Mohawk called the Englishwoman Bright Waters. They said she'd been taken from the Abenaki.

She must have been a slave to the Abenaki. No wonder she had gotten prickly when he mentioned that. But then she was twice the fool to be walking about with nothing more than a corn stick. He didn't want to think what the devils had done with her. Unless, of course, she had been held for ransom. Then they would have left her unmolested. Otherwise, he hoped they'd taken her when she was a child.

She should have been Iron Wood's property. But she had bartered almost a year's lessons in English and muskets for her freedom.

Jan suspected there was more to it than that. Iron Wood probably knew owning her would anger his English allies. They would have made him give her up eventually. So he got what he could. And knowing English would place Iron Wood in a better position to trade and negotiate. Och, but Iron Wood was smart.

ON HIS WAY OUT of the village Jan stopped by Crazy Rabbit's longhouse. Iron Wood was the war sachem. But Crazy Rabbit was the peace sachem. It didn't matter who currently ruled, a trapper needed to have good relations with both sachems if he wanted to trade with a village. Jan always gave Crazy Rabbit first look at the goods he traded.

Crazy Rabbit was not there, but his wife Willow was.

"Ah, One Who Keeps Them Awake," she said. "I'm about to eat succotash with venison."

"And maple syrup?" asked Jan.

"Of course," she said. "Come sit and tell me if you have a son. Or better yet, a daughter."

She wanted one of his children to marry into her family. "Neither," said Jan.

"Barren?"

"Well, she never stayed around long enough for me to find out."

Willow clucked and shook her head. "Huron cannot be trusted. I told you."

Jan shrugged.

"Why don't you come into my family? I have daughters and

granddaughters who would keep you warm. You can have your pick. Mix your blood with that of a real human and I cannot imagine the sons you'd grow. My warriors would be the talk of the five nations."

"It's a great honor," he said. She'd invited him into her family before. "But you know I cannot."

"Bah!" she said. "I do not want to hear your excuses. You are wasting your seed. Lie with one of my daughters. Sons with your strength, your *orenda,* would send the Abenaki and Huron running for the caves."

He had considered her offer the first time. She thought the *orenda,* the spirit that was in all things, made him large and quick. But he could not lie with her daughters. Not that he was the most pious man. But fornication was clearly forbidden by the Holy Word. If Jan's grandfather could die by the hands of Catholic armies for his beliefs, Jan could certainly keep his urges buttoned up.

He would not marry into her family and become part of her longhouse. And it *was* her longhouse. The Iroquois were strange this way. They traced their genealogy through their mothers. The mothers ruled the longhouses. The Wise Mothers of each clan chose the sachem. But it wasn't just that the mothers controlled everything on a local level. He wasn't against a woman ruler. After all, many a land had been ruled by a queen.

The problem was that he would then be a Mohawk. He would have to fight their wars and live here in this village. He didn't want to live in a European settlement. Why would he want to live here?

"My guardian spirit tells me not to," he said.

"I do not like your guardian spirit then."

"I'll marry someday," he said. "And then we shall see." And perhaps he wouldn't marry. It seemed the good Lord wanted to make a monk out of him whether he was Protestant or not.

Jan ate his succotash and told her the story of a German man who awoke one morning to find his cow wearing his pants. Then he told her about Ulysses and the sirens. She always asked for his stories. They all did. That was how he had gotten his name.

"That's a powerful magic," she said. "We have a powerful magic. Perhaps it is time to use it on you to help you find a wife."

Jan suspected she wanted a medicine woman to come chant over him.

"I will call the bone breaker to help you find a wife."

"I don't need magic," he said. The last thing he needed was an Indian witch placing some curse on him. "No amount of blowing tobacco smoke in my face is going to make me any prettier."

Her brows furrowed. "You won't give me sons. You won't take my magic. Maybe the One Who Keeps Them Awake does not want to trade with this village anymore."

Was she threatening to prevent him from trading? She could influence the council. She was Crazy Rabbit's wife and the mother of the Turtle Clan. There were others they traded with, but Iron Wood's village traded the most with him.

He decided she *was* threatening him. "What do you propose?"

"A small tattoo."

A tattoo? That was all?

"Where?" he asked.

"Here," she said, and poked him beside his eye.

It was only a tattoo. And it would secure her goodwill, at least for one season. However, he was convinced that nothing but God's grace would produce him a wife. "Fine," he said. "As long as it comes with more of your succotash."

JAN SLEPT in Willow's longhouse that night. The next morning a very old mother came into the tent. Tattoo lines and triangles crisscrossed her forehead and cheeks. Tattoo spiders clung to each of her index fingers.

"This is our healing woman," said Willow.

Jan had never seen her. But the village held about seven hundred people. Maybe he'd missed her. It was possible.

"I know you," she said. "I dreamed about you."

Jan doubted that. These Indians were always trying to read meaning into their dreams. They could dream of horse farts and still think some guardian spirit was trying to communicate with them.

She uncovered a bowl of pigment that smelled bitter. She made him sit on the ground next to the fire. Then she placed a small white bone in a clay pot and placed the pot in the coals.

"Where's your awl?" asked Jan.

"Shush," she said. Then she lit a pipe and blew smoke in his and Willow's faces. After that she chanted for quite some time in an unfamiliar language.

Jan was wondering if she was going to chant all afternoon when she took the hot bone out of the pot and broke it. She changed her chant and, with the sharp points of the bone as an awl, scraped the pigment into his skin.

It burned. But he told himself it would only make him more acceptable to the clans.

The old mother finally stopped her scraping and chanting and sat back and watched him. Willow wore a huge grin. She gave him a small looking glass, then rose and left the longhouse.

What he saw was a bright red line that spiraled around itself five times. Its small tail connected with the corner of his eye. He thought the red was his blood, but when he touched a finger to it, he realized it was the color of the pigment. He looked at the pigment bowl the old woman had used. It was not red.

"Does this change color?" he asked.

"When the *orenda* has run its course," the old woman said.

For a moment Jan wished he had not let them do this to him. But he told himself it was an investment, a piece of flesh for a good trading contact.

A few moments later Willow returned with her thirteen-year-old daughter, Moon. She motioned at Jan. "What do you think?"

Moon looked at him then shook her head and looked away. This was the daughter Willow had offered him before. Moon had not wanted him then. She obviously did not want him now.

Willow grimaced. She turned to the old woman, who shrugged.

Perhaps Willow thought Jan would be more agreeable if Moon showed more interest in him. If that was true, she was wrong.

"So what's this supposed to do?" he asked.

"Make you more appealing," said Willow. She looked him up and down. "It's his hair, isn't it?"

"Corn does not grow in a day," the old woman said. "The magic will gather strength over time."

Willow grabbed a basket with a flint knife. "But we can clear away the weeds to help it grow. With that beard and pelt on your head, you look more like an animal than a man. Let me shave it off."

"No," said Jan. This was exactly why he couldn't live in her longhouse. She would be telling him how to blow his nose before too long. "Shave my hair and I lose my power."

"Ah, I've heard that story from the children." She nodded. "Then at least take some bear grease to tame it."

"I'll ask my guardian spirit for approval," said Jan.

Willow frowned and shook her head.

"I thought this was powerful magic," said Jan.

The old woman spoke. "We don't bend the bones of our ancestors to unnatural magics. This will not force a yearning for you upon anyone. It will simply help your beauty shine forth."

"And nobody can see that beauty underneath an animal's hide," said Willow. "If you cover it, you bury the magic."

"Hair is the mantle given us by the creator," said Jan.

He could tell none of them believed that, but he wasn't going to shave. His hair covered his birthmark and scars. And he wasn't going to go about plastered with stinking bear grease.

"Don't waste the *orenda* from those bones," said Willow.

"I wouldn't think of it."

WHEN JAN LEFT the village later that day, he saw the English-woman again. She was showing five children how to pack a musket. Perhaps she wasn't as helpless as he thought. If she had lived any amount of time with the Abenaki, she would have to know more of the woods than any number of ladies fresh off the boat from the old land.

He watched her. She was not a proper woman. But that wasn't always a liability. She knew how to load a musket. And quickness would be good to have at your back if you needed to defend your home.

She looked over at him.

After a moment he realized he was simply standing there looking at her, so he waved a fare-thee-well.

She acted like she didn't see him at all and turned back to the children.

So much for the magic of Iroquois bones.

Jan walked down to the path that followed the river. He wondered where she would go when her bargain was completed. One thing was for sure. She'd better go out walking with more than her courage and a corn stick next time, or she just might not fulfill her bargain. A dog and musket would be a good investment.

JAN'S TATTOO EARNED HIM some remarks when he went into the trading post. He never told them how or why he got it. Let them guess. In the end, they made up a better story than any he could think of. He heard from LaRue that all the traders thought it was a sign of a contract between him and Iron Wood and the principal reason why they were having such a difficult time moving their goods.

Jan replied that they all could get the tattoo if they just asked for it. Of course, it would cost them each a child.

He trapped for the next few weeks on his own. When he came back to the settlements, he began to notice women offering him furtive glances. A few days later came unabashed smiles. He told himself that the women had always been so friendly, and he only noticed it now because of the fuss Willow made with her tattoo.

But not long afterward English Pete stopped him at the trading post.

"Have you found gold then?" asked Pete.

"Gold?" asked Jan. Why would anyone think that?

"It's being noised about that you're preparing to build an estate."

"The rivers are fatter this year than I expected, and I've made back all the wampum my last wife stole from me. But it's hardly a treasure trove."

"No," said Pete. Then he lowered his voice. "It's said that Jan van Doorn has happened upon a great Iroquois fortune."

"Pete," said Jan, "you and I both know that the Iroquois are not gold diggers. There is no Spanish treasure in the north."

"Well, then I can't figure it out."

"What?"

"Either you've become handsome or rich. Looking at you I can see that you're ugly as ever. So I have to guess that it's because you're rich."

Jan had no idea what he was talking about. "Pete, you've been drinking bad whiskey."

"Van Doorn, I'd hide the gold if I were you. Not everyone is as honest as I." Then Pete walked off.

Jan turned into the trading post and soon found out what Pete was babbling about. Both Gordon, the post owner, and Lancaster were there. It seemed the baker's wife, the spinster Patrice, and the widow Millard had all expressed an interest in him.

"I don't even know the baker's wife," said Jan.

"You're about the only one who doesn't," said Lancaster.

"She's married."

"That hasn't stopped her before. What I can't understand is how you found the gold."

"There is no gold," said Jan.

"Then don't let anyone know or you'll lose your advantage. If it were me, I'd warm the spinster first. She has a fine stout figure."

Jan realized they all thought he had found gold because that was the only reason anyone would take an interest in him. Suddenly he did not want an advantage. He did not want to warm anyone. He didn't want their smiles.

Then he thought of Willow's tattoo. Was there actually something more to it than chanting and smoke? Jan had an easy way to find out.

He turned to Gordon. "I need some scraps of cloth."

"Not another dress," said Gordon.

"No, I need an eye patch." Except it wouldn't cover his eye. It would cover the tattoo. When he'd stitched together his patch and tied it about his head, he visited the baker's.

The wife stood at the counter dripping honey onto buns. She looked up and smiled at him. Then he shut the door behind him and slid the patch over the tattoo.

Her face changed. It was slight, but the welcome was gone.

He looked her in the eye. "I've a hunger for something sweet and warm," he said.

"No," she said. "I can't. I've baked nothing today."

"Perhaps tomorrow."

"No," she said. It was barely a whisper.

Then he moved the patch off his tattoo.

She looked intently at him as if she'd noticed something strange or was confused. Then her demeanor changed. She placed her hand over her breast. "I think the light from outside affected my vision. I'm sorry. What did you want?"

"I've a great appetite."

"You're a large man."

"That has its advantages," he said.

She arched an eyebrow and grinned. "I should imagine."

It *was* the tattoo. Of course, it helped that she was as unsteady as March sunshine. Jan slipped the patch back over the tattoo and watched her wanton look turn all to business. Then he walked out.

He tried his experiment on the spinster and widow and a few others along the way. All but the chandler's wife reacted in a similar fashion, but it was said a pickled heart beat in her breast and she couldn't be relied on in matters of love and friendship. Whether that was true or not, she was certainly immune to heathen witchery, for he planted himself next to her in the apothecary for at least two minutes, and she didn't so much as bat an eyelash.

And witchery was what it was, plain and simple.

He'd been a fool. They could have performed any manner of Indian devil craft upon him. This was exactly how a man lost his soul.

That evening Jan sought out a minister and inquired how he might remove the evil. The minister told him that if his hand offended him, he should cut it off. If his eye offended, he should pluck it out. Surely, his tattoo should be sliced off. No miracle would do him any good as long as he displayed an open invitation to Satan on his face. It seemed the procedure for casting out devils had changed somewhat since the days of the Apostles. Jan had been hoping for a simple blessing, a painless take-thy-bed-and-walk approach.

Perhaps the patch wasn't such a bad idea.

He thanked the minister and left.

The next day he trekked out to Iron Wood's village. When he found Willow, he demanded she remove the curse.

"If I had wanted to curse you," said Willow. "I would have ordered the healing woman to put a yearning on you for your horse, or maybe a bear."

"Curse or blessing, I want it removed."

"I cannot remove it."

Perhaps the minister was right. "Then I'll cut it off."

"That might have worked the first few days, but that won't stop it now. The *orenda* is in your bones. It will stay there until you let it run its course."

"And how long will that be?"

"Until you are complete."

"It's unnatural devilry," he said.

"It's how you are made," she said. "Your own stories say it was not good for the first man to be alone. He needed a Wise Mother. And only when she arrived was it good. There's a piece of you missing, and until you find it, you won't be whole. Now come see my daughter again."

"I'm not going to deceive her," he said. "Or anyone else."

"It is not deceit."

"And will she say that on the day the *orenda* runs its course? No, she will look at me and despair."

"Bah," said Willow. "That happens to every pair who feel the fire of passion. One day the roaring fire burns down. Did the passion deceive them? Was it unnatural? No, it took its course and burned down to something you can cook with, something useful."

Jan could not see the fault in her argument, but he knew it was wrong. It simply wasn't honest. Besides, such things could not be from God. He'd read about the gift of miracles, tongues, and charity. But not the gift of glamour. And so if it was not of God, it must be of the devil. And Jan did not want to owe the adversary even a nit's teaspoon.

"No good can come of this," he said.

Her looked softened. "You do not listen, One Who Keeps Them Awake. When one bathes in the river and braids his lock of hair before meeting his beloved, is that dishonest? Your own women wear painful clothing to appeal to the silly European sense of beauty. Is that dishonest?"

It wasn't the same, but Jan couldn't explain the difference.

"All we've done is highlight what's good in you. Now come let my daughter see what I do."

"No," said Jan. "I cannot."

She looked hard at him then. "So be it." Then she dismissed him with a flick of her wrist. He could tell she was exasperated. But he could not reconcile witchcraft with girdles and perfumes. And he was sure he didn't want to lure a woman into his bed. Jan was determined: he would have a wife honestly or would not have one at all. It seemed he would have to carry the devilry in his bones, but it couldn't be considered a sin if he didn't profit from it. So he wore his patch and traded as he normally did. Sometimes when he saw the spinster Patrice he was tempted to walk about without the patch. But he never gave in.

The days passed and he began to think more about the English-woman. She was the only European woman he'd found who had looked at him with something other than pity or fear. Perhaps she was beyond the powers of the tattoo. It was possible. Not all the women in the settlements had inquired after him. And the healing woman had said the magic would not force anyone.

In August he found out who she was. He went to the post to get powder and beans. He was drinking a glass of whiskey when Lancaster said, "Have you heard about Devil Jack's daughter? She was out teaching the savages the Bible."

"Isn't that a bit dangerous?" someone asked.

"Well, I guess not for the daughter of Devil Jack," he said.

Devil Jack had been renowned from New York to Ticonderoga for killing more Indians than any man. He'd taken twenty arrows and lived to tell about it. He was as bloody a man as had ever lived. And he'd had eight sons just as bloody as he.

"I thought him and his were all killed by the Abenaki," said Jan.

"That's what we all thought. But apparently he had a daughter that was taken as a slave. That was nine years ago. She was recovered just last autumn by a Mohawk raiding party and bargained for her freedom."

"What did she bargain with?" someone asked.

"You figure it out," said Lancaster.

Devil Jack's daughter. Surely this was the same woman he met earlier. It would explain her bite.

"I would not be so hasty to smirch her name," said Jan. "It wasn't that sort of bargain at all. I talked with those who took her, and they wanted her English."

"What for?"

"Think a moment," said Jan. "How might it profit a sachem when he realizes that he doesn't need us anymore, that he can go directly to the traders in New Amsterdam and speak their language?"

That caught their attention.

"What's her name?" asked Jan.

"Shannon," Lancaster said. "Shannon Burke."

"Has she gone savage then?" someone asked.

"No," said Lancaster. "I was just down in New York. I hear she's living with an aunt there."

"It's a waste," someone suggested. "Who would want an Indian-used woman?"

"I would not dismiss her so hastily," said Jan. There was a spirit in her that was very appealing. "She's got a bit of her father's fire."

Then he told them all about his beavers and getting clobbered on the side of the head. He decided to embellish a few of the details.

"That's not quite the version I heard earlier this summer," English Pete said. "I think at least three warriors were added to the count this time."

Pete and his memory took all the fun out of it.

"You must have heard wrong," said Jan. "I'm telling you there were nine."

IN SEPTEMBER, before the river froze, Jan helped guard a load of goods down the river to New Amsterdam. He still could not bring himself to call it York. Why the King signed it away, he'd never understand. The Dutch had, after all, won the war.

The trip down might have been pleasant, but the cook put something evil into a soup that made him vomit for three days. However, by the time they arrived, he had recovered enough to get off his deathbed.

The city was grand. In the last three years it seemed a thousand more houses had been built. The English were multiplying here like rabbits. He had two days before the ship sailed back up. During the first day, Jan ate enough fritters and crullers to make a man sick. He bought a Protestant Bible and a copy of a Dutch translation of a story about a crazy man in Spain who thought he was a knight. In the evening of that first day, he thought he saw Devil Jack's daughter hurrying down Wall Street holding a basket. He tried to follow her but lost her when she called at a house and went inside.

The next day he found out from a Lutheran minister where Shannon lived and thought of making a call. But then rethought. Why would she want to see him? He could bathe and shave, but that would only show more of his scars and birthmark. They had not met in favorable conditions. Still, he'd never met a woman quite like her.

That first night he did not sleep well and he couldn't decide if it was the fritters or the woman that kept him awake.

He did not have much to offer a woman. He lived alone in a small house far from such a splendid city as New York. Here it was safe. There she might be molested, again. Still, she was a brave woman. She knew the tribes.

Sometime before the sun came up, he decided he'd call on her. The first thing he did was go to the bathhouse. Then he paid a barber to trim his beard and hair up short. But when he exited the barber's, he despaired. He had not called on a proper woman before. He did not know the rules. He'd never known the rules. He supposed he should bring some gift but had no idea what that would be.

In the end he settled on a fine cheese.

When he stood on the porch of her house, he realized he would have to make conversation. But what would they converse about?

A woman opened the door. Her eyes widened and she took a step back. He had always had that effect on women. They always acted like he was going to eat them. He'd hoped the haircut would have made him more of a gentleman. Obviously, Willow's advice did not help with Europeans. He thought about uncovering the tattoo but decided against it. He cleared his throat. He could tell she did not trust him. "I'm here to see Miss Burke."

"And you are?"

Och, he was so clumsy with these things. "Jan van Doorn."

"She's not here right now," she said.

"I see," said Jan. He had been a fool to come. "Perhaps I could wait. I have a cheese."

The woman looked confused by his last statement.

"For her," he said.

"Oh, I can take that. Did she purchase it from Zwaart's?"

She thought he was a delivery boy. "No, I wanted to bring it to her myself, as a gift. I met her among the Mohawk and thought I might speak with her. I'm leaving back up into the interior tomorrow, and, well, I—"

"I see," the woman said. She tried to suppress a smile, but the corners of her mouth gave it away.

A cheese must have been the wrong kind of gift.

"I'm Shannon's aunt. She's out gathering firewood, but you can wait on the porch."

"Of course," he said. It wouldn't be proper for him to wait with her alone in her house. This was proving more difficult than he imagined.

He waited on the porch with his cheese sitting next to him and watched two boys run up and down the street trying to fly a kite. He did not see or hear Shannon arrive. Just when he began to wonder if he would have to wait on that porch until dark, the door opened again and the aunt said, "Will you come in, Mr. van Doorn?"

Jan rose. He ducked into the doorway but then he couldn't straighten back up. Whoever had built this house had been exceedingly short.

"Please sit here," she said, and motioned at a chair that looked as if it was made for a child.

"Are you sure I won't break that?" asked Jan.

She looked him up and down. "No, not entirely."

He almost offered to sit on the floor, but thought better of it. The chair wobbled and creaked when he settled onto it. He could feel if he shifted his weight just a little that it would indeed crack.

Shannon came in then wearing a plain lace covering over her hair and just about stopped his heart. She did not wear fine clothes. She was not shaped like the spinster Patrice. And yet she was beautiful.

Jan rose and thrust the cheese out in front of him. "I thought you might enjoy this," he said.

"I'm sorry," she said. "I don't believe I ever heard your proper name."

Jan thought back. She was right. She didn't even know who he was. And here he'd come calling. "Van Doorn," he said. "Jan. I grew up outside Rotterdam."

She took the cheese from him and handed it to her aunt. A meaningful look passed between them that Jan could not fathom.

They talked then about the Mohawk and trading and living with the English. He could see a tattoo on her left ear, the marking of a slave. He had not noticed that before. That meant she had not been held for ransom, and he wondered how the Abenaki had treated her.

He showed her the Bible he'd purchased. When she asked him if he'd ever read the Bible, he told her that his mother taught him to read Dutch, starting with Genesis. He knew all the stories. That made her smile. They talked more about their homelands and he found out she was not English after all, but Irish.

The aunt came in and joined their conversation. He was telling them both the story of the time when LaRue tried to turn a foundling moose into a packhorse when someone knocked at the door.

It was a man with black boots and a green overcoat. The aunt introduced him as Michael O'Day, a farmer just outside the city and from the same town in Ireland as Shannon.

He looked at Jan and then walked straight to Shannon, caught up her hand, and kissed it.

"And who is this great fellow?" he asked.

"A trapper I met while among the Mohawk," Shannon said.

The aunt laid her hand on Michael's arm. "Shannon and Michael are to be married in the spring."

Jan's heart sank. "Oh, I see. Well, then. You've found yourself quite a woman, Mr. O'Day. Quite a woman."

He suddenly didn't know what else to say. An odd silence hung in the air and he said, "I think I must be on my way. But I give you one warning, Mr. O'Day. If you're ever in a fight, never let her near a corn stick."

Shannon smiled.

"A corn stick?" asked O'Day.

"She can tell you," said Jan. "Enjoy the cheese for dinner." And then he picked up his hat and coat and left. He told himself it was probably better this way. A farmer would provide a stability that he never could.

On the way back to the ship he felt a bit unsteady and wondered if he really was over the illness that had afflicted him on the trip down. So instead of visiting a tavern, he reported to the captain and slept onboard. In the morning they shoved off before daylight.

THAT WINTER was colder than the last. The snows drifted in some places higher than his head. On Sundays, he took his books to the post and read to the men who were there. Lancaster said he'd heard there was a song of songs in the Bible. But Jan acted like he didn't know what he was talking about. He simply did not want to read them the Song of Solomon. In fact, there were ministers who thought it didn't even belong in the Holy Book.

When he read about Elijah calling fire down on the priests of Baal, English Pete commented it was a shame no prophet was alive today to call fire down on the French. LaRue protested, but most of the men at the post were English and they shouted him down.

IN JUNE THE Mohawk and Abenaki skirmished with one another. During that time Jan heard that Shannon had reappeared among the villages. With all the battles and various parties skulking in the woods, it was not a safe time for her to return.

A few weeks later Iron Wood asked for crates of powder, balls, and muskets. Jan brought a mule loaded with the contraband. He also made sure to pack a special musket with crows carved in the stock.

Crow Child did not disappoint him. He proudly delivered a mixture of wampum and beaver and then whooped when he saw the special musket.

Of course, the first thing Willow did was grab Jan's face and turn it toward her to look at his tattoo. Then she shook her head and walked away.

It seemed, despite all his efforts, he was making her into an enemy.

He took his mule out to pasture and saw Shannon at the river washing clothes on a rock. He walked up behind her. "Miss Burke," he said.

Shannon turned in fright and walloped him upside the head with her soap.

"Och," he said, and wiped the suds away from his eye.

"Do you scare all the women?" she asked.

"Oh, I scare them all, but it seems you're the only one who intends to make me pay for it."

She turned back to scrubbing her clothes.

"It's a dangerous time, Miss Burke, or should I say Mrs. O'Day?"

"It seems I was bred for such a life."

"And where's Mr. O'Day?"

"Sleeping with his pigs." She said that with no love. He felt better about this. He wasn't the only one who struggled at the beginning of a marriage.

"Is he here then? Trading pigs?"

"No," she said. "He's back in New York. He called it off."

"The engagement?"

Shannon nodded.

Why on earth would the man do that? He looked at her. She didn't show any sign of feeling sad. But she wouldn't. She'd lived with the Abenaki.

He wouldn't say anything. He knew what it was like to have the lads at the post poke at such a loss. It was all in good fun to make him feel better, but it never did.

Jan's mother always told him that the finest gift he ever gave her was the day he'd done her wash. So instead of saying something, Jan took Shannon's basket of washed clothes and asked her where her line hung. He stood hanging up a petticoat when she joined him with the rest of the wash.

"So you've come back to the Mohawks for good?"

"It seems they don't care about my past," she said.

She was right. The Mohawks would prize her father. "Devil Jack was a bloody man," said Jan. "But sometimes a man has to be bloody to survive."

She looked over the clothesline at him. "He said he didn't want dirty undergarments."

"What?"

"O'Day."

And the Dutch were marked for their fastidiousness. But then that didn't make any sense.

"So you were a poor housekeeper? He could have hired a maid."

"I was with the Abenaki as a young woman," she said.

Ah, he was so slow sometimes. Her ear tattoo was that of a concubine. He should have made that connection. But wouldn't O'Day have known that when he engaged her? Perhaps O'Day suspected some things. But then, for some men, knowing what happens in general is not the same as knowing specifically what happened to the woman you're to marry.

If O'Day was that type of a man, he was a fool.

"Do you have a child then?" asked Jan.

"I did. But my husband sold him away to humiliate me."

"The Abenaki are worthless dog turds," he said.

"Only some of them," she said.

And then he realized her son was probably still among them, sold to another village. Besides, she had once been Abenaki herself.

"You are right," he said. "There are devils among all men."

THAT NIGHT IRON WOOD and most of his warriors left. They returned the next day with much shouting and hung fifteen scalps on their palisades at the entrance. Many wore French hats. This would bring a reprisal. The French would seek revenge.

He found Shannon outside the city cleaning muskets. "Do you not think it a good time to leave?" he asked.

"And go where?"

Jan didn't have a good answer to that.

"I'll stay here. They can use my skills."

"A teacher can't do much in a time of battle."

"I'm no fine lady, remember?" She picked up a musket that stood in a round stack and with amazing speed half-cocked it, poured in the powder, inserted the ball, withdrew the rod, rammed the ball home, and then replaced the rod. A person could not load a musket that quickly unless they'd done it hundreds of times.

"I'll stand upon that wall," she said. "I have five of these children trained to load the musket. Do you know how many balls I can put in the air?"

Jan looked at Shannon with new eyes. By the Holy Mother, Devil Jack did have a daughter.

"I can't imagine. I've never met a woman quite like you," said Jan. "You're something of an inspiration. Maybe I'll stay."

"You have no ties here," she said.

He thought about that. He didn't have kin here, but then again, this was the closest to family he had. These savages and the lads at the post. And if he had to choose, well, he'd rather stay with the savages.

"You're right," he said. "But then I've no love for the Abenaki either."

"It's a good thing this village purchased what powder they did," she said.

"Yes," he said. "I'm thinking they were waiting for my load before going off on that raid. I can tell you one thing, these fields will run with blood."

"One of these days," she said, "it will be my son who comes painted for war."

THE ABENAKI AND French came just before dawn. A village boy went out to the stream to check his weirs. He managed to yell twice before they cut his throat.

A warrior on the rampart heard him and gave the warning cry. Flaming arrows flew over the palisades and into the roofs of the longhouses. Jan saw one bury itself in a woman's back as she ran away.

The warning had come almost too late. The Abenaki were within yards of the entrance when Iron Wood's warriors poured out of the village to meet them. Warriors ran up the ladders and fired muskets and arrows.

Jan decided to stay back by the entrance. The ends of the palisades overlapped here so you could not get a straight shot into the village. If any of these devils wanted to get in, they'd have to go through the Dutch Bear. And by William, he'd smash them to pieces.

The two sides on the field clashed and mingled. Not wanting to hit their own, the archers and musketeers on the wall ceased firing.

Then a cluster of Abenaki broke the line and ran for the entrance. Their faces were painted in horizontal white-and-black stripes.

It had been too long since Jan had seen any real battle, and he could feel himself begin to quail. There was only one solution to that. Jan raised his musket and shot one of the demons in the belly. Then he took up his war club.

The first one to close with him leapt like a deer. Jan's war club was longer than most of those the Iroquois used. So he was able to smash the inside of the man's elbow as he came at him. Then he stepped out of the man's path and with a roar crushed the side of his head.

The Iron Wood warrior next to Jan fell, then began to drag himself back into the village. A yell rose from the far end of the village. Jan glanced back. Archers ran along the rampart back toward the noise.

He hoped Iron Wood's runners were fleet. And then he realized they ran because the village was surrounded. The runners had probably not made it more than twenty rods into the trees.

The Abenaki in front of him began to retreat, and Iron Wood's men chased after them. Something was not right. They never broke off the attack so quickly. And then Jan realized he'd seen no French. He looked at the woods. The farther the warriors ran, the more room they gave someone lurking in the woods to make for the village. A handful of warriors could defend the village from the inside. It took many more to attack.

It was a ruse. The retreat was a ruse.

He yelled to the archer above him to prepare for an attack from the forest. The archer barked orders to the others on the wall and then let out a yell. It was the call for retreat. Others on the wall took it up.

A few of Iron Wood's warriors turned. And then the main body stopped its chase. The woods boiled with men. French and Indian came rushing out. They were half the distance to the village before the warriors in the field caught up with those in the rear. There was no way Jan and the seven who stood with him could hold the entrance. There had to be two hundred French coming down upon them.

The French line stopped and fired a volley that dropped four of the men with Jan and sent chips of wood flying. One chip struck him on the cheek. Another few inches and it would have put his eye out.

He retreated into the village. Women and children stood on the walls armed with bows. Shannon was among them with her five boys. She shot and took a ready musket from the boy behind her, shot again, took another, shot again.

He needed to find the barricades. The village kept them close to the entrance. He and the other three lifted them into place. They set the fourth just before the French broke upon them. The arrows and musket fire rained down upon the attackers, but there were simply too many of them and they reached the barricade. The first two men over were shot with arrows. Jan finished them off when they reached the ground.

He heard a cry and an Iron Wood woman fell from the wall and crashed almost at his feet.

More men tried to leap the barricade with the same result. And then he heard a volley of muskets crack at his back. He turned and saw a dozen French loading muskets. They'd broken through the other entrance. Two of them took arrows and fell.

A group of young warriors rushed those remaining. Only lads. He hoped they had learned their killing lessons well. Jan searched for Shannon on the wall but saw only her five loaders. His heart fell. She must have been shot.

In front of him more French and Abenaki tried to break through. He and the other warriors rushed up the barricade to meet the attackers, but they could not hold. Too many men got past them.

And then Jan found himself back in the village swinging for his life. He downed five men and then saw some Abenaki running for a ladder.

He turned to chase them and found Shannon had reappeared. She stood with her boys, blood smeared down her cheek. She must have taken only a grazing.

One of the attackers threw a tomahawk that struck one of Shannon's boys in the head. She turned her musket down the ladder and blew the first man off; she took another musket and did the same to the second. But the enemy in the back of the village gained the rampart and now ran toward Shannon.

"Shannon," Jan yelled, and pointed.

That distraction cost him. He saw someone out of the corner of his eye. He was fast enough to avoid getting his shoulder crushed, but he was not quick enough to avoid the sharp point of the man's war club in his back. Jan swung his war club into the man's face. But then another Abenaki stood before him. Jan roared and charged. The warrior was quick as a snake. He ducked Jan's swing twice and then smashed Jan's fingers. Jan dropped his club.

The man drew back for a killing blow.

Then there was a wet thud and half of the man's neck disappeared. Another shot took out the one behind him.

Jan looked up. Shannon hadn't missed a beat. She handed her smoking musket to one of her four boys and took another.

He picked up his war club with his left hand and limped to the barricade. He found Frenchmen penned in by those above, Iron Wood's warriors coming back from their chase, and those who fought inside. The attackers died in that spot.

A yell of victory rose from the other end of the village. The warriors there must have chased the attackers out of the far entrance. Many of the surviving French and Abenaki had retreated to the woods.

The villagers regrouped. Jan stood at the entrance and waited for another charge. They came, the French in their pretty lines and the Abenaki yelling like devils. There were still so many of them. He felt weak in his knees and fell to the ground. He tried to crawl out of the way but didn't get far. He lay there watching the backs of the warriors.

The attack broke upon the village. He looked for Shannon and found her. Then his vision started to blur. It was very possible that too much of his life had already leaked out his back.

Men and women yelled all about him. Musket smoke clouded his vision even further. An Abenaki fell crossways over his legs. Someone scuffed dirt in his face. And then another cheer rose up from the walls and the noise of the attack broke off.

"They're running," someone said.

"Don't let them escape!"

Then all went black.

HE FOUND HIMSELF on his stomach in a longhouse. Willow sat on the floor below him.

"We drove them?" he asked.

She turned and smiled. "We slaughtered them from here to the river."

Jan looked at his splinted fingers. He remembered Shannon on the wall. "And Bright Waters?"

"She's a demon," said Willow. "All the warriors want to take her as wife. But I don't think she'll accept."

"Why?" he asked.

"Because all she's done is come in here and check on you."

He suddenly suspected Willow. He reached up to feel his patch. It was still there.

She smiled at him.

Then he brushed his cheek. There was no beard. He felt his chin, then the top of his head. He had no hair at all. She'd shaved him.

"What have you done?"

"Saved your life," she said. "Be grateful."

"You haven't been bringing your daughter in to look at me, have you?"

Willow smiled. "Of course not."

He didn't trust her. He asked her to fetch him a looking glass and held it up to his face. He looked like a fright with his tanned brow and cheeks all surrounded by the white skin that had been hidden under his hair. But the tattoo had not changed color.

THAT EVENING HE FELT well enough to walk so he got up and shuffled outside. He must have been asleep two days for he saw none of the dead. One of the longhouses was now nothing more than ash.

He saw Shannon. She stood with her back to him grinding corn with a foot-long pestle. He walked up behind her, but not too close. "Miss Burke," he said.

She did not startle this time but turned and smiled at him. "Come here and sit by me," she said.

"Is it safe?"

"What were you expecting?"

"A clop with that murderous pestle."

"And you would have received one," she said. "But it seems you've learned it's bad manners to sneak up on people."

Jan sat down on the bench beside her as she ground corn into meal. She'd stitched the gash that went from her cheek to one ear.

"That's quite a wound you have there."

"I'm afraid it won't do in proper society."

"Hang proper society."

"Yes, but I will miss the cheeses."

He looked over at her. There was a playfulness in her expression. But he didn't know how to build on it, so he changed the subject. "Was your son among the dead?"

"No," she said. "He's not old enough yet to fight with the men. I wonder if I'll even recognize him after his growth comes upon him."

"You'll know him."

"But not from a distance," she said, and then was quiet for some time.

She emptied out the bowl full of meal and then looked over at him. "Why do you wear that patch?" she asked.

"I've got a mole the size of a mushroom growing there."

She reached up for it, but he held her hand. "No," he said.

"It's not a mole," she said.

"It is."

"Do you take me for a fool?"

"Fine," he said. He'd tell her the truth. He doubted she'd believe it. He wouldn't have. "It's a bit of Iroquois devilry to help me find a mate."

"I know," she said. "Willow showed it to me."

Willow. First it was a shaving and now this.

"I've seen something similar twice before, while I was with the Abenaki."

She knew what it was. He felt ashamed. It was a weak man who tried to buy or trick people into liking him.

"Why cover it up?"

He didn't want to explain it all to her. "It's devil craft."

"I would think the power to magnify the beauty found in unlikely places is a gift from God." She smiled at him. Her expression was full of warmth. Or was that pity? He'd mistaken pity for kindness before and paid dearly for it. Of course, Shannon did not seem to be one of those social ladies who smiled at and touched on the back of the hand every man they met.

"You don't believe it's witchcraft?"

"I believe that our Lord rains his gifts on the heathen as well as the just."

She reached for the patch again.

This time he let her move it aside.

HOW THE BURKINA FASO BICYCLE FELL APART

K. E. Duffin

I guess the little straps of leather dried
to beef jerky or ligaments of shriveled toad
while it still looked ready to hit the (tiny) road
from its home on a shelf next to a Blue Guide.

Admired, even as its dusty tendons were loosening,
it dissembled well, until one day, it dis-
assembled into the hectic chumminess
of true collapse, wires released from miming

mechanical form so you could no longer discern
what had just been handlebar, mirror, kickstand.
Even the naked wheels couldn't be spun.
An artist, not some hack, made it by hand

and couldn't have intended such a grim display
of how easily attachments fall away.

FORWARDING ADDRESS

K. E. Duffin

Summer afflicts me with a certainty:
if I return to Rome I will again meet gnomic Ruth
at Piazza Cairoli, typing the gossipy truth—
not dead at all—about days with Carlo Ponti,
Sophia, and the Master (we smirked) who gave her the rules
for living a Hindu life, still calling us "girls"
and warning us about "boys" who might ask for a date,
their syringes trashing her sixteenth-century gate.
Rome was Ruth's—she taught us *diciassette,*
the melted scream of Giordano Bruno's story
showed us glittering swordfish in Campo dei Fiori,
the Sistine before the soot was cleared away,
and angels in Trastevere's Santa Maria.
Ruth of the catacombs, not trattoria.

SLIDING

D. M. Gordon

Shadows slip down driveways—
bears wandering at night,
disappearing behind stop signs, moaning,
silver-tipped visions rocking paw to paw.

All the world is sliding—
rain on green mountainsides, soft shoulders
of old women, the sloping arms
of pine, vanishing laps, birth canals and old age,
those worn wet trails. I too slip
down sluices of wet moss.
There goes an old millworks. Sliding.
A row of neat houses, a museum, a parliament.

A blind boy slides on his bedroom door,
equipped with the latest paraphernalia,
air tanks and dry rations. There are omens
he has seen in sudden clearings.

Here's a yellow grizzly standing broadside
in our way, wet-tufted and musty. The boy banks
and vanishes. I prepare to crash.

Here is a glass door,
a brown bear on the other side, dressed
in a pinstripe suit with waistcoat.

I open the door for him, and he tips his bowler hat
as he pads upright on soft bear feet across a marble floor,
    to my great relief,
for last night I heard the banshees sing,
and I thought, for a moment, they were singing for this
    world.

YOU WERE NEITHER HOT NOR COLD, BUT LUKEWARM, AND SO I SPIT YOU OUT

Cara Spindler and David Erik Nelson

. . .

WITH LOVE TO MOJO

ONCE UPON A TIME THERE WAS A FAMOUS AND TALENTED Horror Author with a problem: His wife was a monster in bed. The Famous and Talented Horror Author would scream himself awake in the morning with his wife, who slept soundly asleep next to him, soft and naked and warm and human and oblivious.

In the dream her face would turn fiery red and melt like wax, like Santería candles whose smell of rotting roses might fill a tiny *mercado* and murkily remind shoppers of a great-aunt's house on a sleepy Sunday afternoon. Her eyes would turn charred and black, velvety and endless pools in which he'd scream and thrash and drown. Her touch was a thousand knives, abrading his thighs with a deep, epidermal ache, a burn that crawled across his whole body in a sudden phalanx of pain.

In the dream his wife sucked great chunks of his soul as he clawed and cried in his sleep. His soul was pink and viscous, like hot, unstretched taffy, and having it sucked felt like she was digging into him with a tiny, serrated scoop. In the dreams she was a terrible and boneless tentacular thing, a clinging inescapable ache. A squeeze. If a heart attack were to be incarnated, it would be as this thing he dreamed his wife became.

AT FIRST THIS NOTION evaporated in the day's clarifying light, and by the time he stepped into the bathroom to take that first morning piss, it was utterly dissolved. But after a few weeks of reduced sleep the nightmare began creeping in around the edges of his day.

Did I really dream that she was a tentacle thing digging out my flesh with razored suckers, with fangs and venom-slavering maw? he would wonder, sitting before his idle computer, Did I dream that? In the evening, after dinner, he would clear the table and surreptitiously watch his wife, her delicate hand tucking a stray hair behind her ear as she labored over her laptop, and dismiss the dream as ridiculous. Then he'd fix himself another Jack on the rocks to ward off dreams.

And then things went deeper. There was strange grit in between the sheets. Windows he was sure were latched when he went to bed, he found unlatched in the morning. Dots of blood on the bedclothes, not toward the middle of the bed like a period uncalculated, but up near the pillows and down at the foot, and not menstrual-dark, but a light cordovan, sometimes still sticky fresh when he went to make the bed in the morning. The carpet seemed cooler under the window, just a little damp to his feet, but when he drew his hand over the carpet, it was dry. Sometimes he found wet leaves in the bedcovers or on the windowsill. Once one was plastered to his cheek.

By some mechanism unknown to him—but presumably a byproduct of matrimony—the Author found that he knew the terrible things she did out in the world after sucking him soulless. Like frescoes on the vault of his skull, he saw them painted among the candlelit shadows in his head, visions unbidden and awful: crushed cats, toes raggedly torn from clean seashell pink feet, blood in the jaws and teeth smashed against brick schoolyard walls. The high jabber of fear, the begging: first for salvation and mercy, and then just for death. The violations of the night.

Sitting on the toilet, or leaning over the kitchen sink rinsing out the coffeepot, the Author would suddenly find himself gripped by one of these visions, these impossible memories of his wife's monstrous hungers, and he would freeze with the fear of it, of her. Often he wept, helpless, until it passed.

His wife might come into the kitchen, cheery for the morning, smart in her grey business suit, leather attaché case swinging in her arm.

"Just coffee and an egg," she might call to him. "Gotta get to the office double-quick." And then glance up to see her husband at the sink, ghost-white and red-eyed.

"Hon," she'd say. "Oh, hon. What's wrong? What's wrong?" and she'd go to him, to stroke his hand, to comfort him, and he'd jerk away, as though she was hot or sharp.

"*Nothing!*" Too loud, too quick. "Nothing." Calmer. "I . . ."

She drew her hand back. "Were you crying?"

"I was . . . just. I just thought of something sad, from when I was a boy. It's nothing."

Nothing.

AS HE WASN'T REALLY sleeping anymore, the dream took to creeping up on him suddenly, when he shut his eyes over the computer at work in the drowsy hours after lunch or when he took a late-night walk and the streetlight happened to go out.

His disturbed and disturbing thoughts—his million-dollar thoughts, thoughts that petrified and drained his heart when in his head but made him the Famous and Talented Horror Author when on paper—had always had a habit of creeping up on him throughout his days. These flashes of terror—gut-wrenching, adrenaline-pumping—had always been fun thrill-panic, like when he was a little kid and had watched a scary movie and *knew,* just *knew* that two nights from now after playing Capture the Flag or videogames at a friend's house he would get that horribly-pleasantly sick feeling walking home alone, and he would swear to himself to never, ever again watch a horror movie.

But these strange brood of his dream about his wife were something different, and getting worse. They had even started to creep up while his eyes were open, as he waited in grocery store lines, or when he answered the phone and the caller took just a second longer than normal to reply to his *Hello?* Sometimes, when his wife wasn't yet home from work, he would let the phone ring and ring, because he dreaded what grave-moss voice might speak to him through the miles of roadside copper. Sometimes, when she was home, he let it ring and ring because he dreaded being distracted by the caller, dreaded the tentacles catching him unaware. It had happened in one of the dreams, he was sure. She looked normal, like her heavy-eyed two A.M. self, hair askew. And then she opened her mouth, and out came a voice deeper than the holes under waterfalls, rougher than a lion's tongue or shark's blood-hungry hide. It had scraped him down to the bone.

And so he let the phone ring.

The dream had crept from the back of his mind and now it perched on his shoulder, sometimes gently playing its taloned, toothed suckers across the back of his ears. The dream was so real and horrible that he started to consider the possibility that his whole life was actually a pleasant dream and the true reality was the monstrous, sucking wife-thing that tortured him at night. Memories? All the hours in his sunny home office with its dark-varnished bookshelves, garnished with sunny pictures from his honeymoon to Aruba with his brown young wife? All those other memories that made up a successful, contented childhood of family camping trips and a brother who had marshmallow-toasting contests with him? Those were all memories that had been pinned into him, and were not really a part of him at all, not nearly as real and solid as the tentacles and doll's eyes, as the thing his wife became at night.

In his dazed, sleep-starved stupor, the Famous and Talented Horror Author's mind gently bifurcated. Half perseverated over those classics he'd read in college—*Beowulf* and *Gilgamesh* and the *Odyssey*—and what had to happen to Grendel and Marduk and Cyclops. The other half of his mind thought of guns. He'd never owned a gun—never *touched* a gun—but all day he thought of guns, of holding one in his hand, of slipping one under his pillow and gripping its reassuring weight as he slept, of slipping the barrel into his mouth.

NOW, THIS MAN had a brother, the Club-Footed Janitor. Since Cain and Abel, all brothers have been the same: in every pair, each is equal, but one succeeds and one fails. Sometimes this affects their love and affection, as it did with Cain rising up left-handed, and sometimes it doesn't. It was fortunately the latter case with the Famous and Talented Horror Author and his brother, the Club-Footed Janitor: They had loved each other dearly as boys, and loved each other dearly as men, despite the divergence in the paths of their lives.

Also, ever since Cain and Abel, brothers have always had secrets from each other. The Club-Footed Janitor was not really a janitor, although he worked every day mopping floors, cleaning toilets, vacuuming thin industrial carpet. Innocuous. A relief because he was not the classic mentally retarded janitor who just can't seem to understand the importance of using the right size can liner, who speaks to us with his moist, garbled, mentally deficient voice, cheery and vacuous, an idiot man-child unable to take the world's manifold sufferings and ecstasies in his stunted grasp. Not that kind. Hardly worthy of note at all.

But, unbeknownst to the Famous and Talented Horror Author, and largely unbeknownst to himself, the Club-Footed Janitor worked for the Central Intelligence Agency. He killed people for the Central Intelligence Agency. It didn't make sense, really, that this brother ended up in law enforcement, because when the man and his brother were younger, the Author had always been the athletic one, not due to any sort of natural talent on his part but because his brother had been born with that horrible clubfoot, so reminiscent of the turned ankle the Irish wish on their enemies so that they might know them when they see them coming down the street.

For the Club-Footed Janitor, the younger brother, it wasn't his body the CIA needed, but his mind. Much as the Famous and Talented Horror Author had just the exact right type of mind to be what he was—overimaginative, fearful without being timid, arrogant and yet terribly insecure, paranoid—his brother had just the right mind to kill for the CIA: his brain was a set of rooms whose doors he could open and close at will, and in which he could hide from others and from himself; a warren, like the tunnels of the Vietcong or al-Qaeda or rabbits. No one could force from him the details of his orders, because he kept them locked away even from himself, and only let them come out of the room at their appointed time. When the office rats with their Franklin planners confused him with his coworker, the aforementioned idiot manchild, and spoke to him in an exaggeratedly slow and loud voice, using sign language of their own devising, never did it cross the brother's mind to slide under their SUVs, clutch the chassis to his chest, and ride it out to the suburbs, past the gates and guard dogs and fences, and wait until the opportune moment to sneak upstairs, unbidden, unseen, and open a vial of ground glass onto their shower floor—not just one shower, but all the showers: the white marble of the wife, the pink tile of the daughters. Never, because a door is either open or closed, and when the brother was in his janitor room, he could not be in his killer room.

The Author could not know his brother for what he was, because the Janitor himself didn't know who he was. Just a crippled janitor, just a bright and quiet boy who had amounted to nothing.

But a boy who became a man who dwelt in rooms and knew the truth only to be that which he saw directly in front of him, in the room with him. A man who had smothered the infant sons of drug lords, stomped and electrocuted the wives and daughters of terrorists, slowly poisoned the aged, bedridden, and enfeebled patriarchs of white-supremacist klans. A man who slept easily in a comfortable room with no windows and all the doors firmly shut. Some doors lead to weenie roasts with his parents still alive, others to procedures performed in soundproofed windowless rooms, but all doors are either open or closed.

SO THE FAMOUS and Talented Horror Author went to the anonymous, dark-eyed office building where his brother worked. He ducked in through the loading dock, walked through the cool halls, heard the water fountains humming metallically. The shadows were dusty and still; it was a place where it seemed completely preposterous that a face-sucking demon could hide. He took the freight elevator to the caged basement maintenance office where his brother sat in a wobbly-wheeled office chair, his twisted foot propped on the scarred top of his cast-off desk, listening to quiet tango music waft from a plaster-caked portable radio.

The Author was brokenhearted about his monster wife: a face-sucking demon in his semi-sleep, a perpetual draining worry on his sleep-fuddled brain and heart, a beast that hung in the back of all of the family photographs and sunny afternoons, of his gross sense of reality. His whole nuclear family—Author, wife, 2.5 as-of-yet unconceived children—was crumbling before it had even started, somehow broken down on a schoolyard where one brother played soccer and the other hung out on the swings with the girls. He had nowhere else to go.

He'd almost left his wedding ring in the glove compartment of his car, he explained. Almost pulled it off as he boosted himself through the loading dock, almost handed it to a moon-faced jani-

362 *Cara Spindler and David Erik Nelson*

tor laboriously changing the bag on a vacuum cleaner, telling him, *Keep it for me, wouldya?* because it felt like her, warm and smooth, and maybe it, too, could connect to the netherworld and the horrible monster would find out about his plans, another function of that strange machine of matrimony.

Because even if the Author's brother was a failure, even if his family hadn't been very close, he could still believe in things that we all need to believe in: our family will always love us, and help us, and offer support—be it financial, mental, emotional—or answer big questions, like *Should I kill my wife? Should I kill myself?*

THE CLUB-FOOTED JANITOR, the assassin, leaned back in his creaking, paint-splattered chair, deep in some office building, in the bowels of some city, some late afternoon, somewhere in America. The Author poured out his story, his months of quasi-not-sleep, the gathering intensity of the dreams, the way shadows ran alongside his car, like the monster pacing him leisurely.

The Famous and Talented Horror Author realized he was babbling (a frequent complaint of his critics, he quipped nervously) and so he asked his brother, who stared at him for an endless moment afterward, if he should kill his wife or kill himself, since he believed that she was now—or perhaps always had been—a hideous, primal monster.

The Club-Footed Janitor laughed. "You've been reading too many of your own books, bro."

The Famous and Talented Horror Author said nothing.

And his brother asked, "What do you want to do?"

"I don't know," the Author said. "That's why I asked you."

"Either you do or you don't," said the brother, "and you're in my office, now, telling me that you think that your wife is a monster. So you have to decide what to do. What you want *me* to tell you is what *you* think is true."

The man didn't know what to say, or what it meant, and so he waited.

"What is true," said the Club-Footed Janitor slowly, cracking his knuckles, "is what you see, and hear, and touch. You know what you have to do. Don't ask me to make that decision for you." The Club-Footed Janitor pushed back from his desk, easing his deformed foot down, and limped to a filing cabinet atop which sat a steaming tea kettle on a hot plate.

"It's always struck me as funny that it's a man's world," he said idly, glancing into a mug and blowing out some dust. "All through nature, it's the females calling the shots, in beehives and baboon troops, with lions. Species to species, males are lazy: drones built only for fighting and mating." He opened the top drawer of the cabinet, dug out a box of Lipton's tea bags.

Doors were opening in the Club-Footed Janitor's head.

"Different in humans, somehow," he remarked, selecting a bag. "Don't know why. Maybe that explains misogyny, spousal abuse, all these God-the-Father religions. We're the only species that's inverted the ladies-on-top order, and it takes a lot of crazy hoopla to keep the drones on top of a social order and the queens down." He deposited the tea bag into the empty mug, set it atop the cabinet, and gingerly poured in the boiling water. "But one thing is for sure: you hit your mid-twenties"—he looked significantly at his brother, who was twenty-nine years old, and then rolled his eyes, as he himself was twenty-six—"without killing or making a baby, then you've certainly become an evolutionary aberration."

The Famous and Talented Horror Author, who had a keen ear for dialogue—the fans *love* prosaic dialogue in horror stories: it builds tension—felt his brother's speech building to an overwhelming question. He waited. He watched.

The Club-Footed Janitor stood at his filing cabinet, staring into the middle distance. He sipped his tea reflectively. "You know those descriptions of the old monsters? Dragons and vampires, Bigfoot and the like? You ever notice what they have in common? The size and the fangs, the strength. Lotsa times they have scales, have wings. Just the sort of things little tiny mammals are afraid of, aren't they? Imagine what a hawk looks like if you're a deer mouse. Imagine what a four-inch rodent thinks of a four-and-a-half foot boa constrictor, and all of a sudden dragons make a lot more sense, don't they? You know the way people react to snakes. It's silly, for a hundred-ninety-pound man to scream and dance around like a little girl when he catches sight of a six-ounce snake, but they do. You ever seen how chimps react to snakes?"

The Famous and Talented Horror Author shook his head, but his brother didn't see: the Janitor's eyes were turned inward, to memory, and he remembered standing on the dirt floor of a tin-pot African general's compound, a cool Atlantic breeze blowing back the curtains and making the mosquito net sway around him, standing over the general, a hypodermic needle of warfarin buried in the general's neck, the Janitor's finger on the plunger. An autopsy was unlikely, but one clan assassinating another's warlord with rat poison was hardly unheard of in Sierra Leone. No questions.

What was this man, this lone man with his drug-addled army of children? Why was he important? Why did he need to be liquidated? The Janitor didn't even open the door to the room where those questions paced off their shuffling, senile lives.

No questions.

The general, eyes huge and shining in the night-dark, talked, talked, talked, on and on in Krio, about snakes and bees, about drones and dragons, about women and men. Trying to buy his life with words, but only buying time. The Club-Footed Janitor, curiosity piqued, listened, and then pushed the plunger, watched the general buck and vomit and weep blood from eyes and anus. And then he left.

The next day he'd left his hotel—with a middle-of-the-road digital camera and lots of sunscreen—and gone sightseeing to a local preserve, had seen what chimps do to snakes. "They go nuts, whirling and screaming and smashing the thing with rocks and logs, even if it's harmless, even if it's dead. Hell, they'll go nuts and slaughter a garden hose. They hate snakes. They hate monsters. It's a deep memory, an old memory. Genetic. And good. There's more than just dragons and Bigfoots out there.

"But it isn't the females, even though they'll go wild and tear you apart if you come near their young. They're strong, and they have the capacity for violence. But they don't go after snakes. They don't hunt monsters.

"This is separate from fighting and fucking, another job just for us drones: killing monsters."

The Club-Footed Janitor took another sip of tea, then took several long, awkward strides back to his desk. He opened the drawer and brought out a dull grey revolver, placed it heavily on the desk before his brother.

"In case it doesn't go without saying," the club-footed brother said, settling back into his chair, "I believe you."

"This is ludicrous."

The Club-Footed Janitor smiled broadly. "You know that *ludicrous* comes from Latin, right? From *ludus:* play. So it may be ludicrous, bro, but it's still the world. Some hate the player, some hate the game, but it's still the world."

And so the Famous and Talented Horror Author walked out of the somber, now-darkened office building, and drove home, the gun awkward and heavy in his pocket.

HIS WIFE WAS already in bed, asleep, peaceful and beautiful. The Author peeked in on her, and then took a walk around the block. He knew that as long as he stayed awake she would be peaceful and beautiful, her skin would be smooth and warm and soft, the way that it always was, and she would move over, in her sleep, when he crawled into bed. And the man also knew, after almost a year of thin-sleep nights, that as soon as he fell asleep she would, as on every other night, be a vicious, sucking, hideous beast that would hurt him and make him scream until he woke up sweating and sick to his stomach. She had always slept lightly, but now it had become his job to hear the alarm clock's chirps, to shake or kiss her awake. He wondered if he really did scream in his sleep. The dryness was there, the whisper at the edge of his speech. He wondered why his shoes would wake her on the hardwood and his screams could not.

As he had turned to leave the office, his brother had told him that we are all monsters, under the surface, and whatever this is— the Janitor had gestured around the dusty office, at the table made of a door atop sawhorses, at the broken fans and shelves of grimy, anonymous parts to anonymous, colossal machines—the waking part or the dreaming part, it's the part where we try our hardest not to be monsters, to shove back whatever is evil and wicked about ourselves, and do the best we can to hide our monstrous selves. Hearing that, the man had known what he had to do about his wife.

The gun was heavy in his pocket.

AS HE WALKED, the man thought through all of the stories he'd written, post-apocalyptic zombie worlds, vampire morality plays, houses bent on revenge, and the ghosts of cutthroats cast out of air locks in the Great Nothing between the stars. He could imagine solutions for all of those imaginary people, those old schoolteachers and outcast teens and lonely widows. He could imagine a solution to this.

The Famous and Talented Horror Author closed his eyes, letting his feet and habit guide him over jagged sidewalk and irregular curbs, and he imagined himself and his wife, in bed, the shades gently shuffling in the breeze, the moon etching the curves of their sleeping backs beneath the sheet. He saw them breathe together, slower and slower, more and more shallowly, and then both relax liquidly, like quicksilver, into each other, flatten and bulge and quicken into the rolling wolfsquid that burst up to pace frantically across their hardwood floor, throwing sheets asunder and wadding the rag rug beneath their tentacular paws, building momentum for their leap through the window. Outside, he could see their silvered night lawn, and beyond that the tree line, and in the cut-felt shadows of the trees he saw the slither and tense, the whirl and lurch of everyone else, all of the other mate-monsters out in the midnight world, tearing through trees, running down lone joggers and lost cats and stoned teenagers out past curfew.

He knew then, knew in his heart of hearts, that Aristophanes had been completely right in the most completely wrong way possible: in Plato's *Symposium* Aristophanes had suggested, puckishly, that once upon a time everyone had been four-armed, four-legged, two-faced wagon wheels of love—some male, some female, and some hermaphroditic—that these beasts were too content in their perfectly partnered bliss and had thus been cleaved in twain. Henceforward, each half-a-being had spent his or her days looking for his other half, his better half. Gay men were the two half-a-males seeking their whole, and lesbians were two half-a-females seeking their whole, and straight folks—with their strange hunger for imperfect difference, for the unity that is unending strife and friction—they were the cleaved descendants of those strange, rolling hermaphrodites. The Author had always taken this bit of the *Symposium* to be metaphorical, fantastical, and convenient in its encapsulation of Greek sexuality and secular, homosocial morals. He had never taken it for what it was: the kernel of truth at the heart of the world. He saw that now, finally, saw that beneath the skin of the world there was nothing but gristle and savagery, and was afraid, was awed; for just a moment it was as though he had slipped the surly bonds of earth and touched the face of God.

In his walking dream the Famous and Talented Horror Author became live to the fact that he was not being attacked by his wife, but embraced by her, devoured by her. Ensconced in her, he became her, and they together coursed out through the night: a wolf and a squid, vicious and hungry, supple and strong, pale and invisible in the darkness, velvet-eyed and noxious and strange and far more terrible than any image that had ever accosted Lovecraft from some dreamless sleep in a dimension beyond time. A World Eater. They tore through the fabric of the night and sewed themselves in; they were the terror embroidered into the velvet between the stars, the dim, rusted razor-wire at neck height across decrepit cellar steps. There is little lovely about love.

The Famous and Talented Horror Author came back in silently, to his home, to his wife. She was cozy in bed, naked, sleeping, and he slid out of his clothes quickly, eager to be naked with her, to join together and go out into their night. Dropping his rumpled khakis to the boards he heard the revolver *clunk* dully and didn't like the idea of it there, on the floor in his pocket, or in a drawer. If his wife happened on it, it would worry her. A lot. That seemed cruel, so he dressed again, quiet as a church mouse, and headed back into the night alone.

THE FAMOUS AND TALENTED Horror Author felt fortunate to catch his brother stumping across the office building parking lot. His brother lived far out of town, and driving to his cabin was time-consuming and dangerous this time of the year, with the bucks reckless to rut and heedless of the dark road's passages through their forest.

"Hey Jess," he called, "Jess."

His brother stopped, turned. "Fancy seeing you twice in one night. Your biggest fans must envy me."

"Yeah. Well, the . . . uh, *thing* you lent me? I don't need it after all." The Author looked over first one shoulder, then the other, and then did his best to slyly palm the bulky revolver to his brother, who remained unmoving, hands cradled in his denim jacket's pockets.

The Author stood there, lamely, hand out.

"You sure about that? Wife feeling better?"

"Naw. It's just, well, I rethought all of that. All of everything we talked about. I figured some things out, is all."

"But she's still a monster, right? A soul-sucking, murderous inhuman thing."

"I'm fine with that."

There was no pause; the Janitor shook his head. "I'm not."

The Author let his arm drop. "What?"

"Don't worry. Not everyone has the guts for this sorta thing." The Janitor reached out, eased the gun from his brother's hand. "I'll make the calls tomorrow morning," he said as he ejected the cylinder and checked the rounds, then snapped the gun shut and pocketed it. "There's proper folks for resolving this kinda thing, anyway; I just thought you'd want a shot at it first, maybe. On account of your line of work."

And the Famous and Talented Horror Author thought about lines, the lines between Cain and Abel, and swings and soccer, the twisted line of a deformed leg. It occurred to the Author that maybe he and his brother had never been that close, anyways.

The Janitor smiled broadly. "*Shot.* Get it, *take a shot at it.* It's a pun, bro." He slapped the Author's shoulder and turned to go.

Despite himself, the Author was dimly aware of his brother's real job and associations in some low and reptilian corner of his own capacious haunted mansion of a mind. If drones are only for fucking, fighting, and monster hunting, then it doubtless behooves them to, in some dim way, truly know what is in the world.

"I don't want anyone to kill my wife," the Author said lamely, softly.

"Don't worry," the brother called over his shoulder, unlocking his rusted Honda's driver's side door. "We've got it covered." And the Janitor climbed in and drove away.

THE FAMOUS AND TALENTED Author raced home, quickly and quietly came into his bedroom, slithered from his clothes, and slid between the body-warm sheets. He lay himself down, breathed deep,
breathed deep,

and willed himself to

calm

willed himself to

sleep

and

shockingly

he dozed off, slipped the surly bonds of earth, slipped deep into his bed and sheets and wife and life and then, and then . . .

. . . and then he and his beautiful wife, they bloomed into the full snarling wheel of themselves, of their more perfect union, bloomed like the bloodgold blossom of fire blooming from a plane-struck tower, like the gout of blood from the leaping stag's heart, like the lick of flame from the sniper's barrel.

Out from their bed

Out into the night

Out through the crisp autumn forest

They had to roll fast to beat their brother, their Club-Footed Janitor, their bloodmate back to his home, to his phone, to the copper lifeline that silently binds the web of his own dark family, spread thin over the surface of the earth, the political crust of arbitrary lines and colors that's the veneer of every schoolroom's globe.

They tumbled and roared and tore and, of course, their arrival was in just the nick of time, catching the brother crossing from detached garage to lonely little clapboard cottage, halfway across his muddy lawn, out in the middle of woods deep and dark.

The face of the brother remained unchanged as they bore down on him—perhaps nothing could surprise him anymore, much like the Famous and Talented Horror Author himself. Perhaps he, too, had seen too much, had supped full of horrors, and this final serving was no affront but just more of the same.

It is a tiring world for we fuckers, we fighters, we monster-hunting drones, that look might say. *All right,* it might say; *This is what we do,* it might say; *Let's roll,* it might say.

Maybe Cain rose up because he'd found himself a girlfriend and there was no room in that tiny half-past-Eden world for a warped stray, not in the land of pairs two-by-two. Maybe Abel wasn't so much favored by God as he was an aberrant freak, a half that could never find its better half because it had been born malformed, *half*-formed, *quasi-modo,* twisted and stunted at birth.

Maybe all of our stories are really about love, are really warnings echoing down the library halls of human history, saying "Beware: This is the terror that is love. Here there be monsters."

Maybe every little boy who thinks girls are gross and icky is more right than any man might ever expect.

And maybe the handfasted squidwolf of the Author and his wife, maybe that's not the real monster here.

The Club-Footed Janitor brought up his good right arm, the solid sanity of his gun, and coolly breathed in, relaxed, aimed, took up the slack of the trigger and *squeezed, squeezed, squeezed, squeezed, squeezed, squeezed.*

But what hope had those little lead bullets, each no bigger than a toddler's severed toe? What could those tiny full-metal jackets do to love's twin hearts? A thousand waters cannot drown love, nor fires destroy love. If a man were to offer all of the riches of his house for love, he would be utterly scorned. A dollop of lead? A mushrooming of metal? The pathetic crack of air collapsing back into its vortex? What hope had it against the awful abomination that tore out of that night set to unsolve its only problem?

There was never any hope for the brother, and the final mercy of his life was that, seeing this and being who and what he was, the Club-Footed Janitor was able to slam every door to every room in his labyrinthine mind and walk away before the beast had even brought to bear the most glancing blow of the least of their razored tentacles, and long before their fangs sank mortally deep, before they shook their sleek head in a spine-snapping nicker, before the feeding began in earnest.

But even with all of that, even with the body little more than a vacant lot just going fallow, it was far from a clean kill, and the Author and his wife—the feculent wax monster that tore—felt obliged to press the brother's face in the mud and hold it long, to tear at his corpse until it was far beyond utterly unmade: to be sure. And then to feed.

THE NEXT DAY the Famous and Talented Horror Author awoke next to his soft, sleep-sighing wife, their sheets mud-draggled and the warm blood still tacky on their body, and for the first instant in his life he was truly alive to what love is.

This is a love story, he decided. That made all the difference.

CONTRIBUTORS

HILYAIRE BELLOC stopped answering our e-mails before the first issue came out. We keep hoping to hear from him instead of his lawyers. Who are lovely people, but still, Hilyaire, come on, it's been *ten years*!

DAVID BLAIR lives in Medford, Massachusetts, with his wife, Sabrina, and daughter, Astrid. He is an associate professor at the New England Institute of Art.

GWENDA BOND lives in Lexington, Kentucky, with her husband, writer Christopher Rowe, and their rowdy dog and cat. She is pursuing an MFA in Writing for Children and Young Adults at Vermont College and often posts about books and writing at her blog, Shaken & Stirred (http://gwendabond.typepad.com).

JOHN BROWN wrote the first draft of "Bright Waters" in Orson Scott Card's Literary Bootcamp. Having lived in the Netherlands, he has a particular affection for the hero of this story. John won first prize in the *Writers of the Future* (13) under the name Bo Griffin. He is at work on an epic fantasy novel about a boy, a girl, and a wayward monster. He lives in the hinterlands of Utah.

RICHARD BUTNER is a slow-moving, tree-dwelling mammal who hangs upside down from branches and feeds on leaves and fruits. Small Beer published a chapbook of his short fiction, *Horses Blow Up Dog City & Other Stories*.

DAN CHAON's books include the novel *You Remind Me of Me* and the short-story collection *Among the Missing,* which was a finalist for the National Book Award. Chaon's stories have appeared in many journals and anthologies including *Best American Short Stories, The O. Henry Prize Stories, Year's Best Fantasy and Horror,* and *The Pushcart Prize.* He is most recently the recipient of the 2006 Academy Award in Literature from the American Academy of Arts and Letters.

BECCA DE LA ROSA's fiction has appeared in *Strange Horizons, Ideomancer,* and *GrendelSong.* She is the proud owner of a collection of Venetian Carnivale masks that continues to frighten friends and visitors. She lives in Ireland.

K. E. DUFFIN's book of poems, *King Vulture,* was published by the University of Arkansas Press. Her work has appeared in *Agni, Chelsea, Denver Quarterly, Harvard Review, Hunger Mountain, The New Orleans Review, Ploughshares, Poetry, Poetry East, Prairie Schooner, Rattapallax, The Sewanee Review, Southwest Review, Verse,* and many other journals. Her poems have also been featured on *Poetry Daily* and *Verse Daily.* A painter and printmaker, Duffin lives in Somerville, Massachusetts.

DAVID FINDLAY is a pornographer working in text, audio, visual art, and digital media. A proud Clarion graduate, David is based in Toronto, Ontario, Canada, where he resides with a far more prolific writer, almost enough books, and too many computers. He should only be taken on the advice of a physician.

AMY BETH FORBES bets you're wondering what it's all about. Answers might be found at www.smolderingink.com.

The Girl in the Glass, a novel from HarperCollins (2005), and *The Empire of Ice Cream,* a story collection from Golden Gryphon

(2006), are JEFFREY FORD's most recent books. In 2008, look for a new novel, *The Shadow Year,* from Morrow/Harper Collins and a new story collection, *The Night Whiskey.* He lives in New Jersey and teaches Composition and Literature at Brookdale Community College.

KAREN JOY FOWLER is the author of two collections of short fiction, *Artificial Things* and *Black Glass,* as well as the novels *Sarah Canary, The Sweetheart Season, Sister Noon,* and the bestseller *The Jane Austen Book Club.* Fowler cofounded (with Pat Murphy) the James Tiptree, Jr., Award. She lives in Davis, California.

NAN FRY is the author of a book of poetry, *Relearning the Dark,* and a chapbook of translations, *Say What I Am Called.* Her work has appeared in *Poet Lore, The Healing Muse, The Journal of Mythic Arts, Plainsong, Calyx,* and the anthologies *The Faery Reel, The Year's Best Fantasy and Horror,* and *Poetry in Motion from Coast to Coast.* She teaches occasionally at the Writer's Center in Bethseda, Maryland, and lives in the Washington, D.C., area with her human and canine companions.

GEOFFREY GOODWIN works in a bookshop outside Boston, Massachusetts. He writes for Bookslut.com. LCRW has published a number of his stories. He is not worried by this.

Previously an equestrian and a chamber musician with a master's degree in music, D. M. GORDON owes her literary education to the auditor's program at Smith College. Her prizewinning short stories and poems have appeared in a variety of journals, including *Nimrod* and *Northwest Review.* She is a 2006 finalist for the Massachusetts Cultural Council Artist Grant in fiction, and a 2004 finalist for the same in poetry.

THEODORA GOSS teaches at Boston University, where she is completing a PhD in English literature. Her short-story collection, *In the Forest of Forgetting,* was published in 2006 by Prime Books. Her short stories have been reprinted in a number of anthologies, including *Year's Best Fantasy, The Year's Best Fantasy and Horror,* and *Feeling Very Strange: The Slipstream Anthology.* She lives in Boston with her husband and daughter, in an apartment filled with books and cats. Visit her Web site at www.theodoragoss.com.

SEANA GRAHAM is a bookseller in Santa Cruz, California, and a closet scribbler of long standing. Her work has appeared or is forthcoming in *Red Wheelbarrow Literary Magazine* and *Eclipse.* LCRW is the first zine she's been published in, and she believes appearing here will significantly help her "coolness quotient"—that is, if anything actually can.

GAVIN J. GRANT is the editor, gatherer, and polisher of this tiny zine. Sorry to say he is allergic to you and your pet.

NALO HOPKINSON has lived in Toronto, Canada, since 1977, but spent most of her first sixteen years in the Caribbean, where she was born. Her novels include *Midnight Robber, Brown Girl in the Ring, The Salt Roads,* and *The New Moon's Arms.*

How do we get our stories? We start with the set of people who read. Then we split out those who write with a butter knife (or some other blunt instrument). From these we filter out those who write well (and can hold their breath underwater). Lastly we ask our neighbors to bury the stories in the garden for at least one season. We print whatever stories might still be legible.

Daughter of the world's preeminent forensic anthropomorphologist, ANNA SUNSHINE ISON holds an MFA from the University of

North Carolina at Greensboro. Her work has appeared in *Cross-Roads: A Southern Culture Annual*, *The GSU Review*, *I to I: Life Writing by Kentucky Feminists*, and *Urban Latino*, among other publications. She is currently writing a book about Venezuelan beauty pageants and is studying Vietnamese in preparation for her upcoming move to Ho Chi Minh City.

JAN LARS JENSEN is the author of a novel—*Shiva 3000*—and a memoir about the crazy time finishing that novel, *Nervous System*. He lives in Halifax, Nova Scotia, where he is working on his LLB and becoming more nostalgic with each passing day.

JENNIE JEROME, aka Lady Randolph Churchill, produced *The Anglo Saxon Review* for about a year. Apparently it is awesome. Anne Sebba's new biography will be published in autumn 2007 by W.W. Norton (U.S.) and John Murray (UK).

JOHN KESSEL is perhaps best known for his career as a leafy vegetable. He is director of the creative writing department at North Carolina State University in Raleigh. Speculation is rife that he is descended from the Apostle Simon the Zealot. His stories have received the Nebula, Theodore Sturgeon, and James Tiptree Jr. awards. His books include the novels *Good News from Outer Space* and *The Pure Product*. With James Patrick Kelly, he recently edited *Feeling Very Strange: The Slipstream Anthology*. He lives with his wife and daughter in Raleigh, North Carolina.

LCRW now calls Northampton, Massachusetts, home (previously Boston, then Brooklyn) and considers the following bookshops top vacation spots: Atomic Books, Baltimore, Maryland; Avenue Victor Hugo Bookshop, Boston, Massachusetts; Book Cellar, Chicago, Illinois; Borderlands Bookshop, San Francisco, California; Broadside Books, Northampton, Massachusetts; Downtown

News & Books, Asheville, North Carolina; Dreamhaven, Minneapolis, Minnesota; Elliott Bay, Seattle, Washington; Mac's Backs, Cleveland Heights, Ohio; McNally/Robinson, New York, New York; Pandemonium, Cambridge, Massachusetts; Powell's, Portland, Oregon; Prairie Lights, Iowa City, Iowa; Quimby's, Chicago, Illinois; A Room of One's Own, Madison, Wisconsin; Shocklines.com; St. Mark's Bookshop, New York, New York; and Mark V. Ziesing, Bookseller, California.

DOUGLAS LAIN recognizes that he is a member of the entertained public—a public that Guy Debord described in his 1978 film, *In Girum Imus Nocte et Consumimur Igni,* as "dying in droves on the freeways, and in each flu epidemic and each heat wave, and with each mistake of those who adulterate their food, and each technical innovation profitable to the numerous entrepreneurs for whose environmental developments they serve as guinea pigs." Last week Lain drank six Starbucks coffees and daydreamed about revolution 12.5 times. Douglas Lain lives in Portland, Oregon, with his wife and four children.

KELLY LINK is the Co-Editrix of this adventure. (Also: Hunter, Armtwister, and Shiner.) She'd like a cat, please.

IAN McDOWELL is the author of the novels *Mordred's Curse* and *Merlin's Gift* and various short stories. His most recent publications include the English language version of *Chiba Vampire: The Novel* for TokyoPop. The most traumatic day of his adult life was when he was stalked by clowns. Several years ago, he spent a Saturday morning in jail, where he got into an argument with a Crip as to whether the guy with a mullet who hangs himself in *An Officer and a Gentleman* was Patrick Swayze.

SARAH MICKLEM is the author of the fantasy novel *Firethorn* (Scribner) and has published short stories in *Triquarterly,* LCRW, and an anthology of science fiction erotica, *Sex in the System.* After many years as a graphic designer, she now teaches creative writing at Notre Dame and is working on *Wildfire,* the second novel of the Firethorn trilogy, forthcoming in 2008. Her website is www.fire thorn.info.

DAVID MOLES was born on the anniversary of the R.101 disaster. He has lived in six time zones on three continents and hopes someday to collect the whole set. David was a finalist for the 2004 John W. Campbell Award for Best New Writer. His fiction and poetry have been published in *Polyphony, Say . . . , Rabid Transit, Flytrap,* and *Asimov's,* as well as on *Strange Horizons.* He coedited *All-Star Zeppelin Adventure Stories* with Jay Lake and *Twenty Epics* with Susan Marie Groppi.

SARAH MONETTE is the author of the novels *Mélusine, The Virtu, The Mirador,* and *Summerdown* (forthcoming). Her short stories have appeared in *Ideomancer, Strange Horizons, Alchemy,* and *Postscripts,* and will be collected in *The Bone Key.* She collects books, and her husband collects computer parts, so their living space is the constantly contested border between these two imperial ambitions.

MARGARET MUIRHEAD wore a tiara to our Oscar party. She lives with her family in a dry town in Massachusetts. Her first picture book, *Mabel,* is forthcoming from Dial Books for Young Readers.

DAVID ERIK NELSON is a cofounder and editor of *Poor Mojo's Almanac(k)* (www.poormojo.org) and purveyor of fine prose, poetry, and advice from the Giant Squid. Mr. Nelson is startlingly accurate with a small caliber pistol, and he is Cara Spindler's husband.

On Selling Out: Yes, we will, thank you. Would we take the opportunity of having a larger platform to throw our zine (reimagined as glossy with chocolate-bar pullouts and ads for the latest solar cars) out into the reading masses? Offers to the usual address.

SARA ROJO PÉREZ (Madrid, 1973) is an award-winning illustrator and fine artist whose works have been exhibited widely in both group and solo shows, and have often been National Prize selections. Previously the artistic and creative director of Sopa de Sobre, an animation studio working in both publicity and film for clients such as Canal +, TVE, and Tele 5, she now devotes herself full-time to illustration and fine art. A regular contributor to newspapers and magazines such as *MAN, Diario 16, Mestizaje,* and others, she has illustrated numerous books for children, such as *The Free and the Brave: Poems About the United States, La aventura de Cecilia y el dragón,* and *Manual Práctico para viajar en OVNI.*

PHIL RAINES and HARVEY WELLES have had stories published in *Albedo One, Leading Edge, On Spec, Aurealis,* and *New Genre* as well as the recent collection of new Scottish fantastic fiction, *Novia Scotia.* Philip lives in Glasgow, Scotland, and is a member of the Glasgow Science Fiction Writers Circle. Harvey lives in Milwaukee, Wisconsin.

DEBORAH ROGGIE's short stories have appeared in magazines and anthologies including *Fantasy: The Best of 2004, Realms of Fantasy,* and *Eidolon.* "The Mushroom Duchess" first appeared in *Lady Churchill's Rosebud Wristlet* 17, was short-listed for the 2005 Fountain Award, and was included in *The Year's Best Fantasy and Horror* 19. Roggie lives in New Jersey with her husband and son. She is currently working on a novel.

MARK RUDOLPH is a poetry coeditor for *Strange Horizons* and publisher/editor of *Full Unit Hookup.* He is a graduate of the Clarion Writers' Workshop. His work has appeared in many diverse venues, but he writes very slowly and submits infrequently, which explains why you have to look very hard to find it. He lives in southern Indiana with his faithful dog, Monty.

KAREN RUSSELL is a graduate of the Columbia MFA program and is the 2005 recipient of the Transatlantic Review/Henfield Foundation Award. Her fiction has recently appeared in *Conjunctions, Granta, Zoetrope, Oxford American,* and *The New Yorker.* Her debut collection, *St. Lucy's Home for Girls Raised by Wolves,* was published by Knopf. A native of Miami, she lives in New York City. "Help Wanted" was her first ever publication.

JIM SALLIS's books include the Lew Griffin cycle, a biography of Chester Himes, and a translation of Raymond Queneau's novel *Saint Glingin,* as well as six other novels and multiple collections of stories, poems and essays. His most recent books are *Drive* (called by *The New York Times,* "a perfect noir novel"), *Salt River* (the third and final installment of his Turner series), and the story collection *Potato Tree.* He was a longtime columnist for *The Boston Globe,* regularly reviews for *The Washington Post* and *LA Times,* and contributes a quarterly book column to *F&SF.* His website is www.jamessallis.com.

VERONICA SCHANOES is a writer and scholar whose work has previously appeared on *Endicott Studio, Jabberwocky,* and *Trunk Stories,* as well as LCRW. Her poem "The Room" was recently published by Papaveria Press. She does not like cats.

LAWRENCE SCHIMEL is a full-time author and anthologist who's published more than eighty books, including *Two Boys in Love, The Future Is Queer, The Drag Queen of Elfland,* and *Fairy Tales for Writers,* among others. His *PoMoSexuals: Challenging Assumptions About*

Gender and Sexuality (with Carol Queen) won a Lambda Literary Award. He has also won the Rhysling Award for Poetry and his children's book *No hay nada como el original* (illustrated by Sara Rojo Pérez) was selected by the International Youth Library in Munich for the White Ravens 2005. His work has been widely anthologized in books such as this one and also *The Random House Book of Science Fiction Stories, The Best of Best Gay Erotica,* and *The Random House Treasury of Light Verse.* His writings have been translated into Basque, Catalan, Croatian, Czech, Dutch, Esperanto, Finnish, French, Galician, German, Greek, Hungarian, Indonesian, Italian, Japanese, Polish, Portuguese, Romanian, Russian, Slovak, and Spanish. He lives in Madrid, Spain.

DAVID J. SCHWARTZ's first novel, *Superpowers,* will be published in 2008. He usually tips 20 percent. Find him online at snurri.com. Please do not send ninjas. The bodies disintegrate, but the shurikens keep clogging up the garbage disposal.

WILLIAM SMITH makes spanky new books and sells dusty old ones. Find him at trunkstories.com and hangfirebooks.com.

CARA SPINDLER lives in Michigan with her family and teaches high school. Her writing has appeared in *The Driftwood Review, Z Magazine, Poor Mojo's Almanac(k),* and *Spinning Jenny.*

RAY VUKCEVICH's collection, *Meet Me in the Moon Room,* was published by Small Beer Press, and his novel, *The Man of Maybe Half-a-Dozen Faces,* by St. Martin's. He also works as a programmer in a couple of university brain labs in Oregon.

ACKNOWLEDGMENTS

Inspiration (past, present, and future, and in no particular order) and thanks: *Doris, Roller Derby, Peko Peko, Bitch, Leeking Ink, Xerography Debt* (née *Xerox Debt*), *Western Lore, Factsheet Five, A Reader's Guide to the Underground Press, Broken Pencil, Full Unit Hookup, Say . . . , Kiss Machine, The Match, Plotz,* Vince McCaffrey, Bill Desmond, Joe Bills, Cassandra Silvia, Eben Taggart, Edward Osowski, Brian Morrison, Mai Tyuet La, Paradise Copies, *Ben Is Dead, Clamor, The Urban Pantheist, Cooking Rock, The Free Press Death Ship, Flytrap, Electric Velocipede, Strange Horizons, Kitty Magik, Supermonster, Murder Can Be Fun, Beer Frame, Shimmer, Lenox Ave., Revolution SF, Don't Shoot It's Only Comics, The Baffler, The Third Alternative, The Anglo-Saxon Review, Herbivore, Alchemy, Sybil's Garage, Ideomancer, Punk Planet.* Anyone else we missed: You know it was always a secret between us.

ABOUT THE EDITORS

GAVIN J. GRANT began publishing *Lady Churchill's Rosebud Wristlet* in 1996. He cofounded Small Beer Press in 2000 (see below). He coedits *The Year's Best Fantasy & Horror* (St. Martin's Press), cohosts a monthly reading series at NYC's KGB Bar, cohabitates with coeditor Kelly Link, and freelances all by himself. Originally from Scotland, he has worked in bookshops in Los Angeles and Boston. He was a senior content coordinator for the American Booksellers Association/BookSense.com. He has written for the *Los Angeles Times, BookPage, Time Out New York, Hartford Courant, Rain Taxi, Review of Contemporary Fiction,* and *Clamor,* among others.

KELLY LINK cofounded Small Beer Press in 2000. She coedits *Lady Churchill's Rosebud Wristlet*. She is coeditor of *The Year's Best Fantasy & Horror* (St. Martin's Press) and edited the anthology *Trampoline*. Kelly is the author of two collections, *Magic for Beginners* (*Time Magazine, Salon,* and *Village Voice* Best of Year Lists for 2005) and *Stranger Things Happen* (a Firecracker nominee, Village Voice Favorite, and Salon Book of the Year). Her stories have won the Hugo, Nebula, Locus, Tiptree, and World Fantasy awards. Her story "Stone Animals" was selected for inclusion in *Best American Short Stories* 2005, edited by Michael Chabon.

Grant and Link live in Northampton, Massachusetts.

ABOUT THE TYPE

This book was set in Bembo, a typeface based on an old-style Roman face that was used for Cardinal Bembo's tract *De Aetna* in 1495. Bembo was cut by Francisco Griffo in the early sixteenth century. The Lanston Monotype Company of Philadelphia brought the well-proportioned letterforms of Bembo to the United States in the 1930s.

SINCE APPARENTLY WE CANNOT SUCCESSFULLY FOMENT REVOLUTION WE WILL MAKE A SMALL PAPER OBJECT AND SPREAD GOOD FICTION FAR, WIDE.

These are a few of the choices that have been offered to make LCRW arrive at your door. We also take suggestions. We liked the one about sending green eye shadow with each zine (thanks, Katya, we're working on it). Some of these might even still be valid (check lcrw.net/lcrw/subscriptions.htm).

LCRW AND THE STUNNINGLY REGULAR DELIVERY SERVICE

LEVEL	PRICE	TAG	INGREDIENTS
1	$5		Sample issue
2	$20	Subscribed!	4 issues: U.S. & Canada
2a	$32	Airmail	4 issues: International
2b	$1	Zip	as no. 2 except without the zines
3	$35	Chocolato	as no. 2 & a good chocolate bar each time
4	$39	Huh!	as no. 3 & a chapbook of our choice
5	$51	Fresh	& a T-shirt
	$82	Sewy	& a hand-sewn zine bag
	$99	Comforting	& a warm feeling inside
	$99.95	Smudgy	& finger-painted covers
6	$185	Jammy	& pajamas (cotton) and a robe (probably tartan)
	$200	Rebate	& a $165 rebate
7	$222	Futurist	& dinner with yourself next Tuesday night
	$500	Theoretical	& an evening of self-reflection and doubt with each delivery

LEVEL	PRICE	TAG	INGREDIENTS
8	$1,600	Annoying	& at some point in your life a knowing smile on the subway from someone neither of us knows. Don't wait for it.
	$2,500	Bargain?	& everything we have in print forever
	$2,600	Zither	& a used musical instrument—**ask to see our broad selection!**
	$2,700	Zombie	& William Smith and Kelly Link update your zombie contingency plan
9	$4,000	Crumbly	& an obscure European first edition
	$5,000	Visiting	& all issues hand-delivered (in the U.S. and Canada)
10	$5,995	Saturnalia	& an old car
	$16,500		& 2 return tickets on the Trans-Siberian Railroad
	$25,000	Not stinky	& a Toyota Prius for us and a big round of thanks for you
11	$100,000	Diebold	& any election you choose (please write check to GOP)
	$1,000,000	Bicontinental	& a studio apartment in an okay neighborhood in Tokyo or quite a nice flat in Edinburgh, Scotland

LEVEL	PRICE	TAG	INGREDIENTS
	$75bn	Monkey	*& El Presidente thinks. Thinking is hard. Here's Karl! Karl says war. Karl is great! Boom! Monkeyboy wears uniform. Monkeyboy loves Karl. But! Not in Pennsylvania way, no sir!*
	$300bn	Depressing	& the USA goes to war with the country of your choice
12	$38	Friendly	4 issues for you + 4 for someone else
	?	Offer	You tell us.
	$4,999	Ha ha	the whole damn magazine (*add a folly for only $10,000 more!*)
	?	Bouncy	lifetime supply of LCRW when you buy and ship us a full-sized trampoline

Send checks/money orders, etc., to Small Beer Press, 176 Prospect Ave., Northampton, MA 01060. Send calls for impeachment to the White House, 1600 Penn. Ave., etc.

SUBTLE CONTINUING SUBSCRIBER PLEA:

Papa needs a brand-new bag. Papa needs a new pair of shoes. Papa needs a new RV. Papa needs a new book. Papa needs a new government. Papa needs a new flashlight. Papa needs a new pair of wings. Papa always needs another pair of shoes. Papa needs all these things. But Papa doesn't need your new address when you move. LCRW does.